CW00405338

Dear Reader,

This month I am delighted t[...] novel by best-selling author Patricia Wilson, who is, we know, very popular with romance readers. And we're sure that Julie Garratt's second book for *Scarlet* will greatly please her existing fans, and capture the interest of many new readers. In addition, we are glad to offer you the chance to enjoy the talents of two authors new to the *Scarlet* list: Jean Walton, who lives in the USA, and Michelle Reynolds from the UK.

One of the many joys for me when I select each month's books for you is that I am able to look forward to hearing *your* reaction to my selection. Of course, as *Scarlet* grows, the task of choosing new stories to offer you is becoming ever more interesting as so many talented authors are keen to join our list. Naturally, this means that it is also more of a challenge for me to get the balance of the four books right for you. As always, I invite comments from readers, as such feedback is vital in helping me do my job properly – so I look forward to hearing from *you*.

Till next month,
Best wishes,

Sally Cooper

SALLY COOPER,
Editor-in-Chief – *Scarlet*

About the Author

When she was at school, **Julie Garratt** always came top of the class for writing stories! In the early 90s Julie gained a City and Guilds qualification enabling her to teach creative writing and has since often been employed to take courses in the county.

Julie is the author of four published romance novels and claims that her holidays serve a dual purpose: – 'holiday *and* research trip!' She is married with two grown-up children, and lives at the top of a steep hill, which overlooks a valley dividing Nottinghamshire and Derbyshire. Her hobbies include photography, driving, antique book fairs and music. Julie also has a much loved garden where she can 'sit under the trees to write my novels . . . or play with my dogs!'

JULIE GARRATT

CHANGE OF HEART

SCARLET

Enquiries to:
Robinson Publishing Ltd
7 Kensington Church Court
London W8 4SP

First published in the UK by Scarlet, 1997

A copy of the British Library Cataloguing in
Publication data is available from the British Library

ISBN 1-85487-933-2

Printed and bound in the EC

10 9 8 7 6 5 4 3 2 1

Thanks to
Tom Leonard Mining Museum
Skinningrove, Cleveland
and
Heanor Haulage
(Stephen and Andy)

PROLOGUE
Australia

Melbourne was sweltering under the hot January sun. In the parks, huge fig trees cast their giant shadows while jacaranda and azalea scorched. The city never slept though, not for heat or cold or torrential rain. Kids congregated and couples made rendezvous on the steps of Flinders Street Station at all hours, and trams jammed up the streets despite the heat.

At the birthing centre it was cool and air conditioned and the dark-haired girl leaning over the sterile crib, smiled and watched the baby as it grasped at her finger. She'd marvelled for days at the perfect being she'd created.

But there was a sadness about Kirsten because deep inside she knew that Ryan ought to be here, and he wasn't. Ryan was thousands of miles away in England, where he'd gone with the cool blonde English girl. For some reason, Kirsten found she couldn't feel any bitterness towards Sera.

Six months ago, if anyone had asked her for the name of one person she could rely on implicitly, Ryan Farrar would have instantly sprung to her lips. Now though, she was puzzled and vaguely disillusioned; it was going to be hard bringing up a baby on her own – a baby Ryan didn't even know about.

Anger surged briefly in her heart, quickly followed by regret – regret that she hadn't been there in Queensland with Ryan when his father was killed, regret that she hadn't told Ryan she was pregnant before she left for Melbourne and, too, for that dream job in television.

Phone calls and letters were no substitute for being there, face to face, sharing, caring, and knowing that nothing in the world mattered except Ryan's love.

Was it too late? Even now, she wondered as she left the crib and walked over to the window. Couldn't something be salvaged from a relationship that had once been the most important thing in both of their lives?

She gazed and gazed at the city, shimmering under the heat. She tried to focus on the people down there but her eyes misted up. Holly was coming to see her this afternoon. Her lips twisted in a wry smile. You could always run to big sisters when you needed help, and Holly was no exception.

She felt her spirits lifting a little. Holly would know what to do – even though, so far, she'd shown no sign of forgiving Ryan for running out without a word of explanation.

To Kirsten's mind however, he hadn't run out! There just had to be a reasonable explanation. Ryan had loved her.

There was only one thing for it. She made up her mind on the instant, to go to England. She'd follow him, and find him, and tell him she loved him.

But a little niggling doubt crept into her mind. Could she face a second rejection? What would she do if she

2

discovered he'd had a change of heart and was now in love with Sera?

There was just no way of knowing – unless she could see him again, look into those eyes that could devastate her at a single glance, and ask him what had gone wrong between them.

What worried her most of all though, was how she was going to tell him about his baby girl. She turned her back on the window and strode across the room to the crib. She leaned over it and picked the baby up carefully, still new to the experience of cradling the tiny stranger in her arms.

Fiercely she whispered, 'He's got to be told about you! He has a right to know . . .'

sensitive to the cold as he was, she asked, 'Are you okay?' and concern for him clouded her eyes.

'I'm cold, dammit. That's all. Freezing cold!'

'Go back to the car then and switch the engine on. Come on – I'll take you.' She reached her hand out and grasped his arm, but he dashed her away angrily, and she heard him give a deep growl of impatience as he started pacing up and down the frost-rimed pathway across the back of the house.

Biting down hard on her lip to prevent an angry retort, she remembered the promise she'd made to herself – not to be over-protective with him. It was the last thing he wanted – somebody perpetually fussing over him as if he were a child! She gave all her attention to her surroundings trying to ignore Ryan's thin, stooping figure, with its pale face and haunted eyes, but it was difficult to do that. Even the garden had a sad and sombre look about it today, with its trees bare of leaves, and the damp trellis decked out only in fat rose hips and withered frosted buds. In that moment, she found herself hating the English winter, and she longed again for the sunshine of Australia, and for things to be as they'd always been when Don – Ryan's father – had been alive.

And as if he could read her thoughts, Ryan said in a dull voice, 'I'm glad it wasn't like this for you when my dad died.'

Clasping her hands together, and hardly conscious of the fact she was doing it, she twisted the ring on her left hand that was hidden by her leather gloves, and said, 'The weather doesn't really make any difference, does it? But I must admit it was different at Don's funeral. I really cared for him . . .'

He came over and placed his arm round her shoulders. 'It was all so unfair,' he said gently. 'So damned unnecessary too.'

Not wanting to be reminded of what had happened six months ago, she gazed up at the wide, square-paned windows of the old house, at the mellowed pale pink brickwork and the shallow roof with its covering of grey slate, and without warning, a warmth began creeping into her heart. It was a warmth that had been too long denied her to be ignored now, on the day of her father's funeral.

Wintersgill, that proud old house, had been her home, and whatever her father's faults had been, nothing could make her forget that. It was a long, squat, two-storey building with a tangled mass of honeysuckle leaves half smothering the porch, and ancient stone troughs underneath the windows that had always been filled to overflowing with a riot of dahlias in the old days. Today though the troughs were bare of colour, the soil cleared of autumn's old foliage, but on a wild rockery outside the French doors of the dining room, green tips of crocus were just beginning to push their way through the rich moorland peat, and snowdrops drooped their dainty heads in the long grass under an apple tree on the other side of the garden.

And suddenly, a fierce longing swept over her, almost frightening her with its intensity. This was her home, and it had been ten long years since she'd last seen it. She felt choked with emotion, and knew she'd never be able to steel herself to get rid of the old house which would surely pass to her now that her father was dead.

Ryan's arm fell away from her, and he began pacing up and down in long-suffering silence and, watching him, she was worried as always by his pallor and the dark shadows under his eyes, and knew his future was inextricably linked with hers now. But they could both live here, she reasoned, just the two of them. They didn't have to go back to Australia; there was nothing there for either of them now. And Wintersgill was big enough for them to lead entirely separate lives if that was what he wanted.

Somebody had to take responsibility for him, she argued to herself. And she owed it to Don to do her best for him.

'Ryan!' she pleaded on a deep sigh of resignation. 'Don't be a pain. Do as I say. Go get in the car – you're asking for trouble, standing out here and getting so cold.'

He swung round and glared at her, his long, dark hair, stubbled chin and bushy black brows making his thin face appear fiercer than it actually was. 'Don't "baby" me,' he ground out. 'For God's sake, I'm not helpless.'

She had to agree with him on that point at least. He looked far from helpless – standing there like an untamed wolf who'd been cornered. He was six feet tall with sharp honed cheekbones, deep-set eyes, and a torso as lean and long as a rake. If he'd been a stranger to her she could easily have missed the drawn look beneath his tanned features, and again, if she hadn't known him so well, the tiny lines between his eyes could have been explained away by the mere fact that he'd lived for most of his life in a place where the sun was merciless. As it was though, she knew the truth about him; that was why he was here with her, on a freezing cold January day, on the north-eastern edge of the Yorkshire moors. She hadn't dared leave him on his own in Australia, not so soon after his father had been killed.

The sound of a car engine had her lifting her head and listening. And her heart took on a bleakness as she heard the vehicle stop on the moorland road – somewhere on the other side of the house.

'They're back! *She'll* be back too. Mari Wyatt.'

9

He glanced at her. 'Well – don't look so gutted, you've got every right to be here. This is your home – remember?'

'But she's lived here since I walked out ten years ago. Mari Wyatt! She's been Dad's . . .' she swallowed painfully, 'his *mistress* all this time. Hell, I feel sickened by it all. I wish I'd never bothered to come home at all. I wish I'd stayed in Queensland.'

He grabbed hold of her hand and squeezed it. 'It's *your* home,' he stressed. 'You shouldn't feel uneasy about coming back. I think "mistress" as a word though, has gone out of fashion, kiddo. Maybe you should think more in terms of her being your dad's "partner" or something like that, huh?'

She nodded and couldn't entirely suppress the little laugh that had in it a note approaching hysteria. 'Best foot forward then? Is that what you're saying?'

'We can't put it off, Sera. You've got to meet up with her sometime.'

He swung her hand, linked in his, back and forth as they strode through the wintry garden towards the house, and Serena's spirits lifted fractionally as she felt him beside her, glad now that she'd brought Ryan with her, for she had the feeling she was going to need some moral support in the next few hours.

Serena had been shocked at Mari's appearance when she saw her getting out of the funeral car. Ten years ago her father's secretary had been a plump and pretty forty-five-year-old with laughing blue eyes and a bubbly personality. Now though, as Mari carried a tray containing tea, and sandwiches into the cosy parlour overlooking the garden, she looked tired and below par. Her blonde hair had faded from its once gleaming goldness to a pale straw colour and

10

her forehead was lined. Her eyes too had lost a lot of their brightness, though Serena was forced to admit to herself that Mari had never lost her incredibly good sense of dress. The black cashmere suit with cowl-necked tunic of dark tan underneath it was ideal wear for a funeral on a cold January day.

Mari placed the tray on a low coffee table in front of the leather Chesterfield where Serena and Ryan had seated themselves. Then she eased an armchair forward a little before sitting down herself so that she'd be near enough the table to pour out the tea.

Serena noted that little had changed inside the house since she'd been there last. The heavy old-fashioned furniture was familiar, and the dark panelled walls still gleamed as richly as ever in the glow from the blazing fire. Central heating had been installed in her absence, but the slimline radiators were discreetly positioned so they didn't look out of place. On closer inspection, she saw that the windows were new, and were also double-glazed, a fact that hadn't been apparent from the outside of the house. It was only when she discovered she couldn't feel the old familiar draughts whistling round her ears that she'd even suspected they weren't the same windows that had been there for more than a hundred years.

Mari had good taste – Serena had to say that for her, for she knew it would be Mari who had implemented the alterations. Her father had never had either the time or the inclination for that sort of thing. His concern had been only for the works, for Caindale, and his *other* family – the workforce of the foundry and the tenants of his fifty or sixty little houses that littered the hillsides in the valley of Caindale, twenty miles away from

Wintersgill. Caindale had always been his life; his very reason for existing.

Serena felt some sort of explanation was needed for their lateness.

'I'm sorry we didn't get here sooner,' she apologized. 'I wouldn't intentionally miss my own father's funeral, but there was a misunderstanding about the car I'd hired and we had to wait around at the airport for almost two hours till they got it all figured out.'

'It was sweet of you to come at all.' Mari smiled. 'I know only too well what hold-ups are like at airports though. Sugar and milk?' she asked, leaning forward then, her hand hesitating over the rose-patterned china jug.

'No sugar for me.' Serena shook her head. 'Just a little milk.'

The man beside her nodded for both, and Mari heaped sugar into his cup, milk into all of them, then carefully poured out the tea.

'I thought perhaps there'd be a lot of mourners coming back here.' Serena knew her voice was strained. 'I hadn't expected you would be here alone.'

'Everybody in the valley turned out to see the cortege,' Mari said gently at last. 'You see, although Max seldom talked about death, I knew he'd want his last journey to take him to Caindale, past the foundry and then round by the harbour and sea shore. That place was his life. But you'll remember that, of course.'

Serena nodded, her face stiff and polite. 'But nobody came back here with you.'

'That was how I wanted it. I'm arranging for a memorial service to be held at the chapel in Caindale so his "other" family can pay their respects properly to him right there where he was so well thought of.' Her lips twisted ironically, 'He always called the people from the valley his "other" family,' she explained for Ryan's benefit.

'They were only his employees,' Serena said in a flat voice.

'A little more than that, I think.' Mari picked up her cup and sipped at her tea. 'In their own way, they all thought your dad was a grand man.'

There might have been an awkward silence then, but Ryan obviously saw it coming and cut in quickly with, 'Guess I'm an outsider, but I'm looking forward to seeing all the places where Sera grew up around here.'

'Well – this is the house she was born in. You're very welcome to take a look round, Mr Farrar.' Mari seemed happy to get off the subject of the funeral, Serena thought, and try as she might, she herself was finding it hard to actually dislike the woman who had taken her mother's place in her father's affections all those years ago.

'Hey – my name's Ryan. You don't have to call me "mister".' Ryan grinned in a friendly fashion at Mari.

It was all getting too cosy, Serena decided. 'We can't stay long.' She placed her cup and saucer back on the table.

'Have a sandwich. You must be hungry. You've come a long way in the past two days, my dear.'

'We did manage to grab some breakfast – but it was rushed,' Ryan said.

Serena felt herself flushing, and she wished Ryan hadn't said that. It made it seem as if she'd not been in any particular hurry to get to Wintersgill for her father's funeral, and that hadn't been the case at all, though she knew she'd never convince Ryan of that. The truth was, she'd been worried about the effect the long flight might

13

have had on *him* for she was well aware that he had to avoid stress of any kind. It was for that reason alone, she convinced herself now, that she'd insisted on having a break for a meal that morning. 'If only we hadn't stopped,' she said, 'We would probably have arrived in time . . .'

'It was a nice service,' Mari said awkwardly. 'I had some music played that Max liked.'

Serena could never remember a time when her father had been interested in music. All at once she was interested. 'Oh?'

'Nothing mushy. Max wasn't like that. He was a very practical man. He did like the "Anvil" chorus though.' Mari smiled reminiscently. '*Il Trovatore*, you know. Verdi. I've always loved Verdi myself. There's something so very positive about his music.'

Iron! She might have known it would be something that reminded him of his blessed iron. She muttered with as good a grace as she could muster, 'How appropriate.'

As if sensing the antagonism in the air, Mari said, 'Maybe now's the time to let bygones be bygones. Max is dead, Serena.'

Dead and buried! Yet still Serena couldn't bring herself to grieve for the man, and she felt an almighty guilt settling upon her.

'It was his wish that he should be cremated, my dear,' Mari explained softly.

She caught in her breath, thinking again how fitting that was for a man like her father. Fire had been his life – red hot molten iron was his chosen occupation – and fire had been bred in his heart and was the driving force behind his personality. He'd passed on many of his fiery tendencies to her. Like her father, she was quick to anger, and

14

grievances, though she had few, were slow burning with a white hot core that made them hard to extinguish.

Mari was speaking again. 'I did exactly what Max had left instructions for me to do. He left all his affairs in order. He was a very meticulous man and had made a will several years ago.'

Ryan leaned forward and helped himself to a sandwich. Serena guessed he didn't really want it, but just needed to stop Mari talking about death and Max's funeral as he said, 'Mmm. These are good. You should have something to eat, Sera . . .'

She rounded on him impatiently. 'I don't *want* anything.'

Mari gazed from one to the other of her two visitors, and Ryan gulped down the rest of his sandwich and said, 'Mrs Wyatt – maybe I shouldn't have come. I'm not much good at times like this . . .'

His voice broke off, and Serena, seeing the expression of utter pain in his eyes, explained quietly to Mari, 'Ryan lost his own father a few months ago.'

'Oh, my dear – I'm so sorry. And here I am, going on and on about Max . . .'

'It's okay.' Ryan dusted crumbs off his jacket, but Serena could see he was remembering the shooting in Queensland, and it was upsetting him, making him jumpy.

'How long are you staying in England?' Mari asked on a quick change of subject.

Serena frowned. 'Just as long as it takes to get Dad's affairs settled, I suppose.'

'The lawyer will see to everything,' Mari said. 'Mr Andrews and his partners are very good.'

'There's not just the house to think about though, is there? What's going to happen to the foundry – and the

15

people who live in the valley?' Turning to Ryan, and seeing the haunted expression still there on his pale, thin face, she knew she had to give him something other than his own troubles to think about. 'It's a hideous place – Caindale!' she said lightly. 'It's a deep gorge in the hills leading down to the sea. It's rocky and barren, and the water in the creek is red because it runs over the ironstone rocks. There's an old mine too – where ironstone used to be worked, but it's derelict now. And then there's the foundry with its black smoke belching out, killing what little vegetation there is on the hillsides. Honestly, Ryan, you'll hate it when I show you what it's like at Caindale . . .'

'It's not so bad now,' Mari broke in. 'You're remembering it all from ten years ago, but there are new regulations governing smoke and fumes now. It's a thriving little community is Caindale. It's the only decent place to work for miles around here. If there were no foundry, there'd be no Caindale folk left. It's a lifeline for them. And your father was a good employer . . .'

Serena rose to her feet abruptly, seeing Mari bite down hard on her lip as she obviously remembered things that had happened at Caindale in the past. Would Mari ever be able to forget, she wondered? Certainly Serena knew that she herself never could. No matter how far away from Caindale she went, she would always feel the same hot shame she'd felt for years past now, would always regret the stupid things she'd done. She'd never be able to forgive herself – even if she lived to be a hundred – she just knew she wouldn't.

It was something she'd never spoken about to Ryan, but now he was looking at her with a puzzled expression and it was painfully obvious that she couldn't keep him in

16

the dark about this. Staying as they would be doing for the next few weeks – so near to Caindale – it was highly probable that there'd be somebody left who would remember and tell him what she'd been like in her rebellious teens. And she didn't want him hearing it from anybody else. All the same, it was difficult to talk about such things – especially in front of Mari – but it had to be done.

She faced him again. 'I did some terrible things when I was younger,' she said quietly. 'And if I'd had my way, Caindale would have vanished off the face of the earth by now. Ryan, you don't know me at all. I'm not proud now of what I did, but I tried every trick in the book to wipe the place out . . .' she laughed harshly, and continued, 'In my teens I was one hell of a rebel. I set out on a mission – a mission to topple the king of Caindale – my father, and to rid the world of Caindale because I hated it so much.' She paused briefly for breath, and to entwine her fingers together in front of her, and look down, and away from his astonished face, before continuing. 'I broke into the foundry and smashed machinery. I set fire to chemicals in the works' paint shop; I wrecked water pipes and flooded the place; I stole one of my father's rifles and meticulously potted out every window in the office block. I took Daddy's keys and locked every door at the works – then I threw them away, and production was held up for half a day while the other keyholders were contacted . . .'

She glanced up briefly. Ryan was gazing at her, stunned at her words.

'But why?' he asked at last. 'Why did you do those things, Sera?'

'Because Caindale belonged to my father,' she said, turning to look at Mari again, 'And because I was jealous of the time he spent with that "other" family of his – the workers – the people who lived there.'

Mari struggled to her feet then stood there, shaking her head. 'No,' she said, 'That wasn't the real reason, was it, Serena?'

Serena faltered, 'I – I don't know what you mean . . .'

'It was mainly because of me that you rebelled! It was because your father took up with me after your mother died . . .' Mari held out her hands imploringly.

The words were out before Serena realized she was going to say them, 'You mean *before* my mother died,' she cried, 'Not "*after*", Mrs Wyatt.'

Mari reeled back from her, and her voice was a hoarse whisper as she asked, 'How . . . how did you know . . .?' and her mouth dropped open.

Dazed at her outburst, Serena nonetheless knew that once started she couldn't pretend those words hadn't been uttered. She said in a hard tone, 'I saw you! Both of you! You were here in this very room on the day my mother died.'

Ryan was on his feet, tugging at Serena's shoulder. 'Hey,' he was saying softly, 'Sera, love – don't start any trouble.'

'Trouble!' She spun round to him. '*Trouble!*' She laughed crazily without any joy in the sound. Then wearily her shoulders sagged and she said, 'She was in Daddy's arms and he was kissing her. They were laughing. They were happy. And my mother had just died . . . it was obvious even to a kid of my age that something had been going on between them for a long time . . .'

Mari's face crumpled. 'I never knew . . .' She shook her head again, this time in an obvious attempt to clear it of

18

past memories. She stared hard at Serena and said, 'How did you come to be there? Max had taken you over to the Manleys' house that day. He took you there early in the morning because we knew your mother was dying. The doctor was with her – she had a nurse too. They both said it would be best if you were . . .'

'Out of the way!' Serena was breathing fast. Her hands were clenched at her sides. She felt very defenceless though, and her gaze suddenly dropped to the floor. 'Out of the way,' she whispered. 'Nobody asked me what I wanted, but I knew I'd never see my mother again if I was compliant enough to fall in with your plans. I wanted to be here . . .' She raised her eyes to those of Mari, 'Can you understand that? I wanted to be with my mother, so after Dad left me at the Manleys', I came back. Mrs Manley had given me a pill and left me lying down in one of the bedrooms, but I pretended to sneeze and under cover of doing that I spat the pill out of my mouth. I convinced her though that I'd swallowed it, and then I made her think I was asleep when she came in a few minutes later to check on me. It was easy after that to creep out of their house and run back home across the moor. And I saw you . . .' Her head jerked back, her eyes blazed at the woman across from her. 'I saw you in my father's arms, and you were both laughing!'

Mari seemed to sway on her feet. She closed her eyes briefly, then opened them and whispered, 'I never wanted to hurt you. I don't want to hurt you now, but there are things you don't understand . . .'

Sarcasm flew from Serena's lips. 'Oh, please – don't try telling me he was madly in love with you or anything like that. I just couldn't stand that.'

'He needed somebody – and no, my dear, your father was never madly in love with *me*!' The older woman drew herself up proudly. 'I loved him though. He was the only man I ever looked at after Harry Wyatt died and left me a widow. No! Max wasn't the sort to lose his heart; he always let his head rule him. But he needed a woman – and Catherine . . . your mother . . . she'd been ill, and no wife at all to him for a long time . . .'

There was a searing pain inside her that had no physical connections, and suddenly she wanted to get rid of that pain and pile it on Mari instead of lugging it around herself any longer. She jeered, 'So it was just sex he was interested in with you!'

Calmly, Mari nodded. 'A man like your father . . .'

'Oh, God! Spare me the details.' She felt Ryan's fingers digging into her shoulder through the thick double wool jacket she was wearing. He was trying to tell her she was going too far, she knew, but she took no heed of him. All her attention was fixed on the woman in front of her.

'Your mother had suffered so much towards the end,' Mari said quietly. 'It was a relief to know that it was all over.'

'A relief for *you* too – knowing that you'd got what you wanted . . . or at least that very soon you would be doing just that.'

Mari put her hands up to her face and started to cry softly.

Serena didn't know what to do then. She was shocked; it hadn't been her intention to rake up the past like this. Ryan jerked her round to face him. 'Idiot,' he snapped. 'Today's not the time for opening up old wounds, Sera.'

She swallowed painfully. She was scared – scared that she'd said things that could never now be un-said, for in her heart she knew that Mari was the one who had been used. If blame were being laid at anybody's door, she knew her father should have been the one to account for his actions.

He must have encouraged Mari when he'd known she was in love with him. He was a hard man. And what had Mari got out of the relationship anyway, she asked herself? Her father had never married the woman, had he? And there'd been nothing standing in the way of marriage for either of them.

One thing was becoming clear to Serena however. She was at last beginning to understand herself a little more, and to realize what it was that had driven her to act the way she had done in her teenage years. Unable to vent her anger on the woman who had stolen her father away from her, she'd poured all her hate out on the works, on the foundry, and on Caindale – all inanimate objects that couldn't hit back at her, but whose damage would surely hurt her father.

Mari was mopping at her eyes with a tissue now. Her mascara was smudged. Serena suddenly felt incredibly sorry for her. And for one wild impetuous moment, wanted to fling her arms round the older woman and say she was sorry.

Ryan said, 'We ought to be going,' and the moment was lost.

Mari's face was ravaged as she looked up, 'But where will you stay? I thought perhaps you'd want your old room here for a while, Serena – I got it all ready for you – aired the bedding and polished the furniture. And it wouldn't be any trouble to do the same with the guest room for your friend . . .'

21

'Here!' Serena didn't know whether to laugh or cry at the thought of staying under the same roof as Mari, 'Oh no thank you,' she said. 'No! We'll find an hotel somewhere. It shouldn't prove too difficult, getting a couple of rooms at this time of year. North Yorkshire's not noted for its mild holiday climate in the middle of winter, is it?'

Mari's face was pinched. 'But you'll let me know where I can contact you?'

Serena nodded, and she relented a little. 'I'll ring you tonight. I suppose there'll be things to sort out about the house . . . you'll need time to find somewhere else to live.'

Mari stood still, looking at her, then slowly she shook her head. 'I think there's something you should know,' she said. 'This is *my* home!'

Ryan caught hold of Serena's arm as her temper flared briefly again. 'Leave it,' he warned. 'Leave this to the proper people Sera. The solicitors will sort it out.'

Serena ignored him and shot the question at Mari, 'Just what do you mean? *Your* home.'

'Max left a will.' Mari's voice was very calm and businesslike. 'He wanted me to have Wintersgill. He knew how much I loved the old house, but all your things are still here if you want them.' Mari's hands fluttered ineffectually, showing her agitation, 'They're all stored in the attic with your mother's belongings.'

'But Wintersgill is *my* home . . .' Serena felt her stomach turning over. Since seeing the old house again this morning, she'd known that this was what she wanted – a haven to return to! A place of her own where she could wake up every morning to see the biggest sky in England above her. There was nowhere in all the world to equal the view from Wintersgill. The stark, bare moors had a grandeur that had clutched at her very soul as she'd driven up to the house today. She'd felt as if she wanted to put her arms right round her home and all her old haunts. Her love and longing for her past had made her feel big enough to do that too. She'd forgotten how solid and dependable Wintersgill was, forgotten too till an hour ago, how happy she'd been there as a child. Those two stone acorns at the bottom of the terrace steps had brought poignant memories sweeping back.

Damn those acorns, she thought bitterly. And damn Mari Wyatt too for whisking everything out of her grasp with that one little statement: 'This is *my* home!' Like hell it was!

'I'm sorry.' The woman spread her hands. 'I really am sorry. But you went away – you left it all. Max was angry at first, then he became worried and he even went so far as to pay somebody to trace you. He couldn't bear to think he'd driven you away. And he wrote to you – when he discovered you were still in England. For years he wrote to you but you never replied. He used to get in the car and drive up beyond the Tees and the Tyne, and he'd tell me how he'd sit watching the little house you'd taken lodgings in, waiting for you to go in and out. And you never knew he was there because Max was a proud man, and he wouldn't approach you – not when he came to realize you wanted nothing more to do with him. And in the end . . .' she shrugged, 'in the end he had to give up and come to the only conclusion possible – that he'd lost you, and you were never coming back either to him or to Wintersgill.'

Serena felt guilty about those letters she'd received from Max now. She'd opened them all and had read them with hatred eating away at her heart. And she'd laughed at the words he'd poured out on paper, the words that had told her he wanted her back. She'd even laughed as she'd torn

23

them up and burnt them. But after every one of them, she'd sat with her head in her hands, sobbing her heart out in her dreary little room, because she knew she could never forgive him. Even with all his pleading for her to come home, she wouldn't let herself believe that her father could have changed so much.

'He cared for nothing – nothing except Caindale,' she flared. 'He treated me like a possession, that's the only reason why he wanted me to come back. But he never cared a jot about me – or about my mother when she was alive. He couldn't have done,' she insisted, 'or he'd never have taken up with you, would he?'

Mari shook her head. 'That's not true, my dear.'

'Oh, but it is! And I hated him for it. I hated Caindale too. I still wish Caindale would disappear overnight. I've always hated it.'

It was Mari's turn to look distraught. 'You shouldn't say that,' she said in a quiet voice. 'You really shouldn't, Serena.'

'Why not?' Serena stood motionless in the doorway with Ryan hovering, ill at ease just behind her. 'Why not?' she stormed softly. 'Just give me one good reason why I shouldn't hate the place.'

'Because,' Mari said, with a haunted expression in her eyes, 'Caindale belongs to you now. Max left it to you in its entirety. My dear, you're going to be solely responsible from now on for the place you hated so much – and for the well-being of all the people who live there.'

'Wha-at?' Serena felt her head beginning to spin.

'It's true, my dear.' Mari took a deep breath before speaking again, 'Caindale,' she said calmly, 'is your inheritance, Serena.'

24

CHAPTER 2

'I shall destroy it!' As Serena drove away from the house with Ryan beside her, she was determined on that one aim to the exclusion of all else. 'It's mine. Caindale is mine, so at last I can finish the job I started all those years ago.'

'You're crazy!' Ryan stared moodily out of the car window. 'How can you talk about destroying a complete village?'

'I can because it's mine.' She flicked a glance at him; her heart was racing madly. She had a feeling of power now, and it was a good feeling. 'I can tear down all those miserable little houses, I can raze the damned foundry to the ground and even dynamite what's left of the old ironstone mine to blazes as well if I feel like it.'

'And then what?' He threw up his hands in despair as over to their right, across acres of damp green meadows, the grey haze of the sea came into view. 'What will you do then?' he wanted to know. 'Will you just turn your back on it all and walk away with vengeance still corroding your heart?'

She thought about his words for several minutes as she concentrated on pulling the car up to the highest point of the moors where the scenery was spectacular.

The sea was a murky line on the horizon today that stretched as far as the eye could see, and the moors were covered in blackened heather which had a sinister beauty all its own under the fast-gathering clouds.

Rough-coated sheep gazed at them as the car sped northwards, but her mind was miles away, at Caindale, where as a child she'd been free to roam all over the steep-sided walls of the wooded valley when her father had taken her down to the foundry with him at weekends and in the school holidays. It had been a safe place in which to play when she was young. There'd never been much traffic to worry about in the narrow streets; Caindale folk couldn't afford fancy cars. And anyway, the valley led nowhere except to the sea.

The main road into Caindale consisted of numerous narrow little bridges that spanned the winding, iron-red waters of the Caindale beck. The beck was a stream that tumbled down from the high moors, then twisted and turned its way through the whole of the valley, splashing over a bed of ironstone rocks. It ended its journey by flowing under the last bridge and out in a wide sweep across the beach and into the sea. That final bridge was hardly wider than a footpath, and it led directly onto the shore where fishermen had built ramshackle boat sheds to keep their nets and lobster pots safe. Along the stony stretch of beach she could remember skipping between the brightly-coloured fishing cobles, playing hide and seek with the children of Caindale . . .

'What *are* you going to do with the damn place then?'

'Just clear it of people, *and* buildings that should have been pulled down years ago.'

'Clear it of Max Corder, you mean?' His gaze was accusing.

'Don't be stupid, Ryan.'

'I'm not being stupid,' he said quietly. 'I'm just trying to make you see sense. Can't you get it into your head that your father is dead? You don't have to fight him any longer. You don't have to try and prove *anything* any more.'

'While Caindale is there though, I'll never be able to forget Dad's treachery. And don't tell me I ought to forgive and forget, Ryan. I can't! Can you even start to understand the heartache my mother must have suffered in those last years. Knowing that Dad had another woman?'

'You don't know for sure that she actually realized your father and Mari were . . .'

'Lovers!' she snapped. 'I don't know. All I do know is, I just want to forget. But Caindale and all its memories won't go away.'

'But is it such a bad thing? Remembering? I mean – even if Caindale disappears, you can't wipe out the past. Okay! Maybe your dad wasn't all he should have been – maybe he *did* have his faults, but is that any excuse for wanton destruction on your part?'

They were high on the moors now, almost at their northern-most edge and about to leave them behind altogether when suddenly she pulled the car in to the side of the road and killed the engine. She turned to him. 'Look – do you want me to take you there now? Would you like to see the place in all its tainted glory? I'm telling you, Ryan, it's a hell hole.'

Wearily he leaned his head back and closed his eyes. 'No,' he muttered. 'I don't want to see Caindale. Not today anyway. I just want to get into an hotel room and put my head on a pillow. Okay?'

At once she was concerned. 'Is your head hurting?'

'Yes,' he snapped. 'It hurts, but you ought to be used to me and my damned nuisance of a head by now.'

'Ryan . . .' Panic edged her voice. 'Ryan – shall I get you to a doctor – or a hospital?'

He opened one eye and grinned at her. 'I've had a pill,' he said, 'so you can stop playing "mummy". I'll be okay when I've had a good sleep – and,' he added meaningfully, 'I'll be even better when you've stopped your eternal nagging.'

'Are you sure you're all right?'

His eyes were closed again. 'Yes,' he said. 'Drive on, Sera, darling, and for God's sake get us an hotel with comfortable beds; I don't care what it costs.'

'We'll have the best,' she said, starting up the engine again. 'After all, I'm a landowner now, aren't I? We'll have the very best rooms in the very best hotel – I promise you that.'

Rivelyn was a tiny seaside town just up the coast from Caindale, and hotels with star ratings, Serena discovered, just didn't exist in that part of the world. They booked in at a huge inn, however, that was built of rugged stone and had ivy clinging to its front. A copper plaque on its wall boasted of it being built in early Victorian times.

Ryan tumbled onto the bed exhausted within minutes of being shown to his room. Serena was only two bedrooms away from him, and she went to see that he was settled as soon as her bags had been brought in.

'Do you want me to pull the curtains across the window?' She sat on the edge of the bed where he'd thrown himself, one arm slung haphazardly across his eyes.

'No,' he said. 'This headache won't last for ever, and a darkened room doesn't help any when I get a humdinger like this.'

'You'll call me if you need me? There's a telephone here beside the bed, see? You only have to dial the number of my room . . . it's a hundred and eight, will you remember that or shall I write it down and leave it here beside the phone for you?'

'Don't fuss.' He lay perfectly still with his eyes closed.

'Let me cover you over with the quilt.'

'I'm warm enough,' he muttered.

She had to admit the room *was* hot – stifling almost. There was a bulky radiator under the bay window, and she could feel the heat from it from where she sat. 'Promise me you'll call me . . .' She was reluctant to leave him.

'For God's sake . . .' He lifted his arm a fraction and his eyes blinked open. 'Go away!' he said. 'Go out somewhere and forget about me for a couple of hours, huh? You know I'm lousy company when I get a headache like this.'

'I worry about you.'

'I worry about me enough for the two of us.' He gave her a wink and a weak smile. 'Just go, kiddo,' he pleaded.

'I'm only two doors down the corridor. Remember that, won't you?'

'Go out, Sera, my sweet. Go look at your valley,' he suggested.

She protested with vehemence, 'I can't do that.'

'Yes you can; you own the damn place, don't you? Nobody's going to arrest you for trespass in a place you actually *own*, woman!'

'I mean – I can't leave you . . .'

'I'm beginning to wish I'd stayed at home in Queensland.'

'Don't say that.' She was hurt by his words.

'Then don't "baby" me. You know I hate it. And you did promise not to go all maternal on me.'

'Don't baby me' was an expression of his she was beginning to know well! She'd had the utmost sympathy with him, knowing how he'd hated it when he'd been in hospital and helpless as a baby last year. It had started as a bit of a joke between them when he'd told her the nurses 'babied' him – meaning that they washed him, fed him, staggered under his weight when he threw the bedpans at them and insisted instead on going to the lavatory on his own two feet . . .

'Okay,' she said. 'Maybe I will have a drive down to Caindale. After all, it's been ten years. Perhaps I'll be pleasantly surprised if I find they've cleaned it up and there are roses growing round every door.'

'Maybe they'll have turned it into a national park, huh? Planted trees, brought in a few koala bears, and sited a few bar-bees along the roadside.'

'You forget,' she said drily, 'They don't have koala bears in England, and the only trees Caindale had were poor stunted things that shrivelled up in the fumes from the foundry. As for barbeques – well, I suppose they *might* have them up here in summer – but definitely not in January.'

'Bring me a steak if you do find one,' he murmured as he drifted in and out of sleep. 'I could just eat a real juicy steak . . .'

She knew the pills he took for the pain were strong, so she tiptoed quietly from the room and closed the door as carefully as she could to avoid disturbing him as his breathing deepened and the arm across his face grew slack. Once outside in the corridor, she leaned back against the door and gazed up at the ceiling. He was getting worse. The headaches were more frequent now. She felt helpless . . .

She drove out of Rivelyn in the damp dusk of a raw January afternoon. Soon it would be dark, she knew. She drove as fast as the road allowed, averse to the idea of visiting Caindale in total darkness. She shivered, and felt goose bumps prickling at the back of her neck even as she thought about the place, and as she turned off the main coastal road, and into the valley of Caindale some ten minutes later, her mouth was dry. Ten years ago she vividly recalled vowing she'd never return to Caindale again as long as she lived.

The road dipped sharply as soon as she entered the valley, and from then on it was all downhill. The little bridges – all made of sturdy concrete, and having tortuous bends – made driving hazardous in the dusk. She tried not to look at the foundry as she passed it, but couldn't help noticing its doors were closed and there was no smoke hanging round it like it did in days gone by. The whole place was in darkness. Then she realized it would be closed today as a mark of respect for her father. A grim smile tugged at her lips. If Max Corder had been in a position to know the place wasn't working, he'd be docking the men's wages, she had no doubt at all about that.

At the end of the road, a few yards away from the final bridge, she parked the car, got out and locked it. The beach was a tiny bay, cut in half by the Caindale beck, and with the two high cliffs, one to the north, the other to the south, making two towering arms that reached out to protect it. She stood and watched the sea and listened to it pounding on the deserted shore and splashing against

31

the foot of the cliffs. In the gathering dusk she could just make out the stone jetty under the north cliff where ironstone used to be shipped out from the valley at the beginning of the century. It had nothing to commend it now, being merely a cumbersome projection of grey granite that served no useful purpose any more.

To the south the cliffs were higher, and had always been safe nesting places for the thousands of sea birds that clustered shrieking around the fishing boats when they came in to the shore. She turned her back on the sea and looked at the road she'd come down in the bottom of the huge cleft between the hills. In the valley of Caindale, that was the only road in, and out of the place. The slopes of the high hills were densely wooded, though at this time of year there were no leaves on the trees. The whole place looked bleak and barren, and she could just make out the rows of terraced houses clinging to their hillsides – grey little homesteads – grey-slated, grey pebble-dashed, and with grey smoke curling up from their chimneys into an even greyer wintry sky. Some had lights twinkling in their windows. Others had curtains drawn across to shut out the cold night air and the draughts.

It was all a far cry from the wide, sun-streaked beaches she'd left behind in Queensland. Strangely though, she found she wasn't sorry to be back home. Memory was a strange thing, she decided. When you started looking backwards in time, little incidents came creeping into your mind that made you realize it hadn't *all* been bad at Caindale. There *had* been good times – good friends.

One friend in particular . . . But he wouldn't still be here, she reasoned. *He'd* had ambition. And the last time he'd looked at her it had been with revulsion in his eyes. She dashed all thoughts of Holt Blackwood from her mind. The past was sometimes left well alone – and where it belonged – strictly in the past.

She began to walk alongside the rusty-coloured water towards the jetty, and as she drew near the massive overhanging north cliff she had to force herself to keep on walking. It was here that Max had died, Mari had told her when she'd called her in Queensland less than a week ago. He'd apparently fallen from the north cliff and was lying on the rocks below, half in, half out of the Caindale beck when one of the local fishermen – old George Cook – had found him. She tilted her head back and looked up at the towering headland above her. Why had he been up there, she asked herself? And how had he fallen? He knew the area so intimately and was well aware of the danger the high cliffs presented. She shuddered as she looked down at the rippling, trickling stream. Behind her a street lamp flickered into life, sending its harsh light sprawling across the shallow water and the beach, emphasizing the redness of the ironstone bed as it churned towards the sea.

She didn't want to think about what had happened to her dad. Yet all that filled her mind at that moment was a broken body, lying there lifeless, its blood spilling out into the Caindale beck – red blood on red stones.

She had that prickling sensation down her spine again, almost as if she was being watched, and suddenly she knew she'd been a fool to come here alone. It was almost as if her father's ghost was standing there beside her, silently condemning her for what she'd said earlier about destroying Caindale. She whirled round from the sea and started hurrying towards the buildings huddled round the shore – the Methodist chapel, the post office, the working men's club. The place was deserted. Up on the hillsides she could see the lights in the houses again and she felt oddly comforted by them. But, she told herself, she should have waited till tomorrow and brought Ryan with her in broad daylight.

She stumbled over heaps of stones that had been washed up by many a turbulent tide, and took a deep gulp of a breath when she finally had her feet on solid tarmac again. She'd spent longer here than she'd intended, she realized, glancing down at her watch as she passed under a street light.

Back in the car she belted herself thankfully into her seat, started up the engine and switched on the headlights. She reversed into a gap between the fishermen's huts, then swung the steering wheel to get a good turning circle. And it was then that the headlights picked out the long, low white building that she'd missed when she was coming down into the valley half an hour earlier. She frowned. It was new – that building. New from ten years ago anyway. Slowly she drove towards it and made out the words carved in a huge chunk of stone across its wide entrance. 'Caindale Medical Centre'!

She pressed on the accelerator and the headlights swept round from the building to a neat white wall alongside. Then she gasped, and all the breath left her body as she stamped hard on the brake to avoid a figure standing beside the wall in the shadows.

And her father's face stared straight through the car's windscreen, not half a dozen yards away from her.

Shock held her rigid in her seat. Automatically, without even thinking about it she found she'd turned off the ignition and her gaze was rivetted on that phantom in front of her.

Then reason prevailed. It wasn't a ghost. Of course it wasn't. Her own common sense gradually took over and interpreted what she could see through the windscreen. Slowly, she unhitched her seat belt and got out of the car.

It was an excellent likeness of Max Corder, she noted, that life-size bronze statue which had sent her mind reeling, though now she was seeing it clearly, she realized it was standing on a marble plinth with a hollowed-out niche behind it and it didn't look human at all. If it *had* been her father in real life, it would have been moving not standing still. Max had been a do-er, not a man who stood around idly watching the tide coming in and going out.

She shifted her gaze from his face. Against his feet was a plaque that informed anybody interested enough to read it, that this was Max Corder, benefactor of Caindale, who on his sixtieth birthday had officially opened the new medical centre which he had been personally responsible for building – exclusively for the people of Caindale.

This was a new Max Corder to the father she remembered, Serena thought guardedly. The old Max wouldn't have given a damn for the welfare of the people of his valley. All that had interested him ten years ago had been getting as big a bank balance as possible behind him. He hadn't cared about the men who worked for him. He'd haggled over every penny he paid them. No! It might look like her father, it might actually be a replica of the man, but the words on the plaque were wrong. That man standing there was a man who'd been a tyrant to his employees – not a kindly patron. Max had always been a thoroughly selfish individual who had put everything *he* wanted before the needs of others.

In the darkness, she heard the sound of another vehicle coming down the narrow, winding road into the valley. It wasn't a car, it sounded heavier than that. She frowned as she saw the beam of strong headlights lighting up the road beyond the trees, and a dark shape came lumbering towards her out of the darkness.

She realized suddenly that her car might be in the way of what sounded like quite a heavy truck. Quickly she ran over to it and pulled the door open, but the other vehicle was coming round the bend now, and coming quite fast. She heard the sound of the engine diminish as the driver went into a lower gear. In the darkness she couldn't make out what was on the back of the lorry, but it was something big and cumbersome.

'Hell! I hope he can stop!'

He did. He was obviously an experienced trucker! He stopped the twenty tonner with ease, then jumped down onto the road, a big man with a tangle of dark hair, and long rangy strides and swinging arms. In the beam of her own headlights she saw he had a shock of black hair streaked with grey. He was thin as a rail with narrow hips and wide shoulders. A hideous purple shirt was tucked into his jeans, and a green and black check lumber-jacket was flung on top of it. Both shirt and jacket were unfastened, and she could see black hair lying thick across his chest. Something about that open-necked shirt, and the black hair unnerved her. She didn't want to remember the past, but it seemed the ghosts were out in force tonight.

Her feet felt superglued to the ground. He looked tough and fierce and her first inclination was to jump back in the car and lock all the doors, but his voice stopped her. She stood still and was forced to listen to the polite words as they made her world rock crazily around her.

'Sorry to bother you, maam,' he drawled. 'But I've got a wide load on board. Could I trouble you to pull over a couple of yards?'

The well-remembered voice played havoc with her heart – it had a lilting northern roughness that she knew she would never forget as long as she lived. The gaudy outfit was unfamiliar, but that voice couldn't possibly belong to anyone else except . . .

'Holt!' she gasped out unsteadily. 'Holt Blackwood!'

She nearly laughed out loud at the expression of stunned surprise that flared in his face. He advanced to within a couple of feet of her, peered closely at her in the semi-darkness, then asked incredulously, 'It isn't, is it? It can't be. Not you. Not after all these years . . .?'

She nodded and let go of the car door so that it swung to and clicked shut beside her. Her knees felt weak, just as they'd always done in the past when he'd been around. Funny really, she thought, she'd imagined she'd grown out of things like that, but now it was here again – that heart-stopping, head-reeling feeling had her in its grip again.

His big hands reached out towards her, hovered just above her shoulders, jigged up and down as if they didn't know whether to touch her or not, then suddenly clamped down hard round the top of her arms and dragged her towards him.

And she clung to him, even as she cursed herself and tried to fight down the elation that was bubbling away inside her as he held her in a bear hug to beat all bear hugs. She tilted back her head, laughing up at him, and then before she realized what was happening she was being subjected to the hardest, clumsiest, most ecstatic kiss she'd ever been given in the whole of her life. She wasn't going to go overboard for him again, she told herself firmly. But her lips weren't listening to her, and neither was her heart. Wantonly, she was kissing him back with a fierce hunger leaping up inside her that wasn't sated until both of them were breathless and reeling with the intensity of the feelings their strange meeting had brought about.

Eventually, she loosened her grip on him and slid her hands up to his chest, but it wasn't to push him away that she did it. She couldn't do that. But she could, and did manage to prevent herself from clinging like a limpet to him any more. He wasn't going to run away, she told herself. He'd been startled by her appearance, but he wasn't angry with her any more. When his lips parted from hers and he held her slightly away from him to look at her again, there was no hard glint in his eyes like there had been the last time she'd seen him.

No! He was genuinely pleased to see her. And the past was a closed door – for the moment, at least.

'Holt!' she said, shaking her head as she looked up at him. 'Holt Blackwood.' There was a tremor in her voice, and she felt as if the smile he'd brought to her face could never be erased.

Gently though, he moved her away from him until he was holding her at arm's length. Then he just stared at her.

Her lips felt bruised all over, her arms, she was sure – despite the thickness of her wool jacket – would bear the imprint of his fingers for days to come. He'd always been impulsive though, and that was what she'd loved about him. She managed a shaky sort of laugh and said, 'Wow! What a welcome.'

'Serena,' he said on a note of pure incredulity. 'What the hell are you doing in Caindale?'

'Dad . . .' she began, but he gave her no chance to say more.

'Yes, of course. You weren't at the crematorium though.' At last his hands fell away from her and her own dropped to her sides. She didn't know whether to be thankful he'd let her go or not.

'Were you there?'

His reply was bitingly critical. '*I* had no grievance with Max. Nobody did – except you, of course. They were all there at the service, but they wouldn't intrude further than that. Mari's arranging a memorial do – here in Caindale. That will be the time for them to really say goodbye to Max.'

'I got held up at the airport . . . I've been in Queensland, you see . . .'

'Australia?' he said, astounded. 'Max never mentioned that you'd gone so far afield.'

'I've been there for the past two years,' she said. 'Doing some research at Cape York.'

'That's some wilderness to hide yourself away in,' he said, and his dark eyes suddenly turned hard as they swept over her. 'What was the attraction in Queensland, I wonder?'

'Butterflies,' she said with an awkward little laugh. 'I got interested in butterflies at the Rothermere nature reserve in Northumberland. I worked there for several years after I left . . . home. It was because of my work there that I got the opportunity to go to Queensland.'

'Australia's a heck of a long way to go just to see a few butterflies.' He hooked his thumbs through a leather belt that was pulled tight round his scant waist, and gazed down on her.

'They were quite special butterflies,' she said a little breathlessly, but she was beginning to feel gauche, and more than a bit awkward when his smoky eyes were smouldering critically at her, and the dark lean face reminding her forcibly of the first time she'd fallen in love – a long time ago.

'So tell me.' His head tilted to one side and his eyes narrowed, though his firm straight mouth was crooked attractively in the merest shadow of a smile.

'Well, one butterfly in Australia was especially lovely – the Ulysses – it's a gorgeous iridescent blue. Then there was the Cairns – as big as a bird with a wingspan of almost twenty centimetres . . .' She broke off, laughed a little self-consciously and said, 'You're laughing at me. I can tell, you're laughing at me . . .'

'No,' he said, 'I just never saw you so enthusiastic about anything in your life before – unless it was when you were causing trouble for your dad.'

'Holt – no. Don't bring that up again.' The smile had been wiped off her face at his words.

He lifted his wide shoulders as if he couldn't care less any more. 'Okay,' he said. 'Tell me more about butterflies – though most folk being given the opportunity to see Queensland would be raving about the barrier reef, not butterflies.'

Almost at once, the light faded from her eyes, and she felt incredibly weary. It had been a long day, she reminded herself, and just at this moment in time she didn't want reminding about the barrier reef. It brought back too many bad memories – memories of Don Farrar, and the shooting . . .

'Hey!' He spread his hands expressively. 'What have I said, lady?'

'The barrier reef is something I'd rather forget,' she said, tossing her head and turning away to her car once

40

more. 'The man I went out to work for – Don Farrar – he was killed there.'

'Hey, I'm sorry.'

'It's okay. I'm learning to live with it.'

'You've come back all alone then?'

'No-o. Not quite. Don's son is with me.'

'I see.' His eyes narrowed again.

He didn't see at all and she wanted to tell him so. But looking at things logically, it really was no business of his at all – who she took up with.

'A kiddy, huh? You sure have some guts, taking on somebody else's little 'un.' Those eyes of steel turned suddenly soft as the wings of doves. 'That was a right nice gesture.'

'Ryan's twenty-seven years old,' she said, 'only a year younger than I am.' And she had to smile at the expression of shock that landed fair and square on his rugged face. She opened the car door and leaned on it to ask, 'What about you, Holt? Have the years been kind? And what on earth are you doing driving that enormous truck?'

He seemed to shake himself mentally before answering, 'Oh, that's just one of many. You know how I always had dreams of becoming a racing driver?'

She nodded. 'Don't tell me they've taken up truck-racing in these parts.'

'I gave up the idea of owning a Masserati or a Ferrari,' he said with a wicked grin, 'when I found out there was more money to be made out of trucking.'

'You own that thing? You actually own it?'

With a bit of a swagger, he said, 'I told you – it's one of many I own. I make my living out of transporting wide loads, long loads, and loads that nobody else wants to know about.'

41

'You do? I seem to remember you were doing something with computers when I went away.'

'I still do things with computers,' he said easily, 'you can't run a trucking business without computers.'

She frowned and glanced at her watch again. 'I have to get back,' she said. 'It's been nice meeting up with you again though.'

'Is that all? Nice?' All at once he was deadly serious. 'You walk out on me ten years ago, then come back and shake my life up, and all you can say is it's nice to see me?'

Guardedly, she said, 'I don't remember doing the walking out.'

'You were a bitch in those days,' he said. 'When I saw what you were trying to do to Max, I suddenly found I didn't like you quite as much as I thought I did.'

Disdainfully, she said, 'Yeah. I remember you telling me that at the time.'

'We could have worked things out,' he said, 'You didn't have to take off at our first major row.'

'I was eighteen,' she said. 'Things were bad at home. Dad wanted to move *your* Aunt Mari into Wintersgill and I couldn't stand for that – not while I was still living there.' She lifted her shoulders in a shrug, 'Then you came down on me like a ton of bricks – telling me I was a spoilt brat, that I ought to grow up . . .'

'You were a spoilt brat,' he said, 'But I could have changed all that, given the chance.'

Airily she said, 'What would you have done? Taken me away from it all?' Her laugh came harshly. 'You were hardly the knight in shining armour type, Holt. We were both of us drop-outs if I remember.'

He couldn't meet her gaze. He looked down at the tips of his boots, rocked back and forth on his heels for a second or two before bringing his eyes up to meet hers again. 'Okay!' he said. 'You're right. I should have snapped you up while I had the chance. Marriage would have been good for you, for both of us, but I was nothing but a waster in those days. I didn't know what I wanted. And Max would never have accepted me as a son-in-law – even though he had given me a job of sorts in the foundry laboratory.'

She smiled, remembering. 'He used to yell at me when he knew I'd been seeing you at weekends.'

'I can't say I blame him. My intentions were not strictly honourable when I was a down-and-out twenty-four-year-old.'

'So what changed you?' She was genuinely interested. In the old days he'd had no job, no prospects till Max had taken him on. He did a bit of fishing, a bit of anything that came his way. But he wasn't the sort to settle down.

'Max changed me.'

'Dad?' She frowned.

'When I showed little or no aptitude for foundry work, Max told me he needed a reliable means of transport for his iron castings. He offered me the chance of humping those great chunks of iron all over the country – providing that I set up my own business and made a real effort to get my life in order.'

'And?'

'He loaned me the money for my first truck.'

'Are we talking about the same Max Corder who was my father?' she asked, her voice heavy with sarcasm. 'Are you telling me *he* did that?' She was suddenly very wary. Max had never – not in her memory anyway – put himself out to give anybody a helping hand.

'We got to be great buddies. That's why I was at his funeral today.'

'Not just to give moral support to your Aunt Mari then?' Her eyebrows shot up.

'That as well,' he admitted, 'though she needed no support from me. She had the strength of the whole valley behind her – men and women alike at the crematorium today. You missed some show there, Serena. It would have opened your eyes. Your dad's going to be sadly missed.'

She shook back her short blonde hair that a light wind in the valley had blown forward onto her forehead. 'Nothing's changed,' she told him in a hard voice.

'Except that Max is dead,' he said quietly.

'That doesn't turn him into a saint.'

'You're still a bitch. I could have hoped you'd had a change of heart by now.'

'I'm late,' she said again. 'And if that's all you've got to say, I guess I'll be going.'

'Back to the boy friend?' He cocked his head on one side as he asked the question.

She sighed. 'Goodbye, Holt,' she said, keeping her temper with difficulty.

'Will I see you again? Before you go back to your butterflies?'

'Very likely.' She pulled the car door open wide and slid into the driving seat.

He walked round to the side of the car and peered in at her. 'I want to see you again,' he said.

'Even though I'm a bitch,' she mocked.

'You've changed in one way,' he said. 'You've had your hair cut. I liked it long and flowing.'

'Well, you've grown yours long and I liked it short,' she said with an attempt at being at least civilized towards him.

He rubbed his hand along his jawline. 'You've changed other ways too.'

'Yeah,' she said, 'I've changed since this morning. This morning I had all my life mapped out. Now though, I find myself responsible for this damned valley.'

'No!' he said, resting one hand on the top of the car and staring in at her. 'Oh, no! Max didn't do that, did he?'

She leaned her head back against the head-rest and looked at him. 'He would, wouldn't he?' she said. 'It's his way of getting even with me – leaving me Caindale and all that goes with it.'

A soft laugh rumbled up from the depths of him, then he pushed himself away from the car, turned away from her to face the statue of her father and lifted one hand to it. 'I salute you, Max Corder,' she heard him say. 'This could be the making of your wayward daughter.'

'It's not funny,' she yelled as she started up the car.

He swung round to her again. 'It is from where I'm standing, Serena my sweet.' He threw back his head and roared with laughter, and that was the last sound she heard as she stamped down hard on the accelerator and pulled the car away from him, having to drive on the grass verge to get past his truck, and then to speed out of the valley.

CHAPTER 3
Melbourne, Australia

Kirsten laughed softly, and the baby's wide blue eyes swung towards the sound. 'Bonny baby,' she whispered. 'What shall I call you?'

There was no need for her to ask herself that question. The answer had been there in her mind all the time she'd been pregnant.

A voice from the doorway asked quietly though, 'Yes, what *will* you call her, Kirsty? And what about her surname? Have you told *him* about her yet?'

Kirsten disengaged her finger from the baby's clutching hand and straightened from the cot to face her sister.

'Holly! Hey – this is great. I didn't think you'd be able to get away from the studio today. And there was me – preparing myself for a really boring afternoon while this little one sleeps herself silly for the next few hours.'

The dark-haired girl walked into the room, letting the door swing to behind her. 'They'll be chucking you out of here soon, I suppose, now that junior's finally graduated out of her humidicrib.'

Kirsten's eyes danced. 'Mmm. I'm going to be a full time mummy – for a while at least.' A shadow crossed her

46

face. 'I won't be able to come back to the studios for a while. I hope they understand?'

Holly sighed. 'I can't really see you coming back at all, Sis. You're in love with that kid already. Do you really think you're going to be able to trust anybody else to look after her while you go back to the hard graft of a television studio, with its long and unsociable hours of working?'

'I'll have to.' Kirsten turned her back on the cot, then invited, 'Come and sit down by the window and let's talk. I've got to start getting my life sorted out, haven't I?'

They might have been twins, Kirsten and Holly, but Kirsten was the younger by two years, and the softer, gentler one of the two. She sank down into a leather-backed chair and looked out over one of the city parks. 'It looks real hot out there today.'

'January usually is!' Holly said drily as she perched on the end of the bed and crossed her slender ankles. She fixed the younger girl with a hard stare. 'You don't know how lucky you are in here. The heat out there is stifling. It's sure brought the midgies out in force.'

'Hooray for air conditioning.' Kirsten grinned.

'Tell me about it!' Holly rolled her eyes up towards the ceiling. 'But I'm not here to talk about the weather, am I? I want to know what you're going to do when they chuck you out of this birthing centre.'

Kirsten relaxed in the chair and looked dreamily over towards the baby's cot again. 'I guess I'll just take things easy for a while till I get back into my stride. I'm still getting used to the "new" me – the one who's not carrying a heavy bump around my middle any more. It's absolute heaven being able to get back into proper clothes. Thanks by the way for dropping those frocks off for me yesterday.'

'I left them on reception when they said you were taking a shower. Sorry I couldn't wait and see you. It was one of those days at the studios.' Holly pulled a face. 'I had a very temperamental prima-donna to interview – and boy, was she hard work!'

Kirsten laughed softly. 'I bet she met her match in you though, Sis.'

Holly glanced over at the crib, then changing the subject, asked, 'Well, have you told him about the baby? You ought to, you know. He has a right . . .'

'Hey! Don't spoil things. Let me live in cloud cuckoo land for a little while longer, huh?'

'No, Kirsty.' The other girl shook her head. 'You've got to face facts. And *he* must too. He's the kid's father, for heaven's sake. He'll have to help you. And if you won't tell him, then I will.'

'You can't.' Kirsten was determined she wasn't going to be rattled. She relaxed even more, stretching out her long legs in front of her. 'He's gone away. Gone with the girl to England.'

'God! And you let him? You knew he was going and you never said a word to stop him?'

'When I left him he was still in Queensland, love. I didn't even suspect I might be pregnant when I came to Melbourne for that interview at your TV studio.'

Holly's brows drew together. 'So how do you know he's gone away?'

Kirsten tapped the telephone on the low table at the side of her. 'I tried ringing him last night. I had a touch of conscience and just wanted to see if he'd talk to me. Well, you know how he's been since he threw me over, don't you? Every time I tried to phone him I got the same treatment – silence on the other end of the line. Honestly,

48

Sis, it was plain bad luck that I wasn't there when Don was shot. It sometimes seems as if he blames me for not being there. After all, it was right after the shooting that he rang me and told me he didn't want to see me again, wasn't it?'

'Don't be silly, Kirsty. He can't possibly blame you for not being there. Heck, you might have stopped a bullet as well if you'd been at the house when that junkie broke in looking for cash to fuel his filthy habit.'

Kirsten considered her sister's words for a few moments, then she said, 'Sera phoned me first, just a few days afterwards, and she was the one who told me Ryan had got a grazed head from a bullet as he tried to take the gun off the man who killed Don. She said it was nothing serious though – not serious enough for me to travel all the way back to Queensland to see him.'

'So?' Holly shrugged. 'What does that prove?'

'I don't know.' Kirsten frowned. 'I wish I *had* gone back though. It was more than two weeks before I was able to get to talk to Ryan on the phone about his dad. I *should have* gone back, Holly. I sensed it at the time . . .'

'But I talked you out of it. Yes! I know I'm to blame, love, but I wasn't to know he was going to wreak havoc with your life, was I? And you did get the job at the TV studio. You just couldn't walk out on that when you'd only been there five minutes, could you?'

Kirsten pulled a face. 'Not after all the strings you'd pulled to get that job for me. No, I couldn't. I was desperate for work. I'd started to think all my studying had been for nothing, and I'd be taking seasonal jobs in holiday resorts for the rest of my life.'

'Do you really think Ryan's not there – in Queensland – any more?'

Kirsten spread her hands, 'Look – I spoke to the woman who's taking care of the Farrar bungalow. She wouldn't lie to me. She said the English girl got some disturbing news and took off for home, taking Ryan with her. That, in my book, points to only one thing – she and Ryan have something going between them. Why else would he go with her?'

'He has a responsibility to *you*, for heaven's sake . . .'

'But he doesn't *know* about the baby,' Kirsten cut in. 'I've been here in Melbourne for over seven months.'

'So you're left high and dry. Is that what you're telling me?'

'Yes. It's beginning to look like it.'

'He's a rat.'

'That's nothing to what I called him when I was giving birth to junior last week,' Kirsten said with a grin.

'You shouldn't have been so pig-headed. You could have had an easier time than you did if you'd taken the dope they offered.'

'I wanted a natural child-birth.'

Holly shuddered. 'You're plain crazy. I'd have let them knock me out and cut me open.'

'And miss all that fun?' Kirsten cocked an eyebrow at her sister and began to laugh.

'I tell you – you're crazy! Crazy for letting him get away scot-free.'

Kirsten shrugged. 'So? I'm crazy. But I've got one beautiful little girl over there in that crib. And who needs a man anyway?'

'So what are you going to call her?'

'There's only one thing I can call her. Reanne! It's the nearest girl's name to "Ryan" I can think of.'

Her older sister slid off the bed abruptly and marched over to the cot. 'Yeah!' she said. 'She looks like him, so she might as well have a name that sounds like him. Is that what you're thinking?'

'I just don't want to forget him. Ever. I loved him, Sis. I still love him, and I always will.'

Holly swung round to face her, flinging her hands up in the air and protesting, 'He told you – over the phone, and again in that letter – that he never wanted to see you again. And what had you done? Nothing! That's what. Nothing! He's just a rat, Kirsty. A dirty little rat who upped and ran once he'd got what he wanted . . .'

'No,' Kirsty replied evenly. 'You're wrong. He did care for me. There was no reason at all for him to act as he did after Don was killed. If only I'd been there at the time, maybe I'd understand better why he turned against me.'

'But you weren't there. You were here in Melbourne with me. He got tangled up with *her*! With that bitch from England. She must have taken advantage of the fact that he was cut up over his dad's death. She was there – right there with him, and she obviously got her claws into him when he was at a low ebb. That's all the reason you need my dear little idiot of a sister.'

'No,' she said again. 'He told me about the girl, and I'd met Sera *and* his dad. There was never anything like that between Ryan and her. Well, it wouldn't have been right, would it? Not under the circumstances.'

'So what do you put his change of heart down to then?' Holly walked slowly to the window and stared out.

'Something happened,' Kirsten said thoughtfully. 'Something *must* have happened that I don't know about.'

Holly flung up her hands in despair. 'You just won't hear a damn thing against him, will you?'

Steadily, Kirsten said, 'No, I won't. But I'll get to the bottom of it when I've had time to think things out.'

'How will you do that?' Holly turned away from the window and looked disparagingly at her sister. 'You really have been a prize fool, but you know that without me telling you, don't you?'

'Ryan's not a bad person, love . . .'

Exasperated, Holly ground out, 'Oh, for God's sake!'

'I shall find him.' Kirsten pushed herself to her feet and walked over to the cot as the baby began to grizzle. 'If I can find him, and actually talk to him, face to face . . .'

'How? I'll ask you again – how will you find him?'

Kirsten leaned over the cot and picked the baby up then straightened and looked at her sister. 'I shall go to England and find him.'

'Over my dead body!'

Kirsten smiled at her sister over the baby. 'You could always come with me,' she said. 'You've always said you wanted to travel. Surely Melbourne television won't grind to a halt just because you're not there to pander to its prima-donnas?'

Holly sighed. 'I'm producer of one of the longest running daytime programmes they put out,' she reminded her sister. 'I can't just take time off because I might feel like a holiday. Anyway,' she walked back across the room, reached out towards the baby in Kirsten's arms and touched its face gently with one finger, 'why's junior still wearing that stupid beanie hat?' she asked.

'Because prems lose heat through their head. But you're just trying to get me off the subject of England, aren't you?'

Holly deliberately ignored the jibe. 'But she's making up weight now, isn't she?'

Kirsten nuzzled her face against the baby. 'She's doing just fine.'

'You want to keep it that way, don't you? You can't take *her* to England. England's cold. Everybody knows that. And what'll you use for money?'

'England's only cold in winter. We could go around March when it's warming up there.' Kirsten raised her eyes to those of her sister. 'And we still have that five thousand dollars in the bank that Mom left for both of us. Remember?'

'You're crazy!'

But Kirsten's eyes were radiant. 'Let's blow the lot on a holiday in England, shall we?'

'I *said* you're crazy! What's wrong with you. Aren't you hearing me properly?'

'It might be fun, *Sis.*'

'And it might be a complete waste of money.' Holly had always been the practical one.

'You've not had a holiday in years. That's what's making you so bad tempered and crochety. You work too hard. You *need* a holiday – right away from the TV studio. Right away from Australia.'

'I am not bad tempered . . .'

Kirsten became serious. 'Help me,' she pleaded softly. 'Help me with this, Holly. I have the feeling it's vitally important we should go to England.'

'That money was supposed to be put aside for a rainy day. You know what Mom always said.'

'They do say it rains something awful in England,' Kirsten teased, though underneath the humour she was deadly serious and holding her breath in anticipation that her sister wouldn't refuse her the chance she needed to make things up with Ryan.

Holly scowled, but Kirsten knew she was beginning to weaken when she said off-handedly, 'Okay! We'll think about it. But I don't want to hear another word about England *or* Ryan Farrar till you're out of this place and your hormones are back to normal. Okay?'

England

After a restless night during which Holt Blackwood invaded her dreams as well as her waking moments, Serena wasted no time in going to see her father's solicitor in Middlesbrough, and as she drove back down the coastal road to Rivelyn the next day she was in no doubt as to where her duty now lay.

'You're a very lucky young lady,' old Mr Andrews had congratulated her. 'You have inherited a thriving foundry as well as a close-knit community – the like of which we don't often come across in these uncertain times.'

'I could get rid of it though? If I didn't want the responsibility?' she'd asked, panicking somewhat at the thought of being shackled to a place like Caindale for the rest of her life.

'Oh, no, my dear.' He'd gone on then to read directly from the will that Max had made, and Serena realized with a sense of shock that if she refused the challenge Caindale presented, then the whole of her father's estate would pass in its entirety to his lover, Mari.

It had sickened her enough that Mari had been left Wintersgill, the lovely old house on the moors. How much worse would it be, she wondered, if she herself now admitted defeat at the first obstacle, and handed over everything else Max had possessed, to the woman she'd once despised?

But as for having the change of heart Holt had hinted at . . . well, that in her estimation, was just about as probable as her setting foot on the moon!

54

As she drove into Rivelyn town centre, then headed off towards the old inn where she knew Ryan would be waiting for her, her mind was in turmoil at the thought of what now lay ahead.

Ryan was alone in the lounge bar, relaxing in front of a roaring fire. She swept in and flung off her coat, tossing it onto a chair beside him, then she stalked over to the fire and held out her hands to the blaze. 'God, it's cold out there today.'

'It's great in here though.' He grinned up at her then patted his stomach, 'And that breakfast was really something! I don't think I'll be able to move for a week.'

'You need feeding up.' She scowled at him. 'You always were too thin.'

'Thin's healthy.' His mouth twisted in a little grimace. 'So sayeth the dying man, huh?'

She spun round on him. 'Don't say that. Don't ever say that,' she flung at him. 'It's not something you should joke about.'

'It's true though, isn't it, my sweet Sera? And we have to face facts.'

'No we don't. We have to fight.' She sank down on her haunches in front of him. 'You mustn't give up, Ryan. You mustn't even *think* of giving up.'

'It's easy to say that when you're not the one who's sparring with the grim reaper,' he teased.

'Ryan . . . don't,' she pleaded, laying a hand on one of his.

'Tell me how you got on with the stuffed shirt then,' he said easily. 'And for heaven's sake get up, woman. I can't bear it when you start looking at me with those big sad eyes.'

She rose to her feet and said, 'Mr Andrews is *not* a stuffed shirt.'

'All lawyers are stuffed shirts.' He grinned.

She went to the other side of the fire and sat down in a comfy armchair directly opposite him. She stuck her legs out in front of her so she could feel the warmth from the fire through the sleek black trousers she'd put on that morning. 'He told me I had a choice,' she said in as casual a voice as she could muster. 'I either take Caindale on, or I throw in the towel and let Mari have it.'

He burst out laughing, then, when he'd sobered, said, 'Your old dad sure had a sense of humour, love. I wish I could have met him.'

'He had a *bizarre* sense of humour.' She sighed and let her head fall back against the cushions of the chair, feeling as if she'd like to close her eyes and sink right through the cosiness of it – all the way back to Australia, and sanity! 'I ought never to have come back to England,' she muttered. 'I must have been mad.'

'You would still have inherited your blessed valley,' he pointed out. 'Distance makes no difference to the outcome, does it? Your father died and left you the one thing you always wanted to destroy. When you think logically about it, there's a kind of ruthless justice about it all, isn't there? You might have driven him to distraction when you were young, but in the end, he had the last laugh, didn't he?'

She looked at Ryan through half-closed eyes. 'You think all this is damned funny, don't you?'

'Nope!' he said, 'But I must admit, when I woke up this morning, for the first time in months, I hoped I'd live to see another day.'

'A day when I finally mess up my life for good?' she asked, hardening her heart against him, and refusing to face the inevitable when he wouldn't be around to see anything any more.

'A day when you come to your senses,' he said in a more serious tone. 'Because that's what this is going to force you to do. You can't just walk away from your father again, can you? You've got to face up to what he's done.'

Slowly she sat up and gazed across at him. Then she shook her head and said, 'I can't fight a dead man, can I? There's just no contest. Why the heck didn't he leave *everything* to Mari. She'd know exactly what to do with Caindale. She was Dad's secretary for years – she knows how to run a foundry. I don't!'

'Ah well, it was nice while it lasted – my fond dream of you taking charge of your life at long last,' he said. 'So – when do we fly back to Queensland?' Chewing pensively on the corner of his mouth, he said, 'I reckon we could perhaps make it by the middle of next week, don't you?'

'Hold your horses,' she snapped. 'Who says I'm going to walk out on this mess?'

He lifted his shoulders in a lazy little shrug and said, 'Well, you didn't seem all set for a fight when you came in just now. In fact, quite the opposite. By your attitude I'd say you'd given up . . .'

'I don't give up!' She glared hard at him.

'You're a cussed woman,' he replied on a note of ill-concealed sarcasm. 'You're also the original "Mistress Mary, quite contrary" but I guess you'll never change. You've always been headstrong and pig-headed.'

She leaned forward. 'You want me to stay here, don't you? You want to see me become a laughing stock because I don't have a clue how to deal with Caindale?'

He leaned forward too now, and his eyes were blazing as he said, 'I want to see you make something of it, you idiot. You can win and you damn well know you can.'

She shook her head. 'This is something I know nothing about.'

'Then learn,' he bellowed. 'For God's sake *learn*! Don't just take the easy way out like you have done in the past.'

'Ryan!' She jumped to her feet and stood, hands on hips gaping at him. Her temper was rising. He had no right to talk to her in such a way, she fumed. 'Don't you dare speak to me like that,' she warned him softly, her eyes narrowing, 'Don't you dare say that I always take the easy way out.'

Slowly, he hauled himself out of the chair and stood straight and lanky in front of her. 'Hit me,' he said, sticking out his chin. 'Go on – hit me if I'm not telling the truth.'

Her hands fell to her sides. And though her eyes still spat sparks of fire at him, she would not be goaded into doing as he said. 'Sit down,' she said at last.

But he didn't. He stood there and confronted her with her past life. 'Think about it,' he said. 'You couldn't get the better of Max so you left home. Easy way out number one! When he set up home with his paramour, and got a private detective to do his dirty work for him and suss out where you'd escaped to, you upped and ran again – this time to Australia. Easy way out number two! Out there, your life was nice and ordered. You did what you were told. You lived with Dad and me and though Cape York was no picnic, you put up with swamps and snakes and monsoon rains. You faced innumerable dangers out there – intense heat, poisonous spiders, and the ever-present risk of bush fires. But it was a safe bolt-hole wasn't it?

Your dad couldn't get to you there. You'd found your refuge – your last hiding place . . .'

Suddenly her eyes filled with tears, but she dashed them away angrily with one hand. 'Until we returned to Don's bungalow on the eastern shores of the great dividing range . . .'

Softly he said, 'You're no coward, Sera. You proved that when you tackled the man who killed my father – the man who would have killed me too if you hadn't barged at him like a bat out of hell and knocked the gun out of his hand. Don't be a coward now, love,' he pleaded. 'Don't turn your back on this latest problem – bewildering though it is. I want to see you win through, Sera. I want you to beat your demons and finally lay your father's ghost before I go . . .'

She flew at him, beating him about the shoulders with her clenched fists, then shaking with rage and with tears pouring down her cheeks she sobbed, 'You're not going anywhere – not if I can help it . . .' and her breath came out in jerky little spasms as she finally grasped hold of his sweater and shook him as hard as she knew how.

He let her anger burn itself out before taking hold of both her hands and disengaging them from him. She stood before him, bowed then, and trying vainly to stop the weeping that had taken control of her. He drew her to his body, his arms going right round her as he held her close with her head against his chest and her tears soaking through to his shirt. 'Sera! Sera! Sera!' he muttered gently.

Her voice was hoarse and ugly. 'I – don't – want you to – die.'

'The thought doesn't exactly fill me with elation,' he said drily above her head, 'But we have to face it, Sera.'

She eased away from him just far enough to look up into his eyes. 'I thought I had faced up to it,' she said. 'But I just can't . . .'

'This is something neither of us can run away from.' He managed a smile. 'There's no hiding place for me, love.'

She drew in a deep breath and pushed him away from her, to ask, 'Do you want to go back to Australia?'

'I can't,' he said simply. 'How the hell could I go back to Kirsty with this hanging over me?'

'She would have stuck by you. You know that, don't you? You had no right to make her believe you didn't want her any more.'

His laugh was low and bitter. 'She'll forget me this way. I couldn't bear to have her heaping pity on me.'

'You'll regret it, Ryan. And when she finds out the truth, she'll never be able to forgive herself . . .'

'She had the chance of a new life – a new job in Melbourne with her sister.' He spread his hands helplessly. 'What right had I to tie her down to me? Who knows how long I can last? I can't do a proper job any more. I could go blind – be paralyzed even. You know the risks. What girl would want to be lumbered with somebody like me?'

'Kirsty would,' she said, quietly. 'You know damn well she would. I've never in my life seen a couple who were so well suited as you and she were – nor a couple who were more in love with each other.'

'You're nagging again.' He turned away from her and walked to the door of the large room where he just glanced back before opening it and said, 'I warned you before – if you start talking like this, I'm just not going to stay around to listen.'

'Okay! Okay!' she yelled, stopping him as he would have left the room.

He spun round. 'Truce then?'

She nodded. 'Truce! Don't go though. I need to talk to you. I want to show you Caindale too.'

'In this weather?' He shivered.

'It's January,' she said. 'This weather could last until March, and we don't have enough money to stay in digs like this for ever.'

'What do you suggest then?'

'Caindale,' she said, her shoulders sagging. 'There must be *somewhere* we can bunk down at Caindale. It's the only solution.'

'You said the place was a dump.'

'It is.'

'We'd better go see it then,' he suggested. 'And right now seems as good a time as any, don't you think?'

CHAPTER 4

They walked along the deserted shore, with the jagged face of the north cliff towering above them.

'It's fascinating,' he said. 'I don't know why you called it a dump. I like it. It's melancholy – just like me, in fact.'

'It's hardly the ideal holiday resort though,' she retorted brightly, refusing to let him wallow deep in the well of self-pity.

'It's more – much more than that.' Enthusiasm suddenly filled his voice. He seemed not to notice the biting cold wind and the wet drizzle that was damping down on them. 'Look at that monstrosity over there.' He pointed in delight at the huge stone jetty whose two gigantic grey arms stretched out from under the cliff face. 'What on earth is it?'

'We used to call it the "jetty" when we were kids. I suppose really though, it's a harbour. It's where the iron-stone was shipped out from Caindale almost a hundred years ago. There used to be a railway line that led onto it.'

'This is fascinating stuff, Sera.' He shot her a wide grin, then loped off ahead of her, leaping over iron-red boulders that littered the beach, his arms swinging at his sides in the long overcoat he was wearing, his booted feet swift and sure as he skirted rock pools and banks of mud.

62

She stood still beside the rust-red water of the Caindale beck and watched him scramble up onto the jetty.

He turned round, cupped his hands to his mouth and yelled, 'It's here! It's still here – that railway line you were talking about.'

She laughed, but the keen wind carried the sound away. It was good to see him taking an interest in something again at last. She strode out towards him and joined him on the jetty.

'I always liked the other side best,' she said. 'That's where the cobles used to dock after a night's fishing.'

'Those boats back there?' He jerked his head in the direction they'd just come. 'What was it you called them?'

'Cobles,' she said.

'I'd like to own a coble.' He turned to her, serious all of a sudden. 'Did you ever go out on the sea in one?'

She shook her head. The wind was stronger here where they stood exposed to the elements above the cold north sea. 'Not me. I was only a kid when I used to hang around with the other children of Caindale, remember. We'd play around the boats, and imagine we were sailing the seven seas, but we never actually went out to sea. It was too dangerous to go out on the ocean with the fishermen – or so my father said.' She pulled a face. 'He was very protective – over-protective in fact where I was concerned.'

His dark brown hair was blowing into his eyes. 'He must have loved you very much,' he said, 'to have left you all of this.'

'You have to be joking,' she said. 'My father knew I'd grown to hate Caindale as I got older.'

'Perhaps he realized you needed something like this though,' he said slowly as he turned round to look at the sea. 'Something enduring. Something of your very own. Something to care about.'

'Somehow, I don't think he would have such deep and meaningful thoughts as you do,' she said with a little laugh. 'My father was a purely practical man, Ryan. Think of a bar of iron, and you have Max Corder. Think of a plain stone jetty like this, and you have Max Corder. But think of a flower or a butterfly, or a whimsical thought, and you definitely do *not* have Max Corder!'

'The world though, has been shaped by such men,' Ryan said thoughtfully.

'And also by men who dream dreams, and paint beautiful pictures,' she pointed out.

He shrugged. 'It wouldn't do for all of us to be the same, would it?'

'I suppose not.'

She watched him as he walked purposefully to the end of the jetty and the end of the railway lines, then he turned and came back.

'I like Caindale,' he said, looking up at the tops of the cliffs, then letting his gaze sweep down over the sheer face of them to the shore again. 'There's a cave,' he said, lifting his hand to point again.

She nodded. 'It's been there a long time. We used to make up stories about mermaids living in it when we were young.'

His face brightened. 'Maybe *we* could doss down there, huh? You and me? We could live off fish I'd catch in my coble, and build driftwood fires to keep us warm.'

Her easy laughter rang out. 'When the tide comes in, the water reaches the roof of the cave.'

His forehead creased. 'Not such a good idea then? Living there.'

She delved one hand into her pocket and brought out a bunch of keys. 'A house would be a better idea.'

'You have a house?' The amazement on his face made her laugh again.

'Mr Andrews told me there are two houses empty. He gave me the keys so I could look them over. He says they've been on the market for some time but there have been no enquiries about them. He doesn't hold out much hope of a sale. Caindale isn't exactly a property buyer's paradise.'

'Where are they? These houses?'

She took hold of his arm and pulled him round to look across the small beach that made a sheltered bay between the north and the south cliff. Between where they were standing and the south cliff, the Caindale beck trickled its way over rocks and boulders into the sea.

'Do you see the little grey houses – up there? On the south cliff? We passed under them as we came down the road into the valley.'

He screwed up his eyes. 'Those that are half way up that ruddy great hill?'

She nodded.

'How the heck do we get up there?'

'There's a road. To be more precise, a track.'

'Can we get the car up? Or is it to be the long hard hike, with both of us flaked out by the time we reach the houses?'

'We can get the car up. Just! It's narrow, but it widens out in front of the houses.'

'Thank God for that. I have visions of me sleepwalking right off the edge if we go to live up there.'

'You couldn't do that. There are iron railings to stop you falling.'

'You really expect me to jump at the chance of living up there, don't you?' he asked incredulously.

'It's either that or we'll have to get down to some serious waterproofing of that cave.' She tucked her hand through his arm. 'Come on. Let's get back to the car, and I'll give you the ride of a lifetime.'

'Promises, promises,' he said, but his face grew pale as she inched the car round the hairpin bends of the south cliff and they went higher and higher. 'God – I'm getting sea-sick,' he muttered as he risked a glance out of the window to see the ground falling away sharply from the road.

'You can't get sea-sick this far above sea level,' she pointed out.

'Do you have to be so logical?' he asked with sarcasm.

'If you can think of an alternative to living in this eagle's nest, just tell me,' she said.

'I can't think at all at this altitude, the lack of oxygen's getting to me.'

She heard him breathe a heavy sigh of relief when they reached the row of houses, and the road widened out before them. Now, instead of a miniscule grass verge on the side of the precipice, there was a narrow pavement and – as she'd promised – substantial iron railings. She pulled the car up outside a small house with a faded 'for sale' sign hanging drunkenly off the wall.

They got out of the car. The wooden estate agent's sign, was tap-tap-tapping against the house in the wind. Ryan reached up and pulled at it, and it came away in his hand, showering them with crumbling cement from between the bricks.

'That was dangerous,' he said. 'It could have fallen off and hit somebody.'

'I told you the place was a dump,' she said, but he shook his head. 'No. I like it.' He bent down and leaned the sign against the house wall, then dusted his hands on his coat.

The inside of the house was even colder than outside. Wallpaper – blackened with damp and age – was peeling off the walls, she saw, as they walked directly off the street into the sitting room. A staircase led up from a passage that connected the sitting room with the kitchen. Serena shivered as she looked up the dark stairs. The doors had all been stained with a very dark varnish. In the kitchen, which was a brighter room, there was an old black cast iron fire-grate with an antiquated boiler on one side for heating water, and an oven on the other side. The kitchen window looked out over a small back yard, two outhouses, and an overgrown garden with a view of the sea.

'Dare we go upstairs, I ask myself,' Ryan murmured, hunching himself into his overcoat.

'It's creepy, isn't it? Shall we find the other house that's for sale and see if it's any better than this? It's at the other end of this terrace, I believe.'

Ryan said, 'I like this one. Being the end house, it overlooks the harbour. It must have a sea view from all its rooms. Does the other one have a sea view?'

She shrugged. 'I don't think so. It's nearer the centre of the village and the foundry. Like you – I think I prefer this one.'

'It's not as if you've actually got to hand over hard cash for it, is it?' he said, looking at the problem in a purely practical manner. 'I mean – you *do* own the place – lock, stock and barrel, so you won't be losing anything even if we decide we hate it after a couple of weeks.'

'It's not exactly cash in hand though, is it?' she said. 'What I'm getting at is the fact that we'll need money to do this place up, and I have precious little of that.'

'What did the stuffed shirt suggest when you went to see him this morning – cash-wise, I mean.'

'He said I could have what I wanted – providing of course that I take Caindale on. The foundry, apparently, is making quite good profits from its full order books for such mundane things as manhole covers, drain fittings and "street furniture"!'

'What the hell is "street furniture"?' Ryan burst out laughing.

'Heaven only knows. Probably lamps. Iron railings. Even seats, I suppose.'

He suddenly turned thoughtful. 'Sera – we could do this place up and make it habitable.'

'Ye-es.'

His face fell. 'You don't like it, do you?'

'I hate it,' she admitted. But she grinned at his glum expression and said, 'Only teasing. Actually, I couldn't bear to live in a cottage that's near the foundry – I'd be forever reminded of Dad! Shall we look at the bedrooms. Perhaps they'll be better than the downstairs rooms.'

'You go up first,' he suggested. 'I can't stand dark places.'

She sighed. 'Are you a man or a mouse, Ryan Farrar?'

'Eeeek!' he said, so she pushed past him and ran up the staircase laughing.

On the landing she threw all three doors open to let some light in from the bedroom windows, then she went back to the top of the stairs and yelled, 'Okay – it's safe. There are no spooks.'

He stamped up the bare wooden stairs. 'I could strip this wood down,' he mused as he got to the top. 'Get rid of all this dark varnish and then it'd look okay with a plain jute carpet – and *that* wouldn't be too expensive.'

'You haven't seen the bedrooms yet,' she warned. 'There are two big ones and another that at first sight looks not much more than a cupboard. It's got the tiniest of windows.'

'A bath and shower room,' he said when he popped his head round the door of the smallest room. 'That's what we'll have here.' He walked inside. The miniscule window was high up near the ceiling. He paced out the floor, widthways then lengthways. 'Approximately two and a half by three metres, I'd guess.'

'More expense!' she grumbled, staring round in exasperation. 'Honestly, you'd think Dad would have installed decent sanitation in his workers' houses, wouldn't you?'

'Look – don't go blaming your dad for everything. This house must have been empty for fifteen or twenty years, and we can do most of the work ourselves, Sera. We'll just need a plumber and electrician to do the fiddly bits.'

'Skilled workmen cost money,' she said drily.

'But there must at least be one qualified electrician working at the foundry – maybe he could do a spot of re-wiring.'

Bitingly she retorted, 'You're right. Shall I put him on overtime for the next six months and work him round the clock until this place is habitable?'

'You need somewhere to live if you're going to oversee the foundry,' he reasoned. Just look at it a different way, will you? All the people who live in these houses were employed by your father. The houses were kept in good repair by him . . .'

'All except this one, it seems – but I get your meaning,' she said thoughtfully, 'the renovation can, quite legally, be paid for out of works profits.'

He nodded. 'Let's look at the bedrooms.'

They decided he'd have the front one overlooking the harbour, and she would have the one at the back of the house that had a view of the overgrown garden, the open sea to the left, and about half a mile inland, but still on top of the cliffs, a turretted church and small graveyard. The arrangement suited her for it effectively meant she wouldn't be quite so constantly reminded of Caindale if all she could see was a flower garden, a church, and open sea beyond her window.

'I'll make an old English garden out there,' she mused, 'but first I'll ring Mr Andrews as soon as we get back to the inn and ask him how I go about getting the house cleaned up and made ready for us.'

'I take it you don't have any more surprises for me right now, then?'

She couldn't help laughing as they went back down the stairs, saying softly, 'I sure let you in for something when I dragged you all the way from Australia to this, didn't I?'

He closed the front door firmly as they left the house, then turned the key in the lock before handing it back to her.

They walked across the road to the car where she paused before unlocking it to tell him, 'There really was never any question of me *not* taking Caindale on, Ryan.' She raised her eyebrows and tried to inject some enthusiasm into her voice as she continued, 'I signed all the papers quite willingly when I went to see Mr Andrews. Nobody held a gun to my head. I accepted Dad's challenge, so it's all fair, square and legal now. Caindale really does belong to me!'

She could tell he wasn't surprised at her news.

'I'm real glad to hear that,' he said, reaching out to grab

hold of her hand and squeeze it tightly. 'Real glad, Sera. But I knew all along you'd do it.'

They drove back out of the valley and turned towards Rivelyn. Ryan laughed at some of the outlandish names on signposts and street corners.

'Just look at that one coming up on your side! "Cow Lane"! Is it real?'

Her eyes went automatically to the rear view mirror to check that nothing was too close behind her, then she pressed gently on the brakes and brought the car to a halt on the grass verge at the side of the road. She sat and gazed at the little lane running from the main road across the top of the north side of the Caindale valley.

'Well,' she said softly, 'I'd forgotten all about that. How could I do such a thing?'

'It brings back memories, I take it?' He squinted at her face that was half-turned away from him.

'There was a house,' she said, seeing it again quite clearly in her mind's eye. 'It was down there – right on the cliff top in an overgrown mess of a garden. It had a deep sloping red roof with missing tiles, and nearly all its windows were cracked or broken. I don't think its wood-work had ever seen a coat of paint in its life. We called it the "ugly house"!' She smiled reminiscently. 'An eccentric old lady lived there all alone with her cats, and we children used to think she was a witch because if any of us went near the place she'd come out shrieking at us, waving a broom.'

He laughed softly. 'Do you want to go down that lane and see if it's still there?'

She chewed absently on her bottom lip for a second or two, then shook her head. 'It makes me shiver just to think of it,' she said. 'And if it's still there it must be derelict by now.' She turned and grinned at him. 'I'd still be as scared today, I think, as I used to be all those years ago – if she came out and chased us.'

'Maybe another time then, huh?'

She nodded. 'Maybe. Although some things are best left alone, aren't they? It doesn't always do to go raking up the past.'

Even as she spoke the words, Holt's image sprang to her mind, and she knew that one place she *would* be avoiding was the other cottage down that same narrow lane, where *he* had lived with his Aunt Viv. She wasn't going to risk bumping into *him* again, and neither was she – at this moment – going to mention Holt's name to Ryan.

Vivian Blackwood and Mari Wyatt were the sisters of Holt's father, and Holt's had been a tragic childhood. She could still remember the day her father had read out the headline in a local newspaper – 'Air crash in France – two killed'!

Holt, just a boy not even in his teens, had been staying with his Aunt Viv at the time. Mari was already married to Harry Wyatt and lived in Middlesbrough. Viv, slightly younger than Mari – and with a heart condition – had never married, so it had seemed natural at the time for Holt to stay with Viv, and be brought up by her when he was so tragically orphaned.

She wondered now if he still lived with Vivian, and thought that it was very likely that he did. After all, if he'd had to rely on Max loaning him the money to start his own haulage business, she imagined he'd be hard pressed to buy a place of his own in which to live. From the way he was talking when she'd met him the other night, she guessed all his income went straight back into his business anyway.

Viv's cottage was situated a couple of hundred yards back from the little footpath off Cow Lane that led to the 'ugly house' – and though Serena was curious to know if the 'witch' still lived there, she definitely didn't want to run the risk of meeting Holt again – not just yet.

She was so lost in her thoughts of the past that she didn't realize she must have been staring unseeingly through the windscreen until a hand came up and waved back and forth in front of her face. She blinked and jerked back in her seat.

'Wake up,' Ryan said. 'You were miles away and day-dreaming.'

She shook herself. 'Sorry! It gets to be a habit in a place like this. I don't seem to have been away five minutes, let alone ten years.'

'Your thoughts weren't the happy kind though. You looked sad,' he said. 'That's why I decided to bring you back to the land of the living.'

'Oh, I was there all along.' She smiled at him. 'All the old faces will still be here,' she said. 'But there are some I'd like to meet again, and others I wouldn't.'

'A man?' he asked, cocking his head on one side and looking at her seriously.

Her laugh had a slightly bitter ring to it. 'Max Corder thought nobody was good enough for his daughter,' she told him in a flat voice. 'He wouldn't approve of me taking up with just any Tom, Dick or Harry.'

'That sounds as if you'd tried to,' he said.

Airily she replied, 'I had lots of boy friends.'

'Just to spite old Max, I suppose.'

Surprised at his insight, she said, 'You know me better than *he* did, Ryan.'

'You forget,' he said, 'We've been like brother and sister to each other for the last two years – you and me.'

Her eyes softened. 'I wish you had been my brother. I always hated being an only child. And if I'd had a brother, *he* would have taken over Caindale – not me.'

'Drive on, love,' he said wearily. 'My head's starting to thump again.'

'Oh, God! No! Not twice in as many days.'

'They're getting worse, these headaches. You've noticed it too, haven't you?'

He leaned back in his seat and closed his eyes, and his face, she saw, had gone deathly pale.

'Maybe it's the long air journey – jet lag,' she consoled, not daring to think that he could be worsening so soon, and so quickly.

'Two years,' he murmured softly as she pressed down on the accelerator and pulled out onto the road again. 'They said I *might* just last another two years – if I'm lucky – so I guess you could say I'm into my last eighteen months now, huh?'

She couldn't answer. What was there to say? Words wouldn't help. But she was beginning to feel she'd been foolhardy in bringing him with her half way across the world, the state he was in. She'd have to insist that he rested more she decided. And maybe he would, once they were installed in their own little house.

He was soon asleep – or in that semi-conscious state he lapsed into more and more often just lately. And she vowed to herself there and then that she wouldn't worry him with *her* troubles, he had enough of his own to cope with.

74

Even so, she found herself thinking that some of the pressures she was experiencing now, might have been avoided if she hadn't let a hopeless sense of guilt lure her back to England for the funeral of a man she despised.

CHAPTER 5

Serena soon discovered that Max had practically run his office single-handedly except for a bright-faced little teenager called Jackie who typed his letters.

When she asked to be shown how the computer worked however, Jackie didn't have a clue, and said so quite candidly.

'*Nobody* touched that except Mr Corder. I just typed letters and answered the phone. Mr Corder said he'd think about sending me on a course one day . . .'

'But the wages must have been done on computer!'

Jackie nodded and smiled apologetically. 'Mr Corder did all that side of things!'

'What about invoices, accounts, production and purchasing?'

'Mr Corder! He was always ever so busy.'

'Incoming orders? Costing?'

'All there.' Jackie nodded across at the computer on Max's desk and said again, 'Mr Corder was very organized. Me? I wouldn't even know how to switch that thing on. I never got any "A" levels.'

'Hell!'

In an enthusiastic voice, Jackie informed her, 'Mrs Wyatt could help you. *She* knows how it all works. Odd times, she'd come in to the office and help out when we were busy.'

So that was that.

Serena tried again. 'Where are all the files kept? Past records. Schedule of work. That sort of thing. It might give me some idea of what I'm supposed to do if I could see how it had all been done in the past. After all – I don't want to make sweeping changes around the place, I just want to keep the foundry running smoothly.'

'Oh, Mr Corder kept the main customer files at home; I do a bit of general filing here – copies of the letters I send out reminding customers they haven't paid their bills, and all that sort of thing, but nothing of any real importance. I'm not very clever, see. Mr Corder knew that . . .'

'At Wintersgill? He kept his files at Wintersgill?' she asked, her spirits plunging.

Jackie nodded again. 'Mr Corder had another computer at home as well as this one. He used to say they could talk to each other – the computers – but I think he must have been kidding me. Computers don't talk, do they?' Her face crumpled a little. 'He was a lovely man, your dad, Miss Corder. He gave me this job when nobody else would take me on . . .'

'Don't be sad. He wouldn't want that,' Serena said gently, and as Jackie sniffed and composed herself, she sat down heavily at her father's desk. When she tried to open its drawers however, she found they were securely locked.

She didn't need to ask who had the keys. There was only one thing for it. She knew she'd have to approach Mari and ask for her help, but she baulked at the idea of telephoning the woman while Jackie was in the office listening to her.

'Do we have a tea and coffee machine – one that *isn't* linked up to the computer?' she asked, trying to bring a smile back to Jackie's gamin little face.

The girl beamed at her. 'We've got a nice little kitchenette just down the corridor.'

'Do you think you could make a drink? I have a phone call to make and I'm gasping for a coffee.'

The girl looked at the clock on the wall. 'Mr Corder used to say I couldn't do the first brew up till ten o'clock. Ten in the morning, three in the afternoon. That's tea-break times, and right now it's only just after nine – but maybe he wouldn't mind . . . not for you.'

'I've taken over from Mr Corder,' Serena said firmly. 'We'll have a drink right now, I think.'

Jackie jumped instantly to her feet with a wide grin spreading across her face. 'Yes, Miss,' she said. 'But we have tea as well if you want to change your mind about the coffee. Mr Corder used to say my coffee tasted like cat p..'

'Tea then, but no sugar,' Serena broke in, shuddering inwardly. She could well imagine her father saying something like that, and decided, for once, to respect his judgement where Jackie's coffee was concerned. 'Make one for yourself – and for whoever else you usually make tea for.'

'Right-e-o!'

Jackie sailed out of the room and as she flounced down the corridor in her short skirt, Serena heard a series of wolf whistles follow the girl from the small drawing office opposite, and then some more from the glass-sided general office next to it. She'd have to go and introduce herself to the people in those offices, she reminded herself. Just now though, it seemed of paramount importance to at least start getting to know how to pay the workers in the foundry before she did anything else.

She drew in a deep breath, picked up the phone and dialled her old home number.

Mari answered within seconds, and Serena had the uncanny feeling that her father's lover had been sitting there beside the phone waiting for the call. Wryly, she realized that for the moment, Mari had the upper hand. She had the information that was of vital importance to the running of the foundry and the offices.

'Mrs Wyatt,' she said, forcing a pleasantness to her voice that hid – or so she hoped – the desperation she felt at being dropped in at the deep end. 'It's Serena. I'm at the works, and I need some help. Do you think I could pop over to Wintersgill later this morning and talk to you?'

It was strange, entering her old home, and this time knowing that she could never look on it as *her* home ever again. At least, she thought, when she'd arrived for Max's funeral, she hadn't been aware of the fact that Mari had inherited Wintersgill.

She knew she was still smarting from the blow her father had dealt her by his willing of the old house away from her, and she realized also now that she had been too complacent in thinking she'd always have somewhere to return if life didn't work out the way she wanted it to.

Mari met her at the front door, and for that Serena was thankful. She didn't think she could have borne the indignity of having to stand outside ringing the door bell like some stranger.

'Is it okay if I leave the car on the road?'

'Of course, my dear. We don't get much traffic – or visitors – up here on the moors in winter. I was quite

79

pleased when you telephoned this morning.' Mari led the way inside, hesitating in the hall to say, 'Now – I think I'd better take you straight through to Max's study, don't you – as this is obviously a business call? You'll want the works' keys and all that sort of thing, no doubt, and you'll also need putting in the picture about everything that's going on at the foundry at the moment.'

'Jackie Welland was a bit vague about wages, and sooner than have a strike on my hands if the men don't get paid . . .'

Mari's laugh was warm and genuine. 'Don't worry, love. I've done the wages for this week, but I doubt you'd have had a strike at the foundry even if I hadn't. There's never been a strike at Corder's. The men know they'll always get paid, no matter what.'

'You've done them? The wages?'

Mari nodded. 'Just as I have for the past fifteen years.'

'Oh!' Serena was taken aback. 'Jackie said that Dad . . .'

'Max liked to give the impression he had everything under control. And that's the way it should be,' Mari said happily. 'He was king of his little empire, after all, and he was a good leader to the men in the foundry. But . . .' she sighed heavily, 'Max was only human and he couldn't possibly do *everything*. He used to bring a lot of paperwork home, and I'd sort it all out in the daytime while he was down there at Caindale. Well, it is rather lonely out here, and too far for friends to keep dropping in for casual visits and cups of tea. And speaking of tea – let me warn you to stay well clear of Jackie's coffee.'

Serena laughed and the strained atmosphere she'd been expecting at Wintersgill was instantly dispelled. 'Oh, Jackie warned me against it herself.'

She followed Mari into her father's study, and was glad of its familiarity. Only the computer was new. That hadn't been there when she'd lived at Wintersgill. The leather-topped mahogany desk was the same though. Max, she remembered, had loved its bank of little drawers with shiny brass handles down one side of it.

With an empty feeling in the pit of her stomach she remembered how he used to hide little surprises in those drawers for her when she'd been a child – a bead necklace, a new dress for her Sindy doll, a colourful tube of Smarties . . .

'Are you all right, love?' Mari was looking at her strangely, and Serena suddenly became aware of a wetness behind her eyes. It had caught her unawares – that desk. With all that had happened over the years she'd forgotten all about Daddy's desk drawers and the goodies he used to hide in them. Somehow, she realized with a shock, she'd succeeded in pushing the happier memories she'd had of him right to the back of her mind.

Huskily she said, 'I'm okay. I'm just being silly. Coming in here just made me remember things.'

'He was a good man, Serena.' Mari looked steadily at her.

'Yes.' She blinked rapidly and turned away to stare out of the window. The study was situated on the side of the house, opposite the orchard. There was one particular apple tree . . .

Oh, God, she thought miserably, dragging her eyes away from the window, this can't be happening.

Mari's gaze had followed hers. 'The swing rotted away,' she said, her voice tinged with sadness. 'Max had to take it down last year and it really upset him to do that.'

'Last year?' Serena stared at her aghast. 'But he put that swing up for me when I was just a little girl – and even though it was still there when I went away ten years ago, I never imagined he'd leave it hanging on the tree all this time . . .'

Mari chuckled. 'He used to say there might be grand-children one day who might want to play on it.'

Serena turned her back abruptly on the window and faced Mari, an unutterable weariness sweeping over her all of a sudden. Her shoulders sagged.

'Am I going to be able to cope?' she asked in a small voice.

Mari went behind the desk and sat down; the computer, Serena saw, was already switched on and there was a spread-sheet on its screen.

'Pull up a chair beside me,' Mari said. 'And take your coat off – this is going to be a long job.'

By four o'clock that afternoon, Serena was convinced that running the foundry at Caindale was going to be a twenty-four hour a day commitment. She and Mari had taken an hour's break for a bite of lunch in Wintersgill's comfortable kitchen, and now Serena leaned back in her chair and said, 'I never realized there'd be so much to learn.'

Mari said, 'It's a good job you've used a computer before. You're a quick learner.'

'I think I'll move my bed into the office,' Serena said drily.

'I'll help with any of the office work – if you want me to,' Mari said quietly.

Serena sat up straight and looked quizzically at her. 'You'd do that?'

'Of course I would. I think we could work together – you and I. We haven't done so badly today, have we?' Mari flashed her a quick smile.

Serena looked down at her hands that were clasped together tightly now on her lap. Then she raised her head again and said, 'I don't deserve that, you know. There's no reason why you should want to help me. I was a bitch to you in the past.'

'I can't let everything go under that Max worked for, can I?' Mari looked straight at her. 'Don't get me wrong, Serena, I'm not against you – I never was – but we're not going to be the best of buddies in an instant, just because I've helped you understand a few of the jobs around the place, are we?'

Mari's statement took a few seconds to sink in, then Serena said, 'Does that mean you don't *want* us to be friends?'

'Could we ever be that?' Mari's face twisted comically into a semi-tragic grin. 'Ten years' bitterness can't be wiped out in a single day, can it?'

Strangely, her words cut deep into Serena. And suddenly, she knew she was seeing Mari in a totally unprejudiced way for the first time ever in her life.

'You obviously made Dad happy,' she said, struggling for the right words. 'And I think I've realized since coming back that you're not the . . . the sort of person I'd always imagined you to be . . .'

'The "gold-digger"? Oh, yes, my dear, you can say the words. I know they're the ones you're trying to avoid.'

Serena felt herself flushing to the roots of her hair.

'Oh, God! I'm not being very diplomatic about this, am I?' But before Mari could reply, she went on, 'What I'm trying to say is – I never thought for an instant that

83

you had carried on working for him after you and Dad . . .'

'Started living together?' Mari relaxed in her swivel chair and swung it round so she was facing Serena directly. 'Look, love,' she said, 'We'd better get one thing out in the open – I was Max's secretary all those years ago. I made myself indispensable to him at the foundry, but when I moved in here after your mother died, there was a lot of talk about us around Caindale. The result was that Max wouldn't have me working down there any longer – which annoyed me more than I can tell you. I'd loved my job, you see, but Max wanted his home life and his business life keeping strictly separate.'

'And you wanted things to carry on as they had been doing?'

Mari nodded. 'I wanted to have my cake and eat it, as they say. And eventually I managed it. Max started to bring things home for me to sort out – after he'd discovered he couldn't find another secretary as competent as I had been.' Her mouth twisted in a slightly sardonic way. 'There's been a never-ending stream of "Jackies" in his office for the past ten years,' she revealed. 'The girls never stayed more than a few months because they'd get bored and irritated when Max never allowed them to do anything but the most menial of jobs. All the important stuff comes here. To me. Now though, all that must change. And as I said before, Serena – I'll help you.'

Watching the older woman through slightly narrowed eyes, Serena said, 'And then what?'

A bit flustered, Mari said, 'I – I don't know what you mean?'

'Won't you still want to be involved? Even when it gets to the point where I'm competent enough to do the job?'

Mari's blue eyes dimmed slightly. 'I shall miss it,' she said. 'I'm in my mid-fifties and I've always had an active mind.'

In that instant, Serena made up her mind.

She took a long, deep breath and plunged in. 'Mr Andrews suggested I might like to offer you a partnership. He hinted you'd be more than receptive to the idea.'

The air was charged with tension, until breathlessly, Mari said, 'I told him he was crazy to even think of putting that idea to you.'

'I thought he was crazy too – until today.'

Mari stared at her as if she'd lost her senses. 'Today?'

'We've not done too badly to say we've spent almost five hours together. At least we haven't torn each other's hair out.' Serena leaned forward in her seat. 'And I did make the first move – because when I sat in Dad's office, I realized what a job it was I'd taken on.'

'You're capable of doing it though.' Mari smiled in a slightly defeatist way. 'You *are* capable, Serena. You could make a good job of it – and you could do it alone and by your own efforts if you put your mind to it. You don't have to take on an old woman like me to do your accounts.'

'But I need somebody. Somebody I can trust.' Serena stared down at the desk and all the print-outs Mari and she had been working on. 'I can't be there all the time you see. I have other . . . commitments.'

Shrewdly, Mari said, 'The young man?'

Serena nodded and fidgeted with the ring she wore on her left hand, but made no attempt to enlighten Mari about her relationship with Ryan. 'It's something I can't explain to you at the moment,' she said. 'But I *have* to put Ryan first.'

'It's understandable my dear.' Mari sighed. 'After all, I did the same thing with your father . . .'

'No! No!' Serena was vehement. 'It's not like that. And I've told you – I can't explain . . .'

It was true, she thought wearily. She'd given her word to Ryan that she wouldn't tell anybody what was wrong with him. He'd hate it if people started feeling sorry for him. Illness of any kind had always infuriated him. When his body didn't do exactly what he wanted it to do, he got angry and frustrated. In the past he'd always been so healthy, so full of life, but now . . . She shook her head to chase away the memories of the past few months.

'You care very deeply for him though, don't you?'

Serena found she couldn't meet the other woman's steady gaze.

'Yes,' she muttered, 'I care for him. But Ryan's not the be all and end all of things.' Her head came up sharply. 'We have to think about the best way of carrying on the job as well, don't we?'

Mari pushed herself to her feet and leaned over the desk to start clearing up the papers. Not looking at Serena at all as she shoved all the things into the top drawer of a filing cabinet, she said in a completely detached sort of way, 'There's nothing I'd like better than to retain some interest in Max's world.'

Serena too got up. 'It's my world too now,' she said. 'Think about it, Mrs Wyatt. But be perfectly sure you want to join me for the right reasons. Dad's dead, but the lives of those people in the valley just have to go on.'

Mari closed the filing cabinet drawer quietly, then turned and faced her. 'It's for their sake that I want to be your partner,' she said. 'I can't for the moment, rid myself of the fear that you might run out on them, Serena – just like you ran out on Max . . . and me.'

Serena held out her hand. 'Can I tell Mr Andrews you're interested then?'

Mari grasped her hand and they shook on the deal. 'I'm interested!' Her voice was warm and firm. 'But,' she said, 'I think it would be best if we just worked together for a few months first – before we make any definite arrangement like a partnership.' She allowed her gaze to sweep over the room, 'I would like an office of my own at Caindale though if you don't mind. I'm getting tired of all this clutter here at home. Max isn't around to worry if people talk about our relationship any more, and to tell the truth, I don't think people *will* gossip behind my back any more. I've been hiding myself away for far too long, and it's time I came out into the open again.'

'I can understand how you feel.' Serena's hand fell to her side as Mari let go of it. 'There must have been plenty of talk about me too – when I tried to wreck things down at Caindale all those years ago.'

'We've both of us been rebels in our time.' Mari smiled, then glanced at the small gold watch on her wrist. 'Heavens! It's way past five o'clock. Would you like to stay and have a bite of supper with me?'

'Ryan's expecting me. We usually have a meal around seven at the inn.'

Mari's brows drew together in a worried frown. 'You could both come here, you know. You don't have to stay there . . .'

'We've decided to move into Caindale,' Serena said quickly.

Mari closed her eyes in apparent despair. 'Oh, no! Not one of those awful little houses that have been empty for years! They must be in a dreadful state. They're the only ones in Caindale that haven't been modernized. Max never would do anything about them. Well, you know your father don't you, my dear. He wouldn't just throw money away, and as those two cottages had been empty for so long, he often said it would make more sense to pull them down than to have to rip the insides out of them and start again from scratch.'

'Ryan likes the end one with the open views of the sea.'

Mari lifted her hands, horrified. 'But it's dark and damp and . . . well, it's just not what you've been used to, Serena.'

'It will do us fine.' Serena smiled.

And it wouldn't be for long, she told herself. The day she'd just spent with Mari had convinced her of one thing – Mari would cope admirably with the work at the foundry – especially if she were a partner in it. And that, Serena realized, would take some of the pressure off herself. She would have more time to spend with Ryan and, hopefully, she'd be able to take him back to Australia – if that's what he decided he wanted – now she was going to get help with Caindale.

She couldn't tell Mari that, of course. Not just at the moment anyway, because she couldn't make any plans that were absolutely foolproof. She'd take one day at a time, she decided. That was the only way to get through.

It was no use looking too far ahead. Ryan didn't have much time left, but she knew she had to be there for him while he needed her.

CHAPTER 6

Holt sipped appreciatively at the mug of hot coffee his
Aunt Viv had placed on the kitchen table in front of him.
He was careful as he replaced the mug on a coaster, it
wouldn't do to stain the spotless white tablecloth with its
delicate blue scalloped edging.

Vivian pulled a chair out opposite, sat down herself and
stirred sugar into a Royal Albert china teacup. She
shuddered delicately as she watched him place the mug
back carefully on the coaster.

'Horrid things! Mugs!' she muttered, 'Aren't you ever
going to get yourself civilized and drink from a cup?'

His grey eyes twinkled as he glanced up at her. 'Can you
imagine *me* holding something as delicate as you've got
there? China?' he asked, with a soft little laugh.

Vivian was blonde and pretty. She had the figure of a
woman half her age, and she knew it, he was sure. Her
china-doll face was practically unlined, and her hair was
still the same style as it had always been – shoulder-
length and tipped up at the ends. It was thick and
unruly, that blonde mop of hers; it had a mind of its
own and was just as wayward and unmanageable as
she'd always been herself, Holt thought fondly. He
looked at her, and noted that although it was scarcely

ten in the morning, she'd applied a light covering of make-up, a smudge of coral lipstick to her perfectly shaped mouth, and mascara to emphasize those gorgeous laughing blue eyes of hers.

Tiny clusters of pearls clung to her ear lobes, ropes of pearls hung in three loops around her neck, and nestled against her dove-grey cashmere sweater. She lifted a smooth pale hand to wag a finger at him in a cautionary gesture, and her fingernails were glossy and polished in the same shade as her lips.

'You'll never get yourself a decent girl unless you take yourself in hand,' she warned.

'I don't like decent girls,' he growled pleasantly. 'I much prefer the other kind.'

'You really are a rogue,' Viv declared, smiling in spite of herself. Then she sighed and said, 'I'd like to see you settled before . . .' She let the rest of the sentence hang in the air.

'Now don't start that again,' he said, impatience tingeing his words. 'You're not going *anywhere*, Aunt Viv. And I certainly don't intend hitching myself up to the first "decent" dame that comes along just so you can dance at my wedding.'

'Me? Dance?' Her baby-blue eyes widened. 'Now that will be the day, dear. I've never been able to dance. My heart wouldn't let me – you know that. When I was young I could never do the things the other girls of my age did.'

'Just keep taking the pills they gave you at the hospital,' he said gently. 'You know your heart stays reasonably under control if you do that.'

'I hate having to rely on pills to keep me alive.' She pouted and picked up her tea cup again and looked at him over the rim of it. 'I don't know why they can't give me a transplant,' she said. 'Lots of people have them nowadays, don't they?'

'You'd still have to take pills though,' he argued.

'Oh, I've heard all the arguments. Anyway, I don't think I'd like to go in hospital and have an anaesthetic.'

'Lots of people take pills,' he said in a practical tone.

She let out a long drawn-out sigh. 'I'm forty-nine years old,' she said, 'and since I was old enough to know what I was doing, I've had to take those blessed little pills to keep my heart in check, day in day out. There are times when I get fed up with remembering to take them.'

'I know,' he said.

'They make me sleepy. They make me forget things.'

'They're intended to slow you down,' he said. 'That's how they work to keep your heart steady and your high blood pressure down. The specialist at the hospital explains it to you every time you go for a check-up, Aunt Viv.'

She sighed again. 'They make me feel like an old woman sometimes though.'

'Well, you're not an old woman. You've got the face and figure of a fashion model, and you know it.'

'But I've never had a husband.' She pulled a face at him. 'Nobody ever wanted to marry me – not when they found out about my wobbly heart. I never got the chance to have children of my own like a normal woman.'

He reached out a big hand across the table to her. 'Hey,' he said, 'It was probably because you'd got a second-hand kid that nobody asked you to marry them. It could have been me who scared them off.'

She pouted. 'Our Mari managed to get herself two men. And one of them a big fish around these parts,' she stated with a forlorn look at him.

'But Max Corder never married her,' he said in a level tone.

'He was going to.' She scowled. 'Mari popped in to see me a month ago, and she was full of it – news of the wedding. Max had succumbed to my dear sister's charms at long last.'

Her lips had curled just a trifle maliciously, as she imparted the news, Holt thought.

'You should have been glad for her,' he said. 'Aunt Mari hadn't had all that easy a life until she met Max. And then she was the object of all that gossip after Corder's wife died.'

'She's not done too badly though.' Viv toyed with her cup, tipping it this way and that. 'She and Max had got it all planned for a springtime wedding – and after they'd been living in sin for ten years. I told her – she ought to be ashamed of herself . . .'

'Aunt Viv! People do that sort of thing nowadays. It's the fashion to live together. Not everybody wants a commitment so binding as marriage, especially if they don't intend having children.'

Suddenly he was exasperated with her. She'd always had this streak of puritanism in her, he realized. It had driven a wedge between her and Mari ten years ago, and the rift had never been properly healed between them, although on the surface, they kept up an appearance of friendliness for most of the time. Mari had never abandoned Viv completely though, he knew. Mari was the easy-going type who would never knowingly stir up a hornet's nest just for the fun of it.

'Our Mari will probably let herself go now that she's got no man.' Vivian frowned again. 'Some women just *have* to have a man in tow, don't they? But she could come and live here again.' She brightened momentarily, 'I told her so – right after they found Max dead on the beach, I offered her a home.' She tossed her head. 'But she's always been pig-headed,' she continued. 'Wouldn't dream of returning here! She reckons she's going to stay at Wintersgill – all on her own in a big house like that, and in the middle of the moors.'

'I don't think you need worry yourself about Aunt Mari,' Holt said, downing his coffee in one go, and pushing his chair away from the table and rising to his feet so he towered over her.

She looked up at him. 'What do you mean?'

'Hasn't she told you? She's going back to Caindale to work – she's having her own office at the foundry.'

'Work! At her age?' Vivian stared at him aghast.

'Oh, Aunt Viv! She's not that much older than you are . . .'

'Too old to be gadding around all over the place like a spring chicken,' Vivian said, lifting her hands in despair. 'And what does she want to *work* for? She doesn't have to work! Heaven knows, Max left her a rich woman. She could live in the lap of luxury for the rest of her life if she wanted to.'

'Aunt Mari *needs* to work,' Holt stated. 'And she and Max's daughter have got together and . . .'

'Serena Corder! That chit of a girl?' Vivian frowned and got unsteadily to her feet to face her nephew and demand, 'What's *she* doing back here? Doesn't she know her father washed his hands of her years ago? Nobody wants her back around these parts, I'm sure.'

'Max left Serena the foundry – the whole valley in fact. The foundry and everything in Caindale now belongs to Serena, and according to Aunt Mari, she's taken lawyer Andrews' advice and asked Mari to go into partnership with her. Mari though is waiting a while before agreeing wholeheartedly to go ahead with the partnership.'

'Well!' Viv sat down heavily again on her chair, murmuring to herself in a tone of hurt indignation, 'Well – now I know why our Mari didn't want to come back and live with me! Just wait until I see her again. I'll give her what for.'

Holt felt sorry for his Aunt Viv. She looked so defenceless sitting there alone at her table. He went round to her and putting his hand lightly on her shoulder, leaned down and dropped a kiss on her forehead.

'Don't take it so hard,' he said quietly. 'Aunt Mari will still drop in to see you like she's always done. She won't forget all about you.'

Slowly, she lifted her head and looked up at him.

'You had a thing about that girl though, didn't you? Years ago? Serena Corder?'

His laugh was hard. 'That's over and done with, Aunt Viv. You know damn well it is. We both had a change of heart.'

'You should have married her.' Her voice was flat and devoid of emotion. 'You'd have had Corder's millions by now if you'd done that.'

'I think not, Aunt Viv.' He walked to the door. 'Look,' he said, 'I have to go now. I've got that earth-moving equipment to shift to Huddersfield this afternoon. You will remember to feed Gray, won't you? I've left a tin of cat food out on the kitchen work-top, and there's plenty of milk in the fridge.'

'I never forget to feed Gray,' she said, smiling up at him.

'It's not too much for you, is it? To go to the house and see to her?'

I'm not a complete invalid! Not yet,' she snapped, 'So don't treat me like one, my boy. I do realize that your stupid cat is the love of your life – why else do you think I pander to her every whim?'

'She's completely spoilt.' He grinned across the airy kitchen at his aunt.

'She makes whiskers everywhere! Ugh! I don't know how you can stand it. I just couldn't have a cat around my house.'

'You had worse than that when I was a boy – muddy boots, a bike in the hall, goldfish and hamsters . . .'

'That was different. I wanted to make you think you'd never be able to survive without me.'

'You did a good job. I can't – not even now,' he said laughing. 'Why else do I come every day for my mug of coffee?'

'I wish I could drink coffee.' Her voice was plaintive again. 'Coffee's on my forbidden list though. It has too much caffeine in it. Did you know that?'

He nodded. 'Yes, Aunt Viv.'

'And you know I'm not allowed caffeine.'

She was playing for time, he knew. She didn't like being left alone so much. She didn't have many friends. He suspected it was because she was so outspoken on some subjects, and also because she liked talking about herself so much.

'Look,' he said, 'I'll call in again tonight when I get back from Huddersfield, but I really must go now, Aunt Viv.'

She turned in her chair and her eyes were dancing as their gaze rested on him. He knew she was proud of him.

Softly she said, 'Don't worry about Gray, love. And be careful driving that great big lorry, won't you?'

'I'm just going along for the ride today. Ken's doing the driving. I have to see some people in Huddersfield about clearing that opencast coal site of heavy plant next month.'

'Just take care. I don't know what I'd do without you. I worry every time I know you're out on the road in those awful lorries.'

'I never take chances,' he said to placate her. 'I always take care on the road. My livelihood depends on me taking care.'

'Money, money, money,' she said, shaking her head. 'It's all that some people think about nowadays.'

Laughing softly, he closed the kitchen door on her and strode out into the open air, giving a great sigh of relief to be free of her clinginess once more.

For the past few days it had snowed intermittently. Today was the coldest day they'd had since returning to England and Ryan had been sniffing and sneezing when he'd come down to breakfast that morning.

Serena laid the law down and refused to let him leave the inn. It was always warm and cosy there, she'd argued, and there was no sense at all in both of them freezing to death on the cliff top. She was quite capable of going to inspect the little house in Caindale to see how work was progressing, she'd told him decisively.

And anyway, they'd be expecting her to drop in at the foundry afterwards and there was no room for him there.

She, Mari and Jackie were having trouble not bumping into one another, sharing Max's office which was unbelievably cramped with three of them trying to work in there.

Jackie had cheerfully offered to move into the drawing office, but Serena knew if she did that, Jackie and her short skirts would hold up production more than an all-out strike would do!

A store-room was being cleared so that Mari could have her own office, but it was going to take until the end of the week to clean it up, give it a coat of paint, and have the computer from Wintersgill installed there.

'How's the house coming along?' Mari asked as Serena walked into the office.

'Fine! I reckon we'll be able to move in sometime next week.'

Jackie slid out of her seat. 'Here! Sit down in my chair, Miss Corder. I'll go and make a drink, shall I? You look like a block of ice.'

'I feel like a block of ice, love.' Serena and Jackie had to skim sideways past each other to enable her to get behind Jackie's desk.

As the girl left the office, Mari looked up and said apologetically, 'I feel as though I'm pushing you out. It's you who should be sitting here at Max's desk, not me.'

Serena flashed her a wide smile, and pushed Jackie's typing chair back to the radiator as she huddled into her coat. 'I don't mind. You're better at it than I am. I'll take over this afternoon as planned, shall I?'

Mari nodded. 'It's absolute murder – two of us trying to work in here. There isn't room to swing a cat.'

'I'll have a cup of tea with you, and you can tell me what needs doing this afternoon. Then though, I'm going to go back to Rivelyn to see how Ryan is. He seemed to be going down with flu or something this morning.'

'He doesn't seem very strong.' Mari looked up, an expression of concern on her face. 'Do you think he ought to see a doctor or something?'

Serena said quickly. 'Oh, he's okay.' And as she recalled her promise to Ryan, not to talk about his illness to anybody, she tried to make her voice sound casually normal as she added with a grin, 'A couple of aspirins, and lots of hot lemon drinks should do the trick. That was always Dad's favourite remedy for a cold.'

Mari laughed. 'Don't you mean hot lemon laced with whisky, love?'

'Well – he did have a weakness for his bottle of Irish malt, didn't he?'

Gently, Mari said, 'I'm glad we're able to talk together about him like this, Serena.'

Serena pulled her hands out of her coat pockets and slowly removed her gloves. 'I wouldn't have believed it a couple of weeks ago,' she said. 'But we're not doing at all badly, are we? You and I?' Her eyes came up to meet Mari's in an honest and straightforward gaze.

'We've got to pull together.'

'For Caindale! Yes, I know.' Serena sat forward in her chair and fidgeted with the pair of leather gloves on her lap, then unexpectedly, she asked, 'Are you coping all right, Mari? At home? Without him?'

The older woman was silent for a minute or two as she finished what she was typing into the computer, then she said, 'I'm a survivor, Serena. I shan't go to pieces. Though at first I was absolutely devastated.'

'Yes. You must have been.'

Mari heaved a great sigh and said, 'Viv keeps trying to persuade me to go and live with her.'

'Oh?' Serena's heart gave a sudden lurch. The mention of Mari's sister Viv, stirred up memories of Holt, Casually though, she forced herself to say, 'Would you like to do that? It's a very small house isn't it, where Vivian lives?'

Mari nodded. 'Cow Lane Cottage! It would drive me mad, I think – living with Viv. She worries about everybody and everything, you know. And she seems to think I'm helpless. But honestly, Serena, it's *me* who should be doing the worrying about *her*. She's never been strong. She's always had this funny problem with her heart. She took it real hard – Max's death. In the week between him being found dead on the beach and the funeral, she was really ill. I got quite worried about her but suddenly she seemed to pull herself together again and was right as rain.'

'It must have been a shock – even to her. You and your sister were very close to each other at one time weren't you?'

Mari leaned her elbows on the desk in front of her and propped her chin on them. 'We'd lived together since our parents died – right until the day I married Harry Wyatt and went to live in Middlesbrough. Then of course, our brother and his wife were killed in France, and Viv took young Holt to live with her. Well, there was nobody else to care for the lad and Viv had always doted on him.'

Serena longed to ask for more information about Holt, and here was her chance, but as she opened her mouth to speak, the moment was lost as Jackie kicked the door opened and barged in with a tray full of cups.

'We've run out of sugar,' she breezed. 'Sorry about that, Mrs Wyatt.' Her eager little face screwed up in a grimace. 'I can't stand hot drinks without sugar. I'll have to get some on my way home tonight.'

'Have a sweetener, love.' Mari held up a tiny white box.

'Ugh. Are them things all right? Aren't they loaded with "E" numbers or something?'

'I haven't a clue.' Mari laughed. 'All I know is I like my tea sweet, but my figure doesn't take kindly to sugar.'

Serena slowed the car as she approached Cow Lane. She wasn't driving fast; the roads were icy and quite dangerous on the hills. She pulled onto the grass verge again, however, and turned off the engine. Then she sat staring across at the little unmade road that she knew ran for several hundred yards before finally coming to a halt a field away from the edge of the cliffs. It must have been down here that her father had come on the day he died, she thought silently to herself. But why had he been there, she wondered? And for what reason had his car been parked right at the very end of that road? And what had happened when he'd walked out onto the cliffs? Had he accidentally fallen? Or could it have been something a lot more sinister than that?

Her mind shied away from the thought of suicide though. Max just wasn't the type! And there was no reason at all why he should take his own life.

It was a desolate spot. And he'd have been forced to drive right past Viv's cottage, and then the 'ugly' house. She shivered. She'd always hated that house – even though it had held a shivery kind of fascination for her. She'd never been up really close to it. The old woman who had lived there hadn't encouraged visitors. She smiled as she

100

remembered being chased endless times by the 'witch', when as children they played games of 'dare' up on the cliff tops. Her father, she realized now, would have locked her up at Wintersgill for a month if he'd known what sort of things she used to get up to with the children of Caindale. It was how she'd met Holt though – up on those cliffs . . .

She got out of the car and hurried across the road. It was bitingly cold outside, and snow was falling again. She pushed the car keys into her coat pocket just at the same moment she realized she'd left her bag on the passenger seat. She glanced back, decided it would be safe enough there, then set out to walk the length of Cow Lane.

Viv's cottage stood back from the road with a pretty front garden of neatly pruned bare rose bushes and a few clumps of snowdrops showing through the ice-rimed soil. Snow was ledging in the corners of the square paned windows; there was no sign of life though, and she didn't know whether to be pleased or disappointed about that. It might be nice, she thought, to see him again – and this time in daylight. Often during the last week or so, she'd wondered if she'd dreamed that last meeting in the darkness of Caindale – with the statue of her father silently observing them.

She felt prickles of apprehension running down her spine as the steep red roof of the 'ugly' house came into sight beyond a bank of trees. Her breath was steaming on the frosty air and snow was powdering her eyelashes as she hurried along the rutted track.

The house stood to the right of her, some distance away in a deep dip in the hills that rolled out towards the edge of the cliffs and the headland. It had always been surrounded by shrubs and trees so that many of its windows were almost obscured, and as she stared across the fields at it, she saw that it looked just the same as the last time she'd been here.

Upon closer inspection, however, she realized that what windows she could see, weren't broken or cracked any longer. And the woodwork wasn't peeling either. It had been given a fresh coat of mossy green paint that blended in with the greenery all around it. To her over-active imagination though, it was still a desolate place, and one to be approached with a deal of trepidation.

She came to the path that led to the house and the cliff top. When she'd been here last it had been overgrown with brambles and weeds, and barely the width of a man. Once when she'd been with Holt, he'd had to hold back the thorns that had snatched at her denim skirt. Now though, she saw that the path had been widened and the bushes cut well back. And more than that, there were car tracks in the solidified mud, heading towards the house.

She stood still, wondering if she'd be accused of trespassing if she went any further. She listened, but there was no sound at all except for the raucous cries of sea birds as they soared high above her, and the rumbling of the ocean thrashing about at the foot of the cliffs hundreds of feet below.

She came at last to the driveway and peered at the house through a tunnel of bare branches where snow flakes were filtering down through the trees. She could see little of the building however, for it sat solid and unpretentious in its niche in the hills overlooking the sea, concealed by its cloak of oak and evergreen, and with devil dark ivy clambering over its walls.

She became more and more intrigued with what had happened to the house over the years, and slowly she began to walk towards it, between the trees. There was no sign of habitation as she came up to it. Its towering roof and its gables were oppressive though, and she felt again the fear she'd experienced as a child. She stared up at the chimneys, noting that the roof had been skilfully repaired with new red tiles that only somebody scrutinizing it closely – as she herself was doing – would notice were not the original ones, they blended in so well.

It had a solid front door inside a rugged porch. The door had a massive cast iron ring sealed into its exact centre as a knocker, and fanning out from the ring was a pointed zig-zag design, also in cast iron. She moved nearer to examine it in more detail. She'd never seen such a fantastic door in her life before. In the dimness of the porch it seemed almost medieval – and yet, those points – why, they could be symbolic of something altogether different.

Witchcraft was what sprang to her mind, and suddenly she knew she oughtn't to be standing there at all.

But before she could move away, she heard a noise, and the door started to move. She felt her heart thudding in her throat. She wanted to scream but no noise would come. Her breath caught on a petrified gasp. Then she became aware of somebody standing there – looking at her – just inside the house.

Her eyes became rivetted on the figure dressed, not in a long cloak and pointed hat, but in jeans and a dark-coloured sweater.

'God! What are you doing here?' she cried. 'You scared me half to death.'

103

Holt looked her up and down and slowly smiled. 'I was expecting you,' he said softly. 'I remembered how intrigued you always used to be with this house. I somehow knew that if I waited long enough, you'd come back to it one day.'

CHAPTER 7

'What *are* you doing here?'

Her eyes, she knew, had widened with surprise at the sight of him – the last person on earth she'd expected to see emerging from the 'ugly' house.

He laughed. 'I live here.'

'At the "ugly" house?'

He sobered instantly. 'Why – that's what we used to call it, isn't it?' With a far away look in his eyes, he said, 'Do you know – I'd forgotten we'd lumbered it with such an awful name.'

Involuntarily, she shivered. 'I don't know how you could. Live here, I mean. It's so isolated.'

'I lived in even more isolation when I was doing the place up,' he said. 'I had a caravan on the cliff top.'

'No!' She began to laugh.

'It was quite a sizeable one,' he admitted. 'One of the sort you'd call a mobile home. It was connected to the electricity and water.'

'I wish I could have seen it.'

'Why don't you come inside and take a look round the house?' He pulled the door open wider and stepped to one side, indicating with one hand that she should enter the house.

'No. Oh no.' Her glance flew again to the emblem on the door and she said, 'It's a bit scary isn't it? The door.'

'The compass?' His dark brow wrinkled attractively.

She stared hard at it again, and saw he was right. It *was* a compass, not anything sinister at all, she realized now she could see it more clearly.

'Oh, heck,' she said. 'I thought it was something ominous when I first saw it – you know – I was thinking about the old woman and the broomstick when we were kids . . .'

He shook his head and laughed at her. 'Serena Corder,' he said, 'I never thought you'd be taken in by jiggery pokery black magic stuff. You were always far too level-headed for that in the old days.'

'It is a strange door – you must admit that.'

'Yes. It's a prototype that never quite made the grade.'

She was intrigued. 'I've never heard a door described as that before.'

'We had an idea – Max and I . . .'

'You and Dad?'

'Hear me out, will you? Business at the foundry hasn't always been as good as it is now. Max had this idea about fancy doors and wondered if it could take off in a big way. The doors would be damned heavy though with all that iron in the middle of them.'

She nodded. 'Yes. It looks heavy.'

'It should have taken off and made him a cool million,' he said. 'It was a great idea, but the doors proved too costly to manufacture. And they didn't always come out as they should have done. They couldn't get the seal between the wood and the iron to fuse. This was the only one that survived.'

'Would it have been a viable proposition though? If Dad had spent more time on it?'

He shrugged. 'Who knows? Business picked up at the foundry and Max never had the time or the spare man-power to go into it more thoroughly.'

'Were things really bad at the foundry?'

'Quite bad. Max wasn't worried for himself, but he would have moved heaven and earth to keep the men in work.'

'Not the Max Corder I remember,' she said flippantly.

'I suppose not. He changed after you went away. He softened a lot, Serena. He missed you like hell.'

'It wasn't exactly a picnic for me,' she retorted.

'It nearly put an end to his friendship with Aunt Mari.'

'Did it?' Suddenly she was concerned.

'Yes,' he said. 'Normality went out of the window. Max was half out of his mind with worry.'

'Events these past few weeks haven't been exactly normal either, have they?'

'Your dad?' he asked gently. 'That's what brought you home?'

She looked at him again. 'Yes,' she said. 'I guess that's also why I left the car back there on the main road and came prying around here. It was up here on the headland that he fell, wasn't it?'

'Yes,' he said.

'Had he been here, Holt? To see you?'

'I was away at the time,' he said. 'Up in the wilds of Scotland, delivering a Harland and Wolff locomotive to a theme park.'

'Do they have theme parks in the wilds of Scotland?' She couldn't tell if he were teasing her or not.

'I wouldn't have taken a low loader up some of those hills if I hadn't been absolutely sure there was a theme park at the end of the journey,' he assured, watching her closely.

'Dad could have called here that day though,' she said. 'I mean – he didn't know you were going to be away, did he?'

'Sure he knew. I don't make trips like that without a whole lot of planning, Serena. We had to have a police escort through some of those villages up there. I'd mentioned to Max only the day before that I'd be away until the weekend.'

'I'm sorry . . . I didn't realize . . .'

'Just what are you getting at, lady?' His eyes narrowed.

'I'm curious. Why would Dad have come to the cliffs on a cold January day? And another thing puzzles me – he knew his way blindfold around the place; he wouldn't have lost his footing or anything like that.'

'So! What are you saying? That somebody pushed him?'

'Hell, no! I – I wondered if he had anything on his mind, that's all. If he were worried – or ill . . .'

'Worried or ill enough to commit suicide?' he asked in a hard voice. 'Forget it,' he said then. 'Max was made of sterner stuff than that. You know damn well he was. And anyway – what's all this concerned daughter act all of a sudden? You hated his guts. You always did.'

She felt sickened and wretched at what he was saying, but the last two weeks had brought about a softening in her attitude towards her father. It had come too late though. She couldn't say 'sorry' to him now.

She swallowed painfully and said, 'You never did pull any punches, did you, Holt? You can be a real rat when you put your mind to it.'

He leaned his head back, stared up at the overcast sky for several seconds, then brought his gaze back to rest on her face.

'Okay!' he said. 'Suppose I give you the benefit of the doubt, huh? Suppose I believe this "new" you. A Serena who is at last admitting to having a conscience where her father is concerned. What good is all this poking and prying going to do for you? Or for Max, come to that. Max fell! There was a post-mortem, and an inquiry by the police. If there'd been anything suspicious about Max's death, it would have been discovered.'

She blinked away snowflakes that were misting up her eyes. 'I just couldn't take it if he'd gone and done something . . . stupid – because of me,' she said.

'You didn't know your dad at all if you could think he'd do that,' he said.

'But I *didn't* know him.' She half turned away from him. 'That's why I'm concerned. I *should* have grown up a long time ago,' she muttered. 'I realize now that I've been behaving like a spoilt child for the past ten years and that takes some admitting.' She flashed him a derisory glance. 'I'm going up to the cliffs,' she said. 'I've just got to go up there and see the place . . .'

Whirling away from him, she began to run back down the drive, between the trees, till she reached the little track again. Then she turned in the direction of the high cliffs and the headland – the way she ought to have gone in the first place, she chided herself, angry now for wasting time on the 'ugly' house at a time like this.

She heard running footsteps behind her and slowed down to turn and see him following, struggling into a heavy-looking leather jacket as he raced towards her.

'You are not going up there on your own,' he said as he caught up with her.

She shrugged. 'Why waste your time on me?' she asked as she turned her back on him and began trudging out across the open land beyond the house.

Snow was falling heavily now but he paced along at the side of her, studding up his jacket but leaving the collar open.

She glanced at him. 'I asked you a question. Why are you wasting your time on me?'

'One accident on my land is one accident too many,' he snapped. 'I don't want another.'

'You know me better than that,' she said, rounding on him.

'Do I?' His voice was borne away on the buffeting wind.

She stared at him for some seconds, then walked on, and when they got near the edge of the cliffs overlooking Caindale bay, he suddenly reached out and grabbed hold of her arm. 'Not too near,' he warned. 'The ground's icy.'

'I need to go to the exact spot – right above the Caindale beck. That was where Dad was found, wasn't it?'

He bowed his head into the driving snow and muttered, 'Yes. But I don't know what you think you're going to see from there.'

She spun round to him and shook his hand off her arm. Her face was frozen and smarting from the sleet and snow blowing into it.

'It's something I've got to do,' she told him furiously. 'Don't you understand? I can't get physically close to him any more. I can't even tell him I'm sorry . . . I just want to be there . . . It's something I have to do – stand in the place where *he* stood, the last place on earth he stood while he was alive . . .'

His big frame suddenly slumped and he pushed his hands into his pockets and stared at her, coming to a standstill as she backed away from him.

'Okay!' he said. 'I get the message. I'll stay here – but for God's sake stop walking backwards, will you?'

'I'm nowhere near the edge. You forget, Holt – I too know these cliffs like the back of my hand – as did my dad.'

He nodded silently and watched her as she turned and walked away from him. She was glad to be alone, and the icy weather was a reflection of her too-long frozen heart. She was surprised when she reached the spot from which her father had fallen, and she felt nothing. What she'd imagined she'd feel, she just didn't know. Had she expected to hear his voice on the wind, she wondered? Absolving her from blame? Bidding her a fond goodbye and telling her he understood what had driven her away from him?

She stared down at the Caindale beck, foaming its way down to the sea now, and being churned up by the east wind so it didn't look red with the tinge of ironstone any more, but white and frothy, with snow gathering along its sides, covering the stones on the beach with a downy whiteness that looked as soft as a feather duvet.

The tide was high and smashing against the shoreline and the foot of the cliffs, then swirling out again to meet the next incoming surge, and hurling plumes of water thirty and more feet into the air. Spray misted the air, mingled with the falling snow and softened the outline of the razor-sharp rocks below her.

A cruel east wind brought tears to her eyes, but they were still not tears for Max, she realized. Deep inside her was something that would not free her from guilt and let her mourn his passing as a daughter should. Sadly she turned away from the edge of the cliff and made her way back to the spot where Holt was still waiting for her.

'There's no magic answer,' she said stonily as she came up to him.

'No,' he said. 'I didn't expect there would be.'

'Will you be at the memorial service that Mari's arranging?'

He gave a grim nod. 'Yes. Will you?' he asked, sarcasm edging his voice.

'Mari wants me to go.'

'Then that alone is enough to make you stay away.' His voice was surly.

'Oh, for God's sake. Don't be like that. You must surely know by now that Mari and I have come to a sort of understanding.'

She began walking back the way they'd come, trying to place her feet in the exact footsteps she'd made in the snow coming here, and avoiding his gaze. She knew what he was thinking, and she couldn't blame him, she supposed. He still remembered her as the spoilt brat. The bitch. He couldn't guess at the little girl lost beneath the hard veneer she'd built up around her in the past.

When they reached the drive up to the 'ugly' house again he asked her if she wanted to go in with him for something hot to drink.

'I'm sorry, I can't,' she said quickly. 'I don't have enough time to do that – I have to get back to Rivelyn. I promised Ryan I'd have lunch with him. Then, this afternoon I've got stuff to do at the works.'

'So you're staying here?' His lips curled into a twisted smile. 'How long will that last?' he asked, his tone flippant. 'How long before you up and run again?'

'The men in my life sure have one hell of an opinion about me,' she said.

112

'I wasn't aware I was still one of the men in your life,' he drawled, watching her with narrowed eyes.

'You're not. But you were once.' She felt herself flushing and was uneasy in his company because she knew he still hadn't forgiven her for what she'd once been. She wished she could put things right between them, but the realization came that it was too late to do that now. Maybe he'd got somebody else in his life after all these years. 'Look,' she said, more gently than she'd spoken to him before, 'I really do have to go. I was just passing the end of the lane and . . . and suddenly I wanted to see where it was that Dad had . . . fallen . . .'

The half smile left his face. 'Maybe you ought to try and forget what happened to Max, huh?'

'Forget he's dead, you mean?' she inquired, tilting her head and feeling angry with him again. 'Did you forget your parents in a fortnight when they were killed?' she wanted to know.

He had the grace to look ashamed. 'You really are a bitch!' he muttered. 'But that's the kind of comment I should've expected from you.'

'You asked for it.'

There was no softening of the hard man towards her. 'I'll leave you then – if you don't want to accept hospitality from me.'

'I can't stay. I've told you. Anyway – I never liked that house. It always scared me.'

'We used to meet up near here sometimes, didn't we?'

'Including that last time . . .'

His voice was condemning. 'You shouldn't have run out on me like that, Serena. You never gave me a clue that you were going away that night.'

113

Quietly she replied, 'You would have tried to stop me. And things had got bad at home. Mari was moving in. Dad had given me an ultimatum – I'd been ordered to make myself pleasant towards her.'

'There's no harm in Aunt Mari.'

'I realize that – now!' Her mouth twisted derisively. 'I didn't know it when I was eighteen though. I had no option. I left home. I'd caused enough trouble.'

'You sure did that.' He smiled at last at her, and there was no malice in his words as he said, 'I was real glad to see you back though – a couple of weeks ago – that night in Caindale.'

Her heart was starting to thaw towards him, and that was something she didn't want to happen. She drew in a deep breath and as her eyes met his, the old magic flared briefly between them.

'I'll see you around, maybe.' Somewhere a distance away, a church clock was starting to strike the hour. She counted to twelve before it stopped. 'Hell! I'm late.'

He lifted his hand to her and said, 'See you, Serena. Take care.'

And then he was gone, spinning abruptly away from her on his heel, and striding away through the trees up to the 'ugly' house, and she still found it hard to believe that he actually lived there in that monstrosity of a place.

She ran quickly back to the main road, dashing across to her car and jerking the door open to slip inside. When she'd closed it, fastened her seat belt and started up the engine, the windows started misting up from the cold snow that was melting and steaming on her clothing and her hair. She felt cold rivulets of water trickling down her neck.

'Ryan!' she said firmly to herself as she stared out through the windscreen. 'Ryan has to be all that concerns me for the moment.' And her face was grim as she pulled out onto the road and headed towards Rivelyn.

Ryan wanted to know why she was late.

'I went up on the cliffs,' she told him. 'I wanted to see the place where Dad had fallen.'

'What a ghoul you are!' He glanced at her across the little square table in the dining room of the inn where they were staying, then picked up his glass and took a deep drink of red wine.

'No,' she said. 'It wasn't like that. I kept wondering what happened that day. And I've come to bitterly regret that I never made up my quarrel with Dad before he died.'

'That figures,' he said in a less bantering tone. 'But you can't go on blaming yourself for ever.'

'No,' she said, pushing away her plate and toying with her own glass of orange juice. 'But I can try to make it up to Mari now I have the chance.'

'Do you really want to stay here in England? At Caindale? I thought you hated the place.'

'I – did –.' Her voice faltered and she amended the statement to a more positive, 'I do!' but she found unexpectedly that she couldn't meet his gaze across the dazzling white tablecloth.

'Something's changed,' he said softly. '*You* have changed, Sera.' He leaned his arms on the table and tried to look into her face. 'What is it?' he probed.

'Nothing!' She flung back her head and stared straight at him. 'Nothing's changed.'

'You're not happy,' he said. 'Something's eating away at you. What is it?'

'Nothing.' She forced a brittle brightness to the words then grinned at him and downed the remainder of her orange juice in one go. 'Anyway,' she went on, 'I can't stay gossiping any longer, Ryan. I told Mari I'd be back at the foundry by one o'clock.'

'You might as well let Mari have the place,' he grumbled. 'You're never going to make a go of it – you know damn well you won't. You never wanted to come back here in the first place so why not admit defeat and . . .'

'I'm staying, Ryan.' Steadily she looked him in the eye. 'Nobody's ever going to accuse me of running away again.'

'A couple of weeks ago you were hell-bent on destroying the place.' He looked glum and surly. 'What's so different now that you want to stay and make a go of it?'

She pushed her chair back and stood up. 'I have a debt to repay,' she said. 'And there are a lot of unanswered questions about why my father died, and I'd like some answers.'

'It was an accident, for God's sake.' He sounded thoroughly exasperated with her. 'Mari's told you what happened. He went up on the cliffs on a day such as this one. The ground was icy – he slipped and fell over the edge.'

'Dad wasn't stupid,' she stated. 'He wouldn't take risks by walking near the edge.' She threw up her hands in an impatient gesture. 'Why oh why is everybody trying to convince me it was an accident?'

'Everybody?' He frowned.

'Mari and – and – '

'Yes, Sera? Who else?'

She drew a deep breath, then slumped down on the chair opposite him again. She was silent for a few seconds, then she said, 'Somebody you don't know. Somebody I've never mentioned to you. His name's Holt Blackwood – and I guess it's time I told you about him.'

'Are you still in love with him?' he asked when she'd finished telling him about the man she'd walked out on all those years ago.

'At eighteen I couldn't have been,' she said. 'At eighteen I was mixed up. I must have mistaken a passing attraction for "love".'

'That wasn't what I asked you.' Ryan leaned back in his chair and looked thoroughly dejected.

'I am not in love with Holt,' she said firmly.

'What's he like?'

'I told you – he has his own business now. Haulage. And he lives in that horrible house up on the cliffs.'

'What does he look like.'

'Rough,' she snapped.

'Rough?'

She relented somewhat. 'Maybe it's unkind of me to say that,' she said. 'But he's changed. He used to be a lot nicer than he is now. He used to dress well, he had good manners. He taught me about the seashore – the birds, the shells that were washed up on the tide. He was enthusiastic about the fossils we used to find on the face of the cliffs, and computers, and oh, about everything else as well. Now though, he's cynical and he wears sloppy jeans and shirts, and he's grown his hair long . . .'

'What you're saying, love, is that when you went away he was a boy, and now he's a man.'

She frowned at his words, wondering if that accounted for the change in Holt. 'Maybe,' she agreed at last. 'But I think I liked the old Holt better than the new one.'

'When do I get to meet him then?'

'You want to meet him? Why?'

He shrugged. 'No reason. But he obviously meant something to you at one time.'

'We were just friends,' she said.

'If you say so.'

'Oh, hell!' She jumped up from her chair and stared down at him. 'You're beginning to sound just like my father,' she stormed softly.

'Maybe you need somebody to take care of you.'

She gave a hollow laugh. 'I don't need *anybody*, Ryan. 'So don't go getting ideas that Holt is back in my life, will you?'

Pointedly he turned his head and looked at the clock on the wall beside the door. 'You're going to be real late back at the foundry, Sera.'

'Hell!' It was nearly two o'clock. 'Why didn't you tell me? I must have been talking for more than an hour.'

'You have,' he replied. 'Odd isn't it how you can go on prattling away for such a long time about somebody you care nothing about!'

CHAPTER 8

The little house high up on the hillside in the heart of Caindale was almost ready for occupation.

Ryan had spent the past week painting and decorating, and by the weekend it had been possible to have hard-wearing jute carpeting fitted throughout the whole house.

Serena stood at the bottom of the stairs and yelled, 'Come and give me a hand with the kitchen curtains, will you?'

Ryan popped his head out of the bathroom door and called back, 'Do you want this blessed bathroom cabinet fixing on the wall or not?'

'After we've hung the curtains down here.'

He appeared on the top stair and glared at her. 'I thought we'd agreed to do different jobs so we wouldn't get in each other's way.'

'But I can't reach the curtain rail, and you have the only step-ladder we possess up there,' she pointed out.

He came down at last, the metal steps clanking as he set them up in the kitchen. 'Well?' He stood belligerently in the middle of the room, his arms folded and said, 'There are your steps, so what are you waiting for?'

She grabbed them, hauled them over to the window and climbed up them.

'Pass me a curtain,' she ordered, as she rested one denim-clad knee on the top step.

'Hell!' He strode over to a pile of curtains stacked neatly on the floor and looked down at them. 'Which one?'

'The top one.'

He brought a curtain length over to her. 'If you were a gentleman you'd do this for me,' she said. 'You wouldn't let me climb a ladder while you just stood there watching.'

'I thought we were going out shopping to get some pots and pans this afternoon. We really do need an electric kettle, you know. We can't even make ourselves a cup of tea at the moment.

'We're managing nicely on cans of fizzy pop,' she came back at him. 'And we are going shopping, but not until I've hung these curtains – and you have fixed that bathroom cupboard on the wall.'

'You're turning into a slave driver – you really are, Sera. Why can't you let up a bit? You were just the same with that fellow from the works who had to re-wire the place around us while we were stripping the old wallpaper off the upstairs bedrooms. The poor chap must have slept for a week after he'd finished here.'

She laughed down at him from the top of the steps and said, 'Are you regretting this venture? Don't you like the thought of living with a slave driver?'

He scowled. 'I thought I knew you. In Queensland, when you lived with Dad and me for two years you were never like this.'

She grinned down at him when she'd hooked the curtain up, held out her hand for the other one, and said, 'Don looked after me when I was in Queensland. Now though, I've got to stand on my own two feet.'

He handed her the second curtain. 'Do you still miss him? Dad?'

Her face softened as she glanced at him. 'Of course I do.'

'You never talk about him.'

'That doesn't mean I didn't care about him.'

'I hope you did.'

'What are you getting at, Ryan?' She stood still on the step-ladder, looking down at him, thoroughly confused.

'He thought the world of you.'

'I know he did,' she said. 'But Don died instantly. And you needed me, Ryan. I didn't have much time for grieving when your life was hanging by a thread.'

'I *am* grateful, Sera.'

She turned and started hooking up the curtain. In a strained voice, she said, 'Are you sure you did the right thing – getting rid of Kirsten?'

'I know damn well I did the right thing. I don't want *anybody* showering me with pity.'

'I don't think it would have been like that, Ryan. Kirsten loved you. She must have been devastated when you sent her that letter . . .'

'Better that than being lumbered with a vegetable.'

'You're not a vegetable.' The curtain finished with and hung to her satisfaction, she came slowly down the steps and confronted him. 'Ryan – the only one showering you with pity is *you*. Can't you see that?'

'But it's a possibility that I could turn into a vegetable.' He fixed his gaze on the floor as she moved the steps and arranged the curtains neatly, one on either side of the window. 'Wouldn't you be thinking about that all the time if you were in my place?'

She held out her hands to him in entreaty. 'Ryan, I *could* be in the same position – any time, anywhere. Just look at

121

it this way – I could so easily have an accident. I could crash the car the next time I'm out in it, and *I* could be a vegetable. But why should I start worrying about that before it happens? And it might never happen anyway.'

'No,' he muttered. 'I could just drop dead at any minute.'

'Oh, for God's sake!' She whirled round to him. 'Stop playing the martyr, will you?'

His face was stricken, and she immediately felt sorry for saying what she had. It was hard though, looking after him, being as close to him as she'd been for the past few months. And when he got in one of these black moods she knew from experience that sympathy would only send him deeper into it.

'I'm sorry,' she said, more patient with him now. 'Ryan, I'm sorry. But one minute you're saying you don't want pity, and then next you're wallowing in it.'

'Would *you* like to know you were living on borrowed time?' he yelled at her.

'No! Of course I wouldn't . . .'

He rushed out of the room, towards the front of the house and she heard the outside door bang behind him as he flung himself outside. More slowly, she followed, and found him across the road, his arms leaning on top of the car, his head supported by his hands as he stared out at the little harbour so far down below him.

She went across to him, standing a few feet away from him. 'Ryan! What do you want me to say?' she asked. 'What do you want me to do?'

'Nothing!' He still stood with his back towards her.

'Is your head playing up again?'

'No!'

122

Perturbed, she said, 'Come back inside then. It's too cold to stand out here.'

He didn't answer.

'Don't be awkward, love. We've got to get on with our lives.'

His head jerked forward and she could see that something had caught his attention directly below him on the road.

'Hey – there's a little truck loaded with furniture crawling across the bridge down there,' he said suddenly. 'I thought all that stuff wasn't being delivered until next Monday.'

She groaned and walked over to stand beside him. 'Mrs Crabtree said it would be Monday,' she said irritably. 'She said her son didn't have the time to load it up until then.' She peered down into the valley road. 'Heck, it looks a bit precariously balanced, doesn't it?'

'It's only second-hand stuff.' He managed a grin at her. 'What do you expect for a few hundred dollars? A top removal firm?'

'A few hundred *pounds*,' she corrected him, then added, 'Well, it's all I could afford.'

'You should have cooked the books at the foundry. Paid for it out of the profits. We could have had real swish stuff then.'

'It's good hard-wearing furniture. Real wood anyway, not the build it yourself match-stick sort.'

The little truck disappeared beneath the overhang of the hillside and she sighed and leaned back on the bonnet of the car.

They could hear it grinding up the steep incline several minutes later, and she said, 'Oh, well, I suppose I'd better go and shift those curtains off the kitchen floor. I thought I'd be able to get them all hung before Monday.'

She was half way back across the road when he called to her. 'Sera! Stop!'

She turned round. 'Look – I don't have time to stand there gazing at the sea, Ryan . . .'

'I'm sorry, Sera. For the things I said.'

His mood had lightened, and for that she was glad. But she knew it wouldn't be permanent. The depressions came over him more and more often now, and sometimes she wondered how she'd cope if he got any worse. Cope she would though, she vowed. She owed it to Don to take care of his son, and she'd meant it when she'd made a promise to herself that she wasn't going to run away from anything ever again.

'Come here.'

'No,' she said. 'I'm going inside to start planning where to put the furniture. I could strangle Mrs Crabtree! I really needed the weekend to get everything in order.'

He pushed himself away from the car, and loped across the road to her side, grabbed at her hand and said in a low voice, 'I'm sorry, Sera. Am I forgiven?'

'I'm a fool to say "yes" when you've been in such a foul mood – but I suppose I'll have to.' She grinned up into his face.

'Don't know what I'd have done without you, love,' he said gruffly, letting go of her hand and putting one arm round her shoulders and hugging her. 'You're so practical and down to earth about everything. You make me feel good when I'm down in the dumps, and on top of everything else, you've usually got the patience of a saint . . .'

She looked up into his face. 'You're daft,' she said. 'That's what we say in these parts about cranks like you.'

He laughed down at her, just as the little truck with the name 'Crabtree' over its cab came lumbering up the hill towards them. They moved together then towards the house, he with his arm still draped easily around her shoulders, and the truck drew up alongside them.

Then, to her shock, the door opened and a man jumped down – a man with a face like thunder as he looked at the pair of them standing there together in such a familiar closeness.

And that man was Holt Blackwood!

Mrs Crabtree's son Mark walked round from the other side of the cab and beamingly informed her, 'We managed to get it loaded up today, Missis – thanks to this fella offering to help.' He thumped Holt good-naturedly on the shoulder and Holt felt like thumping the young man back – with a great deal more force than was necessary.

He glared at Serena, and took stock of the young man at her side. They looked good together, he had to admit that – the man so dark, and she so fair. She seemed slightly put out to see him though, and he was glad about that as he swung away from her and started untying a rope at the back of the truck that held the tailboard up.

Mark Crabtree came and helped him lower the tailboard, then, grinning at him, said in a hoarse whisper, 'They're not married, you know.' He jerked his head back towards the house, 'But they're setting up home together.'

'Let's get this lot off, shall we?' Holt was fuming inside as he let his eyes roam over the heaped-up pile of second-hand furniture on the back of the truck. All he wanted to do was get away from here. He didn't want to look at *her* with that lout beside her, his arm so proprietorily draped round her shoulders. At the moment he felt not so much like unloading furniture, as dragging the good-looking man away from her and punching him on the jaw.

Something deep inside him was screaming out to him, telling him that Serena belonged to him. Something was tearing him apart, and filling him with hate for the pair of them. How could she do this to him? And then he realized – she hadn't known that he'd be coming here today. It was he himself who had offered to help when he'd seen Mark struggling to load up the truck, and he'd only then discovered where he was delivering the load of furniture.

He'd leaped at the chance of seeing her again. And now he was wishing with all his heart that he'd not come. To see her like this, with the young dark man beside her was more than flesh and blood could stand. And when he thought about them living here together . . .

'Holt. I'd like you to meet Ryan.' She was standing against his elbow at the back of the truck.

Was she real, he wondered? Actually behaving in such an ordinary and mundane fashion – and having the sheer cheek and audacity to introduce him to the young upstart? The enemy? The rival?

'Hi there, mate.' Ryan had taken his paws off her long enough to hold one of them out towards him, Holt saw as he half turned towards them. 'Sera's mentioned you. Glad to meet you. Can I help with this stuff?'

There was nothing for it but to be civilized and shake hands with the thin-faced Australian, Holt decided. But it wasn't with good grace that he did it.

'We can manage,' he growled, eyeing Ryan up and down and noting the way his clothes hung on him, and how the bones in his hands and fingers seemed almost skeletal. He very nearly found himself feeling sorry for Ryan, for he

126

was visibly shivering in the cold northern air. 'You'd better just get back inside and let us know where to dump everything,' he muttered.

'Oh, I'm leaving the setting out of the furniture to Sera. She's better at that sort of thing than I am.'

Serena moved away, and Holt elbowed Ryan out of the way to reach a chair down off the truck.

When he turned round, there was nobody there. Serena and Ryan had gone into the house.

Holt and Mark struggled upstairs with a pine double bed that was in pieces and had to be put together in situ. Serena was standing in the back bedroom – the one with a view out over the tangle of a garden, and the line of cliffs and sea beyond it down the coast towards Whitby, when they dumped the bed down.

'I'll leave you to put it together,' Mark said, handing Holt a screwdriver.

'I'll help,' Serena said quickly as Mark left the room and thumped back downstairs again.

She moved over to the slatted base of the bed and looked down at it. 'It looks much bigger in here than it did in the shop.' She grimaced. 'I won't get much more furniture in the room with it, will I?'

'You won't get two wardrobes in,' he said pointedly, not looking at her, but dropping down onto his knees to fix a hefty wooden leg onto the base.

'I won't need two wardrobes,' she said. 'Ryan's having the front bedroom. He likes the view over the jetty.'

'He'll be okay in that single bed, will he?' All at once he jerked his head up and looked straight at her, a malevolent gleam in his eyes.

He saw a flush creep into her cheeks before she replied, 'I expect so. It's what he's used to.'

'You've got it real cosy in here.' He knew the words sounded bitter, but he couldn't help it if they did. He just didn't want to think of her being alone in this house with another man.

'Ryan did most of the decorating. I didn't have much time for anything other than hanging the kitchen curtains.' She pulled a wry face. 'The foundry takes up a lot of my time.'

He heard Mark stomping up the stairs again and there was a crash as a small chest of drawers hit the doorframe. 'Take it easy,' he snapped as the younger man came into the room again.

'Sorry!' Mark looked apologetic.

'It's okay, Mark.' Serena crouched down beside Holt and picked up the other wooden bed leg as Mark went back downstairs. 'Shall I hold this in place for you?' She smiled up at him. 'Do you remember Mark from when we were kids?' she asked, reminiscently. 'He doesn't throw things around on purpose – he's just one of those people who has big hands that always seem to be dropping things.'

'You're very laid back about his shortcomings,' he said, glancing at her. 'I hope the rest of Caindale's folks are as laid back when they find out that you and the Australian guy are living here together without the benefit of the clergy.'

Her laugh was completely spontaneous. 'Oh heck, Holt. You don't think they're still as narrow-minded as they were ten years ago, do you?'

'Some of them are,' he said, his black eyes under his black brows glowering at her.

'You?' She sat back on her heels, still clutching the bed leg close to her baggy T-shirt that had dust marks across its pale blue front. Incredulously then, she said, 'It's *you* that you're talking about, isn't it? You actually don't approve of me sharing my house with a man!'

He was instantly on the defensive. 'Why should *I* mind? Your life's your own affair.'

He reached across to her and took the bed leg out of her hand, his knuckles brushing the soft cotton of her shirt, just below her breast. He snatched his hand away from her, and positioning the wooden leg, began screwing it for all he was worth into the bed's base, opposite the first one he'd fitted.

'Shall I help you lift the base up to the headboard now?' she asked, scrambling onto her knees preparatory to getting up.

'I can manage.' There was a tingling in the back of his fingers from the warmth that had leapt into them when he'd accidentally brushed against her shirt. As she shrugged and leaned forward he caught a whiff of her delicate perfume, mingled with the scent of her skin.

'I'll go downstairs then. Sorry I can't put the kettle on for a cup of tea. We don't have a kettle yet.'

'Serena – wait . . .' He couldn't let her go like this, he realized. He put his hand out to her and touched her arm.

'Yes?' Her eyes were guarded. She was still crouching, looking almost as if she were ready to spring away from him, but that hand on her arm stopped her.

'Maybe you *could* give me a hand with this bed, huh?'

'Sure!' She rose to her feet and his hand fell away from her.

He watched as she moved to one side of the bed but he lifted it without her aid and moved it bodily up to the headboard.

She laughed a little breathlessly. 'You didn't want me after all, did you?'

Her voice was low and attractive. It made him remember all those good times they'd had when there had just been the two of them. He cursed himself for not claiming her when he'd had the chance, and stood up, the width of the bed between them, parted from her now by nothing more than a few wooden slats. How the hell could she stand there so cool and self-possessed, he wondered, when he was aching to possess her, when the fire inside him was building up to furnace heat and bursting to be set free.

'I ought to go and help Ryan. He's so undomesticated he can't even hang a picture on the wall without . . .' She was stepping carefully round the bed, heading towards the door. But she'd have to pass him first, he realized.

Suddenly he raised one booted foot and aimed it at the open door, slamming it firmly shut as he heard Mark's voice down below again, at the bottom of the stairs.

He leaned his body against the door then as she came and stood in front of him.

'Holt?' Her eyes were wide, but not afraid, he saw. But she *was* wary of him.

'Serena!'

Sounding now as breathless as if she'd been running, she asked softly, 'Hey, what is this? What do you want?'

He held out his hand, and saw her back away a few steps.

'Serena,' he said again, this time in a hushed tone. 'This is no good – you and him . . .'

'Holt! No! Don't say anything you're going to regret,' she warned quietly.

'Tell me you don't want me then.'

Again she shook her head and gasped, 'No!'

The door shook behind him. Mark's voice came plaintively through to them. 'I've got a wicker chair here . . .'

'Leave it on the landing,' Holt called out. 'I've got the bed jammed behind the door. It might take some time to move it.'

She looked hard and long at him as they both listened to Mark going back down the stairs. Then as she didn't move, he pushed himself away from the door and went to her. He took her in his arms, and she tilted her head back and looked up into his face.

His head swooped down and his lips took possession of hers. He pulled her close to him so that she must surely be aware of his basic physical need of her. At the moment, he had no control over that part of his body which was demanding satisfaction.

She pressed herself against him, and slowly he ground his hips and loins into her softness, feeling her response as she grew taut and moved eagerly against him. Her lips were moving too, parting at his insistence, accepting his open mouth that was ready to devour her sweetness. His hand slid down to her waist, fumbled under the blue T-shirt and rested on the bare skin beneath it.

She moaned quietly. He found her breast; she was wearing no bra, and gently he ran his fingers over the softly rounded flesh, then cupped it in his hand and stroked his thumb over the hard nipple. She gasped, and he was drowning in desire for her as he lifted his lips away from her mouth, and plunged them in the hollow against her sleek, white throat. He had a wild hunger for her that knew no bounds. Every desire he'd ever experienced was caught up in the web of wanting that this woman had always been able to spin around him. He'd

131

dreamed about her, yearned for her, but nothing had prepared him for the actual, physical pain of holding her again – holding her, yet knowing she belonged to somebody else.

Mark stamped up the stairs again and battered on the door. Holt threw back his head, and she leaned her forehead on his chest. Her hands were clutching at the leather belt around his waist, as if for support . . .

'Aint you finished that bed yet?'

Holt began to shake with laughter, and softly, she joined in.

'What're you two laughing about in there?'

Holt sobered. 'The bed,' he called out. 'It's only got three legs.'

Serena collapsed against him, forcing her hand against her mouth to stop her laughing so much.

'Three legs?' Mark's voice rose an octave.

'Yeah! Go see if we've left one in the truck, will you?'

All went quiet, then Mark thumped off down the stairs again to be back in less than a minute yelling, 'You're kidding me, aren't you?'

By this time Serena had pulled herself away from Holt, and was smoothing down the blue T-shirt and shaking her head to rearrange her dishevelled hair.

Holt, still wanting her, but knowing now was not the time, carefully opened the door and said, 'Yes. I was kidding, Mark.'

'You made me go up and down these flippin' stairs for nothin'?' Sweat stood out on Mark's forehead.

'Sorry!' Holt shrugged his wide shoulders. 'It was a joke. I didn't think you'd go back and start hunting for it – not when you knew darn well we'd brought the whole bed upstairs not five minutes ago.'

Serena had moved quickly to the bed head and was busying herself with the screwdriver, when Mark poked his head round the door.

'Has he been skiving?' he asked, glaring at Holt with suspicion.

'Afraid so.' Serena laughed up at him. 'He's been taking it easy and leaving me to do all the work.'

Holt nodded agreeably. 'Yes,' he said, lifting his shoulders again. 'I had no option but to let her take over,' and glancing quickly at her concluded, 'the lady can be very persuasive when she puts her mind to it.'

CHAPTER 9

Serena drew up in her car outside Caindale's little chapel that had been built over a hundred years ago near the sea front.

There were half a dozen other cars parked there, and from inside the building she could hear the soft tones of an organ playing the sailors' hymn – so beloved of folk like those of Caindale, who had always lived with the sea on their doorstep.

She could feel her stomach churning as she and Ryan got out of the car. It was too soon, she told herself, too soon after Don's death to be bringing Ryan here, yet he had insisted on accompanying her to Max's memorial service, even though he'd never known her father. Ryan had been in hospital so hadn't been able to attend his own father's funeral, so she hoped today's service wouldn't stir up too many unhappy memories for him.

The starkly plain interior of the old chapel was brightened considerably today by a host of flower arrangements, Serena saw, as they entered. Mari was standing just inside the door, greeting each and every person who had come to pay their respects to Max, and almost every seat was occupied.

Serena recognized many faces from the past – men who had worked for her father and were now old enough to have retired – their sons, their daughters, their wives, and in one or two cases their parents too, had all turned out on a cold day at the beginning of February for the man they had worked for, the man who held a special place in most of their hearts.

Mari said softly, 'Sit here – with me.' She smiled at Ryan and indicated the two spare seats beside the one she was standing against. 'I'm so glad you could come.'

They sat down on the cushioned seats. The old straight-backed wooden pews had been replaced by this much more comfortable arrangement, Serena noted – of rows of beechwood chairs with wide plush covered seats. As she looked around she saw other changes too – a new modern organ, improved choir stalls, a richly-coloured wool carpet running the length of the aisle. The old electric wall heaters – whose elements regularly used to burn out – were no longer there, but the place was incredibly warm, heated now by neat skirting ducts all the way round the old building.

She was pleasantly surprised by it all. In her early teens she'd been persuaded by some of the other youngsters at Caindale to join their youth club at the chapel, and in those days it had been a dark and dismal little place, suffering from dry rot, woodworm in its old piano, and being freezing cold in winter. There had been plenty of laughter though, she remembered, and she'd enjoyed taking her place here, and being one of Caindale's far-flung family – a part, in fact, of her father's 'other' family.

Her eyes sought, and found, Holt. He was sitting right down at the front of the congregation with his back to her. She hardly recognized him in his dark suit, and with his hair more or less tamed. Then, almost as if he could feel her eyes staring at the back of his head, he turned slowly and smiled at her, and that smile started up the jittery feeling in her stomach again. He hadn't expected her to be there, that much was obvious. She could tell by the slightly sardonic way one dark brow twitched as she acknowledged him by a slight inclination of her head.

She looked away from him rapidly. Seeing him again had reminded her vividly of how he'd held her and kissed her in the little house high above Caindale – was it only days ago? It seemed like a lifetime. There had been moments when she wondered if she'd dreamt it all, but she knew in her heart she hadn't. The magic was still there. After ten long years, it was as strong and as potent as it had always been. She dared to glance in his direction again, but he was sitting completely relaxed, staring straight ahead of him, and not looking at her any longer.

By the time the service was about to start, people were having to crowd in at the back of the chapel and stand, packed in there, so many had turned up. Ryan gave up his seat to a girl who was heavily pregnant. She sank down beside Serena with a sigh of relief, and said quietly, 'Oh, the heaven of these comfy cushions on the seats.'

Serena smiled. 'Yes. It's changed a lot from the old days.'

The girl was a stranger to her – a newcomer no doubt, to Caindale.

'We shall miss him. He did us proud – giving the chapel a new lease of life with all the money he spent on it.'

Serena knew she must have looked bemused, for the girl whispered, 'Max Corder, of course, love. Did you know him?'

136

Before Serena could reply, somebody closed the outside door, and the organist began playing a lively march tune.

The minister stood up after that and said, 'Friends – we're not here today to mourn a death, we're here instead to give thanks for the life of a man who dedicated himself to our little community of Caindale . . .'

Holt avoided her, she noticed, after the brief and happy little service was over. As everybody flocked out onto the road, and Mari was surrounded by many people who wanted to convey their sympathy, or offer her their sincere good wishes, Serena steered Ryan towards the car.

He'd been very quiet throughout it all, but as he sat beside her and they waited for some of the traffic to clear before driving off, he said, 'Your friend Holt said some nice things about your dad in there this morning.'

'Yes.' She bowed her head and looked down at her hands that were gloved in black leather. It had been the last thing she'd expected – Holt taking a major part in the memorial service to Max, and speaking with such sincerity about her father.

A tapping on the car window made her jump, but on seeing it was Mari standing there, she was quick to operate the electronics and open the window.

'Sorry to hold you up,' Mari said, 'But I was talking to old Jack Broadbent back there and he mentioned the ironstone mine . . .'

'Is it really still there, Mari?' Serena realized she'd never given the drift-mine a second thought until now.

'Oh it's still there. Nobody bothers much about it though. But Jack says some kids have been hanging around the entrance. He's a bit concerned. I know he's a bit of a worrier, but it wouldn't do for any of the kids to get inside the place.'

'Isn't it capped off or anything?'

Mari laughed softly. 'They only "cap off" the shafts, love – not the drifts. Max had a security gate fitted across the entrance, and about a hundred yards into the drift the workings were sealed with concrete, but even a hundred yards is enough space to allow gas to build up.'

'Do you want me to go and investigate?'

'Holt said he'd go – if you wanted him to.' Mari raised her brows expressively. 'I didn't know if you'd want him to, so I said I'd ask you first.'

Serena frowned. 'I suppose it is really my responsibility . . .'

'Not really a job for a woman though,' Mari said. 'It's bound to be pretty grotty inside the mine after all these years, you know. And Max used to say there were always bats and creepy crawlies in there.'

Ryan stuck his head forward and said laughingly, 'Bats and creepy crawlies hold no terrors for Sera, Mrs Wyatt. She was in her element in Australia with bird-eating spiders and stingers.'

'Stingers?' Mari laughed.

'Jellyfish with long tentacles,' Serena explained, 'but he's teasing you about those, Mari. I kept well away from them – as does everybody else unless they're wearing stinger suits when they swim in the sea in Queensland.'

Mari shook her head, and pulled a face. 'You're losing me with all this talk about stingers and stinger suits.'

'What it boils down to is the fact that Ryan's right,' Serena said, grinning up at Mari through the window. 'I'm not scared of spiders or bats. In fact, Dad used to take me to look at the bats when I was little. I'll go down to the mine this afternoon – just to check the lock hasn't been tampered with or anything. There's no need for Holt to put himself out.'

'I'm sure he didn't look on it that way, my dear . . .'

'I'm perfectly capable of checking that a gate is still locked,' Serena said firmly.

Mari held up one hand. 'All right. I'll tell Holt,' she said. 'Now then – did you enjoy this morning's service?'

Truthfully, Serena had to answer, 'Yes. It wasn't what I expected. I'd been dreading it in fact.'

'Max wouldn't have wanted tears and long faces.'

'No.' She smiled. 'Whatever faults Dad had, he was never a misery or a kill-joy.'

Mari sighed. 'I'm off now to pick Viv up and take her back to Wintersgill with me – that's if she'll come, of course. Our Viv's always been a law unto herself, but she's not been too well these past few weeks so I thought she might like to stay with me for the weekend.'

'I'm sorry – is her heart problem getting worse?'

'No more than usual.' Mari's brows drew together in a frown. 'To tell the truth – I think she often forgets to take her pills.'

'Her health might pick up a bit then – if you bully her into taking them over the weekend.'

Mari tossed her head. 'Nobody could bully Viv. It's usually the other way round and she bullies me. Viv has always been used to having her own way – being younger than me, and more weakly. I must admit, I did tend to molly-coddle her when we were both at home before I married, but she can be very headstrong, and a proper dictator at times.'

Serena remembered Holt often rebelling against his Aunt Viv's archaic rules that meant he had to be in by ten o'clock at night – a rule she never relaxed until he'd turned twenty and had put his foot down and insisted she treat him as an adult and allowed him to have a set of house keys. After that, Viv had slowly seemed to realize he was old enough to take care of himself. Serena wondered how he'd managed to break away from her completely and set up house on his own, she was so domineering.

'She must be glad Holt lives nearby. It's rather lonely down that lane which leads only to the headland.'

'They get on much better with each other now they're living apart,' Mari said. 'And Viv loves looking after Gray when Holt's away on a long haul, so it suits them both now, the way things are.'

'Who on earth is Gray?'

'Holt's cat. Gray came with the house. She was probably a throwback to the time when the old woman used to live there. They did say she had hundreds of cats, but I think that was a bit of an exaggeration. If there *were* hundreds, I don't know what happened to them. Grey was the only one Holt ever found – and she was wandering around and almost starving when he first had her.'

Ryan was keeping remarkably quiet beside her, Serena suddenly noticed. She stole a glance at him and saw his head was leaning back against the head-rest, his eyes were shut, and his face was deathly pale. Traffic was moving away from the chapel now, so Mari said, 'I'd best let you get going then, Serena. But I'll see you in the office on Monday, hmm?'

'Sure, Mari.' She waited until Mari had walked back to her own car and slid inside it before pulling off. The movement of the car made Ryan groan.

'Headache?' she asked gently.

'Umm. First one for more than a week. I was just beginning to count my blessings.' He opened one eye, winked at her, then closed it again.

'We'll soon be home. Two minutes at the most.'

'Just take it easy round those bends.' He opened his eye again.

She grinned at him. 'You'll be okay when you've had a pill and I've tucked you up in bed.'

'With that glorious view of the sea and the cliffs and that jolly little jetty – yes, I'll be okay, Sera.'

She drove smoothly down to the sea front, then took the first of the hairpin bends that led them abruptly away from the beach, with care. 'You still like the house then? Even though you've sat and looked down on that jetty for the past seven days?'

'I love the house. I love Caindale.' His words were slurred.

She drove faster. She knew it was imperative she should get him back to the house and onto his medication before the headache became intolerable.

The ironstone mine was situated almost in the centre of the village of Caindale, and Serena decided she'd go there on foot that afternoon.

First though, she had to make sure Ryan was all right. He didn't want any lunch, he told her. He just needed to get into bed and try and sleep the headache off. Now, looking at the wall clock in the kitchen, and seeing it was nearly two o'clock, she washed up the few bits of crockery she'd used for her own light meal of canned soup and coffee, then went up to her bedroom.

She changed out of the dark tailored suit she'd worn for the memorial service, and pulled on a pair of jeans, sturdy boots and a yellow sweatshirt. Looking out of the window, she saw a few flakes of snow fluttering down, so took her zipped windcheater too and a pair of wool gloves. Next, she sorted through the keys the solicitor had given her and found three keys ringed together under a tag tied onto them marked 'MINE'! She pushed them into the pocket of her jacket, then made her way quietly downstairs and out into the open air.

Remembering from days long past all the little footpaths and tracks around Caindale, she walked along the front of the terrace of houses – of which hers was the nearest one to the sea – till she found the twisty path that led down to the heart of the village. It was steeper here than the road used by vehicles, and as she reached the bottom of the hill she was almost running headlong because of the gradient. From there, she had to cross the Caindale beck, over a narrow wooden footbridge which led to the main road, where she walked for about a quarter of a mile before turning off onto a track that led to the mine.

Many of the disused outbuildings had been pulled down since she was last in this part of Caindale, she discovered. There were wide open spaces beside the red-tinged little river now, on which nothing grew except nettles, thistles, and coarse tufted grass. She remembered the entrance to the mine being hidden by trees and bushes, and as she drew near the copse in the bleak afternoon with its grey skies and bitter wind, and a few scattered snow showers she felt strangely alone. She shivered and pulled the padded collar of her coat up to her chin, fastening the toggled cord more tightly at the neckline, and then pushed her already gloved hands deeply into her pockets as she trudged along.

She wished Ryan could have come with her. He would have been interested to see the drift-mine, she knew. But the headache had been bad by the time they reached home. She tried not to worry too much about him, but realized he was very dear to her – and she had a duty, she told herself, a duty to take care of him – for Don's sake. As father and son, Don and Ryan had been very close, and now, she supposed, she was seeing herself as a mother figure where Ryan was concerned. She'd never thought of herself as being the maternal sort, and she wondered idly if she'd ever dare have children of her own knowing what a worrier she was about Ryan.

Through the trees, she could see the slight incline leading up to the mine entrance. At one time there had been a rail track and a haulage engine house at the site but these were no longer there. She wasn't afraid of being in this lonely spot by herself; Caindale held no fears for her. She had roamed the length and breadth of the valley in her younger days, firstly when her father had taken her with him to the foundry at weekends, and later, when she was older, and had a bicycle so she could get over to the village from Wintersgill on the moors at any time she wanted, to meet up with her friends.

And Holt had always seemed to know when she was around, she recalled with a little smile. Living with his Aunt Viv, in the cottage to the north of Caindale, he'd stand on the opposite headland and watch the road for her. And then he'd race down one of the steep footpaths on the hillside to meet her – accidentally of course – just as she reached the sea shore.

She turned now and looked back through the trees towards the northern ridge of the hills on the other side of the valley, half expecting to see him there. She shaded her eyes with her hand, but the hillside was deserted, so she turned her attention to the mine entrance, striding out towards the steel barred gate that had been put up by Max to keep people – especially children – from wandering inside. It wasn't that anybody could get lost in there. She knew from Mari that the mass of pillar and bord workings were well and truly sealed off, but there was still that hundred yards or so of tunnel, with its ever-present threat of methane or carbon dioxide gas building up.

Mari's fears, she discovered, were groundless. The gate was still securely locked. She peered through the iron bars into the arched tunnel, so bright at the entrance just here, but disappearing into darkness a few yards inside. She'd never been scared of the mine workings. Max had often brought her up here when she was little, and had taken her inside to take a peep at the 'bitty-bats' hanging upside down in the refuge holes at the side of the tunnel. On a sudden impulse she took the set of keys out of her pocket and unlocked the three sturdy padlocks.

The gate was heavy to pull open. She only managed to move it a few inches, it was so stiff from its years of inactivity. She wriggled herself round it and stood just inside, looking up at the curved brickwork of the tunnel that was so splendidly preserved – and glancing again – farther inside at the darkness beyond this first few yards.

Under her feet, the ground wasn't too uneven. In years gone by, crushed stone had been laid to level it off and now this was packed tightly into the ground and made a firm surface. At waist height beside her was the long built-up ramp where the rail tracks had now all but rusted away. She moved a little farther inside, until she reached the first 'refuge' as it was called. This was a small hole hollowed out of the side of the brick-lined tunnel, where – in the era

144

when the mine was a going concern – miners could step safely out of the way of empty wagons that were released at the entrance to run back down into the mine. Her fingers touched the groove in the brickwork on either side of the refuge. Even an empty truck could have killed a man standing in its path in those days.

She shivered, then wondered if there were any bats, those gentle mouse-like creatures, still hiding away in the refuge. She leaned inside the hole, straining her eyes to see, it was so dim in there. Memories came flooding back to her, and she remembered how she'd clung to her daddy's hand when she'd been tiny. She recalled too, bats swooping down low in the dusk of many a summer's evening, and diving inside the cavernous mouth of the old mine. As a five- or six-year-old she'd clapped her hands, jumped up and down with delight on seeing them, excitedly crying, 'More! More bitty-bats please, Daddy. . .' And Max's deep laughter had rung out around the hillside as he'd lifted her up to shoulder height and walked a few paces inside and shown her how the little furry creatures hung upside down in the refuges . . .

'Daddy!' she whispered brokenly now. 'Daddy – what went wrong?'

Tears threatened, but she blinked them away angrily. She couldn't forgive him – ever. She could never banish from her mind entirely, the day her mother had died, and she'd found him and Mari at Wintersgill, in each other's arms . . .

She went deeper into the mine, loving its stark simplicity and the way the old brickwork seemed to wrap itself around her like a protective blanket. It was quiet and cool inside the tunnel – always it was cool, even in the heat of summer. The daylight from the entrance grew dimmer as she felt the safety of the hillside engulfing her. It had been bitterly cold outside, but in here there was no fierce wind making her huddle into her jacket.

Suddenly she caught a glimpse of something glittering on the ground a few yards in front of her. She frowned as it disappeared in shadow again when she moved forward. Then she stepped to one side so that what was left of the daylight might illuminate whatever it was that had attracted her attention. There was a flash of something that looked like metal on the floor in front of her. In that instant, it seemed as if her heart stood still, for she knew what it was she had seen.

'The keys,' she breathed softly. And there before her were indeed, the keys to the works that she'd hurled into the mine all those years ago when she'd been intent on wreaking as much havoc as possible on anything that reminded her of her father. The bunch of keys winked up at her from the stony ground, half covered in the dust of a decade, but there all the same in a niche beside the sloping railway ramp.

She darted forward, and bent down, her fingers closing round the heavy metallic bunch of keys. But there was something wrong. Somehow she didn't seem to have the strength to get fully upright again. She was hot and very breathless, and there was a weight pressing down on her head, making her eyes want to close. She felt her whole body starting to sway and sag towards the ground again . . .

She tried to turn round but her legs didn't belong to her any more. If only she could sit down for a minute – she'd feel better, she knew she would. The ramp! She'd almost reached its lowest point. She'd just sit down on it for a second – just until this dizziness passed. But the effort of moving even a fraction of an inch made her head start to pound alarmingly in time to the ragged rhythm of her heart . . .

And then, through the mists that were threatening to swamp her, a terrifying thought occured to her, and she knew with certainty what was happening to her. How could she have been such a fool? Terror made her heart lurch sickeningly, and she realized that if her legs refused to support her and she did give in to the need to rest, that would be the end of her.

Black damp – one of the miners' greatest enemies was present in the tunnel! It was the gas that was heavier than air – the gas that gave no warning to the unwary that it was there. It had no taste, no smell, and that was why she'd only felt its presence when she'd bent down to pick up those keys. That gas was a killer! How many times had she heard Max say that? And looking back, she remembered her father always testing for gas with a flame lamp before taking her inside the tunnel to look for her beloved 'bitty-bats'.

She felt sweat beading on her forehead and the heat from her body almost choking her. Again she remembered cautionary words uttered by Max.

'If you've ever worked in a mine, you get to know the signs. You can actually *feel* the lack of oxygen. You're hot, sweaty, and get the devil of a headache. You only have seconds to get to higher ground, because black damp's heavier than air . . .'

Higher ground! From somewhere she gathered a surge of energy that was enough to swing her away from the bottom of the ramp and towards the mine entrance again. She was gasping, and trying to take in deep gulping breaths of air as she tottered forward towards that semi-circle of daylight up ahead, and she might have made it had the bunch of keys not slipped out of her hand and fallen to the ground with a thud, and without thinking what she was doing, she dived after them, and scooped them up.

But as she tried to straighten up again, she realized what an idiot she'd been.

Bells started screaming in her ears. Her mind was spinning out of control. She tried to breathe but a terrible lethargy was pressing in on her.

And then her legs just refused to support her any longer. She went tumbling into velvety blackness.

CHAPTER 10

From somewhere far away she heard a panic-stricken voice yelling her name.

'Serena! Serena! For God's sake . . .'

Hard fingers were digging into her shoulders, hands were grabbing hold of her and shaking her. And the ground underneath the length of her body was very cold.

A shudder slaked right through her as she drew in a sharp gasp of freezing cold air, and then she struggled to open her eyes.

Above her was a slate-grey sky, heavy looking clouds, and there was a mist of fine snowflakes all around her.

There was a man too – a lean, dark man with a worried face, kneeling beside her. His over-long black hair was streaked with grey. She only caught a fleeting glimpse of him because without warning he suddenly hauled her over onto her side so she was now looking at the ground beneath her. He started moving her arms and legs, arranging them in what she knew – from her first aid classes of long ago – was the 'recovery' position.

Then his hands were on her head, placing it carefully to one side. He was very gentle with her. Blinking sideways at him, but not yet having the breath to speak coherently,

149

she saw him tearing off his thick waterproof jacket, and then placing it over her to protect her from the snow.

She managed to move her gloved hand and touch his knee. He took that hand in both his big ones and started chafing it between them, gradually making her blood circulate enough for her to say his name . . .

'Holt!'

Slowly his head came up and his eyes were bleary and red-rimmed as they met hers. 'Are you okay?'

The weight had lifted off her eyelids now. She felt as if she'd been asleep though for a long, long time. She asked huskily, 'Are there any after effects?'

'Usually a memorial service!' His voice was ragged. 'Thank God we won't need that, huh?'

'You – saved my life . . .' She stared at him, hardly able to believe what had nearly happened to her.

He stopped rubbing her hand but still kept hold of it. 'Yeah!' he said, his voice rough with emotion. 'That puts you under an obligation to me, doesn't it?'

Meekly she whispered, 'Thank you.'

'I hope it was worth it. I hope you'll start acting a bit more responsibly now.'

She struggled to sit up, and despite his severe expression and harsh words, he helped her, inching round to sit beside her on the ground, and all the time keeping one of his arms firmly round her shoulders for support.

She attempted a laugh, but it came out all shaky and her voice was uneven when she spoke. 'I just never thought.' She shook her head. 'I just can't believe I was so stupid, but I never dreamed there could be gas down there. Not so near the surface. I – I couldn't have gone more than fifty yards in . . .'

'Don't ever give me a scare like that again.' His dark head was bent forward. His free hand came up and swivelled her chin round so his eyes could bore right down into hers and hold her gaze. 'Promise?'

'I feel such a fool . . .'

'You were a fool – going in there without testing for gas first.'

'It was too late when I remembered that Dad used to take a flame lamp down before letting me go inside when I was little. It was only then that I realized what was happening to me . . .'

'Such a basic precaution,' he stated. 'Nobody in their right senses would go into old mine workings without testing first.'

'I know. I know,' she cried. 'Please, Holt, don't keep going on at me. Heaven only knows, I'm cursing myself fit to bust right now for being so stupid.'

'The flame would have been extinguished at the first whiff of gas.' His fingers were digging into the soft flesh of her cheeks above her jaw now. He was hurting her.

'I know! I keep telling you, I know now what I should have done. But it's been a long time since I was there. It just never occurred to me to . . .' She wriggled to free herself. 'You're hurting me,' she managed to gasp at last. 'Holt, you're hurting me. Let go my of chin will you?'

His hand never altered its grip. He stared down into her face, with an expression on his own that told her he'd recently been to hell and back.

'Serena!' he said, sounding as if he were almost tasting the sound of her name on his lips

She put a hand up to his chest. He was wearing a black sweater of some sort; through her gloves it felt soft and

151

thick. His shoulders were covered in a slight scattering of snow, and snow was in his hair too.

'Thank God. I came down to check on that damned gate,' he said, still staring deeply into her eyes.

'Mari said she'd tell you I was going to check it,' she said softly, not able to look away from that haunted expression on his face.

His hand on her jaw relaxed, then fell away, but only so it could close on her shoulder and bring her round to face him fully now. He looked several years older than he had done this morning in Caindale's little chapel, she observed. Even the grey in his hair seemed more pronounced, and the laughter lines around his mouth were scored into deep grooves of concern. But it was his eyes that worried her most, for they were settled on her face in such a hungry-looking manner, that she imagined they could feast on her for ever.

'I'm sorry,' she whispered hesitantly. 'Sorry for giving you such a scare.'

'You won't go into the mine again, huh? Promise me that, at least?'

She shook her head. 'There'll be no need for anybody to go there again. I ought to go and lock that gate though.' Quickly she glanced back at the entrance to the iron mine where the gate was still wedged open, then her hand fell away from his shoulder and she fumbled in her pocket and drew out not just the set of three keys, but the huge bunch she'd found inside the tunnel too.'

'You've got a hell of a lot of keys there for one small security gate.'

She felt the hot colour spring into her cheeks and bowed her head as she replied, 'These are the keys I threw into the mine – all those years ago – Dad's keys belonging to the works. That was why I'd bent down in the first place – I saw them there, just lying on the ground in front of me. That was when I started to feel all woozy, and then I dropped them and bent down again . . .'

He nodded and his mouth grew taut. 'You bent down and it was very nearly the last thing you did on this earth,' he said.

'It just felt like I went to sleep.'

'I saw you tottering. I'd just reached the gate and found it open. I managed to grab you before you hit the ground.'

She turned back to him. 'I'm grateful . . .'

'Serena . . .' His voice was hoarse. 'Oh, God, Serena . . .' Suddenly he dragged her into his arms and cradled her against his chest, rocking her gently to and fro as if she were a child.

She clung to him, the horror of what had nearly happened slowly draining away from her in the safety of his embrace. She felt his lips touching her forehead, tenderly, lover-like, and one big hand reaching up to stroke the gold hair that sprang back with a life of its own from her face. Then both his hands were holding her face, and it was positioned in such a way, and so close to his own, that it seemed the most natural thing in the world for their lips to touch, to savour for a while the recollection of lost years, and then to lock together in a fierce hunger and a burning need of each other.

She could feel the thunderous beat of his heart as he pulled her up close to him. The waterproof he'd placed over her slid with a swish to the ground and the snow drifted down heavily and silently now the clouds had gone and the sky had turned to the colour of lead.

He helped her to her feet, still holding her tight, and close to his side. He swept up the waterproof and somehow, without letting go of her, draped it round her shoulders, and kept dropping little kisses on her hair as he hurried her to the shelter of the trees that clustered around the entrance to the mine.

Once there, she steadied herself against him, looked up at him and said, 'I must get back home.'

She remembered Ryan and his headache, and realized she must have been out of the house for almost two hours. The old familiar fear came racing back. Anything could have happened. He was ill. She should never have left him alone with a headache like that.

Holt's hands fell away from her. He stood and gazed at her. 'Home? Is that what you call that hovel back there?'

'It . . . it's okay. It's not a hovel.'

'I've seen it. Remember? I helped put the bed together.'

'We – we've got the place nice now. Ryan's been busy . . .'

His face hardened. 'I don't think I want to know what Ryan's been doing, Serena. Slowly he backed away from her till there was more than six feet of space between them.'

She shook her head and snow started melting on her hair and running down her face. 'It's not like that . . . not what you imagine.'

His laugh was harsh. 'How the hell do you know what I imagine?'

'I – I don't know,' she faltered, 'but I expect you think it's something like you and I – when we were younger.'

He smashed one clenched fist into the palm of his other open hand and ground out, 'Don't make it any worse than it already is. Hell! When I think of you and him living together up there – I could kill him.'

'No,' she cried, horrified. 'No, Holt. You mustn't say things like that.'

'Why not? You belonged to me – once.'

'A long time ago. Ten years.' Her head drooped forward.

'You *belonged* to me.' His voice was raw.

Slowly she looked up at him again. 'You didn't need me though. And there was nowhere I could turn when I needed somebody.'

'When you decided to leave home.' His eyes were cold now, and his arms were hanging helplessly at his sides, the tenderness, the passion all gone.

'I *had* to go.' Stubbornly she insisted, 'Dad was adamant. I either accepted Mari – or I left home and made my own way in life.'

He made a helpless gesture with one hand. 'You know what Max was like. Hot-headed. He wouldn't have meant what he said. He'd never turn you out.'

'He didn't have to. I didn't give him the chance. Nobody makes threats against me, Holt.' Her eyes blazed as she glared at him. 'I didn't hang around to call his bluff. He'd made it clear that Mari was moving in and my feelings were of no concern to him.'

'You never attempted to get to know her though . . .'

'No,' she broke in. 'I was eighteen. I was hurting like hell inside. I packed a bag and I just went. It wasn't easy, Holt – turning my back on Dad, and on Wintersgill.'

'And me?'

She let out a long sigh. 'That was the hardest part of all. But what could you do? You were living with your Aunt Viv. We neither of us had any money of our own – or proper jobs. I couldn't come to you, could I? What would we have lived on?'

'You forget,' he said in a kinder tone. 'I was at least earning a wage of sorts, Serena. I was twenty-four and I wanted to look after you. Do you think I would have done what I did if I hadn't loved you?'

'Are you talking about that weekend away . . .?' She stared at him, her eyes kindling with remembrance, her heart quickening.

'That – and practically going down on my knees to your dad, pleading for a job.'

'A job that paid next to nothing in Dad's laboratory at the foundry! A job where he knew you'd never be able to earn enough for us to get married. A job you would have been thrown out of if Dad had ever discovered how much we cared for each other.'

'It was a job, dammit. A damn job, all the same,' he said quietly. 'I was still studying, remember? And Max must have appreciated that to let me work only three days a week and have the other two off to go to college. Serena,' he held out a hand pleadingly towards her, 'Serena, baby, I've never been cut out to be a whizz-kid. I'm a practical sort of bloke who never made the grade to get to university. But I was doing all I could to get to the point where I might make something of my life. I loved you, Serena. I always intended for us to get married – and Max knew that – even if he didn't aprove wholeheartedly of me.'

She shrugged. 'But it's all in the past, Holt. We can't change it to wipe out what *I* did. Not now.' Her shoulders suddenly sagged, and she remembered Ryan again. 'I really do have to get back,' she said, shrugging the heavy waterproof off her shoulder, and thrusting that and the mine keys at him. 'Will you lock it? Holt – I'm sorry, but I do have to go home.'

He snatched the keys and coat out of her hand. 'Aye,' he said, lapsing into the broad northern dialect of his boyhood which she had always loved him for, and which he'd never entirely lost. 'Aye! I'll see to it. We can't keep your fancy-man waiting, can we?'

'He's not that,' she protested, but Holt had swung away from her and was striding back up the slope towards the mouth of the mine.

Despondently she turned away and started hurrying back the way she'd come, but he never tried to catch up or walk back with her. She glanced over her shoulder only once, and saw that he was leaning against the metal gate, idly tossing the keys up into the air and catching them again as he watched her go.

He took the short cut back to Cow Lane, up the zig-zag path on the opposite hillside so he could keep his eye on her as she climbed to the terrace of grey houses high above the north sea. She never looked back at him after that first time, and he was sorry about that. If she'd only lifted a hand to him, or hesitated, he might have gone racing after her like he'd done as a lad. But it was like she'd said, he supposed. Those days were gone; it was all in the past.

He glanced at Viv's cottage as he came out across the field at the top of the hill and climbed over the five-barred gate onto the lane. He supposed he ought to drop in and see his aunt. He hadn't called for a couple of days and he felt guilty about that. With a sigh, he strode across the road and in at the little wicket gate. He went round the back of the house, not bothering to knock, but pushing the kitchen door open and yelling, 'It's only me,' as he stamped snow off his boots before entering.

Vivian came out of the sitting room – which led directly off the kitchen – and said, 'Come on in. Don't stand there out in the cold, lad.'

157

His laugh had a genuine ring to it. 'Lad?' he said, moving on to the doormat and meticulously wiping the soles of his boots on that.

'Old habits die hard. You were my lad, remember. As dear to me as if you were my own, anyhow.' She laughed too then and said, 'And don't think I'm the only one to find it hard shaking off those old habits. Look at you now – wiping your boots just as enthusiastically as you used to do when you were a boy.'

'You'd soon have given me what for if I didn't "wipe mi feet" in those days,' he teased. 'You'd have stopped my pocket money for a month.'

'Aye! I would. But you're a great hulk of a fellow now, and it's not for me to tell you what to do.'

He closed the kitchen door.

'Do you have time for a cup of tea? Or do you have to go rushing off to the ends of the earth in one of your great ugly lorries?'

'Aunt Viv – you know I always have time for a cup of tea.' He moved over to the table and sat down on one of the kitchen chairs.

She went over to a spotlessly clean worktop and clicked the switch on the electric kettle.

'Earl Grey or China?' She cocked her fair head on one side and looked at him.

'China!' He grinned. She always had a choice of tea for her visitors, but he knew she had a passion for Earl Grey herself.'

'Jilly Tewson – the home-help woman – you know her don't you?'

He nodded, wondering what Jilly had done wrong this time, and not envying her one bit for being allocated by the county council to his aunt for three mornings each week.

'She did a bit of shopping for me. Brought me Earl Grey in those little bags instead of loose.' She busied herself spooning tea leaves into a china tea pot, then turned her wide blue eyes on him and said astounded, 'I never knew they'd gone so far as putting Earl Grey into tea-bags, did you?'

He tried not to laugh, and said seriously, 'Have they really?'

'I can't abide those little bags.' She pulled a face. 'You can't imagine it's real tea, can you? Not when it's all done up in little bags where you can't see the leaves?'

'You're a finicky biddy,' he said, leaning back on the chair and grinning at her.

The kettle boiled and clicked off, and she poured the boiling water into the tea pot, then carried it to the table.

She wagged a slender, red-tipped finger at him then. 'You should have more respect for your old auntie – calling her a biddy indeed.'

He smiled as he watched her walk over to the cupboards where she kept her china cups.

'You're not an "old auntie",' he said lazily. 'Look at you now. Slim as a wand, and pretty as a picture. Old aunties don't paint their fingernails and keep their hair looking like sunshine – all gleaming and gold.'

'Flattery will get you everywhere!' she said on a droll note. 'But I expect you've found that out from the lasses you've dated over the years.'

'I have not,' he stated, 'come here for a lecture on why I should find a nice girl and settle down and live happily ever after!'

'Jilly says her daughter thinks you're lovely.'

'I agree wholeheartedly with Jilly's daughter,' he said, raising one eyebrow and pulling one hand out of his jeans

159

pockets in order to flick a lock of hair back from his forehead in an affected manner that was designed to make her laugh. 'She must have good taste.'

'Take that sweltering great mackintosh off, lad.' She brought a cup and saucer, and a mug to the table. She tapped a finger on the mug. 'I remembered, see? I don't get a cup out for you now.'

He rose to his feet and pulled off the heavy jacket. 'You can't have a decent drink out of a wavy-edged cup . . .' Something clinked on the floor as she whisked the coat out of his hand and hooked it on the back of the kitchen door.

She turned round abruptly. 'What was that?'

'Keys,' he said, bending down to pick them up and toss them onto a pine dresser behind him. 'Just keys, Aunt Viv.'

She frowned. 'They don't look like your house keys.'

'No! They're the keys to Max's ironstone mine – or ought I to say to Serena's mine, now?'

'What are you doing with them?' She began to pour out the tea, and glanced up at him as she did so.

'Serena gave them to me. It seems there've been some kids playing around the entrance.' He was disinclined to tell her the absolute truth about what had happened that afternoon, and she seemed to accept the explanation as to why the keys were in his possession.

Her face darkened however. 'You haven't started seeing her again, have you?'

'I don't go out of my way to see her – on the other hand, I don't go out of my way not to see her,' he said. 'Caindale's a small place. We're bound to keep bumping into each other.'

'Corders are bad news. I told our Mari the same thing. Several times.' She pursed her lips for a second, handed him his mug, then said, 'I don't suppose you'll take any notice of me though? I suppose you'll go your own sweet way no matter what I say?'

Holt took a long drink of the hot tea, then placed it in front of him on the table again. 'Let's change the subject, shall we?' he said.

'You'll have to get over her – one day. She made it abundantly clear she didn't want you – ten years ago.'

'I said . . .'

'Yes. I know what you said. You still haven't got over that infatuation you had for her though, have you? And it's high time you did. She's no good . . .'

'Serena's a nice kid, Aunt Viv. You never did take the time to get to know her properly.'

'They say she's living with some Australian fellow. Up on the south cliff.'

Quietly he said, 'That's her business. Not mine – or anybody else's business either.'

'She's no good.' She sat down opposite him.

'Has Gray been in to see you today?' he asked, abruptly jerking his head in the direction of a saucer of milk on the floor beside the cooker.

'Holt! Will you listen to me?'

'No,' he said pleasantly. 'I won't, Aunt Viv. And if you don't get off the subject of Serena Corder, I shall go. I'm not going to stay here and listen to you.'

She stirred a spoonful of sugar into her tea with an impatient glance at him. Then she said in a decisive tone, 'Your cat came and miaowed at the door an hour ago. She was a pathetic little thing all covered in snow. You shouldn't have put her out in weather like that.'

'She has a cat flap in the back door,' he said. 'She didn't have to go out. I never make her go out if she doesn't want to, but you know what cats are – they have a mind of their own.'

He stayed for another half hour until, seeing the weather turning worse, and snow almost obliterating the view outside the window pane, got up to go. At the door he turned abruptly to her. 'Call me,' he said. 'If you need me, you know where I am. There's always the telephone if you have one of your turns.'

'Get off with you. And don't let that cat out again tonight,' she warned. 'On the television they said snow was going to cover the whole country.'

He smiled fondly at her. 'I don't know why you don't get a cat of your own,' he said. 'It would be company for you on these drear, dark nights.'

'Ugh. Cats! Nasty smelly things most of them are. I couldn't abide cleaning out those little sawdust boxes you have to keep inside the house for them. Anyway – it wouldn't be fair to a cat – living with somebody like me who might not have much time left. With this heart of mine I could go at any time.'

'Aunt Viv!' He sighed heavily. 'Don't be so morbid. You've got those pills that keep your heart stable. Just don't forget to take them.'

'I don't forget,' she said, exasperated, as she shooed him to the kitchen door.

As he walked down the front garden path, he turned to wave at her as she stood with the lace window curtain held up to see him go. When he'd rounded a bend in the lane and was out of sight Viv let the lace curtain fall back into place and turned back into the room. As she walked through into the kitchen, almost the first thing her eyes

162

alighted on were the keys he'd forgotten to pick up, still lying there on the dresser.

She slipped them into her hand and walked through to the sitting room again and stood beside the telephone. In a few minutes he'd be home. But she could always dial his number right now and leave a message. She thought about it for several seconds, then she looked down at the three keys in the palm of her hand and bit down hard on her bottom lip. A thought had suddenly occurred to her that would fit in well with the plans she was making.

Moving away from the telephone, she walked slowly over to the window again where a wicker needlework basket stood on a small table. With a smile, she opened the basket lid, and carefully slipped the keys inside it.

CHAPTER 11

Kirsten studied the instructions in the phone booth at the airport, then dialled the number she'd memorized by heart from the piece of paper she was holding.

Mari picked up the phone at Wintersgill and listened surprised as a young female voice asked to speak to Serena.

'I'm sorry, my dear. She doesn't live here any more. She moved away ten years ago.'

At one time Mari had taken several calls a day at Wintersgill for Serena, but gradually they had dwindled away to nothing as Serena's friends and acquaintances began to realize she'd left home for good.

'But – but surely they've arrived in England by now?' The voice was unmistakably Australian. 'I heard that Serena had come home, and that Ryan was with her . . .'

'Ah! I see, my dear. You must be ringing from Queensland. Is that it?'

'Not exactly.' The girl gave a huge sigh on the other end of the phone, then said, 'Look – I'd better explain, hadn't I? I *am* Australian, but I'm here in England now. I wanted to look Ry – er, both of them up while I was here. Wanted to give them a surprise – you know? I thought they might be staying with you.'

Mari smiled. 'I'm afraid not. Serena and Ryan were booked in at an hotel until very recently.'

Faintly the girl said, 'Are you telling me they've gone back to Queensland? Oh, no . . . they can't have, surely?'

She sounded so disappointed that Mari gave a little laugh and said, 'Don't worry – they're both still in England, and likely to be for some time, I'd imagine.'

'But where?' The voice spiralled on a note of impatience, and suddenly Mari was wary.

This girl could be just anybody, and it wouldn't do to start giving information about Serena and Ryan's whereabouts to a complete stranger.

She said, 'I'm afraid I can't give you a number to ring. The Caindale house is still waiting for the telephone to be connected.'

'Caindale!'

Inwardly, Mari cursed herself for her lack of thought. She'd been caught off guard – mentioning Caindale like that, but she supposed she could warn Serena that somebody had been enquiring about her and Ryan.

'I could give Serena or Mr Farrar a message. Will you give me your name, my dear? And if you've got a number, I'll ask them to call you back. I shall be seeing Serena soon.'

'We . . . I don't have a number. I'm at the airport, you see – the one called Heathrow – do you know it? We seem to be somewhere near London, I think.'

She sounded young, Mari thought with a touch of compassion sweeping over her as she visualized the girl newly arrived in England, with no friends, and probably not much money either. But then she recalled that she'd started to say 'we' and had very quickly amended it to 'I' a few seconds ago, and once more she became careful in what she was saying.

'Heathrow's a long way out from the north of England, love.' She was playing for time, trying to see if the girl would come up with any information about herself. There was silence on the other end of the line however, so Mari tried coming straight to the point. 'What's your name, dear? If you'll just give me your name, I'll jot it down and tell Serena you called, shall I?'

'I've just got to find Ryan . . . Look – *please* – give me his address, will you? I – I've been out of touch with him – with both of them for some time.' The laugh came over as forced and unnatural, and Mari's suspicions deepened. She had the feeling that something was wrong; the girl seemed so reluctant to say who she was.

Mari gathered her thoughts together quickly. It seemed pretty obvious that Ryan – and not Serena – was the person this girl was interested in. And surely if she'd been a close friend of his, he would, by now, have let her know where he was staying.

'Can I tell Mr Farrar you called? Perhaps I could arrange for him to be here if you can give me a definite time when you'll be ringing again. And it would help also if I knew your name.'

'Mrs Corder, please . . .'

'Hold on,' Mari said. 'I'm not Mrs Corder. Mrs Corder died a long time ago.'

There was a moment's silence on the other end of the line, then the voice asked, 'But – you must be Serena's mother? I – I looked up the name Corder in the telephone directory to try and find her, and . . .'

'Neither Ryan nor Serena gave you my telephone number then before they left Australia?' Mari asked sharply.

'We-ell, no, but I remembered that Serena's name was Corder when she first arrived in Queensland, and I knew more or less where she'd spent her childhood – Ryan had told me . . . Oh, heck. I'm making a mess of this aren't I?'

Mari was worried, but wouldn't be put off. 'I really do think you should tell me who you are.'

The girl didn't answer. Mari listened carefully and could hear whisperings going on at the other end of the line. She caught the tail end of a conversation the girl was having with somebody else who was obviously there beside her.

A woman's voice said, 'You idiot, Kirsty!'

And then the girl whispered in a panic, 'But it's not Serena's mother! She seems to know who Ryan is though. It must be the right place I've got through to.'

Mari spoke loudly into the phone. 'Hello! Hello! Will you tell me what's going on?'

Silence again. And then the phone went dead.

Mari held the receiver and looked at it, perplexed. What on earth was going on, she wondered? One thing had emerged however, and that was the girl's name. Kirsty! That was what the other voice had said. 'You idiot, Kirsty'!

Slowly, she replaced the telephone, then stood staring at it as she remembered the girl saying something about Serena's name being Corder when she'd first arrived in Queensland. It seemed an odd thing to say – almost as though Serena might have changed her name afterwards. But she couldn't have done that, could she? Tears sprang to Mari's eyes. Surely Serena hadn't hated Max so much that she couldn't bear to keep his name? She wished now that she'd questioned the caller more closely. And then, as she was about to turn away, she froze. It could mean something else altogether, she realized. Serena and Ryan could be married.

She gazed at her pale reflection in the mirror, then murmured, 'If that's the case, the girl on the phone might be an old flame of Ryan's – come over here to make trouble!' She looked at her watch. Serena would be at the foundry office by now.

Without any further delay, she picked up the phone and dialled the works' number, knowing she must warn Serena about this Kirsty girl. But she knew she would have to tread carefully, and she mustn't jeopardize the newly-formed friendship she'd built up with Serena by prying into her affairs. At the moment their relationship was based on a mutual desire to keep the foundry running smoothly, and it wouldn't be right to go asking personal questions. If Serena and Ryan were man and wife, Serena must be allowed to tell her so in her own good time.

Ryan walked down the steep hill towards the sea shore.

On his frequent day time walks around Caindale, people were getting to know him now. Everybody he passed or met would give him a friendly wave or else call out to him. Caindale folk, he decided, were amongst the friendliest on earth, and he loved talking to them, especially the older fishermen who had plenty of time now for chatting.

He enjoyed taking photographs of the boats – the cobles – of which the men were justifiably proud. And then there were the pigeons too that fascinated him! He'd discovered that most of the families in Caindale either had an allotment garden, a fishing boat, or one of the brightly-coloured pigeon lofts that dotted the hillsides leading down to the beach.

He stopped now as he saw old George Cook setting a small step-ladder up against his pigeon house. 'Hey,

George,' he yelled, 'You're not going to climb up that thing, are you?'

George chuckled as Ryan rested his hands on top of the sturdy fence alongside the road, then vaulted over it onto the grass of the hillside on to George's side.

'Think I'm too old for this caper, d'ye, lad?'

'What – a spring chicken like you?' Ryan strode out towards George, his expensive camera bouncing against the bright yellow sweatshirt he was wearing that morning under his open leather coat.

'Ye'll scare my birds to death, wearing that bright jumper!' George grumbled as Ryan came up to him. 'They'll think y're a canary from outer space or summat.'

'It's one of Serena's. I borrowed it. Don't tell her though, will you?' Ryan laughed and stood, feet planted apart, observing George as the old man tried to find a level piece of land on which to position the step-ladder. 'Can pigeons really distinguish different colours?' he wanted to know.

'O'course they can. Why the 'eck d'ye think th'lofts up here are all different to one another?'

Ryan's gaze swept the hillside. The little huts were a well tended assortment of buildings in all shapes, sizes and colours. There was a regal purple 'castle' with a front shaped like battlement, a blue one with a Union Jack flag painted on its side, and another one painted half in red, half in white. There were white, brown and grey ones too, and others in more subdued shades, but looking closely at them, Ryan saw that each one had been given a distinctive mark of some kind – often a glaringly obvious circle on the door, or a different band of colour on the main body of the building. Mainly, those little wooden shacks were rectangular, but there was the odd square or octagonal one, and a very striking circular shed with a white roof. As he gazed round, Ryan found himself believing what old George had said – that the pigeons could identify colours and shapes, and in that way knew which was their home. Why else, he wondered, would there be such odd-looking conglomeration of huts littering the green hillside?

'They all know where they belongs.' George paused to take a breather from the task in hand.

Ryan walked over to him. 'Here! Let me do that, mate. You'll be flaked out lugging that ladder around. Where do you want me to position it?'

'Right there!' George thumped the side of his own pigeon house with one hard and calloused fist.

'What are you going to do up there?' Ryan's voice had the attractive upward lilt at the end of each question that branded him a true Australian.

George pointed to the roof and squinted against the winter sun that had started melting the ice and snow on the hills around the harbour. 'See that bit of roofing felt hanging off . . .?'

'You're risking breaking a leg for a bit of roofing felt that's come adrift?'

'It wants sealing down again.' George bent down and picked up a half litre tin of sealant. 'Can't have me little darlin's getting damp in their 'ouse, can I? An' that flippin' wind we 'ad t'other night whipped that bit o'felt off.'

Ryan sighed. 'Okay!' he said, propping the step-ladder up solidly against the wooden building. 'Okay! When I'm up there, give me the glue, will you?'

'It's not just any old glue, y'know.' George studied the tin, holding it up in front of his eyes and peering at it. 'Proper stuff this is. "All-weather sealant",' he read out.

'It must be good if it's all-weather sealant I s'pose, but I bet ye'll need a 'ammer an' flat tacks as well.'

'Well, just you stand by to pass everything up to me,' Ryan said. 'You're the expert on pigeon houses, so tell me what to do and I'll do it.'

''ave you ever done owt like this before?' George asked suspiciously.

'No. But it looks like I have no choice now.' Ryan grimaced as he cautiously inched himself up the ladder. 'I don't fancy plucking you out of a pool of blood when you fall off this rickety old thing and fracture your skull.'

'No. We've 'ad enough o' that sort of thing around 'ere.' George sounded suddenly glum, and Ryan looked at him.

'That sort of thing?' He frowned.

George shrugged. 'That young lass ye've tekken up wi'! Her dad.' He jerked his head towards the nothern hillside across the beach from them. 'Nasty business that!' He shook his head. 'I wuz t'first un who got to 'im. Still alive 'e was then.' His mouth pulled downwards. 'No 'ope for 'im though.'

Ryan ledged himself half on the pigeon loft roof, half on the ladder and stared down at the old man. 'Max Corder? He was still alive when you found him?'

'Aye! Nobbut just though by t'time I got ovver there. I wuz ovver 'ere, see – on this side of th'beck when 'e fell. Right 'ere where I'm standin'. I looked across there, an' saw these two folks up on t'cliff top, and one of 'em just seemed to topple ovver th'edge up there. I tell ye' lad, I went just as fast as me old legs 'ud carry me to see if I could do owt to 'elp.'

'You said there were *two* people up there.' Ryan was suddenly more than merely interested.

'I thought there was.' Old George was frowning now as if he was trying to remember everything connected with Max's death. He shook his head slowly from side to side and said, 'Funny thing was – I canna say whether it was man nor woman up there wi' Mester Corder. It were just a shape, see?'

'A shape?' Ryan felt prickles running all the way up his spine.

''ooded, like.'

'Hooded?'

'Aye! One o'them coats what 'as a 'ood – t'keep rain and snow off. D'ye know the sort I mean?'

'I suppose most people who live round here wear warm clothing – anoraks, duffles, or whatever winter coats are popularly known as in these parts.'

'Men round 'ere aren't namby-pamby,' George said in a disgusted kind of voice. 'They dunna goo in for covering their 'eads up – unless it's wi' a sou'wester. And t'wim-mim, well, if they wear owt at all on their 'eds, it'd be a scarf, or else a felt 'at.'

'But it wasn't a scarf you saw up there?' Ryan narrowed his eyes and looked across at the headland from which Max had fallen. 'Did the police talk to you?' he wanted to know. 'Did you tell them about the hooded figure?'

'Aye!' George clamped his mouth shut, and was quiet for several seconds before revealing, 'They said they were mekkin' enquiries. Enquiries won't bring the poor bugger back though, will they? An' them there bobbies – they're no more than young lads nowadays. They nivver believed me about somebody else bein' up there wi' Mester Corder. I could tell from their faces they thought I was mekkin' it up. Talked about my eyesight, they did. Asked if I was wearing me glasses when I looked ovver there – and then wanted to know if I'd bin in t'pub all mornin'.'

'And had you?' Ryan asked.

George shook a fist at him good-naturedly and laughed. 'I like a drink, lad, but as for wearing specs, well I don't need them except for readin' me newspaper,' he chuckled.

Ryan glanced down at the beach. 'I'd need spectacles myself to read the names of some of those boats down there,' he admitted. 'I don't think I'd be able to distinguish what somebody on the cliff top was wearing.'

George turned round and looked down at the boats too. 'Cobles, they are,' he stated. 'Don't you never go callin' 'em "boats". See that yellow 'un?' As Ryan nodded, George said, 'That's called Mary-Jane. An' that blue 'un with red inside it?'

Ryan laughed. 'You surely can't tell what that one's called – it's one hell of a long way off – almost over by the jetty.'

'Mornin' Star!' George said. 'An' that black 'un with yellow writing – well that's the Lady Caroline.'

'My God! You have eyes like a hawk.'

'No.' George swung back round to him. 'I just knows the cobles by their colours,' he said. 'Same as all these bloomin' pigeons knows where they live.'

'George! You're an imposter.' Ryan's laughter rang out on the still air, but he understood now why the police had not taken George seriously. No one, he thought – letting his glance wander over to the opposite headland again – could have recognized somebody so far away, nor would they have been able to say so emphatically that one of the people up there was wearing a hooded coat. And perhaps the old man's eyesight had played tricks on him, making him just *think* there had been two people up there instead

173

of one – Max Corder. 'Look here,' he said, 'Would you talk to Corder's daughter about her dad's death?' Ryan knew how her father's accident was still haunting Serena. Perhaps if she could talk to somebody who had been with him at the end . . .

'No point in that.' George was looking as if he'd wished he'd kept his mouth shut now. 'The lass wouldn't want it all rakin' up agen, would she?'

'The accident?' Ryan shrugged. 'I'd want to know all there was to know if it had been somebody belonging to me.'

George shook his head. 'It's ovver and done wi'.'

'Did Max Corder speak to you? Was he conscious?'

'Aye!'

'Aye, he was conscious, or aye, he said something?' Ryan asked, becoming more and more exasperated with the old man because he was having to drag every last bit of information out of him.

'Both!'

'Well? What did he say?'

'George shook his head. 'Didn't mek no sense – what 'e said. Bobbies said 'e must 'ave been ramblin' in 'is 'ed 'cause he was so badly injured.'

'For God's sake, man . . .'

'All right! All right! Keep your 'air on. What 'e said was "'eaven 'as no rage, George" – then 'e was a gonner. That's all there was to it.'

Ryan was puzzled. 'That's all he said? Heaven has no rage, George?'

'Aye. He allus called me George. We'd knowed each other a long time. I were a charge 'and in t'meltin' shop at t'foundry years ago, see? 'E were a good man were Mester Corder. A good boss – 'e knowed what 'e were talking about.'

Until his last moments on earth, Ryan thought. 'Heaven has no rage' was hardly the thing for a dying man to say.

'If I'd just fallen off the edge of a cliff, I'd think heaven was full of rage – against *me*,' he said to George.

'Aye! Well! Mebbe we all would. But Mester Corder, 'e was different to other folk. He could allus tek a joke – even against 'imself, an' that day, as he lay there, I'd swear there wuz a twinkle in 'is eye. I don't think for one minnit he knew 'e wuz goin' to pop his clogs like 'e did.'

'Pop his clogs?' Ryan was puzzled.

'Die!' George stated. 'Don't you know proper English when you 'ear it spoke, young man?'

'You're saying he didn't know he was dying?'

'Nope! I'd stake my life he didn't, lad. Didn't seem to be in no pain, anyhow. It gived me a shock when 'is 'ead lolled back like it did, and he stopped breathin'.'

Ryan decided, for the moment, to say nothing to Serena about what George had told him. It couldn't do any good, he decided. And it might even upset her to know that Max hadn't been killed outright. All the same, he was just a little bit worried, because as far as he knew, Mari had never gone into the details surrounding Corder's accident. And one small part of him insisted that Serena ought to know all there was to know about her father's death.

The snow had almost gone when Kirsten – with baby Reanne – and her sister Holly checked into the inn at Rivelyn, and as Kirsten bent over the visitor's book to sign her name, she suddenly gave a whoop of excitement and turned to Holly.

'They were here. Look.' She indicated two names at the top of the previous page. 'Serena and Ryan – they were here.'

175

Holly glanced over her sister's shoulder. 'Separate rooms!' she stated. 'Well, it seems you have nothing to worry about in that direction then, eh Sis.'

In their large room overlooking the market square, Kirsten turned anxiously to Holly again. 'Do you really think there's nothing between the two of them?'

'It's a funny old set up,' Holly said, 'And I still think you've come on a wild goose chase, but . . .'

'But?' Kirsten's eyes lit up.

Holly sank down wearily on the edge of her bed. 'But now we're here, you might as well check him out, I suppose. I suggest we take the bull by the horns, and go to this Caindale place tomorrow. Somebody's bound to know whereabouts they're living.'

Kirsten shook her head. 'Not "we",' she said gently. 'Just me – for the first time anyway. Maybe later when I've seen Ryan, and had a chance to talk to him . . .'

'So I'm just here to mind the baby, am I?' Holly looked vaguely put out, and she glanced over at the cot in the corner of the room. Reanne was now sleeping soundly.

'Do you mind?' Kirsten perched herself on the side of her own bed and looked worriedly across at her sister. 'Honestly, love – I won't "use" you where Reanne's concerned, but I can't just turn up and present her to him, can I? If we're going to get back together, I don't want it to be merely because I've had his baby. Don't you understand that?'

Holly eased herself back onto the pillows, kicked off her shoes and stretched her legs out in front of her on the bed.

'You are an idiot. Of course I understand. But whether you get back together or not, he's got to be made aware of that fact that he's fathered a child. He has a duty to support her.'

176

'I don't want him to know about Reanne just yet though. And I'm certainly not going to barge right in without giving it a bit of thought. I want to find out where Ryan is. Then I'm going to keep watch. I have to see what things are like between him and Serena. There must be *some* reason why he left Australia and came all this way with her – and whatever you say, Sis, I can think of only one good reason why a man would do that.'

'You think that he fancies her – and she's playing hard to get? If that's the case you'll have to face facts, kid. Don't get your hopes up till you know what's what.'

Kirsten sighed. 'I suppose you're right.' She twisted her hands together on her knees. 'Oh heck. I hope I haven't come on a wild goose chase. I hope I don't go and make a fool of myself – and more to the point, I hope I don't uncover something between those two that I don't want to know about.'

CHAPTER 12

'What's wrong with you?' Serena had been worried about Ryan's preoccupation for the past week. 'Are you feeling bad, love? Are the headaches worse?'

'Hmm? What?' he looked up from the newspaper that was spread out across the kitchen table as she came in to tell him she was almost ready to leave for work.

'You've been very quiet all week. Is your head bothering you more than it usually does?'

He flashed her a grin. 'Never felt better in my life before. I'm getting lots of exercise – getting to know everybody who lives around here too. They all talk to me. I don't think they've ever met a real live Australian before. I'm something of a novelty to them.'

'Be careful,' she warned on a teasing note. 'They might just put you in a cage and start feeding you eucalyptus leaves.'

He sat up straight in the kitchen chair and pushed the newspaper away. 'Seriously – I like it here, Serena.'

'You can't stay forever though.' She smiled at him and sat down in the chair opposite. 'Neither of us can make this our permanent home, can we?'

'You can,' he said seriously. 'You have British citizenship. I'm just an out and out Ozzie – over here for the ride.'

'You don't think I'd let you go back alone, do you?' She reached out across the table and laid one hand on both his linked ones. 'We belong together, love. Now Don's not here any more, we only have each other and we should stick together.'

He stared down at her hand and muttered, 'Your life is here, Serena. There are people who depend on you. I can't ask you to go back to Australia with me – if and when the time comes.'

'So – we'll stay as long as we're able, huh?'

He looked up at her. 'Whatever suits you, kiddo. But don't let me stand in your way.'

'I'm sorry I can't spend more time with you.' She withdrew her hand and looked at the watch that was fastened around her wrist.

'I don't mind being on my own. Honestly. Everybody talks to me. I'm not lonely.' He grinned at her a little wryly. 'Not so's you'd notice, anyway. I'm not saying I wouldn't appreciate a bit of female company though – once in a while, but there doesn't seem much of that around here that isn't already spoken for.'

'You're missing *her*, aren't you?'

'Kirsty?' His lifted his gaze to her face.

She nodded.

'Of course I'm missing her. Missing her like hell. But what sort of life could I offer her? She's young. She's full of life. She'll have forgotten all about me by now.' He gave a grim little smile.

Serena thought about Mari's phone call the other day at the office and wondered whether she ought to tell Ryan that Kirsten was here – in England. She decided against it, but the thought did cross her mind that she could try and find Kirsten and tell her the truth about Ryan.

He was watching her face. 'Don't get any ideas about writing to her and letting her know I'm living on borrowed time,' he warned. 'You know I won't stand for that, Sera.'

She felt impatient with him, but replied, 'But don't you see – you're wasting what time you do have, Ryan. You and Kirsten could be happy together. You were once, and that love you had has never died or even diminished, has it?'

He pushed his chair away from the table, leaned his head back and stared at the ceiling. 'At least this way,' he said, 'I can look back on the good times we had – Kirsty and me – and I can be assured that I was never a drag on her.'

'I don't think she'd look on it that way if you made things up with her,' she said.

He brought his gaze back to her again. 'Don't play the agony aunt, Sera. I'm okay. Kirsty'll have forgotten all about me by now – she'll have made a new life for herself.'

'But if she hasn't? What then? If you knew for certain that she was missing you as much as you are missing her . . .?'

'How can I ever know that for certain,' he asked cynically.

'We could make enquiries.' Her shoulders lifted in a shrug. 'There are ways of finding out.'

'No!'

'Ryan – I'm only trying to help.'

'Don't!' he said. 'That's one sort of help I can do without.'

'Maybe I ought to try and have a couple of afternoons off work each week so that you and I could go to places. Get around a bit. You know – enjoy ourselves and do a bit

180

of sight-seeing instead of being stuck here at Caindale all the time.'

'I told you – I like it here. I can wander round the hills and all over the beach to my heart's content. There is one thing I'd like though, Sera . . .'

'Yes? What's that?'

'I'd like you to come down to the shore next Monday morning. I want to take some pictures of this blessing thing they're all talking about in the village.'

'The blessing of the fishing cobles.' She smiled reminiscently. 'I remember it from when I was a little girl. Dad used to bring me down to the beach every year in the spring to join in the singing of the hymns and the prayers for the fishermen.'

'I guess you'd enjoy being a part of it all again then.'

She bit down on her bottom lip and wondered if she would. Again, she'd been reminded of Max, and as with all the other times when she was brought up sharp against childhood memories, it was painful to remember the happy times she'd spent with her father. She realized with a shock that almost all those happy times had been banished from her mind over the last ten years. Knew too that it had been done deliberately on her part – that shutting out of Max after she'd discovered his infidelity to her mother. She'd spent years building up a hatred of him, but now, almost against her will, it seemed, little by little that hatred was being broken down by the very fact that she was having to acknowledge all he'd lived for, having also, to spend her days in the valley that had been his life – his creation.

'We'll see.' She managed a smile of sorts.

'What does that mean?' Ryan's voice was harsh.

'It means what I said. We'll see. I might be too busy at the foundry office to come, but that doesn't mean you have to miss it.'

'I want you to be there,' he stated, making one hand into a fist and bringing it down hard on the table. 'Why do you always have to try and avoid gatherings like that? It was the same with your father's memorial service. At one point, I thought you were going to chicken out of that too.'

'I wouldn't have done that. It would have been very hurtful to Mari if I hadn't been there.'

'At the time though, you did rather hate her guts.'

'Ryan!'

'Ryan!' he mimicked. Then he gave a short little laugh and said, 'Oh, get off to work, woman. Meet me in the pub for some lunch though, huh?'

'Today?'

'So? What's wrong with today.'

She stood up and shrugged. 'You usually like to cook me something revolting towards the end of the week.'

'So meet me in the pub. You can't complain about the house smelling of garlic then. And the 'Old Bachelor' does a great line in fish dishes.'

'I do have to work with other people,' she tried to explain diplomatically. 'And some people dislike the smell of garlic coming from their workmates.'

'It's good for you.'

'I can't win, can I?' She scooped up her bag and made for the door.

'Please! Sera, honey. Meet me in the pub.'

'Okay! Twelve-thirty.' She paused for a moment, deliberating, then said, 'Order for me, will you? That'll save time because I'll only have an hour. I'll have that out-

of-this-world scalloped haddock – Mrs Skelton's piece-
de-resistance.'

'See you twelve-thirty.' He pulled the newspaper across
the table again, and the last thing she heard, as she went
through to the front door, was him chuckling at the
cartoon page.

'They're living together!'

'So what does that signify? They were together here, in
this very building, remember? But they had separate
rooms. You saw their names in that book downstairs.
Even if they're living together, it doesn't necessarily
mean they're sharing a bed, does it?'

Kirsten deposited a handful of plastic shopping bags on the
bed and walked over to Reanne's cot. The baby was sleeping
peacefully. 'Has she been okay?' She twisted her head round
to look at her sister who was sitting in an armchair in the bay
window, an open magazine lying across her knees.

'Reanne's been fine, kiddo. I took her for a walk
alongside the beach. It was pretty cold out there, but I
wrapped her up well and tucked her into her buggy.'

'She has to get used to it. The cold weather. We're here
for another three weeks.' Kirsten glanced out of the
window. 'At least it's stopped snowing – I suppose we
must be thankful for that.'

'Are you going to show me what you've got in the
shopping bags?'

'Oh, one or two prezzies for the folks back home. And a
few odds and ends for Reanne.' Kirsten walked over to the
bed and pulled out the largest of the bags, tipped it up and
shook its contents out onto the quilt.

Holly got up out of the chair and walked over to her.
'What the heck is that? Have you been to one of those

183

"Jumble" things they're forever advertising in the local papers?' She leaned forward, picked up the bulky garment that was lying in an ungainly heap there, shook it out, and held it up against her. 'And who's the lucky guy who will fit into this, I wonder? It's huge, Sis. Who on earth would want to wear a jacket the size of this one?'

Kirsten pulled the coat out of her sister's hands, grinning. 'Me!' she said, slipping her arms into the navy blue nylon material and buttoning the toggles up to her chin.

'Did somebody tell you it suited you? If they did, they were lying,' Holly said drily.

'I didn't even try it on. There was this open market thing in one of the streets. They had all sorts of things on it. This was just what I wanted.'

Holly sat down with a thump on the edge of the bed. 'Okay! Tell me,' she said, 'just what's your game. You can't seriously expect me to believe that something like that is the height of fashion in England at the moment.'

'Camouflage!' Kirsten said, twirling round in front of the older girl. 'All week I've been going down to Caindale on the bus, and I'm looking over my shoulder all the time I'm there – thinking that Ryan or Serena might catch a glimpse of me. In this thing, they won't give me a second glance. Look, it's even got a hood zipped into it. I can pull it right up so it almost covers my face.'

Holly shook her head despairingly. 'You're not a spy, for God's sake.'

'Yes, I am.' Kirsten slipped out of the coat and stood looking slightly dejected. 'That's just what I am – and I'm not proud of the fact that I've been snooping around and being so underhand about everything, but what else can I do?'

184

'You could just come out into the open and approach Ryan – or Serena. She must know you're around some-where – that woman who answered the phone to you will have surely told her you were trying to find him.'

'What could she have told Serena? I didn't even give her my name, remember?'

Holly nodded slowly, then said, 'I suppose you're right. But the woman knew you were from Australia. It won't be hard for them to put two and two together and come up with the right answer, will it?'

'Serena must have made lots of friends back there though. She'd been in Queensland for a couple of years. It could have been anybody – just *anybody* looking her up again.'

'Her suspicions must be aroused though. Anybody who was a friend would have given a name when they rang up.'

Kirsten flung the coat back onto the bed and scowled. 'Oh, you're always so *right*,' she stormed.

Holly grabbed hold of her hand and pulled her down to sit beside her. 'Look, love,' she said gently, 'In my opinion, you're going about this the wrong way.'

'I've found out where they live. I watched the house for quite some time. Serena goes out around eight-thirty each morning. She seems to spend quite a lot of time at the manufacturing place down there. It's some sort of foun-dry, I think. Great big trucks go in and out all the time, loaded up with strange-looking iron things.'

'She's probably had to get herself a job. They have to live, don't they. And there's the rent of the house too, I suppose . . .'

'No. Listen. I asked a few questions around the place.'

'Idiot! That's really going to get you noticed.'

'No. I was quite casual about it. There's a statue, you see – a statue of a man called Corder. It's outside a little medical centre place near the beach.'

'And?'

'I discovered it's Serena's father. Max Corder. Apparently he owned the place where Serena keeps going each morning – and *he* had the medical centre built for the people of the valley.'

'Sounds cosy!'

'Don't be so damned flippant,' Kirsten snapped, suddenly losing all patience with her sister.

'Okay, honey. Okay!' Holly held up one hand. 'Look – we've been here a week already, and what have we got to show for it? I was hoping we could get all this Ryan Farrar stuff over and done with in a couple of days. It's my money as well as yours, remember? And I'd quite like to see a bit more of England than what I'm doing through the damned window of a sea-side pub. I want to see where Shakespeare was born, and where Anne Boleyn got her head lopped off. I'd like to go to York, and to Edinburgh, and the Norfolk Broads.'

'Heck! I'm sorry.' Kirsten was suddenly downcast. 'It can't be much fun for you.'

'Dead right! It's not, kiddo. I say we give it just till the end of the week, and then we move on. How does that sound?'

'I – I suppose so.'

'Don't look like that. I'm not suggesting we go to the damned moon.'

Huskily, Kirsten said, 'I – I might stay here while you go to all those interesting places – if you don't mind.'

'And what about the baby?'

'Reanne!' Kirsten bit on her lip, then nodded. 'She could be a problem.'

'Yeah! One big problem. For somebody so little, she sure creates havoc in my life.'

'Holly, love, I'm sorry . . .' Kirsten turned to her sister, tears glistening in her eyes.

'Aw! Don't cry, kiddo. She's a pet really. I love her. I really do. But time's getting on – and we can't stay here for ever.'

'There's some big thing going on in Caindale next Monday. Give me till then, will you? Maybe I can get near and actually see Ryan. You know how he loves taking photographs of everything. He's bound to be there with his camera. Just give me Monday, Holly. Let me go and see the fishing boats being blessed.'

'The *what*?'

'They're blessing the fishing boats. It's a service of some sort that they hold every year. A minister gives a special blessing to the new boats and everybody turns out to sing hymns and things.'

'You're joking!'

'No.'

Holly started to laugh. 'You really are joking, Sis.'

Kirsten frowned. 'It's nothing to laugh about. They take it real serious – and anyway, I think it's a lovely idea.'

'You would.'

'Okay, Miss Worldly-Wise. You ridicule it if you like. But I'm going to be there, because I know – deep down I know – that Ryan will be there.'

'And if *she's* with him? What then?'

Kirsten shook her head. 'She won't be. I told you, she always goes out at eight-thirty. She wouldn't be interested in something like that. And I've just got to see Ryan – make sure he's okay, before we move on.'

'And if you see him? Are you going to speak to him. Are you going to tell him about that young lady over there in the crib?'

'I – I don't know.' Kirsten looked down at her feet.

'And if he sees you first?' Holly asked softly.

'He won't.' Kirsten was adamant. 'I'll be wearing my disguise, and nobody will recognize me in that.'

CHAPTER 13

The sky was overcast, but a huge crowd had gathered down on the shore by the time Serena and Ryan started off down the hill from the little house in the terrace.

Ryan was fascinated by the sight of so many people, and he urged her to wait while he took a photograph of them all, mingling in and out amongst the brightly-coloured boats on the beach.

'We could watch the blessing from up here, if you wanted to,' she said. 'It would save you having to walk all the way back up the hill when it's finished.'

He was already focusing the camera, but he spun round on her. 'I'm not an invalid, Sera. I am capable of a half mile walk uphill. Look – you're not going to start "babying" me again, are you?'

'Okay!' She swung away from him, turning just to say, 'I get the message. I don't have to care about you. Is that it?'

He flung her a dark glare and muttered, 'I don't want stifling. You know damn well I hate it when you go all protective on me. I'm not a kid any more, Sera.'

She put on a stony face. 'Well, if we're going to join everybody down there, we ought to be going. The service is due to start in five minutes.'

'You go on ahead.' He was giving all his attention to the camera again, focusing the lens, setting the light to just the right degree. He glanced up at her. 'Go on, Sera,' he urged. 'I won't get lost just walking down the hill to you.'

She shrugged and went on ahead of him. It didn't do any good, standing around arguing with him. He was getting into a 'mood' again, and when he did that, he was short-tempered and argumentative for no apparent reason. She knew only too well though, that it probably heralded another of those terrible headaches he'd been suffering, and she couldn't help being concerned. He'd been on a high for days though – ever since he'd come back from spending the morning with George, and had told her he'd been repairing the old man's pigeon loft for him.

She suspected he'd been attempting to do too much and had got over-tired. But he'd been acting strangely too. Countless times these past few days, she'd seen him wander outside the little terrace house to walk across the road and then train his binoculars on the opposite hillside.

'What are you looking at?' she'd asked him once as she'd silently followed him outside and come up behind him.

He'd rounded on her irritably and snapped, 'Do you have to creep up on me like that? And do I have to ask your permission for everything I do around here?'

It hurt her when he spoke to her like that, but always afterwards he was apologetic, and she realized that under normal circumstances he wouldn't have snapped her head off for the world.

She walked down the hill now, forcing herself not to look back and check whether he was following or not. She began to think again of Kirsten, Ryan's girlfriend. She'd been more than a little intrigued when Mari had told her the girl had made a telephone call to Wintersgill, and from that moment had half expected Kirsten to turn up on the doorstep of the little house she and Ryan now shared.

But as the days passed there had been nothing – no knock on the door – not even a letter or a postcard. And though she had asked Mari every single day if Kirsten had called back, Mari reported no more mysterious phone calls.

She heard footsteps behind her, but didn't turn round even then. He caught up with her and fell into step beside her, seeming in a few short minutes to have relaxed into a happier mood.

'I think I got quite a few good shots from up there,' he said. 'It's quite an occasion isn't it – this blessing of the fishing boats?'

'Cobles,' she said, grinning at him and pushing her hands deep into the pockets of her long wool jacket. 'They're cobles, not boats. The ceremony usually pulls quite a crowd though. I think everybody in Caindale – and a lot of folk from some of the surrounding villages – turns out for it.'

Ryan started whistling tunelessly as they walked, but abruptly she said, 'Don't whistle, not near the beach.'

'Oh, for heaven's sake – whistling doesn't hurt my head. Do you have to be such a damned kill-joy?'

'It's bad luck,' she said, rounding on him and coming to a standstill. 'At least, that's what the fishermen think. They don't like anybody whistling near the cobles. I'm only telling you for your own good.' She forced a smile. 'They'd probably lynch you if you did anything to mar the blessing.'

He grinned at her sheepishly. 'I'm sorry, Sera,' he muttered.

'Ryan – I think we ought to get registered with a doctor around here,' she said. 'I think you should get a check-up. You haven't had one since before we left Queensland.'

'Why should I do that?' His chin jutted aggressively.

'You know why. You must realize that you're becoming utterly unreasonable at times. You yell at me for the slightest thing just lately.'

'I'm sorry. I keep telling you I'm sorry.' His cheeks were pale and hollow, and his eyes looked haunted. 'It's not easy for me, Sera – coming to terms with what I know I've got to come to terms with.'

'I know, love.' She almost reached out a hand to touch his arm, but drew back just in time. He'd probably take it the wrong way if she did that. There was no telling nowadays just how he would react to the slightest gesture, the most harmless of words.

'Hey!' He took a step towards her and thrust his arm round her shoulders, pulling her towards him and hugging her close. 'You're an angel – you know that, don't you? And I'm like a bear with a sore bum most of the time. If I were you I'd hate me.'

'I think the saying is "a bear with a sore head" – not a sore bum,' she replied, grinning up into his face.

He gazed at her for a few moments longer, then suddenly said, 'You're good with proverbs and cliches and things like that, aren't you?'

'Am I?' she asked, surprised at the turn of the conversation.

'Hmm! I think you are. I'm hopeless myself. I was always bottom of the class in English studies when I was at school.'

'I've never really thought about it . . .'

'Do you know anything that starts off – "heaven has no rage"?'

She felt as if she'd been hit solidly in the pit of the stomach. For a second, she closed her eyes and waited till she felt she could draw another breath, then said in a choked whisper, 'Where did you hear that?'

'Oh, somewhere.' His hand fell away from her shoulder. 'I forget where. It's just something that stuck in my mind from somewhere.'

'My Dad was quite a ladies' man,' she said quietly, 'but I often suspected he had little respect for them. He was maddeningly patronizing towards what he called – "the fairer sex", and that was one of his favourite quotes – "Heaven has no rage like love to hatred turned, nor hell a fury like a woman scorned". It was one of the very last things he ever yelled at me – when he knew I wasn't going to fall in with his plans to bring Mari to Wintersgill.'

He didn't know how to answer her, she realized, as she stood looking worriedly at him. He didn't seem able to meet her eyes with his own either, but turned away and stood staring at the crowd of Caindale folk on the beach, gnawing at the inside of his cheek with his teeth as if he were deep in thought.

'Ryan,' she said softly, 'Ryan – tell me where you heard that, and under what circumstances.'

Slowly he moved his head till he was looking directly at her. 'I told you,' he said, 'I can't remember where I heard it – and even if I could, what does it matter?' With the words, he loped off ahead of her, leaving her standing there as he turned this way and that, shooting off film haphazardly at anything and everything his eyes alighted on.

He didn't fool her. He had something on his mind. And the thought struck her that maybe somebody had been talking to him about Max. Why else would he bring up that one little poignant saying that reminded her so vividly of the past?

She shivered. It was like a voice from the grave, a ghost come back to haunt her. Would she ever be free, she wondered, from the man this valley had revered? Once more those words ran through her mind, 'Heaven has no rage like love to hatred turned . . .'

It was a fitting epitaph to Max – from a daughter who could not forgive – for there was no rage to equal that which had burned deep inside her when her father had callously betrayed her by taking a stand against her over his affair with Mari.

The dark-haired girl with the sun-browned skin mingled with the gathering of Caindale folk on the beach where the little red river churned its way over the rocks to the sea.

Always her eyes kept turning in the direction of the far southern hillside though, up to that row of grey houses, and when she saw him coming out of the end one with the blonde girl beside him, a smile quivered on her lips.

He was still the same old Ryan that she loved, and just looking at him, even from such a distance made her feel warm inside. He was standing gazing down at the crowd and the boats, and he kept looking at, and fiddling with, his camera. Oh, yes, that was Ryan, she thought – always the perfectionist. He'd have to adjust the light to exactly the right setting for a picture. The camera's aperture would be a major consideration in the most ordinary of photographs.

He wouldn't notice her, she knew. From so far away she'd be no more to him than just another face in the crowd, but she'd have to keep her wits about her if he came down to the sea shore. If she kept her attention rivetted on him though, she'd be able to dodge away the moment he came anywhere near her.

He was talking to Serena now. 'Sera', he'd always called the girl, she recalled with a faint smile. And now it looked as if he was shooing her away, yet it wasn't in Ryan's nature to be impatient; he was the most tolerant of men. She frowned and kept watching him till he grew tired of taking photographs and started hurrying after Serena. Her heart skipped a beat when he caught up with her, and after a few brief words, pulled the blonde girl towards him and hugged her tight. But Serena was looking up into his face, and it seemed to Kirsten that she was giving him a ticking off.

They didn't look like a pair of lovers . . .

She lost sight of them as they came over the narrow bridge that spanned the iron-red waters of the Caindale beck, and as latecomers started jostling Kirsten for a better view, she moved aside and further back so she could be on the edge of the crowd – handy for a quick getaway should the need arise. She didn't want to be hemmed in on all sides, she just wanted to see Ryan and convince herself he was all right. And if, when she did get a glimpse of him at closer quarters, it was obvious that he and Serena were 'a pair', then she knew she'd have to accept what had happened, and leave well alone. She certainly wasn't here to make trouble.

She stumbled on the stony beach and glancing down noticed several small stones that had been worn smooth by the tide. Some even had holes in them from the friction with other stones. She bent down and picked one of them up, marvelling at its marbled colours and its perfect shape as she laid it in the palm of her hand.

A middle-aged fair-haired woman standing nearby said with a smile, 'That's what's known as a "luck-stone". You should take care of it, my dear.'

'A luck-stone?' Kirsten glanced up into a pair of dazzling blue eyes. She noted that the woman seemed oddly out of place in this gathering of the solid, sober citizens of Caindale. Her pale lilac coat with floral scarf to match, her elegant high heels and perfectly made-up face branded her instantly as an outsider, yet she must obviously have some reason for being here.

She tapped the stone on Kirsten's hand with a soft, kid-gloved finger. 'The fishermen fasten stones like that in the stern of their cobles to bring them luck. Those boats over there – they're the cobles that are about to be blessed. Not a single Caindale man would put to sea in a boat that hadn't been blessed once a year.'

'You live around here?' Kirsten was interested, and forgetful for a while of the reason she was here.

The woman looked up at the high cliff behind them. 'Away over there – beyond the cliff top. A mile or more out of Caindale.'

'And you've walked all that way?'

'Oh, no, child. My nephew brought me in his car. I don't walk far nowadays. But what about you? You're from warmer climes than this. I can tell from your voice that you're Australian.'

Kirsten laughed ruefully. 'Guess I'm an open book with this sun tan and my accent. I'm here with my sister – at a place called Rivelyn. We'd always promised ourselves a trip to England.'

A very present-day church organ – one that looked no larger than a piano – had been brought down from the chapel and placed on the jetty. It struck up the introduction now to the sailors' hymn.

'Do we have to sing?'

The woman laughed softly, and brought a small hymn book out of her pocket. 'Here,' she whispered, 'You can share my book if you don't know the words – but I guarantee nobody else down here today will need a hymn sheet. The words of this hymn are drilled into Caindale children at Sunday School almost as soon as they learn to talk.

Serena was reminded of her father's memorial service as the voices rang out from Caindale's little bay, and reverberated around the hillsides that led down to the sea.

'Eternal father strong to save . . . Whose arm doth bind the restless wave . . .'

Ryan glanced at her, then groped for her hand and squeezed it. 'Hey,' he whispered, 'This isn't upsetting you, is it?'

She shook her head, but couldn't bring herself to join in the singing even though the words of the hymn had been stamped on her brain from the earliest of her schooldays. The memory of her father was too poignant, for never a year had passed when Max hadn't brought her down to the sea shore for the blessing of the cobles.

His voice came back to her on the stiff breeze blowing on-shore, through the mists of the years, right back from the very first time she'd stood there beside him on a day such as this one . . .

'Your grandad – my own daddy – he was a fisherman, Serena.'

197

'Did he have a boat, Daddy? Did you go fishing in his boat with him?'

Max's face softened as he looked down into her upturned questioning eyes. 'Yes, sweetheart, he had a boat – cobles they call them though, not boats. It's name was "Dolly Daydream".' He laughed a little self-consciously then and lapsing into the north country dialect he'd been brought up in, admitted, 'My dadda wasna' proud of the fact that whenever I went a-fishing, I was always sea-sick.'

She was suddenly cold, and wished she hadn't come. Angry black clouds were blowing up from the east over the sea. Her mind tried to escape from its memories, but always it was Daddy who filled her thoughts. He'd been her pivot, her mainstay in those years when she was growing up. He was the one who'd always been there for her.

In the storehouse of her mind, he was the firm but kindly guardian, and it came as a shock to realize that there wasn't much to remember about her mother. Mother had been a remote figure, a pale blonde reflection of herself as she was now, Serena thought with a frown marring her features. But mother hadn't had the same kind of stamina as she herself possessed. Mother had freely admitted that she was a butterfly, a decorative addition to the household. Her laughter had been bright and fleeting when her friends were around, Serena remembered. But when she'd been alone with Daddy things had been very different.

Mother had a special frown that she used to put on for Daddy – a frown and a petulant note in her voice. She wore nice frocks and had rings on her fingers and gold chains on her wrists and round her neck. Daddy frequently bought her little packages which she opened with delight, and for a while afterwards she'd smile instead of frown when he was around, and a new bauble would be added to the enormous jewellery box on her dressing table . . .

Serena swung away from the sea shore and away from the fresh-faced young Methodist minister who was well into his sermon now. She fought her way through the silent congregation, past the children who were getting fed up and were scrabbling among the rocks and in the sand or else whining to go home and '. . . watch telly, Mum . . .'

Ryan made a grab at her but she shrugged his hand away and muttered, 'You stay to the end. I'm going to the foundry.'

She ran across the beach when she was free of the people, glad she was wearing leggings and boots as she splashed through puddles beside the shallow, iron-red beck. She heard somebody call out softly to her from the edge of the crowd, 'Serena! Serena – it is you, isn't it, my dear?'

Looking round, she saw Vivian standing a little apart from the main crowd, regal in palest lilac. Could anyone be regal, she wondered, wearing lilac? There was somebody else with her – somebody who swung away almost on the instant Serena had seen Vivian. The figure was wearing a shapeless navy blue anorak. As it shot away from Viv towards the cliffs, it pulled a clumsy-looking hood up over its head.

Serena couldn't ignore Viv's outstretched hand even though she had to stumble over great hulking boulders to reach Holt's aunt.

'Have you seen my nephew?' Viv asked as she came up to her.

'No – not today . . .' Serena was panting hard. She shook hands with Viv. 'It's good to see you again.'

'Mari tells me you've moved into one of those little houses up there.' Viv's glance at the terrace on the south cliff was dubious. 'Why on earth didn't you go and stay with her at Wintersgill?'

'I – I didn't come back to England alone . . .'

'No! I had heard rumours.' Coyly, Viv said, 'A boyfriend is it?'

'No.' Serena gritted her teeth to stop her from telling Viv to mind her own business.

Viv's laugh rang out. 'But of course, that's just the answer I could expect, isn't it?'

'Aunt Viv. That nose of yours will get you well and truly into trouble one day.'

Serena swung round, and almost into the arms of Holt who had come up behind them, with Mari bringing up the rear.

'We've been looking everywhere for you, Viv,' Mari said as she picked her way over the stony ground, clad in a warm tweed jacket and suede calf-length boots.

Viv shrugged delicately. 'I've been here all the time. I was talking to such a nice girl – a complete stranger to these parts too . . .' Viv turned round. 'Well! That's a surprise. She's gone. I wonder what frightened her off.'

Serena's eyes swept over the crowd, then were drawn to a figure clambering up the hillside above them.

Holt followed her gaze, and laughed softly. 'It looks more like a young monkey scrambling up there than a girl,' he said. 'She'll have to be fit to get to the top of the hill without being winded.' He turned to Serena again. 'We did it many times in the past though, didn't we? I remember we chased all over these hillsides when we were kids.'

As the crowd started singing another hymn, Viv said plaintively, 'I'm cold. I think I want to go home now, Holt – if you don't mind.'

Mari stepped forward, smiling. 'I'll take her,' she said, 'I brought my car down from the foundry.' Then she winked at Serena and Holt and said, 'You two go and do a bit of reminiscing at the 'Old Bachelor'. I expect you have a lot you want to talk about – the two of you.'

Protesting, Viv was led by Mari to her car.

Holt stood and watched them go, then turned to Serena and said, 'How about it then? Think you're up to a bit of reminiscing?'

'I – I don't really think we have anything to say to each other, do you?' she asked stiffly. 'And really – I ought to be getting back to the office.'

'Aw! Come on,' he said, and as if the years they'd been apart had never existed, he grabbed hold of her arm and tucked it through his crooked elbow. 'Let up a bit, will you?' he whispered against her ear. 'Let's go grab a corner in the pub. They're singing the last hymn and this lot'll barge in there like a shoal of thirsty eels when they've finished it. Anyway, I've heard that Mrs Skelton's serving up Carlings for the kids today.'

'Carlings?' It was a blast from the past – and something she'd forgotten all about – those fat grey peas drenched in salt and vinegar and served up in all the pubs along the Cleveland coast. 'But it's not the proper day for Carlings,' she said, laughing up at him. 'Carling Sunday's the Sunday before Palm Sunday – and today is a Monday, and nowhere near Easter.'

The wind was blowing his dark hair awry. He was dressed in a navy donkey jacket and had his jeans pushed into green wellington boots. And her arm was linked with his, and his other hand, bare and big and whiskery, was holding onto her hand to stop it pulling away from him.

She didn't want to pull away from him though. And why should she? She never had done in the past. She'd always felt incredibly safe when Holt was around.

Her face broke into a wide grin. 'We'll have to hurry. They're on the last verse.'

'We'll run.' His huge laugh rang out.

'The corner by the fire?' Her eyes danced with merriment.

'Next to the horse brasses?'

She nodded.

'One, two, three . . .'

'And away we go,' she finished for him, as together they raced across what was left of the beach, and onto the wide concrete path that in some sea-side places might be called a promenade, but in Caindale went by the name of the 'parade'!

Across the bay, Ryan wondered where Serena had got to, and what had prompted her to go rushing off like that.

He leaned with his back against a stanchion of the sturdy little bridge that crossed the Caindale beck, and let his eyes roam over the gathering who were now singing the last hymn after the boats had been blessed. Then, he let out a gasp, for over on the almost vertical grassy slope beyond the hundred or so folk who had gathered on the beach, he saw a hooded figure.

It was climbing the hillside with an agility that astounded him. And it was scrambling up there so fast, it would soon reach the exact spot where Max had fallen to his death.

Everything George had said to him suddenly came flooding back, and without even thinking of the consequences, Ryan knew he just had to find out who was inside that hooded jacket.

He set off at a run across the beach, skirting the edge of the crowd. And his gaze was locked all the time onto that figure – so near the summit of the hill now.

But as he ran, he knew he could catch up with whoever it was. He'd tackled rougher country than this in Australia. And there were one or two unanswered questions he wanted to ask about Max's death.

CHAPTER 14

Ryan was only half way up the grassy cliff side when the figure ahead of him disappeared from sight.

He groaned, and paused, his breath coming in great gasps as he realized he wasn't as fit as he ought to be; at one time, and not so very long ago, a climb like this would have posed no problem at all to him. Now though, the inside of his head felt like a volcano about to erupt. He blinked his eyes as darts of light kept flashing in front of him, then he closed them tightly for several minutes while he tried to get his breath back.

The thought of going blind terrified him. He opened his eyes, turned his head and looked down on the crowd that was jostling below him. The people milled into a jumbled mass of colour as they moved in a body, away from the boats and towards the edge of the beach. He tore his gaze away from them, hoping that Serena wasn't down there watching him. He'd have some explaining to do if she were. When he looked up above him there was still some way to go to reach the summit and he realized he couldn't just stay perched here indefinitely. His only hope of catching the hooded figure, he supposed, would be if it too were out of breath, and resting somewhere at the top of the cliff.

He began climbing again, ignoring the sharp bursts of pain that kept stabbing along one side of his head. His vision had cleared though, and for that he was thankful. He could guess at how difficult it would be to climb either up or down from this point on the cliff if he couldn't see properly.

It must have taken him another five minutes to reach the top of the cliff, and by that time, he was again gasping and very conscious of his heart hammering away inside his chest. As he paused on his knees on the cliff top, he knew without a doubt that he'd made the right decision when he'd told Kirsty everything was finished between them. He couldn't bear to have seen the pity in her eyes when the strong, upright, healthy guy she'd fallen for turned into the sort of weakling he imagined himself to be every time he looked in a mirror just lately.

Eventually, as his breath eased he managed to raise his head and look around him. And it was then that he saw the figure, not fifty yards away from him, crouched on the edge of the cliff near the spot – two hundred feet below – where the old jetty jutted out into the sea under a sharp overhang of rock.

Quietly he rose to his feet, and making no sound in his soft-soled shoes, he padded out across the grass, making a wide half circle of his movements so he wouldn't be heard or observed by that figure in the shapeless hooded coat.

But why had it scurried away up the hill, he wondered? What had startled it so much as to make it do that?

Could George really be onto something when he'd talked of a hooded figure being there alongside Max when he'd fallen to his death? If so, had that same figure perhaps seen George down there on the beach this morning and taken fright?

Carefully, making no sound at all now as he closed in on the crouching figure, Ryan held his breath and then took off at a run towards it.

The figure obviously heard something, and jumped to its feet, spinning round on the instant. Ryan couldn't see its face clearly – the hood was certainly all-enveloping – but he noted that it was frantically jerking its head this way and that, obviously looking for a way of escape.

There was none.

Whichever way it ran, Ryan was positive he could head it off. The figure must have realized that too, but as a last ditch attempt at escape, it whirled round towards the cliff edge again and, to his horror, took a tentative step forward.

'No-o-o-o-o!' he bellowed at it. 'No-o-o-o-o!' And he sprinted forward, scared half out of his mind now at the thought of his surprise attack sending the figure tumbling down over the edge of the cliff and either down onto the hard concrete of the jetty, or else the boulders clustered at the foot of the cliffs.

He'd almost reached it when it turned round again and suddenly lost its footing.

Shocked then, he heard a scream of pure terror as it flung up its arms and toppled forward.

Inside the 'Old Bachelor' a coal fire was well stoked, making the horse brasses around the ingle nook gleam cosily in the light from its flames and the subdued lighting that came from little red-shaded lamps around the walls.

Serena pulled off her gloves and pushed them into her pockets, then had to smile as she saw Holt making his way back to her from the bar expertly balancing a large round tray in his hands on which were two drinks and two plates of peas.

'I thought the peas were strictly for the children in the kiddies' room.' She laughed up at him as he inched himself into the corner seat next to her after depositing the tray on the table.

'We're kids at heart aren't we?' He grinned at her, then shrugged himself out of his donkey jacket. 'Kids getting ready to go down memory lane, huh?'

'No.' She shook her head emphatically. 'We are not going to talk about the "good" old times, Holt.'

'If we don't talk about old times, you can't have the Carlings.' He pulled the tray away from her.

The aroma of 'soaky' peas wafted across the table to her. The tang of vinegar was sharp. Steam was rising up from the two plates. She shot out a hand and hung onto the tray, stopping him from putting it out of her reach. There was a lot of noise all around them. The pub was crowded now; most of the people on the beach had headed that way after the service.

'Give me my Carlings,' she demanded, laughing so much she almost couldn't get the words out.

He relented, smiling broadly at her as he sat sideways in the corner, watching her take her plate from the tray and place it in front of her on the table.

She leaned foward, closed her eyes and sniffed the air above her plate. 'Mmmm! Delicious! Why had I forgotten all about Carlings, I wonder?'

She heard his deep-throated chuckle as he cleared the tray, placing a glass in front of her. 'You said to just get you "anything" to drink,' he said, 'and I remembered you used to like lemonade and Martini. Hope you haven't brought the car. John Skelton was a bit heavy-handed with the Martini.'

She shook her head. 'I was going to walk to work today. I didn't bring the car. It looked so crowded down here.'

'Where's lover-boy? I didn't see him with you,' he said in a casual voice as he pushed the empty tray out of the way, under the table.

'He's not my "lover-boy" – Ryan's a friend. Nothing more than that.'

'Do you set up home with all your men friends?' He picked up his spoon, looked at it and said, 'Did we really eat peas with spoons all those years ago?'

'Of course we did.' Her eyes danced as she answered him. 'What's wrong, Holt? Isn't a spoon manly enough for you?' With the words, she scooped up a spoonful of peas from her own plate and popped them into her mouth.

He watched her, the skin at the corners of his attractive dark eyes, screwing up into laughter lines. 'I'm not really a brute beast, you know. In fact,' he said ruminatively, 'I sometimes feel something of a fairy when I order alcohol for a lady, and make do with a pint of tonic water myself because I'm driving. I draw the line at having the slice of lemon though. I take the tonic water macho-man neat! Except for ice, of course,' he finished lamely.

Serena was happy being with him. He was still just the same, she realized, as he'd been all those years ago. He could always, even in the old days, laugh at himself, and she liked a man who could do that.

'I don't suppose you've had a shortage of ladies to buy alcohol for while I've been away.' She glanced up at him, stirring the peas around in the vinegar as she waited for his response.

'You want to know if I've had girl friends?' he asked incredulously, then followed it up by saying, 'It *has* been ten years, you know. I didn't go off and join the nearest monastery when you upped and left me.'

'So who's the latest flame?'

'She just got married.' He pulled a face at her. 'She got tired of waiting around for me to get over a cute little blonde I once fancied.'

'Ha! Ha!' she said, scooping up more peas and chewing them as he started on his own plateful.

'According to Aunt Viv, her cleaning lady Jilly Tewson has a daughter who thinks I'm "lovely"!' He chewed pensively on his peas, swallowed them and said, 'Viv never did have much idea about what kind of girl I liked though.'

'I expect you must still see quite a lot of your Aunt Viv – living so close to her as you do now?'

'What you're really asking is "is Viv still as clinging" isn't it?' He smiled at her a little grimly.

She toyed with the peas in front of her, then looked up and met his eyes. 'Yes! I suppose I am. I remember she could be a little . . . suspicious . . . of some of your friends.'

'A little suspicious!' He laughed softly. 'You're being polite – of course. Viv is, and always has been a force to be reckoned with – especially when you cross her. I should know. I lived with her, and though I'll always be eternally grateful to her for giving me a home, I'm not blind to her faults.'

'She must miss you though. You were with her for such a long time.'

'Yes.' He sighed. 'But it got to the point where I knew I had to get away from the cosy-cottage scene. I realized also though that I couldn't go far away from her. She has this heart complaint, you know.' His eyes darkened, shadowed with concern. 'I feel responsible for her. She and Mari are the only family I have left now.'

Serena nodded. 'Yes, I know. I also remember that Viv was never very strong.'

'It would have been cruel of me to leave her altogether and move away completely. Anyway, I like it around Caindale. Caindale has a beauty all its own.'

'You sound like Ryan. He loves it here.' She grimaced slightly, picked up her glass and took a long drink. 'Me? I must be blind to Caindale's attractions; Ryan always says . . .'

His face turned thunderous. 'Ryan! Always our conversation comes back to Ryan.'

She looked up at him. He was devouring peas as if he wished he'd got Ryan Farrar cut up in neat bite-sized bits on the plate in front of him. She'd finished her own plateful, and sat back.

He glowered at her. 'Okay! What have I said wrong?'

'You're jealous!' Breathlessly she gave a little laugh, while inside she was rejoicing. He still cared for her. And it was obvious he hated it because she and Ryan were living together. She felt guilty because she couldn't tell him why that was so, but, she reminded herself, she'd given Ryan her word that she wouldn't talk to anybody about what was wrong with him.

Holt finished off his peas and pushed the plate away, seemed to be thinking about her words for a moment, then said, 'So? What if I am? Jealous! It's not a pleasant feeling I get when I see you two together, or think about you in that little house up there.'

'You looked absolutely murderous when you brought that furniture up to the house with Mark.'

He nodded slowly. 'I felt murderous. Farrar had his arm draped round your shoulders as if he owned you. It was the first thing I noticed as we drew up in the Crabtree truck. Then – in the bedroom, you were completely different – remember? You let me hold you – just like in the old days.' His voice was low and seductive. 'We laughed together. It was like you'd never been away.' He shook his head then and said, 'Serena – I can't make you out. You've got me all mixed up. Is it him you want, or is it still me?'

It was as if a cloud had descended on her. She said stiffly, 'I can't explain, Holt. All I can tell you is that Ryan needs me, and while that state of affairs continues, I have to be there for him.'

He thumped the table with a clenched fist. 'And I can go to hell? Is that it?' She almost wavered in her resolution not to tell anybody about Ryan's condition, but a promise was a promise she told herself severely. Some people's attitude always changed when they found out somebody was dying, and Ryan was very intuitive. He would surely know if he met up with Holt again, that she'd told him the truth about Ryan.

'I can't tell you why he needs me,' she said, tentatively swirling the liquid around in her glass. 'He just does and that's all there is to it.'

'I need you too.' His face was serious. 'We had a lot going for us at one time, Serena. We could still pick up the pieces and start again – if you wanted to.'

'Maybe. One day.' She drank the remainder of the Martini and lemonade, then placed her empty glass on the table again.

'Do you have to be so casual about it? This is us we're talking about. Our future, for God's sake.'

'I can't talk about a future.' She shook her head. 'Don't ask me to – please, Holt. Not yet. Not just now.'

He stared at her, not understanding, she was sure. At last he leaned back and said, 'Okay! Why are we here then?

If we don't have a future together, why the hell are we wasting our time raking up the past, finding out we still care about each other?'

'You asked me to come here, if you remember,' she reminded him.

Softly, his eyes dark and serious, he said, 'But you came, Serena. I didn't have to use force, did I?'

'I – I did want to talk to you. I've been thinking about something ever since I found out where you lived. Ever since I stood outside your door and you opened it so suddenly and scared me half to death.'

'So? Talk,' he said, lifting his big shoulders in a shrug of impatience.

'It's about that door.'

'My door? You want my door? Is that it? You don't want the man, you just want the door?'

'Listen to me, will you?' She sat forward in her seat. 'I told you – I've been thinking – thinking about what you told me. You know – about Dad wanting to manufacture doors like that one.'

'So?' Brooding, he considered her across the table.

'It's too late now for me to tell him I'm sorry for all I did in the past.' She looked down at the table top where her hands were clasped together. 'What I could do though – what I'd like to do,' she amended, 'is to run some more tests at the foundry on those doors.'

He frowned. 'What will that prove?'

'Nothing!' She sighed. 'Absolutely nothing, of course, but I'd like to feel I finished something off that Dad started. Can you understand what I'm getting at?'

He thought about her words for some seconds, then said, 'I guess so.'

'I found all the drawings in a cabinet in Dad's office. He

didn't just intend making doors with iron compasses in them – there were other designs too, birds, ships, a kind of port-hole with an etching of Caindale beach on it with the jetty in the background.'

He nodded. 'Yes, I've seen them all, Serena. But Max ran tests for months, and always the wood split away from the iron when they tried to fuse the two together.'

'Except in the case of your door.'

He nodded and frowned, 'Well, yes.'

'So what was different about your door?'

'It was the original "witch" door from the "ugly" house.' He grinned at her. 'Maybe the old woman put a spell on it. Who knows?'

'It's oak though. And it's weathered. It wasn't a new door, was it?'

He was looking interested now. 'No,' he said, 'and the design of the compass doesn't go right the way through the wood – because *that* door is twice the depth of today's doors.'

She said, 'I saw from the test results that Dad used oak doors, but they were the modern kind. New wood. And the designs were the same thickness as the doors – so that when the pattern was cut out of the door to make way for the iron, the door had already lost a lot of its strength.'

'Yes,' he said. 'Max was already working on the theory that maybe the iron was too heavy for the wood. Unfortunately – or maybe fortunately for the work force, a new big order for drainpipes etc., came in and all work on the doors had to be shelved. Max never got back to it.'

Her eyes lit up. 'Do you think it would be worth starting up the tests again then?'

He reached across the table and his big hand covered both of her own. 'Hey,' he said, 'Don't give this priority will you? Not over the bread and butter orders you already have?'

'No. I wouldn't do that. But I could put a couple of men on it at the moment. We're not rushed off our feet with work. And I would like to do it, Holt.'

'To make your peace with Max? Is that it?'

The light faded from her eyes. 'I know I can never do that. But if I could feel I'd been of some use . . .'

'After your attempts to sabotage the place . . .'

'God! Don't remind me.' She swallowed and said, 'I'll never forgive myself. As long as I live, I'll never forgive myself for what I did.' Easily he said, 'There was no lasting damage, Serena.'

'Except to my relationship with Dad. And with you.' Her glance rested on his hand, still covering both her own.

His fingers closed tightly round the hand nearest his. She winced a little as the ring she wore on her left hand cut into her flesh.

'Sorry!' He grinned and let her go instantly. 'I don't know my own strength . . .' His voice broke off abruptly as he stared down at her hand, then he pushed himself to his feet and stood towering over her. 'No!' he said hoarsely. Oh, no – I don't believe this . . .'

Too late, she realized what he was staring at, and in vain she dragged her hands off the table and clutched them together on her knee.

'It isn't what you think . . .' she began, but he cut in aggressively, 'Oh, no? That *is* a wedding ring you're wearing, isn't it?'

'Yes, but . . .'

'Just tell me one thing,' he muttered in a savage voice. 'Just tell me you haven't changed your name to Farrar.'

She swung her gaze up to his. And after a silence that lasted an eternity, said quietly. 'I can't do that, Holt. My name *is* Serena Farrar now. I was married twelve months ago in Queensland . . .'

He waited to hear no more. He swung away from her on the instant, and pushed his way through the throng of people towards the door.

'Holt . . .' she cried, lurching to her feet, but he'd gone. And in exasperation she cursed under her breath.

'Damn! Damn! Damn the man!'

CHAPTER 15

Ryan flung himself forward and grabbed at one of those flailing arms as the figure in the hooded jacket, still screaming, lost its footing and pitched forward over the edge of the cliff.

He caught at an arm as he landed flat out and face down, skidding and slithering on his stomach in the long damp grass on which the stranger too had lost its footing.

Desperately he held on to that arm, feeling his fingers sliding down the smooth quilted nylon material of the jacket as the slight frame dangled below him. It had stopped its screaming now, and all he could hear was a terrified whimpering, interspersed with a sobbing that made him all the more determined to save that pathetic figure down there. After all, it was his fault, that all this had happened.

But still his fingers could not get a proper grip, and with every second that passed he was getting more and more horrified at what he had done. Now was not the time for wrestling with his conscience however.

He inched forward, wriggling like a snake across the grass until he could just peer over into emptiness. He couldn't see the hooded figure, it was hidden from his view by tough marram grass and clumps of boulder clay.

He yelled then, 'Swing yourself round! Grab hold of me with your other hand! For God's sake, grab me, will you?'

He was surprised that the figure below him was not heavier. He'd expected a man's weight when he'd grasped that arm, but a man's weight, he knew now, would have dragged him over the edge too. It must be a boy, he thought and he closed his eyes and prayed for the strength to hang on, or to pull the figure up to safety before he lost his grip.

He felt a tug, and his hand started slipping over the smooth nylon quilting again. 'Don't move!' he shouted, panicking, but the jacket was slowly slipping out of his grasp.

And then he felt a jerk on his arm, and he clutched at a hand – a hand that, like his own was naked, its grip fierce and warm. He thanked heaven then that neither of them had been wearing gloves. That would have been yet another hazard, for gloves would have slipped just as the jacket material had been doing.

He locked his fingers round the wrist of the hand that was clutching him. It was a small hand – a smooth hand. He fumbled around in the grass with his free hand until his fingers closed firmly round tussocks of grass growing along the line of the cliff. He'd need a good anchor, he realized, if he was going to attempt this rescue all on his own – and it looked like he might have to, for there was nobody else available to help him.

The wind was blowing keenly off the sea and a light drizzle of rain was coming down. He could feel the figure swaying below him. He drew in a deep breath and yelled again.

'I'm going to try and pull you up. Okay?'

He felt a slight tightening of the grip on his wrist.

'Don't panic,' he yelled again. 'We'll take this real easy –
one bit at a time.'

This time there was no response, except that the
sobbing started up again. It was a sound that caught at
his heart.

'Hey – don't worry,' he shouted. 'I won't let you go.'

Summoning every bit of strength he possessed then, he
tensed the muscles in his arm and shoulder and hauled as
hard as he knew how, until bit by bit, he was able to edge
backwards, away from the cliff edge, first by hauling on
the figure below him, and then by taking a break and
finding a fresh hand-hold in the tough grass.

There were grunts and groans from below him, and
he knew that whoever it was down there, might, just
might come out of this with a dislocated shoulder or a
broken arm – but he reasoned that such an injury was
infinitely better than the only other alternative, which
was a two hundred foot plunge onto rocks below the
headland.

After a long half hour that seemed to go on for ever, with
him straining, steadily pulling, and having frequent breaks
to find a fresh hand-hold on the cliff top, another hand
suddenly appeared over the edge of the steep drop. He
could see it as it fumbled, groped, and tried desperately to
find something to cling onto and help itself back up onto
safe ground.

'Over to your right,' he yelled. 'About six inches.'

The hand found and clutched at the tussocky grass and
Ryan felt the strain ease on his arm. He pulled again, and
the hood of the navy blue jacket tipped the edge of the
cliff. As yet, he couldn't make out a face. The head was
bowed, it inched up higher, the face still turned away from
him.

And suddenly, he realized this was not the end of the battle. That figure was intent on shielding its identity, even now, after all it had gone through in the last half hour.

He gripped that small hand even harder, and gave one last almighty pull. With its own efforts as well, the figure swung a blue denim leg over the edge of the cliff top, then another, after which it rolled soundlessly away from the precipice, suddenly jerked its hand free of him, reeled to its feet and started to run again.

Sheer blind fury shot Ryan to his feet too, and within seconds he was racing after the dark blue jacket that topped a pair of flying legs clad in faded denim.

The cramp in his right arm – from hanging onto that figure and saving it from almost certain death – was excruciating. It hung limp at his side as his long legs – much longer than the other guy's, he noted – carried him forward across the green swathe of grass that was dipping now towards the lower ground and away from the cliff edge, the beach, and the sea.

He caught up easily; caught up and overtook, shooting out his left arm and grasping again at an arm. The figure lashed out at him, and still its face was obscured by that hood. He brought it to an immediate halt, however, hanging onto its arm, jerking it round, bringing up his other hand now that was slowly getting some feeling back into it and reaching towards the navy blue hood.

The figure head-butted him in the midriff. He gasped but still hung onto it. It kicked out, this time aiming at his shins, but he managed to avoid those lashing boots.

'You won't get away . . .' he gasped. 'I'm going to see your damn face if it's the last thing I do . . .'

Another head-butt almost winded him, but Ryan's foot came up, catching the smaller figure at the back of the

219

knees, and knocking it off its feet. Ryan went down with it, determined not to let go his hold of the prey. It was face down in the grass and breathing heavily, but still struggling. Ryan twisted its arm up behind its back and it cried out in sudden pain, and the sound alarmed him.

It was the cry of a woman.

But this one certainly couldn't be called the weaker sex, he thought wryly. This was one tough little female, and suddenly things started falling into place. Max must have met a woman up here! That had to be it. It was a woman that George had seen – a woman wrapped up in a shapeless anorak such as this one was wearing.

And what was it George had told him Corder had said just before he died?

'Heaven has no rage, George'!

And Serena had completed the saying for him, when he'd asked her if she'd ever heard it before.

'A woman scorned, huh?' His voice was savage – totally unlike his own as he ground out the words breathlessly.

The figure on the ground beneath him writhed but by no amount of thrashing about could it free itself.

'"Heaven has no rage, like love to hatred turned. Nor hell a fury like a woman scorned!" I bet that rings bells for you, doesn't it?' Ryan panted. 'Come on now. Explain to me why you were up here with Max Corder? And explain also why he should utter those words as he lay dying?'

He yanked the figure over onto its back, tearing the hood from its head and exposing its face as he did so.

Then all the breath left his body, and he was unable to utter another word as, in amazement, he gazed down into the face of Kirsten Hardie.

'Ryan!' she muttered weakly, and then she started to laugh, but tears were pouring down her cheeks. 'Ryan! Oh

Ryan! I didn't want you to know it was me you were chasing.'

His hands fell away from her. He sat back on his heels, panting and breathless. Then he began to shake his head. 'No!' he muttered. 'I don't believe this. It can't be you . . .'

'I came to find you.' She wasn't attempting to get away from him any more. She just lay there weeping softly and making no attempt to stem the flow of tears. She smiled through them at him. 'It's so good to see you. But I never intended letting you know I was here . . .'

His breathing was ragged. 'How? . . . Why?' His eyes held distrust. 'Serena . . .' he gasped. 'Sera – *she* didn't send for you, did she? I'll kill her if she did . . .'

'Sera?' She frowned and brushed her hand across her face to wipe the tears away. 'Why would she send for me?'

Slowly she began to push herself into a sitting position, while still he crouched, just out of reach of her now, for he'd backed away, though was still hunched up on the grass, watching her.

'Kirsty! Kirsty!' he muttered, 'Kirsty, my darling girl . . .'

Huskily she asked, 'You're not angry?'

'Angry?' He was a lot of things, surprised, astounded, caught off guard, and overwhelmed – to name but a few. One thing he was not, however, was angry! He was relieved, he supposed. And then he was gutted at the thought that he'd very nearly killed her back there on the headland.

He tried not to think of what he might be feeling now if he hadn't managed to snatch at her when she went careering over the edge of the cliff, but the thought was there all the same, and suddenly she was very precious to him.

He reached out to her, and she flung herself into his arms. He rocked her back and forth, to and fro, murmuring her name over and over again.

'Kirsty, sweetheart! Kirsty my darling girl! Kirsty! Kirsty!'

And then his lips sought and found hers, and his body melted into hers, hugging her, holding her, his hands moulding her to him, then moving to cup her face, her sweet darling little face, and he gazed hungrily into her eyes.

He kissed her eyes, smothered the rest of her face, from her forehead to the delicious little dent under her ear lobes, with kisses. He felt like a drowning man, a man with not much time left, who had to make the most of the moment, and take with him a memory to outlive the eternity he was falling into.

When she could, she burst out, 'Why? Why did you leave me? Why did you tell me you didn't want me?'

The question caught him off guard. But she was here. She had followed him half way across the world because she loved him. And in an instant, he realized that no matter how much time he had left, he wanted to spend it with her.

Tears coursed down his cheeks and mingled with hers as he told her.

'I got caught up in the gunfire when Dad was killed by that bastard at the bungalow . . .'

She tipped her head back and her eyes were haunted. She nodded. 'Serena told me when I telephoned. You got a graze on the head . . . but it wasn't serious . . .'

He hung his head. 'That's what I made her tell you.'

'You didn't get a graze on your head?' Her eyes searched his face, his forehead for signs of a scar.

Slowly he said. 'I got a bullet in the brain, my darling.'

'Ryan! No! You could have died.' She stared at him, horrified.

'I'm *going* to die,' he said quietly. 'They can't get the damned thing out without killing me.'

The only sound she made was a silent little gasp. Then she whispered, 'They must have made a mistake. They have to be able to get it out.'

He held onto her shoulders and shook her gently. Their eyes met, hers wide and unbelieving, his own guarded, and for the first time since the shooting occurred, free of fear. He could take whatever fate threw at him now that she was here with him, he realized. With Kirsty beside him, he could accept whatever had to be.

'It's inoperable,' he said. 'And it could move in the tissue surrounding my brain at any time and kill me.'

She placed her hands on his shoulders and stared wide eyed at him. 'You're so thin,' she whispered, the tears starting again. 'You're so pale, you're like a scarecrow.'

He gave a sudden laugh. 'What a thing to say to a dying ma . . .'

'Hush!' She covered his lips with two fingers. 'Hush my darling. If it's true what you say, if there really is no hope, let's just love each other until it happens, huh?'

'You still want me?' He stared at her. There was no pity in her eyes, he saw. But there was plenty of love and compassion.

'We can't let a little thing like a bullet get in the way of our love, can we?' She smiled through her tears.

'Can we make this a permanent arrangement? For as long as it lasts?' he asked her solemnly.

She laughed again. 'That's a lousy way of proposing marriage,' she said.

'Will you marry me?'

She nodded, stars in her eyes. 'I hoped you'd ask me.'

He held her away from him and his eyes devoured her. 'You look absolutely horrific,' he said. 'Where did you get that thing you're wearing?'

'It's my camouflage,' she said ruefully. 'I thought that neither you nor Serena would recognize me dressed like this.'

'I didn't . . .' he said, thinking again uneasily about the hooded figure that had been seen on the cliff top with Max.

'You said some pretty strange things when you had me down on the ground,' she probed gently.

'Yes. It's a long story.' He grinned at her. 'Come back to Caindale with me. Sera will be pleased to see you. She's done nothing but nag at me to get in touch with you for the last few months.'

She laid a hand on his arm. 'I've got something to tell you first, love . . .'

'Can't it wait?'

'No. I have to tell you now. It's important.'

'Nothing's important,' he said, dragging her into his arms again. 'Nothing except having you here.'

CHAPTER 16

When Serena took the phone call in the office that afternoon, her first thought was that Ryan had flipped. Either that, or else the bullet that was lodged in his brain had suddenly made his condition worsen.

'Where are you?' she asked sharply. 'For heaven's sake, speak more slowly and tell me.'

'I'm at Rivelyn!'

'At the inn?' she asked, knowing now that something awful had indeed happened – the obvious explanation being that he'd started with one of his headaches and had wandered away after the blessing of the boats.

He was often woozy and disorientated with the pain in his head, but never before had she known his memory to fail him – as must have happened today. Why else would he be in Rivelyn?

Frantic with worry about him, she could understand in a way, him making for somewhere he'd been staying recently though, somewhere he remembered well. And confident that she had stumbled on the truth of what had happened, she said in a firm voice, 'You must stay there, Ryan. I can be with you in twenty minutes.'

In the background, on the other end of the phone, she

could hear another voice – two voices – and something that sounded like a baby gurgling.

Ryan was laughing now and saying, 'There's no need for you to come, Sera . . .'

'Stay there,' she ordered, knowing that she must get to him before he wandered off again, 'Stay there. I'm coming straight over in the car for you.'

Hell, she thought, there sounded quite a rumpus in the background. The proprietor of the inn must be going crazy, wondering why the Australian had returned. She wondered if Ryan had been trying to force his way into his old bedroom, the one he'd stayed in when they first arrived from Australia. She hoped nobody had called the police to try and get him carted away!

'Sera! Will you listen to me. I've got a baby!' he yelled – so loudly that she winced and held the phone away from her ear.

He really had gone over the top, she thought. Gently, so as not to upset him, she said, 'Have you?'

'Sera! You're not going to believe this . . .'

No, she thought wearily, I am definitely not going to believe this! In a calm voice she pleaded, 'Just stay put, love. I'm on my way. Don't leave the inn, will you?'

'I'll be staying here for quite a while, Sera. There isn't the slightest possibility of me leaving.'

'Yes. Well, we'll see about that when I arrive.'

'Bring me some clothes, will you? From the house? Just a few bits of underwear, some jeans, and a couple of sweaters.'

'Yes! Sure!' she promised, inwardly hoping they wouldn't put him in a strait-jacket before she could get there. Nobody had mentioned he could go out of his mind. Okay – she knew his condition was serious. Knew he could

226

go blind or have any number of other complications, but this was something she hadn't been warned about.

'Sera! I've got a *baby*! Why don't you believe me? It's a perfectly logical and sensible statement. I've got a *baby*!'

'Ryan – I'm coming now. Okay?'

'Her name's Reanne! Get it? The feminine form of Ryan.'

Her heart gave a lurch. Could he be making this up? Suddenly she didn't think so. 'Reanne?' she asked, caution making her voice faint.

At that moment, Mari came into the office, saw she was on the phone and made as if to leave again.

Serena covered the mouthpiece with her hand and whispered, 'No – stay, Mari. It's Ryan. I can't make head or tail of him. He's phoning from the inn at Rivelyn. He says he's got a baby.'

His voice was more insistent. 'Sera! Sera? Are you there? Sera?'

Mari perched herself on the edge of the desk and looked bemused.

'Yes. Yes, I'm here,' Serena said in a firm voice.

'Let me start again, huh?'

'Look – I think it would be best if I came over and brought you back to Caindale.'

'I'm with Kirsty,' he said, loud and clear. 'Kirsten Hardie? Remember her?'

'Kirsty?' She raised her brows at Mari, and Mari who couldn't help but overhear Ryan shouting into the phone, whispered in an enlightened voice, 'Is that the Australian girl who phoned me?'

Serena nodded at her, then asked Ryan, 'Hey, what is this? Can we start at the beginning – and not in such a loud voice?'

He said in very precise tones, 'Kirsty was down on the beach this morning. We – er, we sort of fell into each other's arms.' He gave a self-concious little laugh.

'Kirsty? Here?'

'That's what I said, Sera. And Sera – I've got a *daughter*. A real little beaut. Her name's Reanne. That's what I've been trying to tell you all along. Kirsty's over here with her sister Holly. And they've brought Reanne with them. And like I said, the baby's a real beaut. Sera! I'm in heaven. And Kirsty and me – well, we've got a room here, with the baby. And Holly's going up to Edinburgh in the morning.'

At last, something was making sense. Serena told him she understood, and was happy for him. She smiled at Mari. 'You heard?' she said softly as she put the phone down.

Mari nodded but frowned. 'You seem pleased about it . . .'

'I am, Mari. It makes up a bit for losing Don.'

'Don!'

'I never told you, did I?' Serena bit down on her lip, feeling slightly guilty for not confiding in Mari before this. It had been difficult though, working with the woman who had turned her world upside down at one time, getting to know Mari as a friend instead of the enemy. 'I married Ryan's father six months before he was killed,' she explained.

The little house was lonely without Ryan sharing it, although he had been over from Rivelyn a couple of times, but not yet with Kirsten or the baby.

Serena, on her own now, found she was spending more and more time at the foundry during the following two

228

weeks however. It was easier to take a sandwich to the office, and then make herself a late supper if she needed it, than to go home twice a day and make herself a proper meal.

She worked late, and after hours, when everybody else in the offices had finished for the day. The door project fascinated her, and she found she could make minute improvements and alterations to the drawings of Max's door plans quite easily. She became more and more convinced that if the designs could be streamlined there'd be less chance of the wood splitting when the cast iron was fixed into it.

She'd tracked down a northern manufacturing firm too, which had agreed to supply doors at double the normal thickness, with frames to match at a reasonable cost should they need them, so tests would be able to go ahead in late April-early May when delivery of the first batch of doors would commence.

There was one design however, whose lines could not be softened or streamlined, and that was the compass. She wished she'd taken more note of it when she'd first seen it at Holt's 'ugly' house now. The sharp points of a compass did not take easily to modification. Rounded designs, with no jutting-out bits would fit snugly into new and unseasoned oak, she decided, especially if the iron only went half way through the wood and a good bonding material was used.

But the compass design defied all her efforts to soften its outline. She desperately needed to see the original again, because only by doing that could she perhaps work out exactly how the iron and wood had been joined together and given such an excellent seal. But she baulked at contacting Holt and asking such a favour of him. She hadn't met up with him again since the blessing of the fishing boats, when he'd stormed out of the 'Old Bachelor' bar without a backward glance at her.

Joe Fisher and Terry Madely, the two patternmakers she'd chosen out of the foundry to spend time on the door project were working flat out to make the moulds for the other designs. She could, she decided, discard the idea of making doors with the compass design in them, but to even think of doing that made her feel she was shirking her responsibility and failing her father.

Max had only ever had a single successful door – and that was the one belonging to Holt.

The project became a challenge to her. Max had thrown down the gauntlet – it was as if he was daring her, defying her to pit her wits against his own in this venture. And it was becoming an obsession with her too, to match up to her father, to finish the job he had started. She felt if she could do that one thing, it might, in some subtle way, ease her conscience and make up a little for all the heartache she must have caused him in the past.

And yet, still in her heart, she blamed him for being unfaithful to her mother. And nothing could rid her of the memory of Max and Mari together on the day her mother had died. She tried to forgive him but it was pointless trying to do that. She couldn't forgive. There was a small part of her that blamed him for her mother's early death. Perhaps if he hadn't been unfaithful, her mother wouldn't have given in to her illness so easily.

Even so, there were times when she wished she could shed a silent tear for Max, but that relief also was denied her. It was as if a steel door had closed on her heart, shutting Max outside, and it worried her that she could be so hard, and so unforgiving towards the man who had adored her.

She was working late on a Friday evening, and suddenly it all got too much for her. There seemed no way possible that she could hope to redesign that compass. She flung the drawings away from her, across the desk. There had been no notes made on the construction of the doors or the wood that had been used. It had all been guesswork, and trial and error. Nobody in the foundry had been able to enlighten her either. The one man who had worked on the project with her father was also dead.

Young Jackie at the office, had shrugged and told her that her father had looked on it merely as a kind of hobby – making those doors. Serena knew though, that until he had perfected something, Max would keep his research close to his chest, and it was not in his nature to waste time on hobbies.

Hard work and making money were the two things her father had been good at. In her mind there was no doubt about it – Max had seen an opportunity to make more money, to offer a luxury item to a public that was already tiring of plastic doors and window frames. It must have been a new and exciting enterprise for the man who headed a small firm dealing with the usual unromantic undertakings for drain pipes, water pipes, gas pipes, drain covers and street furniture.

She was weary though, and she yawned and stretched her arms above her head, then rubbed at her eyes and peered at the clock on the wall opposite her desk.

'Seven-thirty! It seems more like midnight,' she muttered.

The telephone stared back at her as her eyes alighted on it. Holt's number was etched on her brain. She'd looked it

231

up and had been on the verge of ringing him several times in the past two days to ask if she could go over to the 'ugly' house and look at that door again.

Why not now?

No.

She decided against it. It was Friday evening. Weekend almost. He'd probably be going out somewhere. Maybe he'd got a heavy date.

The thought of Holt with another woman sent shards of ice slicing into her heart.

But – she ought to ring him, she tried to convince herself. For as well as wanting to see his door again, there were other, more important things that had to be put right between the two of them – she couldn't let him go on thinking she was married to Ryan!

Automatically her hand went to the phone. Then she drew back. He wouldn't want to hear from her. He'd probably give her the brush off if she rang him up. Could she take that, she wondered?

There was, in the end, only one way to find out.

She reached out again, and this time she dialled the number, then sat there waiting for him to answer, with butterflies churning around in her stomach.

'I'll come and fetch you. You can leave your car at the works, can't you?'

Suddenly, seeing her again was the most important thing in his life, and he didn't want to waste any time.

'There's no need. Really, Holt. I've got the car right outside. I can be with you in less than half an hour.'

On his end of the phone, he shrugged. 'Okay, lady! Have it your way.'

'I'm not interrupting anything important, am I?'

He glanced in amusement at the pile of papers on the desk in front of him in his study, and at the computer screen showing next week's work schedule – the long term contract with Danby Brothers, the transporting of their iron girders from Tyneside to Leeds heading the list. Mentally he made a note to put Jim Johnson on that one; it was a relatively easy journey that could be completed in a day with a three-axled unit. Jim's wife was expecting twins at any time now, so short runs were what Jim needed so he could be on hand for the birth.

Then there were the mobile homes to be taken from the Lake District to East Coast resorts. With his free hand he typed 'air suspension unit' beside that entry, then also noted that a police escort had been arranged for the aero engine and wreckage being sent down south for inspection and investigation. It had taken months to plan that route, avoiding low bridges, and tight bends. It never failed to amaze him that some town planners didn't seem to appreciate that loads such as this had to travel by road at times.

'No,' he said easily. 'There's nothing that can't wait. In fact, I was hoping for a quiet night in front of the television, just being lazy for once.'

'You don't mind if I pop over then?'

'Of course not.' He did his best to sound casually uninterested in her. It was difficult. Just listening to her voice was turning him on!

'About twenty minutes then? Is that okay? I have a few things to put away in the office.'

'That's fine,' he said, looking at his watch, 'See you then.'

Slowly he put the receiver down, then muttered to himself, 'Twenty minutes! Just time to have a cold shower! I sure need one when that dame's around.'

* * *

Lamps had been lit all the way up his drive, she saw, when she turned the car onto it. On the day she'd been here before, she hadn't noticed the slim cast iron lighting columns that blended in so well with the trees. Now though she was glad he'd switched the lamps on. It was quite eerie enough in the daytime, going up to the 'ugly' house, how much more spooky it would have been at night, and in the dark, she decided.

He was standing in the porch, leaning complacently against the door frame waiting for her as she parked the car, then walked over towards him carrying a folio case containing the plans for Max's doors.

'You oughtn't to be out here wearing just a shirt,' she said, as she came up to him. 'I'd forgotten what springtime weather could be like in England.'

He grinned. 'Snow's been forecast again. But I don't feel the cold – you get used to it when you work out in it in all weathers. I came out to look for you thinking you might be scared – coming up to the 'ugly' house in the dark.'

She came abreast of him, glancing at him and seeing his hair gleaming damply, and smelling the fresh tang of spicy lemon soap on him. 'You look as if you've been for a swim.'

'Only in the bathroom.' His laugh was dark and sexy. 'I don't go skinny dipping in the sea any more – though I still remember what fun it could be on a balmy summer night, down there in that little secluded cove beyond Caindale.'

She ignored the remark, but felt herself flushing all the same as she was reminded forcibly of those halcyon days – and nights.

He pushed the door wider so that she could enter the house in front of him, saying as she passed him, 'Have you come to stay? Is that your overnight baggage?'

She flung him a look of amusement. 'Even you, Holt, can't fail to see this is work. Dad's plans for those doors, to be exact.'

'Hmm. Yes. You said on the phone you wanted to see my door again. I hoped it was just an excuse actually, and not merely work you had on your mind. I took the liberty of taking a stir-fry out of the freezer for later on.'

'If that's an invitation to stay for supper – you're on. I haven't had a decent meal since Ryan left a couple of weeks ago.'

His eyes narrowed as he followed her into the hall and closed the door behind him. He seemed puzzled about something, she could tell.

'Have I said something wrong?' she enquired.

He walked towards her, passed her easily in the spacious passage, and said, 'Come into the big room where we can talk in comfort – I've stoked the fire up in there.'

The 'big' room was a comfortably furnished sitting room, she discovered, with a high ceiling and book-shelves from the floor up to it in the wide chimney alcoves. He was right about the fire; it was well stoked and blazing away in a low grate above a red-tiled hearth.

'Let me take your coat.' He was standing beside her, taking the folio case out of her hands and placing it on a low table between two cushiony sofas that faced each other in front of the fire.

She slipped out of her coat, conscious of the fact that she was still in her office clothes – slender heeled shoes, slim grey skirt and forest green tunic. The contrast between them, she so neat and tidy, he in casual check shirt and jeans, couldn't have been more emphasized.

He took her coat and placed it over a chair at the back of the room. She stood looking round. It was a pleasant room with heavy furniture – bureau, bookcases, lamp tables, etc., giving it an atmosphere of homeliness. It wasn't entirely tidy. There was a pile of trucking magazines on the seat of an easy chair, a scattering of compact discs beside a stacking hi-fi system, and a grey cat fast asleep on the brown wool hearthrug, lying with its paws in the air and smile of contentment on its face.

'That's Gray,' he said. 'She lets me live here with her.'

'Gray!' She grinned at him. 'You were never much of a one for fancy words, were you, Holt?'

He shrugged. 'She was a bundle of grey matted fur when she first limped into the kitchen,' he said. 'I didn't think she'd make it those first few days so there didn't seem much point in giving her any name except one that was her colour.'

'She looks fine now.'

He pulled a face at her. 'So would you on a diet of fresh fish and chicken. That's all she'll take from me, but for Viv she eats anything – even stuff out of a tin.'

'She probably knows she can't get round a woman the same as she can a man.'

He rubbed his chin thoughtfully. 'You could be right,' he said. 'But she adores Viv. Follows her everywhere – even though Viv professes to hate cats.'

'Shall I sit down?'

'Sure! I was going to put some music on,' he said. 'I also planned to turn off the centre light and put some sexy lamps on around the room.' He laughed a little self-consciously. 'Guess I'm not the romantic type though. I couldn't find any low watt light bulbs, and most of the music I've got is grand opera.'

'I like opera.'

'You do?' He seemed a little put out. 'Ten years ago you liked pop – Shakin' Stevens, Elton John!'

'While you . . .'

'I liked the lady in red.'

'Ah! Chris De Burgh!'

'No – Serena. Remember that dress you used to wear? He gave a little growl of approval. 'Wow!'

Her cheeks flamed again. He'd always liked that dress – always said how much the colour suited her. She walked over to one of the sofas and sat down. He followed and sat on the opposite one, facing her, with the long, low table between them at just the height of their knees.

He said quietly, 'You don't seem upset because the Australian's left you. I heard he'd gone. Some girl from back home – and a baby?'

She smiled and nodded. 'Why should I be upset?'

Scowling he said. 'You're married to him, for God's sake . . .' and he flung his hands up in the air. 'Honestly – I've heard of some things – open marriages and such, but this one takes the biscuit. You lavish all your care and attention on the bloke, then you take his running out on you so – so dispassionately. Didn't you care for him?' He spread his hands out towards her. 'Are you so heartless you don't care for anybody any more?'

'I'm not married to Ryan,' she said softly. 'I tried to tell you that – before you ran out on me in the 'Old Bachelor' that day. You wouldn't listen though. You just wouldn't give me a chance to explain.'

'You admitted your name was Farrar though . . .'

'Yes.' She nodded, then explained, 'I was married to Ryan's father. His name was Don. We were married for six months before he was killed.'

237

He stared at her, his face blank, but his eyes blazing. 'You – you married somebody else? Yet you wouldn't wait for me?'

'There was no question of "waiting" for you,' she said impatiently. 'Ten years ago we had no hope of ever getting married.'

'We would have been married – eventually . . .'

'"*Eventually*" wasn't soon enough for me, Holt. I had to get away from home. I would have married you then and lived in a tent if we'd had to. God knows, I would have gone to the ends of the earth for you.'

'You're saying I let you down?' His chin jutted sharply. 'Is that it?'

She sighed. 'Don't put words into my mouth, Holt. It's just that you wouldn't risk anything in those days. You were only twenty-four and I was eighteen. I was head-strong and impatient, and you were . . .'

'A stick in the mud?' he finished for her.

'You were cautious.'

'Yeah!' he said. 'And that was another word for coward in your book, huh? And all because I wouldn't take your side against Max. Well, let me tell you – I agreed with Max, in my book he deserved some happiness with Aunt Mari. And the things you did – all that trouble you caused at the works, well, if you'd been my daughter, I'd have thrown you out on your ear and disowned you, Serena. It made me mad, the things you did. I began to wonder why I'd ever been attracted to you.'

She looked down at her clenched hands, then slowly lifted her face to his. 'I don't blame you for thinking like that,' she said. 'I've had time to realize what a fool I was. I can understand too why you didn't want to tie yourself down with me.'

'I'd have been finished around these parts if I'd done that. You know I would.' It was his turn to bow his head now, then he glanced up at her again and went on, 'If you'd been in the right though, I'd have stuck by you. You know damn well I would.'

'Yes,' she said simply. 'I know that now. Ten years ago though, I felt that the world was against me – and my world consisted mainly of you – and my father.'

'So you turned to the Australian guy.'

She stared at him silently, then after a few moments said, 'In eight years you never attempted to make contact with me – even though I was only in Northumberland. And slowly, I came to realize you'd washed your hands of me, so when the opportunity to go to Australia came along, I jumped at it. I liked it there, and I liked the man I worked with. Don was a good man. We got on well together right from the word go.'

'I take it he was divorced – seeing that he had a son. Ryan!'

She nodded again. 'He told me about Brenda – how they'd married when they were both only seventeen. She walked out on Don after Ryan was born – leaving him to bring the baby up on his own. It hadn't been easy for him, but Don was one of those people who don't let life get them down.'

'He was quite a bit older than me . . .' she went on, but remembering was still painful; she gazed down at the table top. 'It was his forty-fourth birthday on the day we came home from celebrating it to find an intruder in the bungalow. When the man turned a gun on us, Don pushed me behind him and was killed instantly by a single shot.'

'God! I'm sorry, love.' His expression was one of horror.

'Ryan was shot too. But I managed to knock the gun out of the man's hand before he could have another go at him. When the police cornered him later, he turned the gun on himself. He was high on drugs, they said.'

'What an awful mess.'

'Yes.'

'There's more, isn't there? I can see by your face.'

'Ryan . . .' she said hesitantly.

'Ryan?'

'He got a bullet in his head. It lodged near his brain, splintered his skull. It's inoperable.'

He let out a long, low whistle. 'So that's it! That's why you've been so concerned about him. But why didn't you tell me all this before?'

'Ryan made me promise I wouldn't say a word about it. He had this steady girl friend in Queensland, you see. They were really serious about each other, and then Kirsten got the chance of a good job in Melbourne. It was while she was there that Don was killed, and Ryan . . .'

'He thinks he'll be a burden on her? Is that it?'

'Yes,' she said. 'Partly that.'

'Only partly?' He looked at her steadily.

'Ryan was given two years at the most to live,' she told him. 'The bullet can't be removed because of the splinters of bone that are actually touching his brain. He suffers terrible headaches. He's lost an enormous amount of weight. The doctors say it's inflammation and infection that keeps flaring up. Drugs have little or no effect any more, so he lives on pain killers.'

'And this girl in Rivelyn? Tell me about her?'

'It's Kirsten. She came to find him. She couldn't understand why he'd ditched her. And unknown to Ryan, she was expecting his baby.'

'Does she know about his condition now?'

She nodded. 'Yes. That's why I feel free to tell you all this now. Ryan's been totally honest with her, so she knows what to expect. But Kirsty's a force to be reckoned with. She's staunchly behind Ryan, come what may. In fact, they're getting married just as soon as they're able.'

'Poor kids,' he said softly. 'Not much of a future for them, is it?'

'I told you – Kirsty's made of strong stuff.' A little smile played around her lips. 'If sheer will-power can keep Ryan going, she's got enough for the both of them. And they're both up to their eyes in parenthood at the moment. Ryan adores his little daughter, baby Reanne.'

'God! What a mess though.'

She agreed with him. 'They're so young to have this happening to them. So much in love.' Without warning, tears sprang to her eyes and she dashed the back of her hand across them.

He got up from the sofa opposite and came round to sit beside her, putting one big arm round her shoulders and pulling her against him. 'Cry your eyes out if you like,' he said. 'It must have been one hell of a strain on you these past few months.'

Her laugh was unsteady, 'I don't go to pieces easily. I'm fine now.'

They sat silently for some minutes, then, with an uneasy note in his voice, he asked, 'Did you love him? This Don guy? Ryan's father?'

She rested her head back against his shoulder. 'I gave up on love a long time ago.' She tilted her face up and grimaced at him. 'Don knew that, but we got on well together. We liked the same kind of things. And I never

241

wanted to come back to England – not after I knew that I'd lost you for ever. Don and I were thrown together – we had a lot in common besides being two people whose sane and simple worlds had crumbled. A physical attraction sprang up between us. I wasn't cut out for a single, celibate life, Holt.'

She felt his fingers tighten around her shoulders, but knew that before they could get back on the old footing, she had to be entirely honest with him. 'Don and I were two lonely people; we'd lost our way in life, and we just sort of drifted into a relationship that suited us both.'

'If he were still alive I'd hate him,' he muttered.

'No you wouldn't. You never hated anybody in your life, Holt.'

'Yeah! That's me. A real easy-going bastard.' His words were full of impatience for himself.

She shook with silent laughter.

'What're you laughing at?' he demanded.

'At you.'

'Why?'

'I have this weakness for easy-going bastards, I suppose.'

'Serena honey . . .' his voice was husky with emotion as he gazed down into her eyes.

'Hmm?'

'I never stopped loving you – not even when I despised you.'

She started to laugh again.

'If you don't stop laughing at me, I'm going to have to kiss you.'

She didn't give him time to carry out his threat. She leaned up towards him and touched her lips to his, gently, lovingly.

He closed his eyes and groaned, 'God! I had a cold shower before you arrived.'

'So? What's the problem?'

'It was wasted,' he said softly, bringing his lips down to hers, 'that shower was a complete waste of time!'

CHAPTER 17

She brought her hands up to cup his face and stare into his eyes.

Inside, she was a churning mass of emotions – love, apprehension, and the fear of losing him again being but a few that she recognized. She knew now that she'd never stopped loving him or wanting him. And being here in his arms was what she'd missed most in all those years she'd been away.

She'd shut him out of her life, though – out of her life and out of her mind and her heart. And over the years, she'd convinced herself that he could never, ever forgive her for those crazy days when she'd been hell-bent on making trouble for her father.

But she'd grown up a lot since those days. And she wanted him to know that she was ready now for more than a platonic friendship and the kind of kisses that went with such a relationship.

Huskily she whispered, 'I've been at the office since nine this morning. I could do with a shower myself.'

Carefully, gently, he edged out of his seat, never letting go of her for a minute, and when they were both standing up, his arms went right round her and she found herself melting into his embrace – and feeling as if she had every right to be there.

His kisses were controlled as his hands moulded her body to his. He was hard and straight and strong. She strained against him, feeling a quickening of her heartbeat, and an ache of longing deep down inside her for the lost lonely years.

She drank in the scent of him, the scent of his newly washed body that mingled with the unmistakable man-scent. She closed her eyes and ran her fingers through the hair at his neckline and felt him shudder and press more closely against her. His lips were warm and tantalizing as they mouthed little kisses against her eyes and her ears, then moved back to her lips, to tease her for a few seconds more before invading the hollow beneath her ears, and then her throat.

She arched her neck, tilting her head back, running her hands up the sides of his body, round to the muscles supporting his spine. She wanted to feel him all over, to make sure he was really there, and this wasn't some dream she was going to wake up from, with tears on her pillow . . .

Dreams like that had haunted her in the past, but the past was behind her now she decided. And she was determined on one thing to the exclusion of all else – she was not going to be such a fool again. Happiness as she'd once known it with Holt was too rare a commodity to be recklessly flung away a second time.

Slowly he eased her across the room until they were standing beside the door.

'Where are we going?' she whispered.

'You said something about a shower?' There was a question in his voice. Something that told her more subtly than words, that if she was going to get an attack of cold feet and back out of this tension-charged situation, now was the time to do it.

'I don't need a "get-out-of-jail-free" card.' She opened her eyes and stared at him. 'Did you really think I'd lead you on like this and then not run the course?'

'No,' he said simply. 'I know you're not that kind of girl. You never were. You always went flat out for what you wanted – I just needed to be sure.'

'I want you,' she said softly.

'You *still* want me?' One dark eyebrow rose in a questioning manner. 'After all these years?'

'I want you,' she repeated. 'But first of all I need that shower.'

It was a big shower – built for a big man. It held the two of them easily and there was still room to spare – room to twist and turn and reach out to each other. Room to smother him with lemon soap, and then have him do the same to her. And then their two slippery bodies came together, with soap bubbles running down between them as he frothed up her hair with something out of a bottle with a clean zingy sort of smell that reminded her of the sea shore. It was blue, and fresh-feeling, and again she tipped back her head, laughing now as he took the shower head from its holder and rinsed the shampoo away, his hand delving into her short crop of blonde hair, squeezing and squeaking it, squeezing and squeaking until it was clean and fresh and shining. It was an act of love-making in itself, that erotic cleansing of her hair. She revelled in the feel of his strong fingers as they massaged her scalp. And each time his hand buried itself in her hair, then pulled itself free again, it was like the surge and thrust of a lover.

And then he replaced the shower head, and as she shook the drops of water from her face, she felt him move against her. He lifted her gently, with both his big hands on her waist, almost encircling it. She slid against him easily, gasping when his mouth was level with her breasts, and his lips brushed against one tight, taut nipple.

He played with it, his tongue circling it, his teeth sliding over it. He teased it into a still harder bud and she heard him growl softly as he felt her response to him. Her breath caught in her throat and as he lifted her higher, she wound her legs tightly around his hips so she could stay in the position she liked best, moving slowly up and down against the flat of his stomach, crazily, agonizingly aware of the hard shaft of flesh just below her body that was touching her and growing more taut and insistent each time she moved against it.

Her breathing was sharp and shallow. She heard him give a deep-throated groan, then he was sliding aside the shower screen and carrying her out onto the hessian mat outside it. She grabbed at a towel and rubbed at her hair. 'What are you doing?' he said, lowering her slowly to the ground, sliding her wet body down the length of his. Still locked against him, with his hands resting on her hips, she could feel the strength and power of his arousal. She stood on tip-toe, pressing her body against him, and gave his hair a brisk rub too, thrilling afresh as the friction between them increased.

Her voice low, she said, 'I don't want to wet your pillow.'

His hands slid down to her buttocks and he pulled her close against him. 'Damn the pillows. We can chuck them on the floor.'

She dropped the towel and dug her fingers into the sparse and firm flesh of his shoulders, and a ripple of desire threaded through her.

'Holt!' she said softly, and lifted her face so that his lips might find hers again, and when they did, she murmured against them, 'Love me.'

Somehow, locked together, they reached the bedroom. He clicked a light switch as he pushed open the door. She reached past him, her lips still locked tight on his, and clicked it off again. He kicked the door open still wider to allow them access side by side into the room.

'There's light enough coming in from the landing,' she said, laughing softly. 'We don't need anything glaring.'

'I want to see you properly. All of you. It's been a long time . . .' He gazed down hungrily at her.

They stood still, facing each other, just inside the door. The interior of the room was in deep shadow and she couldn't make out what the furniture was like. She distinguished, however, that it was cumbersome and heavy, and also detected the scent of real wood – old-fashioned wood that had been carefully preserved with bees wax and lavender. Under her bare feet the floor was carpeted with something springy and warm; she curled her toes into it – genuine wool. The house had a warm, cared-for air about it, and knowing Holt as she did, she realized there would be nothing artificial about it, or its contents. Plastic, and glass-topped tables would be out!

He put his arm round her shoulders and walked her right inside his bedroom and her eyes began getting accustomed to the gloom. He let go of her and walked over to the bed.

She didn't want him to leave her. She wanted him right there beside her – wanted him holding her – wanted him inside her.

God! How she wanted him.

He threw several pillows and a duvet onto the floor. She didn't feel wet all over any more, but there was a hotness and a wetness inside her and a lingering ache to have him come back to her so she could hold him again.

He came across the room and she feasted her eyes on the long, rangy body, the wide shoulders, and the dark hair that she knew would still be damp across his chest and down to that narrow vee just above his waist. He was caught in the gleam from the lamp outside the room, and he was hard and aroused more than ever, she saw.

Her heart leapt inside her as she ran to him, and was enfolded in his arms again. He didn't take her back to the bed. He kicked the cushions and quilt into a haphazard kind of order on the floor, then swept her up into his arms and together they went down into the feather-soft nest.

He raised himself on one elbow and gazed down into her face. The light from beyond the door was bathing them both in a subdued glow; the room was warm. The heat seemed to be coming from over by the window where there was a square of night sky and bright stars watching them. Even with the door open as it was, there were no draughts in the depths of their makeshift bed. Warmth seemed to be creeping in and around them like the muted light from beyond the door was doing too. She gazed up into his eyes and he bent and dropped little light kisses on her forehead and her eyes.

She rested her hand on his chest and found the curled mass of dark body hair still damp as she'd known it would be. His flesh moved under her touch as he drew in his breath. He cupped one of her breasts in his hand and bent his head to kiss the rosy nub of it.

She traced a line down to his waist, and with the flat of her hand, smoothed out the curls of hair – smoothed them out straight, pulling them tight under her hand until they reached beyond and below his waist. She felt his muscles tense again, heard the hissing of his breath as he sucked in a great lungful of air. She touched him gently then closed her hand around that most intimate part of him, that throbbing hard shaft, and gently she held it, barely moving her hand at all except for a light movement of her thumb against it.

His kisses became more urgent. He hooked his arm around her neck and leaned over her. His other hand worked round from her breast, delved down to her waist and then spread-eagled itself across the bikini line of fine blonde hair below it. She moved her legs, parting them slightly, and then a spasm of exquisite sensation shot through her, making her arch the whole of her body towards him as his strong, but gentle fingers parted and separated the fount of her womanhood and then slid inside her.

It was like the washing of her hair all over again, except this time it was more intimate, more sensuous. And this time it didn't end with a dousing of water and a squeezing and squeaking. This time it went on and on, until she was spiralling out of control, her body on fire, as it pulsed and strained and obeyed centuries-old laws – laws that demanded and insisted upon her absolute acquiescence.

He was not without regard for safety though. Somewhere during the heady spiralling of all her emotions, she felt him ease his arm from around her neck and slide something against the hand that was still touching him so intimately. Her fingers were quick and nimble, fitting the sheath easily with seconds to spare before he reared over her and plunged inside her.

She was alive. Vibrantly so. For the first time in months, she was no longer tense. With every thrust he was binding her closer to him, and the world started spinning faster – and everything was out of control now.

She cried out, and he gasped her name over and over as they whirled to a mind-numbing pinnacle where thought was stilled, but where the physical whirlpool engulfing them swirled and surged to the ultimate climax of all human passion.

'I never told you I loved you,' he said later when they lay, fingers laced together, bodies abandoned and sated on the pillows strewn over the floor. He jerked over from his back to face her and his eyes were stricken.

'Serena – I never once told you I loved you.'

'You did tell me,' she said. 'We told each other, didn't we?' She wriggled nearer to him until their naked bodies were touching again. 'You told me with this.' She smoothed a path right down his torso with the flat of her hand. 'With your body – and with mine too – we spoke the words that millions of lovers the world over understand. What is that line in the marriage ceremony? "With my body, I thee worship"?'

Slowly, cautiously, he held her eyes with his own and asked, 'Are you going to marry me?'

'Are you going to ask me?' Her eyes were bright as she gazed up at him in the semi-darkness.

'Marry me, Serena.'

'Yes please,' she replied softly, moving rapturously into the circle of his arms again.

CHAPTER 18

Serena gazed around the sitting room and tucked her duster and tin of polish under her arm.

The whole of the little house in Caindale was ready now, she decided, for Kirsty's first visit.

Ryan had phoned her at the office a couple of days ago and asked her if he could bring Kirsty and the baby over at the weekend, and she'd been delighted to tell him he could.

'You don't have to stay at the inn, you know,' she'd told him. 'The house is as much yours as it is mine. We chose it together.'

'It's better this way, love. Two women in one kitchen? You know what they say about that, don't you?'

'But I'm at the foundry all day. It seems a bit silly – you two and the baby having to make do in one room at the hotel. And it's such a waste of money.'

He'd sighed. 'Don't go on, Sera. I can't risk losing Kirsty again. We like it this way – even if we are cramped up in the one room, and with baby Reanne stuffed into a tiny crib at the side of us.'

'I could always move out of the house . . .'

She'd heard him give a snort on the other end of the phone. 'Don't be an idiot, Sera. It's your house, for God's sake. I'm not going to push you out.'

'I think Mari would put me up for a while – just until you two get things sorted out . . .'

'Talk sense,' he'd snapped. 'You'd hate it. You know you would being a visitor in the house that was once your old home.'

Silently she'd agreed with him. It wasn't the best idea she'd ever had, she knew. But she was just so happy now she and Holt had made up past differences that she wanted everybody to feel as euphoric as she did. So far, she hadn't told Ryan that things were working out fine for her and Holt. She'd tell him at the weekend, she decided, when Kirsty was with him. She hoped he wouldn't think she was being heartless – taking up with somebody else when Don had been dead for such a short while. But he'd known of course that her marriage to his father hadn't exactly been a love match.

No! She and Don had been honest with each other; he had never really got over his love for Ryan's mother who had deserted the pair of them, and Serena hadn't hidden the fact that if Holt had offered marriage, then she would never have gone to Australia in the first place.

Ryan would understand; she just knew he would.

Now though, there were other things to think about. She wanted the place to look welcoming for Kirsten and the baby. She turned away from the parlour, satisfied that it was adequately dusted and vacuumed. A small fire was crackling away in the cast iron grate. She frowned slightly, then walked over to it, bent down and adjusted the front grate so that more air was sucked through to the fire and sent sparks crackling up the chimney. Babies needed warmth, and she was forced to admit that there were some almighty draughts creeping into the house through the crevices of the old sash windows. The letter box in the front door clattered up and down too whenever a gust of wind blew up the steep cliffside from the sea. She couldn't do much about the draughts today though, she decided. Maybe later on, before putting the place up for sale again, she'd think about installing central heating, and having new doors and double-glazed windows fitted.

Ruefully she realized that she still hadn't spoken to Holt about her father's plan for making and finding a market for his decorative doors.

But there had been other, more important things on both their minds on that never-to-be-forgotten night!

She heard the sound of a car grinding up the steep hillside, and quickly she ran over to the window and glanced outside. Mark Crabtree operated the only taxi service for miles around, and the familiar and cumbersome big black car was slowly negotiating the tortuous bends of the hill.

She tore off her apron as she dashed through to the kitchen to get rid of the evidence of her super-cleaning spree. That done, she hurried to the front door and flung it open.

Kirsty had the baby in a car carry-seat, and was holding it by the handle – much as people did with a supermarket basket – Serena thought with a silent chuckle. As the Australian girl came bouncing up to the front door, leaving Ryan to pay Mark and arrange for the return pick-up, Serena held out her hands for the baby.

Kirsty tossed back her dark hair and her eyes were sparkling. 'Hi, Serena. It's lovely to see you again.'

Serena took the baby from her. 'It's been a long time since I've known him to be so happy, Kirsten.' Then softly she added, 'I hope you don't blame me for taking him away from Australia – *and* away from you.'

Kirsty glanced back at Ryan, then whispered, 'Of course I don't blame you. He put you in an impossible position – making you promise not to tell me there was anything wrong with him. It must have been awful for you – doubly awful, losing Don like that as well . . .'

The pain of remembrance shot through Serena as she led the way into the parlour, and again she became worried about how Ryan would accept the news she had to tell him. Would he think she was being disloyal to his father's memory, she wondered queasily? Was it too soon to start thinking about another man? Another husband? After all, it had only been a few months . . .

She heard the front door being slammed shut and winced. In a few short weeks she'd forgotten about Ryan's exuberance when he was in a good mood and feeling better than usual.

Outside the house, Mark's taxi was doing a laborious three point turn in the road. Serena placed baby Reanne's carry-seat on the coffee table, and then knelt down at the side of it and pulled aside the shawl that was half hiding the baby's face, as Ryan came into the room.

She drew in her breath and sat back on her heels. 'She is so lovely.' Her eyes met those of Kirsty who was crouching at the other side of the baby.

'She's terrific, isn't she?' Kirsty grinned. 'I guess I'm prejudiced though.'

Ryan had walked over to the window to watch Mark's departure. He turned back to them as the sound of the car engine faded away. 'She's the absolute image of me,' he said proudly. 'Even *I* can see that.'

'Mmmm.' Serena shot a look of mischief at Kirsten, then gave all her attention to Ryan and said calmly, 'Yes. I can see it now. That rosebud mouth, those adorable long silky lashes, and that little snub nose.'

Ryan flushed crimson and threw up his hands in mock despair. 'Trust you!' he said, 'to cut a guy down to size.'

Serena grimaced at Kirsten. 'They can't take a joke, can they? Men?'

Kirsty laughed. 'Not this one, anyway.' But she turned her face to Ryan, and Serena saw the love shining out of her eyes. Softly Kirsten said, 'But I wouldn't swap him. I think he's got me well and truly hooked.'

After a cup of tea, and as Kirsten sat patting the baby's back after giving her a feed, Ryan said, 'Sera – would you mind if we left the baby with you while I show Kirsty around Caindale?'

'Of course not. I'd love to have her for a couple of hours.'

He beamed at Kirsten. 'There! I told you she wouldn't mind.'

Serena still hadn't plucked up the courage to mention that she and Holt were together again, but now was not the right time to do that, she decided.

She had a sudden thought. 'Hey – could I take her over to Wintersgill? Mari would love to see her, and I know she'll be at home this afternoon. She never goes out on a Sunday.'

'Mari?' Kirsten glanced from one to the other of them. 'At Wintersgill? That must be the woman I spoke to on the phone when I was at the airport?'

'Mari was my father's partner,' Serena said without flinching. 'They lived together after my mother died.'

She'd accepted now that Max and Mari had been a pair. They'd been happy together, she knew, and it was

256

senseless blaming them for living as man and wife for all those years. She supposed though that marriage – to her mind at any rate – might have made the alliance a little more respectable. Somehow, although she took it for granted that many couples lived together without getting married nowadays, it still seemed slightly immoral to imagine her own father doing it.

It was crazy, she knew, and it was also like having double standards. But it was too close to home for comfort when it was her own father 'living in sin' – as most of the population of Caindale would see it. She cursed herself constantly for thinking as she did, and for being so narrow-minded, but reluctantly had come to the conclusion that Max had been a law unto himself.

And when her mind turned to that way of thinking, all the old barriers were set up once more, and all the prejudice she'd felt came surging back. Max, she was sure, had broken her mother's heart by his unfaithfulness, and knowing that, she hardened her own heart against him, and could not forgive.

But there was nothing to be gained from hating Mari. Mari, without the benefit of wedlock, had her own cross to bear, she knew.

'That's a great idea. I like Mari.' Ryan bounded across the room, scooped the baby up out of Kirsten's arms and carrying her over to the carry-seat said, 'Come here, Sera. I'll show you how to fasten her in. And then there's this harness affair that slides through the seat belts in the car. You have to make sure it's secure – and in the front passenger seat, with the baby facing towards the back of the car . . .'

Kirsty stood up, shaking her head at him and smiling across at Serena. 'He's nothing but an old mother hen,' she announced. 'Goodness only knows how he'll deal with it when she's old enough to start dating.'

A silence descended on the room. Ryan's gaze dropped hungrily to the face of the sleeping child. 'If I still happen to be around then,' he said softly.

Kirsten walked over to him, grasped his arm and shook him gently. 'Hey,' she said. 'You know what we agreed? We'll live one day at a time, huh? There's no room in this relationship for doubts or self pity.'

The look of utter adoration in his eyes, as he gazed down at the girl he loved, moved Serena almost to tears. She blinked them away rapidly though as she said, 'Okay, "new" daddy! Show me how this thing works then.'

Ryan grinned. 'I'll do better than that. When Kirsty and I get back from our tramp round Caindale, I'll cook us all a meal. How does five-thirty suit you? Can you get back from Wintersgill by then?'

'Sure I can,' Serena said. 'It's less than half an hour's drive across the moors from Wintersgill. You know your way around the kitchen and pantry – so have fun, you two.'

Ryan and Kirsty linked arms and watched as Serena drove away with little Reanne – in her carry-seat – firmly fastened in the passenger seat beside her.

When the car was out of sight round the last steep bend on the hillside, Ryan sighed and said, 'It's strange – seeing somebody else with her. I hate letting her go, don't you?'

'I'm more used to it than you are.' Kirsty grinned up at him. 'You forget – I had to leave her with Holly when I was nosing around Caindale looking for you.'

Ryan groaned. 'Don't remind me,' he said. 'I have nightmares about chasing you the way I did – and then almost losing you when you tripped up and fell over the cliff.'

'Now that *was* scary.' Kirsty shivered. 'It's right what they say, you know. The whole of your life *does* flash in front of your eyes.' Her fingers tightened on his arm. 'While I was hanging there, with you clutching at my hand, I lived through the birth of Reanne again, and then everything that had gone before.'

'You should have told me about her,' he said gently, his gaze misty as it rested on her upturned face. 'I would never have left Australia if I'd known about the baby.'

'You didn't trust me,' she said. 'It's that which hurts me, Ry. Knowing that, as close as we'd been, you couldn't trust me to carry on loving you when you were in trouble.'

'I thought you'd start to pity me.' He pulled her round to face him, and his face was grim as he went on, 'I didn't want you burdening yourself with me.'

'Yet you allowed Sera to "burden" herself.' There was pain in her eyes. 'I still can't understand why you did that.'

He leaned back his head and looked up at the sky. 'Under this bare blue heaven I've had lots of time to think logically about what happened to me.' For long seconds he was silent, then he brought his gaze back to her and said, 'I don't know why I turned to Sera though. I was in a mess, Kirsty. I just didn't know which way to turn, and Sera was somebody I could depend on. God knows how she got us through what happened to Dad, but she did. I guess I knew that there was no danger of her and me getting too close. Do you know what I mean?'

'No.' Kirsty shook her head.

'Well . . .' Ryan let out a long, low sigh, 'Being married to my Dad, and me never knowing my mother, I suppose I looked on her as a kind of mother figure. What I'm getting at is – I'd never be able to fall in love with Sera. I was safe

259

if I stuck with her. I knew she'd take care of me without sentiment – or whatever you could call it – getting in the way.'

'You trusted her.'

'Yeah! I guess so. That must be what I'm trying to say.'

'But I was the one you should have trusted.'

Seriously he looked into her eyes and said, 'I *loved* you, honey. I was crazy about you. I couldn't let you throw your life away on me.'

She went into his arms and buried her head against his shoulder. 'I'll never, never understand you,' she muttered, then, laughing softly, she looked at him again and said, 'You and me – we're alone now. For the first time since I arrived in England. Alone!'

'It's a great feeling, huh?' He grinned. 'I'm missing little honey-bunch already though.'

She thumped him. 'You've got *me*,' she said. 'Do I have to spell it out? We have the house to ourselves for a couple of hours.'

'I'm going to show you round Caindale,' he said. 'We told Sera that's what we were going to do.'

'Sera won't know if we don't do as we said. Sera won't know if we stay here and just be together.'

Amusement danced in his eyes. 'I only had a single bed when I lived here.'

'We can manage with a single bed, can't we?'

'I can't do that. Not here.' His laugh had a gruff sound to it. 'Heck, Kirsty, I couldn't face Sera if we'd . . .'

'Okay!' She placed two fingers gently on his lips. 'Okay, Ry! It was just a thought.' She grimaced. 'Now I *know* there was nothing between you and Sera – you're talking about her as if she really was your mom.'

'In a way she was. She married my dad.'

'And I bet you hid your head under the bedcovers when they went to bed together, didn't you?'

Sheepishly, he said, 'Sometimes. Even though my bedroom was at one end of the bungalow and theirs was at the other.'

'You're funny. You know that, don't you?'

He nodded. 'I guess so.'

'We manage okay at the inn though, don't we?'

He kissed the tip of her nose. 'Baby Reanne's too little to know about such things – and anyway, we always wait till she's asleep.'

'You are very inhibited for a young man of the nineties.' Kirsty gave a deep chuckle.

'We'll go back to Australia – back to Dad's bungalow, huh?'

She nodded, and her eyes sparkled. 'I can't wait. But meanwhile, I don't see why we should let that single bed upstairs go to waste do you?'

It was more than an hour later when Ryan got round to dicing peeled potatoes and carrots with a sharp kitchen knife in readiness for the evening meal. Cubed chicken pieces had been lightly fried and placed in an ovenproof dish beside him on the kitchen table.

'Damn!' he said suddenly, looking up at Kirsty who was sitting with her legs curled under her in an easy chair beside the fire.

'What's wrong?' Her gentle smile was lazy as a sleepy kitten's.

'Don't look at me like that,' he warned, wagging the knife at her. 'Don't go all misty-eyed again. You know darn well I don't have an ounce of will-power where you're concerned.'

'I only asked you what's wrong,' she said with a chuckle.

'No onions,' he said. 'I knew something was missing when I put all this lot out on the table.'

'Can't you manage without onions?'

He gave her a look that spoke volumes and said, 'Look – I know you don't know the first thing about cooking, love, but . . .'

'Okay!' She held up one hand. 'It's not the end of the world though, is it? Having no onions?'

'I need them for the casserole.'

'Aren't there any in the garden?'

He dropped the sharp-bladed knife on the table and growled, 'Of course not. It's a flower garden. Sera planted daffodil bulbs.' He jerked his head towards the window. 'Take a look – lots of lovely daffodils flowering out there, and one or two tulips too, but no veggie.'

'You want me to go get some onions, is that it? I have to go out on a Sunday afternoon and find the nearest super-store?'

He grinned. 'They don't have superstores in Caindale. They do have a great little corner shop called "Maddie's" though that never shuts.'

She sighed and uncoiled herself from the chair to stand up straight in front of him. She shot out one hand. 'Give me the right money then. I can't get the hang of pounds and pennies over here in England. I feel a right nutter having to stand there converting from dollars to pounds when I go in a shop.'

'Onions don't cost as much as a pound.' He started to laugh, and fished in his trouser pocket for some loose change which he tipped out into her hand. 'There! A fifty pence piece, some twenties, tens and twos. How's that?'

'This will buy me some onions?' She cocked one eyebrow at him.

'Tell Maddie you want roughly a pound and a half.'

'Maddie!'

'Maddie owns the place. She's sixty-six, in years, in inches round her middle, and in inches high. You can't mistake Maddie for anybody else.'

'Why don't you go?' She scowled. 'It's a foreign language they speak round here. You understand it. I don't.'

'I'm going to get the oven up to temperature.'

'Big deal.' She screwed up her nose at him.

'Get off with you, woman.'

'I don't even know where the blessed shop is.'

He took hold of her shoulders and steered her towards the front door. 'Oh, come on. I'll point it out to you. You can see it from here, but it's right down near the medical centre.'

'The place where Sera's father stands guard?'

'That's right. It's only just round the corner from there.'

She whirled round to face him. 'Okay! I'll find it. You stay here. Don't come to the door – you'll get cold.'

'I like the way you look after me.' He pulled her to him and kissed her roundly on the lips.

She pushed the money he'd given her into the pocket of her jeans, then hung onto his shoulders with both hands and made him kiss her again. 'I won't be long,' she promised. 'I'll run all the way, if you like.'

'It'll take the gas oven at least twenty minutes to heat up,' he said, gently stroking back the hair from her forehead. 'So don't rush. Have a look round the place. That way you'll be able to talk knowledgeably about

263

Caindale and what you've seen to Sera when she comes back.'

She gave him a knowing look. 'And Sera will never know that we didn't go exploring, like you said we would? Is that it?'

Tenderly he kissed her again. 'We made the bed up again,' he said. 'She'll never guess we stayed in.'

'It was good, huh?' Her eyes met with his in a long look of understanding.

'It was good, Kirsty. It's always good – with you, my darling.'

He closed the front door after watching her go walking off down the hill, then he went back to the kitchen. What was it he'd been going to do next, he wondered? His mind was hazy. On the table were chopped up carrots and potatoes. As he looked at them, their outlines suddenly blurred and a shaft of pain shot through his head.

'God! No!' he groaned. Then, 'Pills. Where are those goddam pills?'

His gaze roved round the kitchen. His brow was furrowed. Everything was jumbling up inside his brain. He made an attempt to sort it all out.

'Gas cooker,' he said firmly. 'Must get it up to temperature.' He walked over to the stove and turned one of the little knobs at the front of it. Gas hissed out of a burner on the top. He shook his head. 'Wrong one! How could I have forgotten so soon?' He bent down and pulled open the door, then knelt in front of the appliance. He turned his head to one side to listen for the familiar hiss again as, his brain fuzzing over, he tried each little knob in turn and finally found the right one. His head was feeling light and strange. It was also thumping, heralding another of those turns that usually resulted in him being flat out in bed for the next half a dozen hours.

The gas was still hissing inside the oven.

'Lighter!' he muttered to himself. 'Where's the damn lighter?'

It was a long metal stick thing, he remembered. You didn't need to use a match, you just had to shove the stick inside the oven, right to the back of it where the gas jets were – and click it to make a spark.

He remembered seeing the safety lighter on one of the units earlier, and rose to his feet. As he did so, pain came, wave after wave of it, like the sea rolling onto the shore in slow motion. He was unable to think straight.

'Pills?' They were in his coat pocket! He always carried them with him. And his coat? Where had Sera put his coat? They'd been in the sitting room at the front of the house when they'd first arrived that afternoon – was that where he'd left it?

He wandered into the passageway that linked kitchen and sitting room together, passing the bottom of the stairs as he did so, and remembering that he and Kirsty had been up there after Sera had driven away.

He climbed woozily up to the first floor bedroom, each step of the way rocketing pain around his head. But there was no sign of his coat in the front bedroom, and the pills were in its pocket, he was convinced of that now.

Back down in the sitting room, he found his coat had fallen off the back of one of the chairs onto the floor. He bent down to pick it up, and everything went black. He came to again, how long afterwards he couldn't guess, but he was sitting with his back against the wall, and his hand was fumbling with a bottle of pills that had a childproof top on it. He couldn't get enough pressure on it to move it, and that frustrated him.

'Damn! Hell! Damn the bloody thing.' He hurled it at the door, but still the top stayed on, and the bottle didn't break because it was made of plastic. He crawled after it, picked it up, then found he couldn't get to his feet. His legs kept folding up under him. He managed to crawl into the little passageway between sitting room and kitchen. There was a funny smell . . .

'God! No! The gas. Must – find – that – lighter thing. . .'

But it was too late. Darkness overcame him again, and he felt himself drifting, floating. It wasn't a bad feeling. It was warm. Of course it was warm, he told himself, there was a ruddy great fire blazing away in the kitchen grate . . .

Serena saw Kirsty striding down the road back towards the sea shore, and slowed the car as she came level with her.

Kirsty yanked the back door open and poked her head inside. 'Thank heaven it's you,' she panted. 'You don't mind if I hop in and have a lift up the hill, do you?'

'That's why I stopped the car,' Serena said. 'But what on earth are you doing here? Have you lost Ryan somewhere along the way? You're almost a mile from the house.'

'Ryan is cooking dinner.' Kirsty flopped into the rear seat behind baby Reanne who was asleep, and fastened in her car carrier beside Serena.

'He sent you out alone? To see the sights of Caindale?' Serena flashed her a smile as she started up the car again.

'No.' Kirsty shook her head. 'It wasn't like that.' She gave a shaky little laugh. 'You're early. We didn't expect you back until five-thirty. Ryan's going to be blazing mad with me for taking so long to go and buy a pound and a half of onions.'

'Onions?'

'He's making some sort of chicken stew stuff. Sent me out to "Maddie's" place for some. He said that Maddie's shop is never closed, but when I got there, the shutters were up and everything was locked up. Maddie must be taking a holiday.'

'So where did you go?' Serena was driving slowly down the road past Maddie's shop now, then round the long bend towards the medical centre also closed for the weekend. She glanced at the bronze figure of her father as she passed it.

'I walked right to the other end of the valley – but there are no more shops. Ryan will have to manage without onions, I'm afraid. Surely it won't make that much difference to the dinner?'

'There are some hanging up in the coal shed,' Serena said with a laugh. 'If only he'd looked in there, it would have saved you a lot of time and trouble.'

'Heck! And I did ask him if there were any in the garden.' Kirsty laughed too.

They could see the house now. Serena was making sure she took the tight bends slowly and carefully as the steep hillside rose in front of them. Kirsty leaned forward and rested her arms on the back of the passenger seat where she could watch the sleeping baby.

Serena just started to say, 'Maybe we'd be better settling for scrambled eggs on toast for tea . . .' when there was an almighty flash up in front of them, and an explosion that reverberated right through the ground underneath them.

'What the . . .' Kirsty gripped the seat as Serena slammed on the brakes.

They both stared in horror up at the place where the house had been. But all they could see now was a gigantic pall of black smoke with flames shooting through it, up to the dazzling blue of the sky.

CHAPTER 19

Holt was standing more than half way down the grassy slope of the north cliff when he saw Serena's car coming down Caindale's main street.

The valley was deserted, except for the figure of a lone girl, walking some distance ahead of the car. As he watched with interest, he guessed that Serena must have recognized the walker, because as she drew level with the girl, she slowed the car and then brought it to a standstill.

Still watching, he saw the girl tug one of the doors open and speak briefly to Serena before climbing into the back of the car.

It must be Kirsten, he decided, for when he'd been at the foundry to pick up a load of iron castings for despatch the other day, he'd paused for a brief word with Serena in the office and she'd told him Ryan and Kirsten were going over to see her at the weekend.

'*You can come over for tea on Sunday as well, if you'd like to,*' *she'd invited.*

Mockingly he replied, 'I don't think that's a very good idea. Does he know that I thought you were married to him? Your Ryan?'

269

'I don't think so. He'd have teased me unmercifully about it if he'd had the slightest inkling about that.'

'Serena – honey – I've been all kinds of a fool . . .'

Her eyes softened. 'No you haven't. You were jealous, and jealous people aren't always the most rational kind.'

'It seems crazy now. I've never been the jealous sort.'

'I don't mind you being just a little bit jealous.'

They'd talked about Ryan and Kirsten and the baby after that, but in the end he'd declined her invitation to go over for tea. Eyes narrowed now, he watched the progress of her car. As it reached the hairpin bend adjacent to the sea, she slowed her speed so as to take it in safety.

His steps were sure on the springy turf of the hillside as he tackled the last part of the steep slope under the headland. She'd be surprised when he turned up, he knew. But it was precisely because they'd talked about the Australian couple the other night, that he was making his way to her house, right now.

Serena had been worried about Ryan and Kirsten having nowhere to live except at the inn at Rivelyn. It couldn't be easy, she'd said, living in one room, and with a baby there too.

He'd thought about her words all week, and gradually, an idea had formed in his mind. And now he wanted to sound her out about it. Wanted to put it to them all, he supposed. But he'd never been the sort of bloke to gate-crash a party, he reminded himself, and the thought of presenting himself on her doorstep at four o'clock on a Sunday afternoon when he knew darn well she was entertaining visitors didn't appeal to him one bit.

But it was important that he talked to them all when they were there together – about the big caravan he'd still got stored at the truck depot – the caravan – 'mobile home', he corrected himself, that he'd lived in while he was doing up the old house. It had been comfortable and spacious – far too big for one man, but to his mind, it would be just right for Ryan and Kirsten and the kiddie. And he could site it again, on the cliff top near his home, it would be nice and private for them there, and the view was stupendous . . .

His feet started to slide in the shale at the foot of the cliffs, and there were boulders too that had to be avoided. He made his way carefully, then glanced across the wide sandy bay where the Caindale beck swept its way into the sea. It was a fine cold day. The sky was blue and reflected its colour in the sea, but the Caindale beck still had that hint of red in it.

Serena's car was taking the hill and the bends slowly, and he smiled to himself, reckoning that travelling on foot, he wouldn't be much more than five more minutes later than she was, arriving at the house . . .

Then it happened!

The flash, the blinding explosion on the opposite hill-side, sent him reeling.

At first, thoroughly sickened to the pit of his stomach, he thought it was her car that had exploded, and invo-luntarily he screamed out her name as he flung himself down the last bit of the hillside and started to race out across the sands.

The Caindale beck – a twelve feet wide rushing torrent – barred his path. It proved no obstacle to his headlong flight however. In his mind, the girl he loved was in danger. He ploughed right through the water. It swirled round his knees. He stumbled and fell over boulders in its bed. But nothing could stop him. He floundered in the water. Tripped over his own booted feet, but miraculously kept his balance. Then he was scrambling out the other side. Thirty seconds, he reckoned, was all it took him. And to have gone round by the road would have taken several precious minutes.

With a sob in his throat, he was able to focus his gaze upwards again, though he dreaded what kind of sight might meet his eyes. But for the first time in years he was able to utter what amounted to a prayer.

'Thank God! Thank God!'

She was safe!

The car had come to a standstill. It hadn't gone up in flames after all. His glance was drawn to the top of the hill, and with a gutted feeling inside him he saw it was the house that had exploded.

Exploded and disappeared.

There wasn't a sign of it, but a cloud of black smoke was where it used to be, and flames were zipping up towards the sky, tongues of orange fire flicking out and upwards, dancing and darting . . .

The car was moving forward again. 'No-o-o!' he bellowed, desperately afraid for her now. Sparks from the flames were peppering the hillside, and huge splinters of burning wood were shooting out of the fire and drifting down on the grass around the pigeon lofts. It only needed one of those firebrands to land in the path of the car and the petrol tank might ignite.

'No-o-o!' He weaved in and out among the boats that were moored on the beach, then clambered up onto the road and followed the car, running in the middle of the road, his arms waving.

'Sto-o-op! Seren-a-a! For God's sake – Sto-o-op!'

The car stopped as it neared the terrace, pulled into the

side of the road, and he saw Serena all but tumble out of it and race madly round to the other side. She flung the door open. The girl in the back seat was also out. They were both leaning inside the car. Why the hell didn't they just get right away from it, he fumed.

'Leave the damn car,' he yelled, breathless now and panting as he came up to them.

'The baby . . .' She bobbed her head out and shouted. And then he saw some sort of harness was hindering them. But they had the baby out now, and Serena was pushing the carrying seat at Kirsten and then spinning round to him.

'I have to move the car,' she gasped. 'The emergency services – this is the only way they can come.'

Kirsten was standing white-faced and shaken, hardly aware of the baby in her arms. She was staring blindly at what had been Serena's house.

'See to her.' he muttered. 'She's in shock. I'll move the car.'

'Holt! It's too dangerous. Look at all those sparks.'

The air was filled with the acrid smell of burning wood. Smoke was drifting down the hillside all around them, and they continually had to dodge aside as burning, crackling debris showered down. He slid inside the car and started the engine, shouting to them to keep clear of it. He reversed it then, back down the hill, till he found a spot where the road widened into a kind of layby that was often used as a vantage point for picnickers. He parked it there, got out and locked it. At least the road was clear now.

He ran back up the hill then, but they couldn't get near the house. The flames beat them back. Kirsten was crying. It was a horrible sound. He wished she'd stop. They were safe, weren't they?

Serena flung round to him, and he saw tears and blackened smoke smudges on her cheeks.

'Ryan . . .' she sobbed. 'Ryan was in there.'

'God . . . no!'. He stared at her. She had to be mistaken. Nobody could have survived in that lot.

Far off in the distance, the whole of Caindale away, he heard the sound of a police car, and the strident siren of a fire engine. He jerked his head round. 'Somebody must have phoned . . .' He stared through the swirling heat mass and saw figures moving about on the other side of the pall of billowing smoke and flames.

'Ryan,' she whispered again, and she moved nearer to the girl with the baby and put her arm round her shoulders and held her tight.

He shook his head to try and clear it so he could think logically about what he had to do. There was only thing he could do, he decided. He started moving forward, towards the heap of blackened bricks, the choking black smoke and the flames that, thankfully, were starting to die down a little. The parlour ceiling was just a twisted mass of smouldering wooden joists. Even as he watched, one giant beam collapsed with a crash.

He heard Serena screaming out his name.

'Holt! No! Come back . . .' but her voice was lost in the crackling and the hissing of age-old wood as he put his arm up in front of his face and ploughed through debris several feet thick that consisted of smashed glass and smouldering window frames, and the bricks, wood and dust that was littering the whole of the street in front of the terrace.

The heat was terrifying. If Ryan was still alive it would be a miracle, he reasoned. But he had to try and get to him if it were at all possible. He could hear the sound of sirens, nearer now. They were coming up the hill. Thank goodness he'd managed to shift the car out of their way. People were milling around him.

'Now't can be saved, lad. Might as well leave it to t'firemen now.'

He glanced towards the voice. George was standing there, shaking his head glumly.

'The guy who used to live there?' Holt snapped. 'What happened to him? Did he get out?'

'Young Ryan?' George's mouth dropped open. 'He don't live there any more.'

'He was there today though. Visiting.' Holt felt like shaking the old man. 'Did you see him, George? Did he get out?'

George shook his head. 'Nobody could get out o' that lot. It were like a bomb goin' off. Some of us were already outside our 'ouses when it 'appened. There was this 'orrible smell of gas, see . . .'

Holt turned back towards the house. There was a chance – just the slightest chance that Ryan had been near the front of the house when the explosion occurred. And if he had been, then there might be some hope of finding him. He raced forward, feeling the heat scorching his face. He pulled at the collar of his coat and held it high up against his face. The knuckles on his hand reddened, but the flames were not so violent now. The gable end of the house had been blown outward. The stairs were lying across a great heap of rubble, and looked like a grotesque and giant see-saw, with one end of them sticking up high in the air. Bricks, beams and a mountain of glass and mortar lay across the middle of the see-saw. Ryan *might* just be down there, underneath the stairs.

Shading his face with his other hand he glanced round at what was left standing of the house – and saw that the only wall intact was that one joined up to the next house along the row. Half way along it, and fifteen feet above the ground, a washbasin clung pathetically to a patch of white porcelain tiles. Water was cascading down the wall where the bathroom supply had been ruptured.

He approached the almost horizontal staircase with care, then almost lost his balance as a jet of water hit him. He gasped and half turned. The fire-fighters were playing water on him and he was glad of it. One of them yelled to him to 'Get out of there, mate! Leave it to us.'

He pointed to the stairs, then wasted no more time, but started carefully moving hot bricks, smoking wood, and anything that was barring his way to the triangular under-part of the staircase. He was joined by a figure in dark protective clothing and a yellow hat, then another, and another. 'Get back to where it's safe,' somebody said, trying to haul him away from the rubble, but Holt had seen something.

'He's there! Look! A hand . . .'

Somehow they got Ryan out, and he was still breathing when he was lifted into the ambulance.

Holt watched as Kirsten went with him. He wiped his face with his hand. His eyes were sore and his throat parched with the heat. Serena was standing with her back to him, watching as the ambulance was driven away. He couldn't see her face. He walked over to her, stood behind her.

'You should get away from here.' His voice was husky with the smoke and the dust he'd inhaled.

She turned slowly round to him, and he saw she was holding the baby's car seat in her arms. It turned his heart over seeing her so, her face taut and drawn, yet with the

276

ultimate of compassion in it as she glanced down at the tiny face swaddled in a blanket.

'Holt . . .!' Her eyes flickered upwards to his. 'You saved him. Nobody knew he was there . . .'

He shrugged. 'It was just a hunch – he couldn't be anywhere else but under the damn stairs. There was nothing else left.'

'I – I don't know what to do. The baby . . . What shall I do with the baby? Kirsten couldn't take her in the ambulance – she just dumped her on me.'

'We can't stand around with her – all this smoke – it's not good for her.' He grasped hold of Serena's shoulder and pushed her in front of him, back down the hill towards her car.

She sank into the back seat with the baby who was grizzling now. He turned round from the driving seat and said, 'You're coming home with me.'

She didn't argue with that but said, 'What about baby food?'

'There's bound to be a shop open somewhere. Most places stock powdered baby milk. I don't suppose at her age, she'll be into MacDonalds Happy Meals yet, will she?'

A flicker of a smile twisted her lips. 'I love you, Holt Blackwood,' she whispered across the baby's downy head.

Holt settled them at the 'ugly' house, put the kettle on to boil, washed the dust from his hands and face, then announced that he was going out to get stocked up on baby things.

He'd only been gone about ten minutes when Kirsten rang from the hospital. Ryan was being taken to the operating room, she told Serena. He needed surgery.

'How did you know where to find me?'

'Sera – it was easy. I saw the look on that guy's face – Holt's – and I just knew he'd take care of you and Reanne.'

'Kirsty . . .?' An unspoken question hung on Serena's lips.

'Ryan's okay for the minute.' The girl's voice was tense. 'They say he's "stable", whatever that means, but he inhaled a lot of smoke, and there are crush injuries – internal . . .' the words tailed off. 'It doesn't look all that good . . .'

'Do you want me to come over?'

'No! No – it's okay, Sera. While you're with Reanne, I know she's all right. I won't worry about her. Are you staying there? Or – I thought you might be going to your old home – to Wintersgill?'

'I'm staying here. It will be easier for everybody this way. It's more convenient being near Caindale than going all that way out across the moors to stay with Mari.'

'I – I'll ring you again, Sera. When he comes out of surgery.'

'Yes. Yes. Do that, love.'

'I shall stay here all night – if they'll let me. Is that okay? Can you manage – the baby, I mean?'

Serena couldn't hold back a little smile. 'Holt's gone out shopping for some things for her.'

'She's usually very well behaved. Well, they all are at that age, aren't they. But don't worry if you can't get her usual brand of milk. It's Sunday, after all. There can't be many shops open around Caindale.'

'Don't worry about her. We'll take care of her.'

'I know you will.'

Holt was back within half an hour, triumphant, with a huge tin of milk, a sterilizing unit and a couple of feeding bottles. He'd also bought talcum powder, baby lotion and soap, and a mammoth pack of disposables.

'For girls,' he said, swinging the plastic shopping bags onto the table in the kitchen and eyeing the nappies with suspicion. 'I didn't know they had "his'n'hers" in that department, did you?'

Despite her fears for Ryan, Serena found herself laughing. 'No,' she admitted, 'I didn't. But I've never had much to do with babies until now.'

'Where is she?' He looked round the kitchen with a worried frown.

'On the sofa, in the big room, packed round with cushions.'

'What about Gray? Cat's and babies don't mix well, do they?' Alarm sounded in his voice. 'You haven't left Gray in there with her, have you?'

'Gray went out when you did – if you remember,' she reminded him.

'Aah! Yes. She'll have gone to Viv's.'

'I rang and told Mari what had happened. You don't mind, do you?'

'You don't really need to ask that.' His hands free of the shopping now, he placed them on her shoulders and shook her gently. 'You don't have to ask my permission for *anything* – understand? This house belongs to both of us – it was destined to be ours, I think, even when we were kids – when we used to hang around on the cliff top, and tell each other spooky stories about it. It held such memories for me, I just had to buy it when the old lady died. It was a little bit of our past, and now it's going to be a whole lot of future for us too.'

She went blindly into his arms, tears stinging her eyes.

'Don't cry,' he said softly against her hair. 'Don't cry, love. The baby needs feeding.'

She gulped back the sobs and began to laugh again. 'Trust you,' she muttered as she wriggled away from him. 'Trust you to bring me back down to earth with a bump.'

'We never talked about babies in the old days, did we?' Carefully he held her away from him and looked deep into her eyes.

'We were young. We had other things on our minds.' She managed a smile.

'You're coping just great with this one.'

She laughed again. 'You've hardly seen me with her. I feel like I'm holding a fragile piece of china when I lift her up.' She grimaced.

'I'd like to think that one day . . .'

'Hey!' She lifted a finger and placed it on his lips. 'It's too early to talk like that.'

Seriously, his gaze searched her eyes. 'I want you. I need to know you're not going to leave me again. I'm talking wedding bells and confetti, Serena.'

'I know what you mean.' Her voice was soft.

'Have my baby, Serena.'

Colour flew to her cheeks, but she nodded and gave him a straight look. 'When the time comes. When we know each other well enough. When we're married.'

'When? Not if?' His eyes were alight with a hunger he could barely conceal, she saw.

'When,' she said steadily. 'I promise it will be when not if!'

He hugged her close, and she leaned her head against his shoulder and wished with all her heart that she didn't have Ryan to worry about.

'Kirsty rang,' she said, the words muffled against his thick, smoke-smelling jacket.

She felt him give a deep sigh. 'Ryan?'

'In surgery.'

'God!'

'She said she'll ring again later.'

'And if he pulls through this little lot? What then?'

'Nothing will be changed.' She put her own happiness on hold in that instant. Soberly, she said, 'What he had before, he'll still have. That bullet lodged in his brain was totally inoperable.'

'Maybe it would have been better if he'd . . .'

'Hush – don't say it.' She clung to him, shivering.

'We don't have a right to happiness just yet, do we?'

'No,' she whispered, loving him for his understanding. 'The time isn't right.'

CHAPTER 20

Holt made omelettes for tea, but neither of them felt like eating. Afterwards he offered to mix up a batch of milk feeds for Reanne whilst Serena went upstairs to bath the baby.

Half an hour later, as she came slowly down the stairs with a sweet-smelling bedtime Reanne in her arms, she paused for a second as she heard the sound of raised voices coming from the kitchen.

Viv jerked her head towards the sound of the door opening as Serena entered the room. She bestowed a tight little smile on her and said, 'So this is the baby you were just telling me about, Holt.'

Serena, silently wishing they could have been left alone for a little while longer and then, instantly chiding herself for being so churlish, hitched Reanne up on her arm, tilted her head to look at the baby and said, 'This is Reanne. Ryan's little daughter.'

Viv walked towards her and inspected the baby. 'Holt was just telling me what had happened. I was worried, that's why I came down the lane to see if he knew what the commotion was all about. I heard police sirens going past the end of the lane, and when I looked out of my bedroom window there was a great cloud of smoke drifting up from Caindale's sea shore.'

Holt came across and took Reanne out of Serena's arms. 'Hey – sit down,' he said. 'You look all in. I was just putting Aunt Viv's mind at rest about the explosion.'

Viv rounded on him and burst out, 'Hardly putting my mind at rest, considering what happened to that poor boy.' She shuddered delicately and hugged her lilac-coloured coat more closely around her. 'I do hope he's going to be all right.'

'Kirsten went with him to the hospital a couple of hours ago.' Serena felt suddenly drained of energy. It was as if the events of the past couple of hours were catching up fast with her. Catching up and overtaking her. The relief she'd first felt when Ryan hadn't been killed outright was tempered with the sobering thought that he had an even bigger struggle ahead of him now. She sank down onto a kitchen chair when she realized her legs were in danger of crumpling up underneath her.

'The girl friend from Australia?'

Serena nodded. 'Reanne's mother.'

Viv looked from one to the other of the two adults. 'So! You're left "holding the baby"!'

'It was the least we could do.' Holt strode over to the kitchen work top where a bottle was all ready and waiting for Reanne, and as she started to grizzle and rub at her tiny nose with her fist, he popped the teat into her mouth. He looked up at Serena and said with a grin, 'It's okay – I tested the milk just before you came in and it's the right temperature.'

She swivelled round from the table and the sight of such a tiny baby, being cradled in those big arms with such gentleness, made her heart turn over. She loved him. Oh, how she loved him. With a smile, she asked, 'Shall I do that? Shall I feed her?'

He gazed down at the baby and pulled a face at it, muttering, 'No. I can manage. It's quite easy isn't it? This baby lark?'

Viv gave a snort of disapproval. 'You're holding her all wrong. You don't have a clue about handling babies.'

He glanced up. 'Reanne's not complaining. And she seems quite comfortable.' He shot a meaningful glance at Serena. 'And I'm quite comfortable too – doing this.'

Viv raised her eyes to the ceiling. 'When is the child's mother coming to collect her?'

Holt looked at Serena. She shook her head. 'I don't know.'

'Nobody knows. Not until we get some more news from the hospital,' Holt said in a calm and practical voice.

'But you can't keep a baby here!'

He said quietly, 'Why not, Aunt Viv?'

Viv glared at her nephew. She spread her hands helplessly. 'Well, for one thing you don't have anywhere suitable for it. And then there's the cat! You can't have a baby and a cat in the same house.'

'Lots of people do.' Holt seemed as if he were digging his heels in, but Serena knew that Viv wasn't really objecting to the baby, she was objecting to her staying here in Holt's house. Viv had always had a streak of jealousy in her. It had been the same in the old days, Serena remembered. Viv hadn't wanted anyone taking Holt away from her.

She cut in quickly, 'It's all right. I can take Reanne over to Wintersgill. I phoned Mari – she said she'd be pleased to have us there.'

'You can stay here.' Holt's voice was tense.

Serena pushed herself up from the chair and walked over to him. The baby had dropped off to sleep. She tried

284

to give him a warning look – a look that told him not to rub Viv up the wrong way.

'Hey – look at that now.' His eyes crinkled as he smiled at her. 'She's fast asleep. She must like me, huh?'

A ready smile sprang to Serena's lips. 'I think she's got wind stuck in her tummy. See how she's pulling faces in her sleep?' She leaned her head towards the baby, then held out her hand for the bottle. 'Let me take that while you hoist her onto your shoulder and pat her back.'

Holt handed over the bottle.

Turning away from him, Serena was shocked to see angry red spots of colour in Viv's cheeks. The older woman was obviously holding herself in check with the greatest difficulty, but it seemed she couldn't resist saying, 'Oh, what a cosy little scene.' And her lips were drawn tight, her eyes hard and brittle as they rested on Serena.

'I think we have a right to our cosy scenes, Viv,' Holt said, sounding suddenly exasperated with his aunt. 'We *are* planning on getting married.'

The explosion Serena anticipated at his words came!

'Married?'

Ignoring the venom in Viv's tone, he answered, 'Yes,' in the most solid, no-nonsense tone of voice that Serena had heard him use in a long, long time.

Viv caught hold of the edge of the table and turned pale. 'You can't. You've got your future to think about. The business. It's barely got off the ground. You can't tie yourself down . . .'

'The business is fine.' Holt came round the table to Serena and handed the baby over to her gently. He smiled down at her. 'We're getting married, aren't we, love?'

285

Taking Reanne from him, she looked up into his dark, serious eyes and nodded. 'Yes,' she said softly. 'We're getting married.'

Viv stared at them both, then looking drained, she said weakly, 'So that's how the land lies!'

Serena felt infinitely sorry for Viv, knowing that the older woman had had Holt to herself for such a long time – and looking at the situation realistically, she knew that Viv had taken over the role of Holt's mother.

She felt she had to say something. 'I shan't take him away, you know . . .'

Viv stared at her, stared through her, then suddenly sighed and pulled out a chair on the opposite side of the table. She sank down onto it and clasped her hands on the surface of the table in front of her and bowed her head.

She was breathing shallowly, Serena saw. She said, 'Holt – get your aunt a drink.'

Holt brought a glass of water to the table and leaned over Viv, placing a hand on her shoulder. 'Your heart?' he asked levelly.

She nodded and fluttered her hands in a helpless way in front of her, then she leaned forward and took several deep gulps of air.

Holt picked up the glass of water but she waved it away. He put it down again, his face distraught, and caught at one of Viv's hands, his fingers going straight to the pulse in her wrist.

'Hell!' he said in a savage tone. 'You oughtn't to get upset like this. There's no rhyme or reason to your heartbeat.'

Viv tried to smile. Breathlessly she said, 'You don't have to tell me about my own heart, my dear . . .'

Holt held onto her hand a while longer, occasionally looking at the clock on the wall as he did so. Finally, he dragged a chair nearer to Viv and sat down.

Serena was beginning to panic. 'Shall I call a doctor?'

Holt shook his head. 'Not at the moment. Let's see if it settles down first. Okay, Aunt Viv?'

Viv nodded, her face ashen. 'It . . . it's steadying a little . . .'

Serena moved quietly away from the table and fastened the sleeping Reanne into her car carry-seat, leaving Holt to stay by his aunt's side and talk soothingly to her. After what seemed like an eternity, some colour came back into Viv's cheeks.

'That's better . . .' She took in another great gulp of air.

Holt grasped her wrist again and for a few minutes there was silence. Then a fleeting smile spread across his face. 'It's slowing. Your heartbeat, and it's a more regular rhythm now.'

Viv nodded.

From across the room, Serena watched them, feeling helpless herself. It seemed as if Holt had faced this particular situation many times before, for he knew exactly what to do. He talked quietly to his aunt, encouraging her to take slow, deep breaths – and taking the same slow, deep breaths himself as she did so. Viv's eyes never left his face, and eventually she relaxed in her chair and closed her eyes thankfully.

'I'm going to take you home.'

'I can walk . . .'

'No way!' Holt rose to his feet.

Viv didn't argue. Serena went across the room and stood by the table. 'Is there anything I can do?' she wanted to know.

Before Holt could answer, Viv said plaintively, 'You must come and stay with me, Serena – you and the baby.'

'Oh, no – really, I couldn't.' Serena's startled gaze flew to Holt.

He too shook his head. 'Serena's fine here, Aunt Viv.'

'Living here? Together? Under the same roof?' Viv's bright blue eyes turned on them both accusingly. 'Before you're married?'

Holt's patience was wearing thin. 'Serena is homeless,' he ground out. 'The explosion blew her house apart.'

'It won't do.' Viv's eyes were blazing now.

'Miss Blackwood . . .' Serena's voiced tailed away as Viv glared hard at her. She finished lamely, 'Look – I've told you, I can always go and stay at Wintersgill. I don't want to cause any trouble.'

Holt threw his hands in the air in impatience. 'Aunt Viv is just being old-fashioned.'

Quietly Viv said, 'Do you want the entire valley to talk about Serena like they did our Mari when she went to live with Max Corder?'

'People won't talk – not in this day and age.' Holt was rapidly losing all patience, Serena could tell.

'Yes they will.' Viv turned her gaze on Serena. 'Mark my words. People will talk – they'll say "like father like daughter" – and Holt has a business to run. You can't afford to have idle gossip flying around when you have a business to run.'

Holt said grimly, 'But Max did. He out-flew the gossip – and it became a nine-day wonder, that's all. Everybody soon took it for granted that Max and Mari were a "pair".'

'They depended on Max for a living though,' Viv said tartly. 'They don't depend on you, Holt.' Turning again to Serena, she went on, 'Are you prepared to risk his haulage business going under, Serena? Is that what you want to happen? So that he'll be dependent on *you*?'

'No! No!' Serena shook her head. 'Look – none of this need have come up if I'd gone straight over to Wintersgill and stayed with Mari.'

'But you'd be miles and miles away from the hospital,' Viv said softly. 'And if they were to send for you . . .'

At that moment the telephone shrilled from the hall, and with a smothered oath, Holt strode out of the room. They listened in silence to his muted voice, not able to distinguish any words, just curt replies, his voice raised questioningly, and then silence.

He came back to the kitchen. 'Kirsty,' he said to Serena. 'She wants you to go to Rivelyn to the hospital.'

'Ryan . . .' she whispered, staring at him.

'He's conscious. And asking for you.'

'Me!'

'He obviously has something on his mind. Kirsty said his blood pressure is sky high and they're worried if you don't go . . .' He shrugged and left the sentence unfinished.

'Oh, no.'

Viv, back to her normal self now, seemed to sum up the situation more quickly than either of them.

'Take her to the hospital,' she ordered Holt. 'Go on,' she urged as he looked worriedly at her. 'Go on,' she repeated. 'I'm all right now. I'll look after the baby until you get back.'

'No. I couldn't leave her . . .' Serena shook her head. 'I'll take her with me.'

'That poor young man won't want bothering with a baby – who might be screaming and fretful by the time you get there,' Viv said, rising from the table and walking purposefully across to the sleeping Reanne.

'I do know how to look after a child,' she flung back over her shoulder. 'What's the matter? Don't you trust me?'

Serena bit down hard on her lip. She didn't trust anyone with Reanne. But what was the alternative?

Holt made the decision for her. 'Come along,' he said. 'Viv's right. She can stay with Reanne while I run you over to Rivelyn. It won't take more than fifteen minutes each way. I can be back here in half an hour. I'll leave you there, and you can always ring me to fetch you back.'

'B-but your aunt . . . her heart . . .'

'Viv's okay now,' he said, walking over to her and placing his hands on her shoulders. He shook her gently. 'She's okay, Serena. Her heart is steady again now.' He glanced over at Viv. 'Right?'

The older woman nodded. 'You have to go, Serena. You know you have to go, so what are you waiting for? A hospital's no place for a baby of that age.'

Serena gave Reanne a last, long look, then glanced back at Holt. 'Half an hour? You'll come straight back.'

'Cross my heart.' He grinned at her. 'Come on, Serena. Ryan needs you.' He held out his hand. 'Let's go.'

CHAPTER 21

Ryan was in intensive care, moved away from, and screened off from the other critically ill patients because he was making so much noise.

Serena could hear him as she hurried up the corridor alongside Kirsty who had been in reception to meet her. He was yelling her name.

'Sera-a-a! Sera-Sera-Sera-a-a-a!'

'He's been like that since he regained consciousness,' Kirsty told her.

Serena felt sorry for the girl. 'I came as soon as I could . . .'

'Yes. I know. And I'm glad Reanne's in such good hands. I don't know what we'd have done without your friend Holt.' Her face puckered up. 'He saved Ryan's life – going into the flames like he did to get him out . . . I'll never be able to thank him enough.'

'What's happened here though? Here at the hospital?' Serena wanted to know as Ryan's voice reached them again.

'Sera-a-a! Sera-a-a! Sera-Sera-a-a!'

'The burns aren't as serious as they first thought. He has internal injuries though. The staircase that fell on him had ruptured his spleen. That's why he was operated on so quickly. He was haemorrhaging.'

A nurse came hurrying towards them, and led them into the Intensive Trauma Unit. Ryan's voice was pitiful to hear.

'Sera-a-a! Sera-a-a! Sera-a-a-a!'

'The doctor thinks it might be best to sedate him again,' the nurse informed them as they went over to Ryan's bed.

Serena was shocked by the sight of Ryan. There were tubes taped to him everywhere.

'He's breathing for himself.' The nurse grimaced. 'As you can hear, of course. Try and calm him if you can.' She smiled and left them.

A screen behind Ryan showed his heartbeat was slightly erratic.

Kirsty whispered in a distressed voice, 'He lost an awful amount of blood.' She glanced at the transfusion bag and shivered.

For the moment, Ryan was quiet, but his head was thrashing about on the pillows. As Serena leant over him, his eyes flickered open and he began to moan.

'Sera! Listen! Sera . . . honey . . .'

'Hush! Try to keep calm,' she whispered softly.

'Figure . . . cliff top . . .' His eyes were wild; they burned into her face. 'Understand?' His voice was raw.

Tears spilled out onto her cheeks. His body was naked down to where a sheet covered him from just above the waist. He was a mass of bruises and lacerations, but surprisingly only his hair and eyebrows had been singed by the flames, though the skin on his face was red and peeling.

'I'm here. Try to sleep, love.' She clasped his hand in hers.

He mumbled, 'My mind, Sera – clear. Got to tell you. Now. Can't wait. Maybe not here for long . . .'

Behind her she heard Kirsty start to sob. 'No,' Serena said firmly, dashing her own tears away with her free hand. 'No, don't talk like that, Ryan.'

'Have to be – practical.' He began to cough, and the effort was painful to him, she could see.

'Don't try to talk,' she whispered.

'Have to . . . Not much time . . .'

She touched a finger to his lips.

'Sera – listen. Don't – talk – just – listen . . .' He was breathless, and straining for her to understand. There was a pallor beneath the redness of his skin that worried her.

'Okay! But take it slowly, huh?'

He tried to smile, coughed again. Then, 'Max!' he said hoarsely.

'Dad?'

He closed his eyes and moved his head slightly to indicate she was on the right track. 'Max! George Cook!'

She nodded. 'George found Dad on the beach after he fell from the headland, is that what you're trying to tell me?'

'Sera!' He smiled weakly.

'But I know that. Mari told me.'

'Max – wasn't – dead.'

For a moment she thought he was delirious. 'Wh – what are you saying?' She frowned.

'Not – dead! Remember – that saying – I asked you about . . .'

She nodded slowly. 'Heaven has no rage?'

He started to cough again. Kirsty leaned forward and wiped his mouth with a tissue. He rolled his head away from her. 'Go away . . . not much time . . .'

Serena closed her eyes and felt all the breath leaving her body. 'You're telling me Dad wasn't dead when George found him? And that Dad said . . .'

'Heaven – has – no – rage . . .'

Gently she said, 'Why didn't you tell me sooner?'

'Didn't want to – worry – you. Wanted to sort it out – myself . . .'

'It might have put my mind at rest, love. Knowing somebody was with him when he died.'

Ryan rolled his head from side to side, closed his eyes and moaned, then opened them and said, 'Not alone – when he – *fell.*'

All the breath seemed to seep out of her body, and she felt cold all over. 'Who – who told you that?'

'George . . .' his voiced faded away and she thought he'd fallen asleep, but after a few more moments he rallied again and said, 'Hooded – figure. Cliff top.'

'You mean . . .?' She couldn't say the words. She felt sick inside, and frightened too. She started to shiver.

'Murder? Could – be. Take care – Sera . . .'

Kirsten was standing on the other side of the bed. Serena felt Ryan's hand go slack in hers. She glanced across at Kirsten.

'He's asleep. He's fine now he's spoken to you.' Look at the monitor. His heart's steadied now. Kirsty leaned over Ryan's inert body and pressed her lips to his forehead, then looked up at Serena and said, 'I think he'll settle now he's seen you.'

'You're not going to like this!' Holt's face was grim in the darkness of the car as he drove out of the hospital car park and turned towards Caindale an hour later.

Her heart lurched. 'What's wrong, Holt? What's happened? Oh, God, not Reanne?'

'Don't get in a panic,' he said. 'Nothing terrible's happened. It's just that when I got back after bringing you to the hospital, Viv had taken the baby to her cottage. She must have been waiting to tell me – must have heard the car coming down the lane, because she was outside her front door, waving me down.' He glanced across at her briefly. 'She'd pulled a heavy old drawer out of the bottom of her old-fashioned wardrobe, and had made a kind of cot out of it. Reanne was fast asleep in it. In the spare bedroom.' He grimaced. 'The room that used to be mine when I was a boy.'

'But she can't keep her . . .'

'She intends for you to go and stay with her. She's made the bed up. Even put the electric blanket on it to air it.'

Serena groaned. 'Oh, no.'

They were turning into the little lane again now. He said, 'Look – if you're adamant about this, we'll go and turf Reanne out of that drawer and take her back to my house.'

With a deep sigh, she said, 'We can't do that, Holt. Viv means well.'

'I wish she'd mind her own business though.' He pulled the car to a standstill outside Viv's house, then turned to her. 'She is so domineering.' He clenched a fist and brought it down on the dashboard. 'Honestly, Serena – I had nothing to do with this. I was so mad when she told me . . .'

'Hey. Calm down.' She closed her hand round that clenched fist and squeezed it.

'She says she's just concerned about your reputation, but . . .'

'Well, maybe she is,' Serena replied logically.

'That's just an excuse, and you know it.' His glance was level as he gazed at her. 'She's a damn nuisance . . .'

'Holt! She's jealous.' Serena sighed again. 'We've just got to humour her a bit. Let her get used to the idea of us getting married, and okay, if it means I've got to stay with her for a few days, then I'll do that. It might be a good thing anyway. I can try to get to know her a bit better.'

'You'll be at each other's throats before twenty-four hours have passed.' He blew his breath out in irritation. 'She makes my blood boil,' he ranted. 'That woman is infuriating.'

'Maybe it would be best if you just dropped me off here, huh?'

He threw his hands up in the air. 'You've got no damn clothes to wear. Nothing. Everything you possessed was burned to a cinder.'

'I'm sure Viv will lend me a nightie.' She grinned at him, loving him for his concern, even forgiving him his bad temper against his aunt.

One strong arm swept round her. 'You wouldn't have needed a nightie at my house.'

She tilted her head back. 'So Viv was right. My reputation would have been in danger?'

He growled and crushed his lips down on hers and she clung to him, wanting nothing more than to stay with him and be loved by him. Eventually though, she knew it couldn't be. Gently, she eased away from him. 'Viv must know we're here,' she said in a low voice. 'It's best if I go in to her, Holt.'

'Damn! Damn!' He glared at her in the darkness of the car.

'I'll be able to see you tomorrow,' she reassured.

He shook his head. 'Not possible, love. I've got a long haul – starting at four in the morning. I'll be in Ireland for four days. Hell! I could do without this.'

296

'No, you couldn't. You have a job to do,' she said in a practical voice. 'Don't you see? This is just what Viv's worried about – that you'll neglect your work because of me. I suppose that's why she wants Reanne and me to stay with her – so that you don't feel responsible for us . . .'

'She had no right . . .'

She placed her fingers on his lips. 'Okay! I agree with you. She had no right to be so high-handed, but I think she means well. She cares about you, Holt. She doesn't want to see you throwing yourself away on somebody like me. She remembers me as I was ten years ago, remember? I did some pretty stupid things then. And I walked out on everybody I loved.'

'But you won't do it again.' His voice was firm.

'No,' she said gently, her hands resting in her lap now. 'I won't do it again. I'd never throw somebody's love back in their face again like I did then.'

He looked down into her upturned face. 'It's been one hell of a day, hasn't it?'

She nodded, then told him quietly what Ryan had said about the figure on the headland on the day her father had died.

He frowned, then said, 'I had heard a rumour about that, love. But the police discounted George's evidence after it was discovered he'd spent that entire morning drinking at the "Old Bachelor".'

She stared at him, then asked, 'But why didn't somebody tell me? Mari never hinted at it, and neither did you. Why all the mystery?'

'I can't speak for Mari,' he said in a calm voice, 'but for myself – well, you never seemed to want to talk about Max. And knowing how you felt about him . . .' He lifted his shoulders in a shrug. 'Maybe I was wrong to keep quiet, and if it worries you so much, maybe we should talk to George ourselves, huh?'

She relaxed a little at his explanation. Then she smiled. 'It's good to hear you saying "we". I'm not alone any more, am I?'

He found her hand in the darkness and held it tight. 'I'll be away for four days,' he said. 'When I come back, we'll talk to George.'

'Perhaps it would be better to let sleeping dogs lie,' she mused. 'After all, if the police didn't take George's story seriously . . .'

He grinned down at her. 'George *does* hit the bottle sometimes.'

'I don't want to think that anybody else could be involved in Dad's death,' she said.

'Then we'll make a few enquiries of our own, huh?'

She leaned towards him and touched her lips to his. 'Mmm,' she said against his mouth, 'but I'm going to try not to place too much importance on it, even though Ryan was half out of his mind with worry. He could have been rambling a bit after the anaesthetic.'

He held her close and kissed her, then put her away from him and said. 'Four days, love. That's all the time I'll be away. We'll look into it when I get back from Ireland.'

'Yes,' she said. 'Four days is no time at all. Nothing awful can happen in four short days can it?'

CHAPTER 22

Kirsty arrived half way through Monday morning to collect Reanne.

'Holt telephoned me at the hotel,' she explained. 'He told me you were staying with his aunt.'

Viv beamed at the girl and asked if she'd like a cup of tea. The kitchen was spotless and shining, with no sign now of Reanne's mushed-up breakfast on the work-tops.

'Thanks, but no. I have to get back to the hospital and see Ryan.'

Serena said, 'I'll run you back to Rivelyn – but what about Reanne? Is it okay for you to take her to the hospital?'

Kirsty grimaced. 'I'll manage. They have a creche . . .'

Viv cut in, 'It's no trouble having her here, my dear. I could look after her for you.'

Kirsty sank down onto a kitchen chair. 'It's okay. Really. But I am grateful for you both looking after her yesterday – and overnight.'

Serena made some tea, and Viv went into the front parlour to fetch Reanne who was having a nap. She placed the baby, still asleep, in her little carry-seat on a chair next to Kirsty.

299

'She's a little love.' Viv's words were wistful, and Serena knew that Viv had indeed enjoyed 'mothering' the little one for the few hours that they'd had her.

Serena enquired after Ryan, and Kirsty said she'd stayed with him and he'd spent a comfortable night.

'They told me this morning that he'd probably be moved out of "trauma" and into a side ward sometime today.'

'That's great news, isn't it?' Serena glanced across at Viv as they all sat round the table with cups of tea.

Viv smiled kindly at her. 'But you'll stay here, won't you, Serena? I mean – you don't have anywhere to live now, do you?'

Serena took a gulp of tea. She couldn't stay here, she knew that. Viv would stifle her, just as she'd stifled Holt when he'd been young. She knew she ought to be more charitable. Viv had, after all, taken them in yesterday and showed them the warmest hospitality. But Viv's presence, she had to admit to herself, was overwhelming.

The house was clean and tidy. Too tidy. Not a thing was out of place. If she got up from a chair in the little parlour, Viv was there behind her, plumping up the cushions again. And while she'd been in the bathroom this morning, Viv had gone into the guest room and remade her bed. Even now, Viv was brushing up grains of sugar from the tablecloth with her fingers, getting up out of her chair and wiping them away in the sink, then washing her hands meticulously with a bar of anti-bacterial soap.

She returned to the table. 'We can't take risks with germs – not when there's a baby in the house.' She smiled brightly, then turned to Serena again and said, 'Now I insist – you *must* stay here with me.'

Serena found her voice at last and hoped she didn't sound hard or unfeeling as she said, 'You've been kind, Viv, but I need somewhere I can take work home from the office. I was thinking of looking at the other house that's empty in Caindale. The one overlooking the foundry . . .'

Viv's face showed horror and surprise. 'You can't,' she stated. 'I really can't allow you to move into a damp and filthy little cottage. Holt would never forgive me. I'm supposed to be looking after you while he's away, aren't I?'

'No,' Serena said firmly. 'I would just be a burden to you if I stayed here indefinitely. I'm coming and going at all hours. Some days I work late at the foundry. It just wouldn't be fair to you – not knowing what time I was coming in or going out.'

'We could come to some arrangement . . .'

'No!' Again, Serena was firm, and she was glad when Kirsty chipped in, 'I think Serena's right. Ryan told me he used to get very frustrated when Serena didn't turn up on time for meals.'

Serena smiled gratefully at Kirsty. 'We had no telephone so I couldn't call him when I was going to be late – and you're right about Ryan – he really would tear his hair out at times when – because of me – a meal was ruined.'

'Perhaps I could come with you? I mean to look at the house?' Kirsty said.

On the opposite side of the table to her, Serena saw that Viv was frowning. 'We could all go,' she said, including Viv in the invitation.

Viv shuddered. 'Count me out,' she stated. 'I don't want to go traipsing round a dark and dismal iron miner's cottage.'

'Is that what the houses up there on the cliffside were at one time?' Kirsty asked, interested. 'Cottages built for the miners all those years ago?'

Viv nodded, and pulled a sour face. 'They're built on the hillside above the drift-mine. Built on boulder clay which is no proper foundation at all. I'm not surprised that gas main ruptured yesterday . . .'

Kirsty held up a hand. 'No,' she said, 'that wasn't what happened at all. Ryan was able to tell me – he had some sort of a blackout, and he'd turned on the gas and then couldn't find the thing he needed to light it.'

Viv rounded on Serena. 'Are you telling me you had one of those old-fashioned stoves that actually need to be lit by hand?'

Serena sighed. 'It was second-hand – like all the other stuff we had. We couldn't afford brand new.'

'So you cut corners.' Viv tut-tutted. 'It never pays to cut corners.'

'I would have replaced it eventually . . .'

'But now you've got to replace the whole house. I stick by what I said, it doesn't pay to cut corners.'

Serena felt like a naughty schoolgirl being told off by an irate teacher, but she realized that Viv was talking sense. It had been a mistake, installing that old stove. She ought to have realized that something like this could happen. But regrets were of no use now. Mark had assured her he would 'see to the stove', and she'd trusted him. Her only excuse now would be to say that she'd never before had to bother her head about kitchen appliances, but she kept quiet. To speak out would only get Mark into trouble. Viv was not noted for keeping her views to herself.

She rose from the table and cleared the cups away. Viv appeared at her side, saying, 'I'll see to those, my dear. I like to scald crockery in hot water for at least half an hour.'

Serena managed a weak smile. Kirsty rose to her feet and thanked them both again for looking after Reanne.

It was only then that Serena realized her car was still parked outside Holt's house, farther down the lane.

Viv, it seemed, could read her mind. 'I suppose you need these.' With the words she unhitched a bunch of keys from a holder behind the door. 'The keys to Holt's house.' She smiled frostily. 'I'll have them back when you've finished with them though, so don't go sailing off with them in your pocket, will you? I have to go down there and feed Gray later this morning.'

'Gray?' Kirsty queried.

'Holt's cat. She follows me everywhere. I expect she's sitting on my back doorstep right now – but I wouldn't let her in today because of the baby.'

Kirsty's face fell. 'I hope the poor thing's not cold. It's quite frosty out there. Really chilly for April . . .'

'Cats have fur coats to keep them warm,' Viv said. 'Don't worry about her. They have nine lives you know – cats.'

Kirsty laughed as Serena picked up the keys, walked into the parlour through the adjoining door to retrieve her coat and bag, and then made for the back door again.

'Surely that's just a myth – cats having nine lives. They don't really, do they?' Kirsty asked conversationally.

Viv spun round from the table, her smile brittle and her eyes bright. 'Gray had a truly miraculous escape when . . .' Her voice tailed off. She made a flurrying kind of movement with her hands, then pressed one of them to her heart and said breathlessly, 'But it's of no interest.'

Politely, Kirsty said, 'I'm sure it would be.'

Viv glanced at her coldly and said, 'No. I think not.' Turning to Serena then, she asked, 'Are you going to fetch the car up here? there doesn't seem much point in both of you going – and carrying the baby all that way?'

303

'Yes.' Serena nodded. 'Yes, of course. I won't be long, but I can't remember where Holt put my car keys so perhaps I'll have to hunt around for them when I get there.'

Viv said in an off-hand manner, 'They're on his kitchen table.'

Serena stared at her. How did Viv know that, she wondered?

Viv seemed for a moment to be a little put out, then she muttered, 'I saw them there earlier. I went down to make sure Holt hadn't left the cat inside the house.'

Something didn't add up to Serena. She thought about it for some moments, then she said, 'But Gray has a cat flap cut into the back door. She can let herself in and out when she wants to.'

Viv shrugged. 'You're right. There is a cat flap, yes. But as you say, it's in the kitchen door. Gray often gets herself shut in one of the other rooms though – and sometimes she'll curl up in the understairs cupboard.'

Kirsty, obviously sensing an atmosphere, gave a little laugh. 'Well, if she's there, she won't be out on your cold doorstep, will she Miss Blackwood?'

Viv laughed too. 'All this fuss about a cat!'

She began running water onto the cups in the sink, and with a rueful sort of glance at Serena, Kirsty said, 'I'll bring Reanne outside as soon as I hear the car coming up the lane, huh?'

Serena smiled. 'Yes. You could do that. It will save us a bit of time, won't it?'

She walked out into the cold morning air after pulling on her warm coat, and was glad of the biting frost that cooled her face after being in Viv's hothouse of a kitchen, glad too to be out of reach of Viv's tongue.

She knew she had to get away from Viv. She couldn't take much more of the woman's outspokenness. She walked quickly away from the house, her breath steaming on the air in front of her.

She saw no sign of Gray as she walked up to the 'ugly' house. And it seemed strange, letting herself into Holt's home with his keys. The main door of the house fascinated her again – as it always did. She ran her hands over the cast iron points of the compass. The bonding between iron and wood was a work of art. Would she herself ever be able to perfect the design enough to make it a saleable product, she wondered?

She made her way down the long passage towards the kitchen and found her car keys where Viv had said they were, on the table. She weighed them in her hand, wondering why – if Viv had known they were hers – she hadn't taken them back to the cottage with her that morning. Holt also, she realized, could have slipped the keys through Viv's letterbox if he'd thought about it, when he left the house earlier at four o'clock.

But perhaps he'd had other things on his mind. It must be a big responsibility having to spend four days taking two gigantic steam presses to Southern Ireland on the back of trucks. They'd be travelling in convoy, he'd told her, he and a co-driver in one tractor unit with a low loader in tow, and two more drivers in an identical vehicle, with a police escort until they reached Liverpool.

As she turned back to retrace her steps out of the kitchen, she heard a faint scratching noise.

Stopping, she tilted her head and listened. A pitiful mewing made her let out her breath in a sigh of relief.

'Gray!' She listened again. The sound was hollow and echoing.

'Gray!' she called out softly. 'Gray! Where are you?'

There was silence. She walked out into the hall, looked up the stairs, half expecting to see a gray furry face staring down at her through the wooden banisters.

Nothing.

Quietly, she started up the stairs, wondering if Gray had got into the airing cupboard in the bathroom, but there was no sign of the cat when she got there.

She heard the mewing again, coming from the heart of the house. And then she remembered. Viv had said Gray sometimes went into the cupboard under the stairs.

Sure enough, Gray was there. She prowled out of the cupboard when Serena opened the door, stretching her legs one by one, tipping her head up and miaowing loudly, her back arched and proud, her tail erect and her whiskers twitching forward. She rubbed herself against Serena's legs, nuzzling her head and ears down towards the ground where she suddenly flopped onto her back and waved all four legs in the air.

Serena laughed softly at the antics of the cat, then bent down and stroked the soft, silky fur under its chin. It seemed to smile, stretching its neck back for more fuss.

'Oh, no, my lady,' Serena said. 'You've got me for a prize mug, haven't you? And I don't have all day to spare playing with you.'

Gray rolled over and crouched facing her. Big green eyes focused themselves on Serena's face, and then the cat upped and darted back into the cupboard.

'Hey! Come back.' Serena dived after her, but it was dark under the stairs. She noticed, however, that there was an electric light bulb fitted to the low ceiling, and on further inspection found a switch against the door frame. She flicked it, and the inside of the cupboard was instantly illuminated.

Gray miaowed again and peeped at her from behind a pair of Holt's boots that stood facing her against a vacuum cleaner and an ironing board.

'Come on out, you rascal.' Gray, Serena realized, was enjoying the game, but time was getting on, and she'd promised to take Kirsty back to the hospital.

'Please, puss,' she begged, bending down again and reaching out towards the cat. 'Come on – I'll give you some milk in the kitchen if you're a good girl.'

To Serena's surprise, the ruse worked. The cat must know what the word 'milk' meant, she thought, as she remembered a cat they'd once had at Wintersgill who had known only two words, 'milk' and 'meat'.

'My old cat, Susie,' she told Gray seriously, 'could tell me what she wanted – milk or meat. I bet you can't do that.'

Gray put her nose in the air and walked off towards the kitchen, and Serena laughed and turned back to the cupboard to switch the light off.

Then she froze, for her gaze had swept round the place and become rivetted on something hanging in the far corner. A coat – a long, navy blue duffel jacket that was hanging up by its . . . hood!

Her stomach turned over.

She whispered weakly, 'No . . . oh, no-o-o!' as Ryan's words came back to haunt her.

'Hooded figure. Cliff top . . .'

And then a cold shudder slaked through her from top to toe, for right after that, she remembered Ryan had added, 'Murder?' and then, '. . . take – care – Sera . . .'

307

CHAPTER 23

Serena stopped off at Viv's house just long enough to return Holt's house keys to his aunt. Then she drove Kirsty to Rivelyn, back to the hospital.

Reanne was grizzly all the way there, which suited Serena, for her mind was in a turmoil, and Kirsty's preoccupation with the baby left her little time for casual conversation.

Conversation was the last thing she wanted. Her mind was reeling. Yet who could she talk to? Who would understand the awful suspicion that was going round and round in her brain?

From Rivelyn she drove straight back to Caindale, down to the sea shore and up the bendy hill towards the terrace of houses. She averted her gaze from the pile of rubble she passed that had once been hers and Ryan's home. Up until a short while ago she'd been happy there . . .

Her eyes started to smart. Angrily she dashed the tears away. Tears never solved anything! But for Holt to have deceived her so . . . Holt who she'd have trusted with her life. It just didn't bear thinking about that he should have been the figure on the headland with her father when Max had fallen to his death!

She had to have time to think. She knew she couldn't return to Viv's house. She drove slowly along the terrace high above the sea until she came to the little house near the other end that had a faded 'for sale' notice in its front window.

It looked drab and dismal. She pulled the car to a standstill outside its peeling front door. The windows were grimy, but through them she could see masses of cobwebs draping themselves across the corners.

She forced herself to get out of the car and walk up to the door, insert the key in the lock, and then go inside. The door swung to behind her. She gazed around. It was worse than anything she could have imagined. Soot had fallen down the chimney and spread itself all over the floor. There was a great gap under all the skirting boards where the floor was sagging. When she walked on the floorboards they bent and creaked.

She told herself it didn't matter. She could manage without a sitting room. She went through to the kitchen.

This was better. The floor was a solid one. There was a black cast iron firegrate that heated water in a boiler on one side, and had an oven on the other. An iron trivet hung drunkenly beside the fire, but that could be repaired she decided, and at least she'd be able to put a pan of vegetables on it to boil.

Upstairs one bedroom was running with damp where tiles must be missing off the roof. But again, at the back of the house, the smaller bedroom was dry – but filthy. A box room had been converted – she laughed at the word – 'converted' didn't start to describe it as a bathroom. There was a low flush lavatory, a handbasin and a narrow, tiled shower cubicle. All the appliances had brown stains marking the porcelain, but they could be cleaned, she assured herself. The brown stains were obviously from the water – the iron-red water that was stored in the tank in a shoddy little airing cupboard on the landing. She hoped, however, that the drinking water downstairs didn't come from the same source!

She ran back down the stairs. She'd move in. She was confident she could manage. But first, Mari had to be told that she needed a few days off work.

Mari listened with growing horror as Serena stood in the office and told her where she was going to live.

'You can't!' she said at last. 'The place isn't habitable, Serena.' What was the girl thinking of, she wondered?

'I shall stay there. What else can I do?'

Jackie had been sent to make some tea. Mari knew she'd be back at any moment. With a sense of urgency she said, 'You're coming with me to Wintersgill.'

'No!' Serena shook her head adamantly.

'Don't be a goose.' Mari got up from her desk and came round to take hold of her by the shoulders and shake her gently. 'Serena! Be sensible. You can't live in that house the way it is. You don't even have a bed.'

Hollow eyes came up to meet hers. 'I – I can't stay with Viv.'

Mari chuckled. 'My dear, I realize that. Viv's a pain in the backside. You'd probably get disinfectant poisoning if you lived there with her for long.'

'Ouch!' That made Serena wince, and smile for the first time since bursting into the office. 'Ouch, Mari. I didn't realize you could be quite such a cat.'

'I know my sister, Serena.' Mari let go of the girl's shoulders. 'That's better. It's good to see you smile. Now just come over to my desk and sit down, will you? I can hear Jackie clattering away up the passage in those ridiculous clompy shoes she wears. Sit down. I'll get rid of her again on some pretext, and then we can talk like two sensible cats, hmm?'

Serena sat down. Jackie brought the tea in to them, then

Mari said, 'Jackie love, do you remember me saying I'd try and arrange that college course for you?'

Jackie's eyes widened. 'You bet I do, Mrs Wyatt.'

'Well, I phoned them this morning, and if you'd like to go over there and pick up the prospectus this afternoon . . .'

'This afternoon?' Jackie yelled. 'You really mean that, Mrs Wyatt?'

Mari nodded. 'You can catch a bus at the end of the road. It'll take you into Rivelyn.'

Jackie gaped. 'You really think I can do it? Learn about computers?'

'Of course you can,' Mari said drily. 'Anybody can learn to get the better of a computer. They don't have brains, you know. They're just silly boxes.'

'Mrs Wyatt . . . I don't know what to say. Nobody ever thought I was clever enough for them to pay me to go to college.'

When Jackie had gone, clutching a five pound note for her bus fare from the petty cash box that Mari kept in her desk drawer, Mari sat back and said, 'Right. Now we can talk.'

Shakily, Serena picked up her cup of tea, and before she knew it, she was telling Mari about the things Ryan had said at the hospital the previous day.

'I knew about George's ramblings,' Mari admitted. 'I think everybody in Caindale did, But there's more to this than you've told me, isn't there?' Shrewdly, she'd observed the way Serena's hands had been twisting themselves together throughout the conversation. The girl's face too was pale and drawn.

She looked away. 'No. Nothing.' Serena's voice was just a mumble.

Mari leaned forward. 'Come on. Tell me.'

311

Serena looked up at last. 'I found a hooded jacket. In a cupboard under the stairs at . . . at Holt's house.'

Mari said. 'You're upset. You're not thinking straight. Holt's not a murderer, my dear. Nobody killed Max. It was an accident. The police said at the time that nothing led them to believe anybody else was involved.'

'I want to believe that.' Serena's eyes were dull.

'You love him very much, don't you?'

The girl lifted her gaze to look straight at her. 'Am I so transparent?'

Mari pulled a little face, then took a long drink of her hot tea. 'You're not denying it, I notice.'

'No!' The voice this time had a hopeless note in it.

'Holt had no reason to kill Max.'

Serena's retort was sharp. 'But did anybody?'

'Not to my knowledge.'

'So?'

'So – we'll have to be very careful about this.'

'You're very calm.'

'Yes, my dear. I've had a lot of practice at keeping my feelings well and truly under control.'

'Meaning?'

'You know, I think, what I'm getting at. My affair with your father, before your mother died.'

'It was a long time ago.'

'And time heals most hurts. Is that what you're saying?'

'It's what I want to feel is true, but I can't. I hate myself Mari – for what I did to Dad. Time can never heal that. I can't forgive myself.'

'Max will have forgiven you by now.'

'We don't know that though, do we?'

'He never said a bad word against you, love.' Mari spoke

312

the truth as she knew it. 'He would never hear a bad word against you either.'

'You're not making me feel any better.' The girl's ice cold gaze rested on her.

'Maybe not. But it's what you want to hear, isn't it? You want to be convinced that Max didn't hate you when he died.'

'I – I couldn't bear it if he did. And if Holt had anything to do with Dad's death, then I never want to see him again as long as I live.'

'Your Dad and Holt were buddies, Serena. Max gave Holt his first big break.'

'Yes. I know. Holt told me Dad had lent him the money for his first truck.'

Mari nodded.

'Could Holt have been in trouble? Money trouble, Mari? Was Dad calling in the loan or anything like that?'

Mari sighed. 'Holt paid back the loan years ago, love. There was nothing like that. Holt has a thriving business, paid for by his own efforts. I don't think you realize exactly the scope of his little empire, do you?'

On the defensive, Serena said, 'Well – I know he has at least two trucks, because he told me there'd be four drivers and two trucks on this run to Ireland.'

Mari started to laugh softly. 'Eighteen truck beds,' she said then. 'Twelve tractor units. Fifteen employees. The units are stored in the old disused railway yard at Rivelyn. Holt's offices are the railway buildings – the station-master's house and the old ticket office. Holt has just had plans approved to open another outlet, this time in the Midlands on the Derbyshire-Staffordshire borders. He aims to employ another twenty men there.'

Serena sagged in her seat and her gaze was rivetted on Mari. 'How do you know all this?'

'Holt's my nephew, love. He often comes over to Wintersgill for a chat.' Mari shook her head but laughed all the same. 'Your Dad and Holt were cast in the same mould – both of them solid and upright men. Men who put their heart and soul into everything they do. Strong-willed men, straight as a die men, and men that any girl should be proud to love. Holt loves you too Serena – don't let anybody convince you otherwise.'

Mari watched as Serena pushed herself slowly out of her chair and stood up. She stood there, straight and tall. 'I believe you,' she said at last, 'But it doesn't alter the fact that there *was* a hooded coat inside Holt's cupboard.'

'I never once saw Holt wearing a hooded coat, girl.'

'Neither did I.' Serena turned away, then abruptly swung back to Mari. 'But that proves nothing, does it?'

Mari got to her feet. 'Come to Wintersgill,' she said. 'If only for the night.'

Serena lifted both her hands in a little useless gesture. 'How can I?'

'You have to sleep somewhere.'

'There's the house on the terrace.'

'But no bed. No furniture. No cups and saucers. Be realistic, Serena. Come to Wintersgill, and if in the morning you still feel the same, we can go and clean the other place up.' Mari suddenly had a thought. 'Tell you what,' she said, 'You could have some furniture to kit the place out if you wanted it. There's oodles of stuff in the attic at Wintersgill – some of it yours. There's a desk, and there's a wooden bedstead – and goodness only knows what else that you might be able to make use of.'

'In the attic?'

Mari nodded. 'Your dad cleared a lot of your mother's things up there too.' Her face clouded. 'At the time I would have thrown them out, but he said maybe one day you'd want some of it.'

'Mother's stuff?'

Mari lifted her shoulders. 'Jewellery! An old Victorian writing box! Even a trunk full of clothes, I think.'

'How insenstive of him. Expecting you to live with all that junk, all those memories.'

'No. Not insensitive. I think he felt the need to hang onto something from the past – especially after you left.'

'You didn't mind?'

Mari gave a sharp laugh. 'Of course I minded. I'm a woman, aren't I? But I loved him. And if I'd started being jealous of a dead woman and a runaway girl, I wouldn't have lasted long with a man like Max, would I?'

'You don't pull any punches do you? Are you telling me you'd have put up with anything in order to hold onto Dad?'

Mari held her gaze for thirty seconds or so, then said, 'Yes. That's just what I'm saying. I wanted Max. Only Max. Nothing else in the world mattered to me, and just as I was about to get the one thing that meant the world to me – his name – he . . . he died.' Mari felt her face beginning to crumple. She firmed her lips, blinked her eyes, however, and took a deep breath to steady herself.

'His name? You mean . . .?'

'He'd asked me to marry him. We'd set the date.' Mari looked up at the clock. It was four o'clock. 'Oh, hang it all. Let's go home. I can't take any more of this place today.'

'You said you'd set the date?'

'It would have been this coming weekend,' Mari said. 'I'll need something to take my mind off it, won't I? So how about you and me doing a spot of cleaning and painting at that little house of yours, hmm?'

'Oh, Mari . . .'

'Oh, Mari,' Mari echoed bitterly. 'Come on. Let's go.'

CHAPTER 24

It was another three days before Serena could bring herself to even think of going up into the attic at Wintersgill.

In those three days, Mari had held the fort at the foundry, letting Serena tackle the more strenuous job of scrubbing out the little house high up on the hillside above the drift-mine, and overlooking the works. It had been hard and dirty work, but Serena was longing for a place of her own again and so set to with enthusiasm.

In the evenings however, she was tired – too tired to even watch television with Mari at the big house on the moors. She tumbled early into bed in what had once been her own room there at Wintersgill, and she slept dreamlessly, and woke refreshed each morning.

Viv had phoned once, petulant and complaining to Mari.

Mari had placated her sister somewhat, however, by telling her that Serena had been forced to come back to Wintersgill to sort out some clothes she'd left behind ten years ago. It was a partial truth. Serena did find that some of her things were not too out-dated – things like underwear and nightwear – but she needed more than that. And before the scrubbing and cleaning had commenced she'd taken half a day off to go shopping in Middlesbrough and get herself some new outfits to replace the ones that had been burnt the previous weekend.

'Are you sure you're going to be all right? Going through your mother's things up there on your own?' Mari asked on the Thursday morning before setting out for Caindale.

'I'll be fine. I'm not going to go to pieces just looking at bits of jewellery and stuff, am I?'

Mari had been concerned. 'You never know. There's a lot of your past life up there, love.'

'But that's just what it is, Mari. Past life. I ought to be looking to the future now.'

Mari smiled. 'You sound just like Max. There's a lot of him in you, you know.'

'I suppose there has to be – for me to take on a place like Caindale.' Serena grinned as she got up from the breakfast table and started clearing it.

'You don't still hate Caindale, do you, dear?'

'No.' Serena turned round from her self-appointed task and laughed gently. 'Hey! Don't look so worried, Mari. It's growing on me.'

'Even though you're going to have to spend your days looking down at the foundry from that cramped little house?'

'The foundry's just a building. I'm getting to know the people, and finding that I like them too. I think they're getting to like me too, though some of them must have long memories and still remember the awful things I did.'

'Holt's due back tomorrow, isn't he?'

Serena's face clouded. 'Early morning, I think – or maybe around midnight tonight.'

'What are you going to do?' Mari leaned her elbows on the table and asked the question directly. 'Are you going to tell him what you found in that cupboard at his house?'

Serena shrugged. 'I'll have to, won't I?'

'Don't make an issue of it, love.'

Serena spun round. 'Why not? I think I deserve an explanation.'

'He's not guilty of any crime though.'

'How do you know?'

'I just do.' Mari looked down at the table top. 'I just do. Trust me, Serena. Don't go throwing wild accusations at him.'

Serena put her hands on her hips and walked back to the table. 'Now what are you getting at?' she wanted to know.

Mari looked up. 'You're headstrong. You fly off the handle. You're like Max. But Holt – well, he's only human, my dear, and I don't want to see you mess up your life . . .'

'Again! You were going to say "again" weren't you?'

Mari looked straight at her. 'Yes,' she said, 'I was going to say that, but only because I know what heartache you've gone through.'

'Don't you think I owe it to Dad, Mari? To ask Holt why he has a hooded coat hidden away under his stairs when – allegedly – the last person Dad was seen alive with was somebody wearing a hooded jacket?'

'But I too have a hooded jacket, Serena.' Mari rose to her feet. 'Do you want me to show you?'

'Don't be silly.'

'Is it so silly? Isn't everybody in Caindale and all the surrounding areas under suspicion if they have a hooded jacket?'

'No! Of course not.'

'Just Holt.'

'No. No. It isn't like that.' Serena was suddenly flustered. She lifted her hands in a helpless gesture. 'Oh, Mari – I don't want it to be Holt who was with Dad on the headland.'

'Holt was away in Scotland when Max died. You know that.'

'Yes.' Serena was subdued.

'But you're still not convinced.'

'He did that run on his own. He doesn't have an alibi.'

'He has a tachograph. That's his alibi – if he needed one. The tachograph chart will tell the name of the driver of the truck, the date and destination, the hours he spent driving, the speed he drove at, the breaks he had, the place he started from and finished at. Oh, Serena, don't you see? Holt couldn't have been anywhere near Caindale when Max died.'

'But we haven't seen that chart.'

'Don't push him, Serena. I've told you – he had nothing to do with Max's death.'

'But you can't say that with absolute certainty.'

'I can, love. Believe me, I can.'

'How?'

'Don't ask, because I can't tell you. All I am telling you is for you to drop this idea you have that Holt was somehow involved. He wasn't.'

'Can I spend the rest of my life not knowing for sure though?'

'Serena – some things have to be taken on trust.' Mari looked at the clock on the wall. 'Look – I have to go. I really do. It's Thursday. The security van's due with the wages at ten. I can't leave it to Jackie to sort all that out.'

'I'm sorry, Mari.' Serena sighed. 'I'm a pain, aren't I?'

'Just get yourself sorted – you and that crazy house you're intent on living in. Do that. Today. We'll get Mark round to shift some furniture at the weekend while you and I go down there with a couple of cans of paint. Okay?'

'Okay, boss.'

Mari chuckled and moved over to the door. 'And don't,' she warned, wagging a finger at her, 'Don't go doing too much.'

'I won't.' The promise came easily, but Serena knew she wouldn't keep it. She longed desperately for a place of her own again, and she felt guilty also for leaving all the work at the foundry to Mari.

She watched Mari drive away, then filled the dishwasher and tidied the kitchen. Mari had a woman in to clean the house three times a week so there wasn't much else left to do after that. She was at the bottom of the stairs contemplating the prospect of going up to the attic when the phone rang.

Kirsty sounded all in. 'Serena! I know I'm taking advantage again, but I've got the most horrendous migraine . . .'

Serena assured her that she could help. 'Yes', she'd come over to Rivelyn and take Reanne for a couple of hours, and, 'No,' she didn't have anything planned that couldn't be left for another day.

She drove swiftly into Rivelyn and called at the hotel. Kirsty had taken a smaller room for her and the baby. It was on the second floor and hadn't much of a view, Serena saw as Kirsty invited her in.

The girl was pale and hollow-eyed. 'It's not much of a place.' Ruefully she indicated the room, 'But it seemed silly keeping the double room on at a double room price when Ryan's not here.'

'If you're short of money . . .' Serena began, but Kirsty waved her protest aside. 'Hey, I'm not hinting at anything. I just feel I can't cope today.'

'It's reaction, I expect, love.' Serena went into the room which was comfortable, but cramped.

Kirsty sighed. 'I've just got to go over to the hospital though. Ryan will be out of his mind with worry if I don't turn up.'

Reanne was gurgling in a small crib at the side of the single bed. Serena smiled down at the baby. 'She seems happy enough.'

'If you could just look after her for me till after lunch . . .'

'Of course I will. I know what I'll do – I'll have a run into Middlesbrough again and do some more shopping. I've only managed one half day so far to try and replenish my wardrobe.'

'Oh, Serena – I never thought of that. You must have lost everything in the fire . . .'

'Don't worry. Look – let's get you over to the hospital, and then I'll take myself off with Reanne. Okay?'

'I don't know what we'd have done without you.'

'Now don't start all that. Ryan's the one we've got to think about.'

Kirsty looked round the room. 'I don't know how we'll cope when he comes out of hospital. I mean – he won't be fit enough to travel to Australia straight away, will he? And to bring him back here . . .'

All Serena's hopes of having a place of her own suddenly dwindled to nothing. She knew she'd have to let Ryan and Kirsty have her own little house – at least while they got things sorted. For the time being she'd have to stay with Mari at Wintersgill.

'They've said he might be able to come home at the end of next week.'

'Ryan? So soon?' This was worse than she'd bargained for. The house was a mess. There was no way those sagging floors could be fixed, the roof mended, and the place made ready for an invalid and a baby.

'He's out of danger. He says he feels fine – except of course for the headaches, but they're not going to go away, are they?' Kirsty's face suddenly creased up and tears started pouring down her cheeks. 'Why this?' she wanted to know through her sobs. 'Why? Why? Why did this have to happen? Hasn't he suffered enough? Doesn't he have enough to cope with?'

Serena went over to the girl and put her arms round her. Kirsty wept like a child in her arms, and Serena knew she could say nothing to soothe her. She let her cry, rocking her gently back and forward, until there were no more tears left.

Kirsty pulled herself away, then groaned, 'Oh, God! I thought I could cope,' and rubbed at her face with her hands, then pushed her fingers through her long, dark hair and stared miserably at her reflection in the dressing table mirror. 'And I can't even ask Holly for help now she's gone back to Australia.'

'You can cope. You have coped,' Serena insisted.

Kirsty sniffed, went over to the washbasin and splashed her face with cold water then dried it on the hotel towel. She gave a great sigh then. 'I've got to keep up,' she muttered. 'For Ryan's sake I can't go to pieces.' She picked up a brush and started hauling the snags out of her hair then turned round. 'Do I look okay? I don't want him to know I've been crying.'

'You'll be fine once you get out in the fresh air – and it is

322

fresh this morning, believe me. A bit of a red nose won't look out of place at all today.'

Kirsty managed a grin.

'And don't worry about accommodation. I've had an idea. I don't think Ryan will have to come back to the hotel when they let him out of hospital.'

Kirsty's face, suddenly became radiant. 'He won't?'

'Look – I can't say any more just now. But don't worry. I won't let you down, I promise.'

It was just after two that afternoon when Serena drove back to the hospital and returned Reanne to her mummy and daddy. Ryan was out of bed and sitting in a day room. He was pale-faced, but on the mend, she could see, and that made it all the more important that she should get back to Wintersgill and start sorting out that furniture in the attic. The little house would have to manage with a quick face-lift, she decided. Maybe Holt could point her in the direction of a fast-working joiner and roofer.

She drove quickly back to Wintersgill in the half-light of a drizzly April afternoon. Reanne had been little or no trouble, but she'd been glad to hand the baby back to Kirsty and Ryan. The trip out though hadn't been wasted. On the back seat of the car were several carrier bags full of clothes and pairs of shoes.

She'd leave them there for the time being, she thought as she reached Wintersgill, for she wanted to make the most of what daylight was left to search through the attic.

There was plenty of stuff in the attic, she decided, some ten minutes later, to basically furnish a house for herself. But if Ryan and Kirsty were going to live at the cottage over the drift-mine, they'd need stuff for the baby as well.

In a corner, she found the old drop-side cot she'd had when she was a baby herself. It was in reasonably good condition, but needed a new mattress. She started making a list on a notebook she'd taken up into the eaves with her. 'Cot mattress,' she muttered to herself. 'And curtains for the whole house.'

There was a rocking chair, a fold-away camp bed, a box of china ornaments. Then she found a complete tea and dinner service – also boxed. She smiled. Her mother had hated it when some colleague of Max had taken to bringing her samples from his pottery. Catherine Corder's taste didn't run to chunky earthenware – Wedgwood had been more suited to her standard of living.

Serena moved over to the desk she'd once had in her own bedroom, and ran her fingers over its dusty lift-up top. It was a child's desk, but she'd never outgrown it. Feeling as if she were opening Pandora's box, she cautiously lifted the lid, but it was empty. Desolation swept over her. She'd half-expected to find pens and pencils, crayons and diaries she'd kept, relics of a past life when she'd been happy and contented. In the cupboards underneath, it was the same. All had been cleared out.

She paused when she found her mother's antique writing box – also dust covered. She knelt down and blew the dust away from it, then opened it, expecting to find that empty too, but it wasn't. Her mother had never kept a diary, but there were writing things in there – pale blue paper, blue envelopes, exquisite slender pens, a gold powder compact that when she picked it up and clicked it open, puffed out a pink, scented cloud that conjured up the unmistakable smell of 'mummy' that she'd forgotten had ever existed.

Light in the attic was fading. She peered into the box again and shuffled the papers about. There was a photograph of her mother, a small studio portrait – postcard size. Across it was scrawled 'Darling Philip! All my love!'

She frowned and turned it over in her hand. There was a photographer's studio name printed on the back with a date stamp. With a shock she realized the photograph was more than twenty years old. She was puzzled. She'd never heard the name Philip before. So – who was Philip? And why should her mother have written that message on the picture?

Her head jerked up suddenly as from downstairs came the noise of a door banging shut. And then Mari's voice was calling to her up the stairs.

'Serena! I'm home!'

Serena jerked her hand up to look at her watch and her hand caught on the edge of the writing box, up-ending it so its contents were scattered across the floor of the attic.

'Damn!' She got to her feet, went to the top of the narrow staircase leading down to the first floor of the house and yelled back, 'I'm still up here, Mari. I didn't get as much sorted as I wanted to.'

Mari appeared below her. 'I came back early to help. It's only half past three but I was up to date on everything in the office so I thought what the hell! Shall I make a cup of tea and bring it up?'

'Please. Then I can tell you about my day.'

'You've been out, I know that because I saw the parcels on the back seat of your car.' Mari laughed.

'I did a spot of baby-sitting too. Kirsty had a migraine so I took Reanne shopping with me to Middlesbrough.'

'Poor you!'

'Babies scare me to death. They're so little.'

Mari chuckled. 'You won't say that when you've got one or your own, I hope.'

Serena thought of Holt again, and her stomach lurched. She dreaded having to meet him and to possibly ask him about the hooded jacket at his house.

Mari obviously saw from her expression what she was thinking. 'Forget it,' she said in a matter of fact tone of voice. 'Think about the babies you and he can make together, not a dratted coat hanging in a dark cupboard.'

'I'm going to forget it. For the time being at any rate. I've got more on my mind than Holt at the moment – I've just knocked something over and there's stuff all over the floor.

'I'll bring a battery lamp up with the tea,' Mari promised. 'It's getting dark. Max was always saying we'd have to have electricity laid on up there, but we never did.'

Serena heard Mari moving away, and then going back down the lower staircase, so she turned back to the attic, and being careful not to step on any of the papers that had fallen out of her mother's writing box, knelt down in the midst of them and started collecting them up.

The photograph stared up at her in the gloom. She wondered again who Philip could be.

The sheets of writing paper were faded on the edges. She wondered if they were worth keeping, but didn't feel at the moment as if she could throw anything away that had belonged to her mother. She stacked them neatly in the bottom of the box, the envelopes followed. There were some postage stamps too – more than a decade out of date.

She opened out a newspaper cutting – a 'Young Farmers of West Yorkshire' gathering! It was a group photograph. Her mother, in dazzling evening dress was gazing up into the face of a very tall good-looking man who had his arm round her.

She folded the cutting and stowed it in the box. West Yorkshire! It didn't make sense. Why would her mother be in West Yorkshire when she lived here on the East Coast?

There were several letters on the floor. She picked up an envelope and saw it was addressed to Mrs Catherine Corder. The postmark showed it had been sent twenty-three years ago from Harrogate. She smiled to herself. 'I'd have been five years old at the time,' she murmured as she turned it over in her hand.

Would it be wrong of her to read the letter, she wondered? After all, it had belonged to her mother. Her curiosity was aroused. Angry though she'd been when her mother had died, and she'd discovered her father and Mari together, it was strange, but all her early memories seemed to be of her father.

She heard Mari coming slowly up the stairs, and sat back on her heels and called out, 'Watch your step. I still haven't cleared the floor.'

Mari carefully avoided all the letters, and placed two steaming mugs on the bare floorboards before saying, 'I'd leave them if I were you, love. Look, let's go back downstairs, shall we?'

'Heck, no, Mari. I've just got to get that house in Caindale sorted. She curled her legs under her and sat down on the floor, picked up her mug and started to tell Mari about Kirsty and Ryan, and how upset Kirsty had been that morning.

Mari scuffed some of the letters aside with her foot, pulled up a small leather pouffe and sat down too.

'So you see – I'll have to let Kirsty and Ryan stay in the house – at least until Ryan's well enough to go back to Australia.'

'Hmm.' Mari's attention was obviously on something else.

'Hey! Haven't you been listening to me?'

'Yes. Of course I have. It's getting dark up here though. Let's go down, shall we? Attics have never been a favourite place of mine.'

'You said something about a battery lamp?'

'Oh! Yes! I forgot to bring it up.'

Serena frowned. 'No, you didn't, Mari. It's over there by the top of the stairs. I saw you put it down a few minutes ago.'

'Oh, that old thing. It needs new batteries, love. Let's leave all this till tomorrow, shall we?'

'Oh, Mari. It's not yet four o'clock. There's still a bit of daylight.'

'Serena – let's leave it!' Mari snapped.

Serena took a gulp of hot tea. 'I can't leave it. All these things belonged to my mother. For heaven's sake, Mari – these are her personal belongings, her letters. I can't just leave them littering the floor.'

Mari drank her own tea down quickly. 'He should have burned them,' she muttered. 'I told Max – he should have burned everything.'

'That's an awful thing to say.' Serena gazed at the woman she'd come to look on as a friend. 'How can you be so heartless, Mari? I know you must have hated my mother, but . . .'

'Hated her?' Mari gave a harsh little laugh.

'It's obvious that you did.'

'Look – Serena, let's not have this conversation.' Mari rose to her feet. 'Let's go down and have some dinner before we both say things we'll regret later.'

'No!' Serena placed her mug of tea on the floor and looked down at the letter addressed to her mother which was still in her other hand. 'No,' she said, 'I'm going to stay here and sort through these letters. I think I have a right to know all about those last years of my mother's life.'

'No!' Mari's voice was little more than a croak. 'Don't do that, Serena.'

Her gaze flew to Mari's face. 'Why not?'

'I – I can't tell you.' Mari turned away and fled to the top of the attic stairs, where she spun round and said, 'Serena – I'm asking you – begging you to leave well alone. Forget you ever saw those letters – I thought that box was locked. Max said he was going to lock it and throw away the key . . .'

'My father said that?'

'Please, love. Leave them. The past is buried.'

But it wasn't. Not in Serena's eyes. 'The past is a mystery,' she said quietly. 'I shall never understand why my father was unfaithful. She was so beautiful . . .' Idly she bent and picked up the photo of Catherine Corder, 'My mother,' she explained, glancing up at Mari.

The pain on the older woman's face was hard to bear. Serena half rose to her feet, then she looked down at the picture again, and then round at the scattered letters at her feet.

Mari gave a sigh that sounded like a sob. 'If that's how you still see her, then stay here – and break your heart,' she said.

And then she was gone, leaving Serena staring after her, with the dreadful feeling somehow that her whole world was going to be torn apart.

CHAPTER 25

Mari waited, tense and troubled, down in the kitchen at Wintersgill.

An hour passed, and it grew dark outside on the moorland. The silence in the house was frightening. There had been no sound from upstairs since she'd left Serena on her own up there.

At intervals, she raised her eyes to the ceiling, straining her ears for the slightest noise. She made no attempt to prepare a meal. Food would choke her, she knew. And the girl? What would her reaction be when she eventually came down?

Mari was scared. She cursed herself for not getting rid of Catherine's belongings once Max was dead. She had baulked at the task though. Had shuddered at the thought of raking up the past by handling those letters. They weren't her letters to get rid of. She had no right to them – no right to touch them even.

Serena was the only one who could have the final say, that was why Mari had never mentioned them. She'd hoped the problem might go away – that the letters might crumble to dust up there before anyone found them again, or the mice – and time – might nibble away at them and render them unreadable. It had been a faint hope of hers that Serena might overlook the writing box, or at the very least that she might dispose of it without looking inside it.

The silence crowded in on her. She propped her elbows on the kitchen table and leaned her head on her hands, then jerked up at a creak, a step on a stair, a muffled sound that could have been a sob or a sigh . . .

She spun round on the seat to face the door. She knew her own face must be haggard even though she had shed no tears. Not yet. There would be a time for tears when Serena faced the fact that an awful truth had been hidden from her for all these years.

Mari waited for the girl to come to her. She had to come to her. There was nobody else . . . nobody except Holt who would be able to comfort her, and he was still hundreds of miles away in Southern Ireland.

She heard the sound of a door being opened almost soundlessly, and half rose to her feet. It closed again quietly.

'No! Oh, no!' Mari was only half way across the kitchen when outside, the car engine sprang to life. 'No . . .' She raced out of the room, down the hall, across to the front door and flung it open.

Icy air from the open moorland hit her in the face as her feet carried her across the garden to the gate, and then beyond that to the road. The car's tail lights were disappearing into the darkness. Mari had a choking sensation in her throat. She pressed a hand to her lips and strained her eyes until the lights faded into nothing.

Back in the house, her fingers trembled as she punched out Holt's number on the telephone. 'Blast! Blast! Blast!' How she hated those stupid answer machines. She left a message, her voice unsteady. She knew it sounded garbled.

'Holt! She knows! Serena! She found all those damn letters from Catherine's lovers! I don't know where she's gone!'

Serena sat in the darkness shivering. She gazed wide eyed but unseeing into the patchy mist that was swirling around her stationary car. It was quiet here, quiet enough to think if she'd been able, but her mind was numb. She left the engine ticking over and warmth from the heater slowly started to creep into her.

Where was she? Although it didn't really matter, she felt the urge to know. She opened the door, pushed it wide, and slowly swung her feet out onto the ground. She stood and looked around. In the distance she heard the plaintive baa-ing of a sheep.

'We're poor little lambs who have lost our way . . .' It had been a popular ballad at one time. A favourite of Max's. He used to sing it to her when she was a little girl. He'd sing it in the car as he drove her to Caindale or to the zoo, or the cinema. She'd join in the chorus when he was driving her over the moors to a party, to a friend's house, on a trip to a department store to buy her a toy. Those trips were endless. And now she knew why. He didn't want her to know what her mother was like. He wanted to protect her when Catherine's lovers came to the house. That's why he had taken her everywhere with him . . .

Her fingers gripped the car door frame. 'Daddy!' she whispered to the darkness of the night. 'Daddy!'

So much was beginning to make sense now.

Feeling slowly started coming back into her limbs, into her mind, and she was beginning to hurt so much inside that she didn't know how she was going to bear it.

Words were drumming in her brain. 'Too late! Too late'! Hideous words they were. Two little words, but hideous and pitiful. The most awful words in all the world. *Too late* to say 'sorry'. *Too late* to say 'forgive me'! *Too late* to say other words too – three little poignant words that would have summed it all up – what she felt for him. She pushed all the words that she'd never uttered to Max, to the back of her mind, burying them there under all the hate and all the pain.

'Daddy!' she whispered again. 'Oh, Daddy!' But her eyes stayed dry, and her cheeks were cold.

Cold as death. Don't think of death. Think of death and those three little words would rush to the surface again, and they'd stick in her throat and choke her, because she couldn't say them now. They had no meaning – not to the man who had idolized her all those years ago.

Somehow, she forced herself to get back into the car. The mist had cleared a little. She looked at the clock on the dashboard. It was nearly ten o'clock. It must be wrong. She couldn't have been sitting on the moor all that time. She revved the engine and headed towards Caindale.

There was nowhere else to go.

The valley was silent and still, and steeped in the soft glow of moonlight as she drove down the narrow little road. Lights twinkled in the houses high on the hillsides. Lamplight was mellow on the red waters of the Caindale beck as she passed over the tight bends of the bridges built above it.

She came to the beach and the tide was far out, the sand gleaming silver-wet on the lonely shore. She parked the car and turned her back on the sea and all its memories. But turning her back made no difference, the memories were still there, memories of all the love that had been lavished on her, memories of the heartache when she'd washed her hands of everybody who cared for her and had run away from everything she held most dear.

Inside she was hurting so much . . .

There was a tight, raw knot of obstinacy though that would not let her give way to her grief. She had to make her peace with Max. She had to tell him she'd been wrong. But how?

Her gaze swept up to the headland from which he'd fallen. Her steps took her falteringly in that direction. She had to find him – get close to him.

'No!' Had she spoken the one word out loud, she wondered as she stumbled to a halt? She was almost at the spot where they'd found him – where George had found him. 'Heaven has no rage, George . . .' That was what he'd said.

Her lips began to move of their own accord, 'Heaven has no rage like love to hatred turned, nor hell a fury like a woman scorned.'

A woman! Was that what Max had been trying to tell George?

If it had been a woman on the headland with Max, that meant Holt was in the clear and had nothing to do with her father's death. Guilt almost overwhelmed her. How could she have ever imagined that Holt could do such a thing? Holt loved her. And she loved him. She knew now that it must have been a moment of madness that had brought such a suspicion to her mind.

She turned away from the red waters of the Caindale beck and headed for the parade. Once there, she walked quickly towards the chapel. It was all in darkness though. She didn't know why she'd gone there.

From the pub – 'the Old Bachelor' – came the sound of singing and she recognized the voice. George was in full flow with 'The Drunken Sailor'!

She walked on, her mind closed. A white building loomed up in front of her. Caindale Medical Centre. She walked past its long, low lines, because the man she wanted was waiting for her.

But he was only a bronze statue.

She gazed up into the face of Max Corder. He didn't see her. Of course he didn't see her. The hurt was welling up inside her again. She wanted to scream at him, but even if she did that, she knew he wouldn't hear her.

He couldn't protect her now. Couldn't hide from her the stark and evil fact that her mother had been nothing but a whore – long years before Max had taken up with Mari.

Catherine hadn't just been unfaithful the once either. Serena felt sick inside as those sheets of paper, those letters, photographs and mementoes mocked her silently from her mother's hateful writing box – discarded now, left there on the attic floor at Wintersgill.

There had been a steady string of 'admirers'! There had been taunts about her father in the dreadful letters. Cruel inuendoes from the man called Philip, saying that Max '. . . wasn't man enough to hold onto the beauty he'd married . . .'!

Catherine had flaunted her power over men. She'd been foolish and vain and many had sought her favours – even men who had been business associates of her father's . . .

Max must have lived a life of hell with her.

Serena's eyes searched the face of the statue, saw the lines of laughter etched there on the stern features. She remembered the absolute hardness of the man, the tough tenacity of him . . . and yet the gentleness of his eyes had been caught by the sculptor, a gentleness that no amount of bronze could diminish.

One hand was pushed deep into his pocket like she'd seen it so often in life. At any minute now she could almost believe it would emerge with a bar of chocolate in it – or mintcake which she'd loved as a child. Tears gathered behind her eyes.

'I'm sorry, Daddy.' The words were easy now. They released the pain. It welled up and broke loose bringing harsh, gasping sobs of torment that wracked her body.

'I'm – sorry – Daddy – so sorry . . .'

Words! She cursed herself. What use were words to Max now?

Tears streamed down her cheeks and into the collar of her coat. They trickled down her neck when she lifted her face to the sky. They came faster then as the futility of her words hit her hard and long. They ran into her ears and damped her hair. Grief swelled up her face and made her eyes sore. Her soul was raw and bleeding. She welcomed the pain the tears brought; it was dissolving the hatred that had been locked up inside her for too long. Her tears were flushing it away, and as it went, a kind of peace was taking its place.

She could grieve naturally for Max at last.

She curled up at his feet. The three words that had been buried in her heart for so long, broke free. 'I – love – you,' she muttered brokenly, and it was true. She knew now that she'd never stopped loving the man who had been her father. Jealousy, anger, and the hot rage of youth had blinkered and blinded her.

But now was the time of reckoning and she was paying dearly for her folly.

* * *

A sweep of headlights came down the road, swishing through the rain that she'd never noticed was falling. She huddled closer to the bronze feet of her father, hiding her face in her hands until the car had gone past.

But she hadn't gone unseen.

Seconds later, running footsteps echoed on the hard concrete slabs of the pavement. Hard hands hauled her up from the base of the statue. A rough voice melted into her mind.

'Serena! Honey!'

She buried her face in his chest as he swept her into his arms and carried her down the road to his car which was slewed against the kerb. Sobs still racked her, but she could feel a calmness creeping over her. He never said another word. He didn't comfort or condone, but on the other hand, he didn't censure her either.

She looked up at him. Rain had plastered his dark hair to his head, curling it against his ears. He looked fierce and protective, and in his eyes there was a world of understanding.

'Mari . . .' she croaked. 'I have to go back to Mari . . .'

Slowly he shook his head. 'No!' he said. 'You're going home.'

'Wintersgill . . .' Tears mingled with the rain on her cheeks. How could she go back there in this state?

'No,' he said, and she felt his arms tighten around her. 'You belong to *me*.' There was a note of desperate fury in his voice. 'The "ugly" house is where you belong, Serena. That's where you're going – and that's where you'll stay till I've made you my wife.'

CHAPTER 26

They'd talked into the early hours. He'd known, of course, about her mother.

'You should have told me!'

'You would have hated me.' They sat on opposite sides of the fire – together, yet a world apart.

'But to find out like that . . .' her voice tailed away, for recriminations wouldn't help, she realized.

'Would you have believed me?' He raised his head to look at her. His big hands were clasped helplessly in front of him between his knees which were splayed apart.

She thought about that question for a moment or two, then sighed. No, she wouldn't have believed him. She said so, and they dissolved into silence.

Now she was alone, and the harsh light of morning was creeping into the bedroom – one she hadn't seen before last night. If she listened hard, she could hear the steady roar of the sea, and the thrashing of it against the foot of cliffs a field and a half away. The dazzling brightness of sky and water played on the ceiling above her head, but the walls were a warm yellow, and a feather-soft quilt co-cooned her.

Somehow it hadn't seemed right for them to share a bed. Not last night. Not after what she'd gone through. She needed time to collect the pieces of her life, but more than that, she needed to forgive herself, and that was something she couldn't contemplate doing just at the moment.

Holt had gone out early. She'd heard him knocking about in the bathroom, on the stairs, then down below in the kitchen. She'd heard the clank of dishes on the kitchen tiles and guessed he was putting food down for Gray.

After that she drifted off into an uneasy slumber again, and now, picking up her watch from the bedside cabinet, she saw it was nearly nine.

She showered and dressed, then made her bed and tidied the room. She went downstairs and put two slices of bread into a pop-up toaster. An envelope was propped up against the tea caddy on the table. Her name stood out boldly on the stark whiteness of it. She put a tea-bag into a mug and made herself a drink, then sat at the lonely table to eat her breakfast, and looked at the white envelope, but didn't touch it.

Gray was purring, eyes shut, on a cushioned chair in the kitchen. The stove was well stoked and the kitchen warm. Outside the window, late April was having difficulty trying to remember it was supposed to be springtime. There'd been another frost. The season was playing a game that found a ruthless echo in her heart, making her wonder if she'd ever waken to summer's warmth again, so frozen were her emotions.

She finished eating her toast and picked up the letter, ripping it open slowly, savouring the moment. What would it contain, she wondered? Had he changed his mind about her? Or would there be a protestation of undying love? She thought not. She flipped the folded paper open and read it.

'*Come to the yard – I have something to show you.*'
His name was scrawled under the enigmatic sentence.
There was a P.S.
'*The old railway goods-station – Rivelyn.*'

Holt whirled round as he heard the crunch of tyres
coming into the yard, and he felt his face creasing into a
smile as she stopped the car only feet away from him and
got out of it.

'What kept you?'

'I didn't have a car, remember? It was still down at the
beach in Caindale.' She laughed up into his face.

He smacked his hand to his forehead. 'Damn! I forgot
about your car.'

'Don't worry. I quite enjoyed the walk along the cliff
top, and the scramble down to the jetty. It blew the
cobwebs away.'

Instantly he was concerned for her. 'Are you okay?'

She pulled a face at him. 'On the surface. But I'll
survive.'

He held out his hand, and she placed hers in it. His
fingers closed round hers. As always he marvelled at how
smooth her skin was – how right it felt to touch her. He
couldn't imagine himself ever looking at another woman –
not now she was back in his life.

She was all he'd ever wanted.

She smelled good. It was that lemon soap. It reminded
him of the time he'd soaped her all over. He felt himself
hardening. Last night had been bad. It had taken all the
will-power he possessed to keep him in his own bed, and
not go next door, into hers.

He took her across the yard where the trucks and tractor
units were parked. There were several spaces between

some of them and he pointed out that the self-load air suspension unit had gone out that morning, and the twin-axled rigid was in the workshop. He explained the difference between a low loader and a semi-low trailer, showed her various tractor units – the cab part of the trucks onto which various trailers could be connected, and in technical details told her how this was done.

And then, away from the trucks and sheltered from the dust and dirt, he led her to a long, cream-coloured caravan.

They stood alongside it and she looked at him questioningly.

'I lived in this for six months – when I was doing up the "ugly" house. I wondered about doing something with it for the young couple – Ryan and Kirsty.' He glanced down at her upturned face, and shrugged. 'Well, they've got to live somewhere, haven't they? He'll need a place to recuperate when they let him out of the hospital.'

'Here?' He could hear the amazement in her voice.

'Heck, no.' He rubbed at his chin with his free hand. 'I could clear the wreckage of the house away. At Caindale. That's what I was thinking anyway.'

He saw a lightening of her expression. 'Hey – that's a good idea, Holt.'

'You think so?' He grinned at her. 'You really think so?'

'It'd take some doing – shifting all that rubble. It was a mess.'

His broad shoulders lifted. 'A couple of days.'

'Is that all?'

'Give or take a day. Then, of course, we'd have to get the water connected, and the drains, and the electrics – and get permission from the borough council but that'll be a doddle.'

342

She started to laugh. 'How long have you been planning this?'

'Since we talked, and you told me about those two kids, and how Kirsty had to take a smaller room at the hotel because of the cost.'

'I – I was going to let them have the house.'

'Your house? The one over the drift-mine!'

'Mmm.'

'It doesn't have a sea view. Do you think anybody could get better looking at a dusty old foundry day after day?'

She thought about his words for a moment, then shook her head. 'You're right, of course. Ryan loved the view out over the jetty. He'd feel stifled gazing at the foundry all day long.'

'I'll do it then? And you'll tell the pair of them they can move in any time after next weekend?'

She gnawed on her lip. 'Won't it be difficult – I mean, this is one big caravan, it must be all of thirty feet long.'

He threw back his head and laughed. 'It's got two bedrooms, shower, kitchen and living room – and you're almost right about the size. But this is my job, Serena. This is what I do for a living. I move "immovable" objects, and it'll be a piece of cake.'

'Getting it round those tight hill bends will be a piece of cake?'

She looked at him warily. 'Are you kidding me?'

'You can come and watch. Believe me, it won't take long.'

'But the demolition of what's left of the house . . .'

'Another piece of cake, love. Come on,' he swung her hand and pulled her round to the yard again. 'Let's get back to the office. I have a couple of phone calls to make now I know you're happy about it.'

'I still think you'll have a problem round those bends.'

'I'll work on that.' He squeezed her hand. 'It's simply a matter of logistics – rigid versus artic!'

'You've lost me.' She shook her head at him. He loved the way that her short blonde bobbed hair gleamed in the pale sunlight.

He faced her. 'Trailers! Rigid – the ones that don't bend – or articulated – the ones that do. I'll have to calculate the rise of the hillside, measure the angle of the bends, but nothing like that has ever beaten me yet.'

She stared at him, and a slow smile spread across her face. 'I think I understand now why you said you still worked with computers. Is that it?'

'Come to the office and I'll show you how it's done, huh?' He bent down suddenly and kissed the tip of her nose. 'I might even get you to ring up and hire a bull-dozer for the demolition.'

Ryan loved the new home.

Serena was waiting there when Holt brought him from the hospital. Kirsty and the baby got out of the car first, then Ryan, looking pale, and thinner than ever, stepped out, looked at the caravan and whistled under his breath at first sight of it.

Serena went down the two steps of the caravan to meet him. She hugged him close, trying not to let him see how worried she was because weight had dropped off him so drastically.

'He needs feeding up,' Kirsty said huskily.

Serena let him go at last, and he stepped back apace and said, 'Wowee! This really is something. Are you sure you can trust me with it?'

344

Shakily she said, 'There's no gas connected this time. It's all electric.'

He reached for her hands, clutched them in his own skeletal ones. 'Sera – you're a marvel.'

'Not me. Holt.' Her gaze went beyond him, to Holt who was leaning lazily against his car and watching the scene before him with interest.

Ryan dropped her hands and turned round. 'Thanks, man!' His voice was warm with emotion. 'I'd got all geared up for living at the other end of the row. I tried to con myself into thinking it would be like living in a Lowrie painting – y'know? All match-stick men going in and out of the foundry, little trucks, little houses – match-stick houses . . .'

'You're talking too much.' Kirsty laid her hand on his arm. 'You need to rest and get your strength back.'

'And grow my hair.' He grimaced at Serena. 'How d'ye like the convict look, Sera? They say it'll grow back, but it's showing no sign so far.'

He did look odd. Serena felt tears prickling at her eyes. The fluffy growth of hair on the side of his head where he'd been burnt was all spiky with little bald spots between it. The rest of his hair had been neatly trimmed to almost crew cut proportions. 'You're okay,' she murmured. 'Come on inside.'

'I asked for a head transplant,' he quipped. 'Seems they don't do them though.'

She gripped hold of his hand and led him into the caravan. Kirsty and the baby, and Holt held back a few minutes.

'How are you feeling?' Serena asked him seriously.

'Okay.' He pursed his lips. 'Good for another six months, I guess.'

'Ryan – don't . . .'

345

'Nothing's changed, Sera.' He looked at her and there was a hopeless expression in his eyes.

She dashed a hand across her own eyes.

'Hey, don't cry.' He grinned. 'I'm not worth it. Demolition man – that's me. I've sure caused you some trouble, haven't I?'

'What are you going to do, love?'

'Marry Kirsty first and foremost,' he said gently, and not teasing her any more. 'It's the most important thing in the world to me.'

'And then?'

'We'll go back to Australia, Sera. It'll be better for Kirsty there when the inevitable happens – at least she'll have her sister . . .'

Serena pressed her lips together, then gathering all the composure she could muster said, 'I'll miss you.'

'Me too, Sera.'

They heard Kirsty talking to Holt as they approached the caravan.

Swiftly, Ryan said, 'Sera – you remember what I told you? About that hooded figure?'

She lifted a hand. 'I – I don't want to take it any further, Ryan. Nothing's going to bring Dad back, is it?'

He shook his head. 'That's just what I was going to say. Maybe it's best if we forget all about it, huh?'

'My thoughts exactly.'

He seemed to relax instantly. 'No good can come of delving any deeper into something we'll probably never understand.'

She said, fixing a smile on her face. 'I agree.'

But in her heart, she knew she could never let the matter rest entirely.

CHAPTER 27

'Do you mind not being a June bride?'

Serena tipped back her head and gazed solemnly up into Holt's dear face.

'June's another month away. Why waste four perfectly good weeks?'

'I can't believe this is happening.' He laughed softly and touched his lips to her forehead.

'We still have to tell Mari – and Viv – that we're getting married in a week's time.'

'Neither of us want any fuss though, do we, sweetheart? And you know what Viv will be like – insisting on buying herself a new outfit and a hat. It's *our* day. That's all that matters.'

'Do we have to tell anybody?' she asked. 'It's not as if I'll be decked out like a Christmas cake or anything, is it? It's going to be a perfectly ordinary ceremony by Rivelyn's registrar in her office at the town hall.'

'You're sure you don't want a white frock?'

'I look hideous in white. And anyway, it's my second marriage remember?'

'Did you wear white for the first one?' His arm tightened round her as they walked down the hall towards the front door of the 'ugly' house.

'No. I wore a denim skirt suit. It was a damp Australian springtime – dull but pretty warm.'

They reached the door.

'I'll miss you,' she said.

'It's only four days.' His eyes crinkled up with laughter.

'Ireland again though. It always seems a much longer absence when I know there's an ocean separating us.'

'I'll call you.' His voice was husky. 'I'll miss you like hell though.'

'I'm back into the swing of things at the foundry. I'll keep busy, then it won't seem so long.'

'You do that.' His arms swept round her and he pulled her to him. His head descended and his lips were warm and urgent against her own. But at last he held her away from him, and his gaze locked with hers. 'I hate to say this,' he muttered, looking hungrily at her, 'but I wish we could keep the wedding to ourselves. Am I being selfish in wanting that?'

A little pleasurable shiver ran through her. 'I feel the same way. I keep thinking if we even mention it to anyone else, something will happen to stop me being so happy.'

'That's a crazy idea.' His laughter seemed forced though, and he admitted then, 'I've been getting the same feeling though.'

In a rush, she said, 'Let's not tell them.'

'Could we do that?'

'Well – let's not mention it unless somebody brings it up, huh?'

'Like Viv, you mean.' His tone was caustic.

She nodded. 'Viv does seem to be a little odd, just lately. Maybe she's feeling pushed out with me being here all the time with you.'

'Perhaps. But she's got to get used to it.'

'You're going to be late,' she warned softly. 'Look at the time. You wanted to be off at dawn to get a good start, didn't you?'

He pulled a face at her. 'Six o'clock *is* dawn.'

'Take care, Holt.'

'You too, sweetheart.'

He opened the door, walked out into the mist-laden garden, then turned just once before unlocking his car, and lifted a hand to her.

Viv watched the lane from her bedroom window. At exactly eight minutes past six, Holt drove past her house, heading towards the main road that she knew would lead him to his depot in Rivelyn. She smiled a little secret smile to herself. He'd be away for four days now. He'd told her when he'd called in last weekend that he was going to Ireland again.

That meant she'd have the girl to herself, and she had a few things to say to that young madam!

She dressed carefully; cool colours suited her. When she was changed into a pale grey woollen suit, she laid her favourite coat – the lilac one, out on the bed. Then she went downstairs and made her porridge which she sat and ate with slow deliberation, going over in her mind what she would say to Serena.

The girl had a reputation for running away from trouble. Well, Viv hoped this time if she ran away, she wouldn't bother coming back.

A shadow at the window startled her for a moment, then she realized it was Holt's cat. She went and opened the door and Gray sidled into the kitchen for her morning saucer of milk.

'You can't stay long today, puss.' Viv crouched down and ran her hand along Gray's sleek back as the cat lapped at the milk. Gray peered up at her, amber eyes wide and sombre. Viv rose to her feet and walked away from the cat. She was getting too fond of the animal, she told herself, and that didn't suit her. Only one thing happened when you started to love someone or something.

You always got hurt.

Viv timed it perfectly, walking straight into Holt's kitchen at half past eight that morning without even bothering to knock, and making Serena spin round from a cupboard, a can of cat food in one hand while the other one flew to her lips as Viv's presence obviously startled her.

'Viv! You gave me a fright.'

Viv noted that the girl's laugh was shaky as she turned back to close the cupboard door, then faced her again and stood clutching the cat food.

She came straight to the point. 'We don't get much chance to talk together – you and I, do we, Serena?'

The girl shrugged, then walked over to the kitchen work-top and started opening the tin of cat food. Viv knew she was playing for time, getting her composure back after the shock of finding someone else was in the house with her when she'd thought she was alone.

Viv went to stand beside her, then leisurely picked up the kettle, filled it with water and switched it on. She turned a bright smile on Serena. 'You don't mind, do you? I've always treated Holt's house like my own, what with having to come up here to see to Gray, and everything when he goes away on those long journeys.'

She *did* mind. That much was obvious to Viv, but Serena busied herself emptying cat food into Gray's dish before saying, 'Did you want to talk about anything special, Viv? Only I'll be going to the foundry in about ten minutes, and Holt isn't here. He's had to go out early this morning.'

'Ireland again. Yes, he told me.' Viv proceeded to spoon loose tea leaves into the pot, then, her eyes bright, said, 'I think maybe we *should* talk, don't you?'

'Now's not a good time, Viv. I really do have to go to work, you know.'

'You don't mind me coming here, do you?'

'If Holt doesn't mind, then why should I?'

'I sometimes like a quiet walk along the cliffs. Holt's garden provides a short cut. I get so breathless if I have to take the longer way round . . .' Viv turned away to reach into a cupboard for cups and saucers. She took them over to the table, glanced up at Serena and saw a deep understanding in the girl's eyes. It made her angry, seeing that expression; she didn't want Serena feeling sorry for her. Her head came up sharply. 'I'm not asking for pity . . .'

'No. Of course not. Serena glanced at the wall clock, seemed rather agitated, and said, 'I really do have to go, Viv.'

'It was a big wrench for me when he came to live here – even though it's only a short walk from my house to his.'

Serena looked down at her hands, then back up at Viv again. 'I'm not trying to take him away from you, you know.'

The kettle boiled and clicked off. Viv went and poured water into the teapot, then carried it over to the table, placed it in the exact centre, and sat down. 'How's your own house coming on, dear? The one on the terrace overlooking the foundry. Will you soon be able to move in?'

'There's a lot of work needs doing on it,' Serena hedged. 'Far more than I'd anticipated. When it's finished though . . .'

'You *will* be going to live there?'

Serena moved over to the table and pulled out a chair. She gazed down at Viv for a few seconds before sitting down, then said, 'I think it will probably be put up for sale when it's been made habitable again.'

'So it's true what Holt told me? That you'd be staying here with him. Living in sin – like you're doing now?'

Colour flew into the girl's face. 'It happens, Viv. People – couples – they do live together nowadays.'

'Because other people do it – well, it doesn't make it right, does it?'

'Is it a sin then' Serena asked steadily, 'to love somebody?'

Viv shrugged. 'Not when it's all done legally and above board.'

'Viv . . .' Serena hesitated, then went on, 'It's different today, to what it was when you were young. Things alter. People change. And surely it's best to find out if two people are suited before tying themselves down for life.'

'It's not what I was brought up to believe. It's not how I brought Holt up either.' Calmly, Viv began to pour out the tea. 'I used to tell our Mari that mother and father would be turning in their grave if they knew how she was carrying on with your father.'

'In the end though – they were hurting no one,' Serena said quietly.

'Well, you've changed your tune, haven't you?' Viv pushed a cup of tea across the table at her. 'Wasn't it the very same thing you're doing now that made you leave home in the first place – all those years ago? If gossip was correct, you couldn't bear to live in the same house as Max and his fancy woman.'

Serena gasped. 'That's a cruel way to talk about your own sister.'

'You only know what Mari wants you to know.' Viv picked up her tea cup and smiled sweetly across the table, a smile that was designed entirely to take any sting out of her words.

'I do know that I was wrong to pass judgement on Dad and Mari,' Serena insisted.

'My dear – you didn't know your father at all.' Viv drained her cup at a single gulp. '*I* knew him. Believe me, *I* knew him. He would use anybody to get his own way.'

'I don't think you should say things like that.' Serena half rose to her feet, but Viv snapped, 'Sit down. Whether you like it or not, you're going to listen to what I have to say.'

Serena sat down heavily and sighed. 'Okay,' she said. 'So tell me.'

'I knew him first.'

'First?'

Viv nodded. 'I first met Max when I was sixteen.' Immediately, she saw she'd caught the interest of her audience.

'I didn't know that. I thought you only got to know Dad through Mari.'

'No. Mari got to know Max through *me*. I used to meet him out there on the headland – walking his dog – a mongrel called Pippin. He lived in Caindale. His father was a fisherman. Did you know that?'

'Yes. I knew that. Dad had lived in Caindale all his life – till he married my mother. He loved the place.'

'He loved *me* too.'

'No . . .' The girl frowned, obviously not wanting to believe what Viv was saying.

Viv nodded her golden head slowly. 'Yes. He did,' she said, 'But I had no money, and that bitch Catherine did. That's why he married her.'

She saw the girl swallow. Then Serena stood up. 'I am not,' she said in a bitter tone, 'going to stay here and have my family pulled to pieces, Viv.'

'It's true though. Your dear father didn't have a penny until he married that . . . that . . .'

Serena broke in, 'I think you've said enough . . .'

'Oh, shut up and sit down.'

'No . . . Look, Viv, I don't want to argue with you, but . . .'

'Like father like daughter. I've said it before and I'll say it again. You Corders are out for all you can get. First him, and now you, and I'm warning you – leave my nephew alone.'

'Holt?'

Viv rose to her feet, her chair scraping and making a hideous noise on the bare floor tiles. 'Leave him alone,' she snapped, her eyes blazing, 'you'll be sorry.'

The breath all seemed to seep out of Serena. 'Sorry?' she asked faintly. 'Just what are you getting at, Viv?'

'Just that.' Viv walked round the table, halting as she came level with her.

Serena said, 'I think you should know that Holt and I are getting married next week.'

Viv was stunned. So soon? They'd arranged to get married, and Holt hadn't told her? Then reason took over. The little bitch was lying; she had to be lying.

She laughed softly, 'A nice try, but you don't catch me out that way. Holt would have told me . . .'

354

'We haven't told anybody yet. We wanted to keep it to ourselves as long as possible. We don't want a big fuss.'

'I don't believe you.' Viv's brain began ticking over quickly. She had to convince the girl she couldn't marry Holt. It didn't bear thinking about – this girl taking him over, lock, stock and barrel. Mari had taken Max away from her after Catherine had died, and now, this bitch, this spawn of Corder's, was going to snatch Holt away too.

'You can't marry him,' she said in a frozen voice.

'I can and I will.'

Viv shook her head. Lies sprang readily to her lips. 'You'd marry the man who killed your father?'

The girl drew in a sharp breath and the colour drained away from her face.

Viv began to relax. So – the bitch already had a suspicion in that direction, had she? She congratulated herself for duping Serena into looking in the cupboard under the stairs the last time Holt had been away. The girl had seen the hooded coat. Now was the time to heap more doubts on her.

'Look in the cupboard – under the stairs,' she heard herself saying.

Serena swayed. 'I . . . I already have done . . .'

'You've seen it, then? The coat? The one with the hood?'

'It wasn't Holt! I know it wasn't Holt . . .'

Viv heard the waver in her voice, knew she had to ram home the fact now that Holt *had* killed Max. The girl must be made to believe it.

'I saw it all,' she said slowly and distinctly. 'I saw the horror on Max's face as he toppled over the edge.'

'No – oh, no. I don't believe this.' Serena shook her head wildly.

Viv moved to stand directly in front of her and ask, 'So what are you going to do about it? What *can* you do about it, Serena Corder? Will your conscience allow you to marry the man who killed your father?'

CHAPTER 28

Viv's hands were trembling when she reached home.

She pulled off her gloves and coat, then whipped the scarf from round her neck. The clothes cascaded to the floor around her as she stood panting and breathless. From force of habit, she began dredging in deep breaths of air through her mouth, pressing her hand to her heart as she did so. Why, oh why had she let that little bitch upset her so, she wondered?

It was too late now for regrets though. She knew she'd said – and done – too much, but she'd been angry – angry and hurt that Holt himself hadn't told her about the wedding. She convinced herself there and then that she could probably have talked him out of it, if he'd been straight with her.

Obviously though, Serena had got her hooks into him. Just as Mari had done with Max. And it wasn't fair. Her heart steadying a little, she walked into her front sitting room and positioned herself in front of the mantel mirror. She was still good-looking, she knew that for sure. She'd been beautiful though at sixteen – absolutely beautiful, but with a heart condition that had scared Max off for good. He'd been keen on her till he'd found out about that.

357

She still hated him for taking up with Mari even though that was years later. Years in which he'd wedded that rich bitch Catherine, had a daughter, and seen his own marriage end bitterly. In some ways she couldn't blame the arrogant Catherine for looking for fun elsewhere. Max was married to his foundry – and his valley. Caindale had been his life. He'd had only one love that was greater than Caindale, and that had been his love for Serena, the daughter he'd adored.

Mari was the one she hated most though. Mari had already had one man, Harry Wyatt, so why should she have another? No, it just wasn't fair. Life didn't share things out equally. Life grabbed at your happiness and flung it at somebody else. Life gave you a heart that needed pills to keep it steady.

She clenched her teeth together and muttered through them, 'It's not fair. It's not fair.'

And now Serena was grabbing at Holt, whisking him out of her grasp, out of her life. And Viv knew she herself would just be expected to take a back seat and let it happen. But she couldn't do that . . . And when Holt discovered what she'd done to Serena, he'd never forgive her. She couldn't face him. She'd been a fool; she knew that now.

There was only one way out.

More composed than she'd been for the past hour, she went back into her spotless kitchen and opened a drawer. First of all she took out a writing pad and a pen, then she picked up a bottle of pills and carried all three items to the kitchen table.

She took the top off the pill bottle and emptied the contents out on the table top. It was a new prescription, collected by Jilly only last week. There'd be over a hundred and fifty tablets left – two a day, and three months supply. If she took the lot . . .

Her stomach churned at the thought. But what other option was there?

Everything had gone wrong. Tears of frustration sprang to her eyes. She looked down at the pills scattered on the table; she'd always hated swallowing pills. She'd choke on them, she knew she would.

Suddenly though, a better idea came to her. What was it Dr Grace had said to her the last time she'd visited his clinic at the hospital and had told him she was heartily fed up with taking pills? She frowned, and his words came back to her.

'Take them religiously, Miss Blackwood. Twice a day and you'll be right as rain. Stop them suddenly and your blood pressure could rocket – resulting in a fatal heart attack or a stroke . . .'

That had scared her. But now it was different. She didn't want to live. Couldn't bear to see the disgust on Holt's face when he found out what she'd said about him. A murderer? And him the gentlest man on God's earth. Tears sprang to her eyes. He'd never want to see her or speak to her again. He was a proud man. And it was obvious he loved Serena, Anger flared briefly.

'The bitch! I hate her. I hate all Corders . . .'

On impulse, she scooped the pills off the table and onto a newspaper, then carried them to the little cloakroom at the bottom of the stairs and flushed them down the lavatory. This way was the best way. A rise in blood pressure . . . and then it would be all over – one way or another.

Holt would be back in four days' time, but by then it would be too late.

She sat down at the kitchen table, and began to write. It was good to see it all in black and white. She'd imagined she could live with her conscience, but she knew now that she couldn't. She addressed the letter to Holt. Holt would know what to do about it. She couldn't trust the Corder bitch. Corder! The very name sickened her.

She wrote it all down exactly as it had happened, starting with the phone call she'd made four months ago to Max, and it was as if that day in January was happening all over again.

'*Max! I've got to see you. Come to the house . . .*'

'*Hell, Viv, I'm busy. What's wrong now?*'

As usual he was exasperated with me. I was angry. '*Mari's told me. Told me about the wedding. How can you think of marrying her? I won't stand for it, Max. I'm warning you – I'll tell her all about us.*'

'*There's nothing to tell, woman. It was all over between you and me years ago. Mari wouldn't believe you anyway.*'

'*Shall we put that to the test? I'll phone her, shall I? Tell her how you took advantage of me and when you got what you wanted, you ditched me.*'

'*It wasn't like that, Viv.*' *He sighed.* '*You know damn well it wasn't like that. I didn't know about your heart then. It would have put your life in danger in those days – being married. It's different now . . .*'

'*So marry me. Not her,*' *she pleaded.*

He was adamant. '*I love Mari.*'

I played my ace. '*How will you feel when I jump off the cliff?*'

Alarm sounded in his voice. '*Don't be so stupid. Viv . . .*'

I'll do it. I'm going there now. I'll kill myself if you don't come and talk to me. Meet me there. Above the Caindale beck. Meet me in an hour.'

'Viv . . .'
'If you're not there – I'll jump.'
'Viv . . .'
I slammed down the phone.

She read through what she'd written feeling bitter and suddenly very tired with it all. She leaned her elbows on the table and supported her head in her hands. Sun streamed through the window and bathed her in a golden pool of light. On that cold January day, the sun hadn't shone . . .

Holt had gone away to Scotland. I told him before he went not to worry about Gray. It was a dark afternoon, but Gray needed feeding. I unhooked the navy blue duffel coat I'd bought for pottering about in the garden, from the back of the kitchen door, and slipped into it. It was ugly and shapeless, but it was warm. I tied a wool scarf round my neck to keep the hood from slipping off my head. Then I made my way down the lane to Holt's house.

In a daze, I let myself in and fed Gray, then preoccupied with my thoughts, I left the house and locked it up. Slowly, laboriously then for the cold air played havoc with my breathing, I made my way to the highest point of the cliffs, the headland above the Caindale beck.

I waited there for him. He'd come. I knew he'd come. And I'd threaten him with whatever it took if he insisted on marrying Mari.

We argued when he did arrive. By that time, Gray had followed me up to the headland. I didn't want the cat there. I tried to shoo it away, but it wouldn't go. It mewed and wound itself round my legs and wanted attention. Max had laughed at it. He'd stood with his back to the sea, actually laughing at the antics of the cat, while I was seething.

Viv began to write again and the pages grew into a pile as she tore them off the pad and placed them neatly beside her on the table.

It seemed as though he was laughing at me – not the cat. I became very angry, and Gray was scared when I started to shout at Max. She scurried away to his side, looked up at him and started that awful mewing again. He laughed and told me he was happier with Mari than he'd ever been in his life before. I shrieked at him to stop saying things like that. It was one big joke to him. I flung myself at him. He stepped back, surprised. Gray was between his legs, he tripped. The cat howled and spat and scratched when Max caught her with his foot. Then Max was going over the edge, and Gray would have gone too – except that I grabbed her. Holt you'd left her in my care. I couldn't let anything happen to Gray – and it was either Gray or Max Corder. Max didn't care for me any more . . . so I let him go and saved Gray instead . . .

Her head was starting to ache. She got up and put the kettle on to boil. She had plenty of time for a cup of tea. And there were more letters to write. She was going to have the last word – make them all sorry. And Holt wouldn't be back for four days.

Serena battered on the door of the understairs cupboard, cursing herself for her stupidity. How could she have been so gullible as to believe it when Viv had said there was evidence of Holt's guilt in the pocket of that hooded jacket?

It had taken only a moment. Viv, for all her frail looks was remarkably strong, she'd discovered. One push from Viv had sent her sprawling into the cupboard, grabbing at the ironing board, then falling onto the vacuum cleaner and bringing the hooded coat down on top of her from its hook on the wall.

Viv had slammed the door, and two bolts had been shot across to fasten it – one at the top, one at the bottom.

It had been galling, sitting there in the darkness, listening to Viv's footsteps running down the hall, and then the front door slamming shut.

Serena remembered the switch beside the cupboard door then, so at least she had some light as she tried to prise the door open. It was sturdy, however, and made of seasoned oak – it wouldn't budge. She yelled for help for a while, then decided shouting would achieve nothing except to give her a sore throat. After a while, Gray came and miaowed at the door and she talked soothingly to the cat on the other side, glad to have some company. Eventually though, it seemed that even Gray got tired of the game, and she must have wandered off, for the silence became oppressive again.

Several times as she sat there panting from her efforts to break down the door, she heard the telephone ringing, and now it had started again. She looked at her watch. It was nearly mid-day. Mari would be wondering about her, she knew. She didn't know whether to hope Mari would come over to the house or not. She was worried as to what Viv might do if she did. And Viv would be sure to see if anyone came down the lane. They'd have to pass her house to get here. She didn't want Mari walking into danger.

Was Viv dangerous? Looking at it logically, she thought not. But Viv *had* locked her in this tiny cupboard, hadn't she? And that could be dangerous – especially if nobody found her for four days, or if the house caught fire . . .

'Oh, God. I'm getting paranoid,' she muttered. 'Of course the house won't catch fire . . . unless . . . Viv . . .'

She banished that thought from her mind. Viv wouldn't destroy something that belonged to Holt, reason told her. Viv would respect his house, the home he'd renovated and repaired . . .

'Like hell!' she said, convinced now that Viv would destroy anything that stopped her getting what she wanted.

Exhausted she eased her position as she sat on the floor facing the door. She closed her eyes and leaned her head back against the panelling. The glaring electric light bulb above her head was comforting to a degree. She wished there was more air in the cupboard though . . .

She woke with a start and began to panic all over again. She scrambled to her feet and beat her hands against the door again in a frenzy. She grabbed the heavy ironing board and hurled it at the door. The wood didn't even start to splinter. She gazed around for small cracks in the woodwork. There were none.

She was hot, and the air was heavy. She was reminded of that time in the drift-mine when she'd lost consciousness and Holt had saved her life.

'Air! Oh, God. I need some air . . .' Wildly she attacked the door again. 'No air!' How long had she been in here? How much air was left? Was the cupboard airtight, she wondered? She sank down onto the floor again, looked at her watch. Half past five. Her chin fell forward onto her chest. She closed her eyes . . . How long could she stand it? Being locked up in this tiny space? How much air would be left in four days' time when Holt returned . . .?

Mari had begun to get worried when, at ten o'clock that morning, Serena hadn't rung in to the office to say why she was late. She tried phoning Holt's house, but there was no answer. She remembered he'd gone off to Ireland again, but surely Serena would be there.

At half past three, Holt rang the office and asked to speak to Serena, and Mari was forced to tell him that the girl hadn't been in to work that day, and she'd tried ringing the house but there was no reply.

'Will you keep trying, Mari? I'll call back later. I've had a breakdown though and had to phone the dealer network for somebody to come out to the truck.'

'Is it serious? The breakdown?'

'Could be. Some kids were playing on a bridge over a main road. They humped a block of concrete down onto the cab. I've got a smashed windscreen and some damage to one of the wheels which ran over the block.'

'Are you okay yourself?' Mari was instantly concerned.

'Yeah! Sure!'

'I'll try to make contact with Serena.'

'Thanks, Mari. Must go. I can see the breakdown boys' yellow flashing light.'

Mari sat and dialled the number of Holt's house again, but still there was no reply. She decided she couldn't sit in the office a minute longer – she just had to get out there and find out if Serena was all right.

As she turned the car into Cow Lane, she saw Viv walking towards her. It was late in the afternoon by now. She pulled in to the side of the road and stopped, then got out of the car.

Viv's face was pale. Her breathing was shallow, her lips a pale mauve colour.

Mari ran towards her. 'Viv. Where are you off to?'

'I – I needed some things – from the shop.'

'But there isn't a shop for miles!' Mari scolded.

'I was going to walk down into Caindale.' Viv seemed edgy, full of unease for some reason. She kept looking behind her. 'I need some milk – and eggs.' She waved one hand agitatedly in the air. She had a small shoulder bag and she kept snapping and unsnapping the fastener.

'You don't look at all well,' Mari said. 'Come on, love. Sit in the car. I'm just going down the lane. Serena's not turned in today – we're getting worried about her.'

'Oh! You won't find her!' Viv laughed a little recklessly. 'She's not at the house. She went out. I saw her. She came past my house – not an hour ago. I thought it strange really – she was walking you see. Not in the car.'

'Not in the car?' Mari frowned, worried about Serena, and worried about Viv too who was all jumpy and nervy, and was gabbling on too long and in too shrill a voice. 'Well – I don't know, I'm sure. Did she say where she was going?'

Viv shook her head. 'I only saw her from my window. But she was definitely walking up here – towards the main road. Maybe she's gone into Rivelyn – or perhaps she caught a bus down to the foundry.'

'No,' Mari said. 'I haven't passed a bus. And I would have seen her if she'd been on foot.'

'Run me down into Caindale – there's a love.' Viv's voice took on a wheedling tone. 'You never know – Serena's probably gone down there too – to see that young couple who are living in the caravan.'

Mari hadn't thought of that. 'Okay,' she said. 'Hop in, Viv. But if Serena's not at Caindale, well, I don't know what to think.'

CHAPTER 29

Serena woke with a throbbing head. The light bulb above her head had gone out. She was in total, absolute darkness. The air was close and hot in the cupboard.

She tried to get to her feet, but she was cramped and her legs refused to hold her. She rolled onto her knees and started hammering on the door again. There was a scratching on the other side, and then Gray's faint mewing.

She had no idea of the time now she couldn't see the watch on her wrist. She sat and listened for what seemed like hours, knowing that eventually the clock in the hall would strike the hour. When it did, she counted to seven. But was it seven in the evening, she wondered, or seven the next morning? She decided on evening. She was hungry, but not ravenously so. She also needed to visit the bathroom. One thing was comforting however. Air must be creeping into the cupboard somewhere, otherwise, she realized she'd be in a worse state than this if she'd been utterly deprived of it since half past eight this morning.

She heard a sound. Could it be wheels crunching on the gravel outside? She tried to shout but the sound came out croaky. Her mouth was parched, her throat sore. She listened intently. Gray miaowed, somewhere close at hand but on the other side of the door. She started talking to the cat. And then there came a noise like the banging of a door, and a cold draught whistled around her in the bottom of the cupboard.

She yelled as loudly as she could. 'Holt! Holt! Help me . . .' Then her voice tailed off as she realized it could be Viv again – Viv, come to see if she were still alive, Viv, who might be planning something else – some more awful fate for her.

She leaned her ear against the door. Gray was scratching at the woodwork again.

'What is it, you old mouser?' she heard Holt say.

A sob caught in her throat. She banged on the door again. 'Holt! Let me out!'

'What the . . .'

Bolts were pulled back, the door flung open. She tumbled out at his feet, and then he was down on his knees, and as she blinked and screwed up her eyes against the light in the hall, he wrapped his arms round her and lifted her to her feet.

'Serena! Honey – what happened?'

'Viv . . .' she squeaked. 'Oh, God! My voice. It feels like I've been yelling and shouting all day . . . It was Viv . . .'

'Tell me!' His face was very dark, very angry.

'Okay – but very quickly. I need a drink, and I must visit the bathroom.' She grinned sheepishly, gave him the gist of what had happened, then said, 'I just can't believe I've been shut in there since half past eight this morning.'

His face was still wearing that thunderous expression, she saw, as she came back down the stairs. He was standing sideways to her, staring at the still open understairs

cupboard. He swung round to her. 'She's got to be stopped.'
His voice was ragged. 'To think – she did this to you . . .'

She went over to him and placed a hand on his arm. 'I
ought to have known better. I should never have allowed
her to get me in there. I think I did it to humour her more
than anything . . . She just kept on and on about that
damn coat . . . and about you being up there on the
headland with Dad.'

His chin jerked up. 'Did you believe her? That I'd killed
Max?'

Calmly she looked up into his face. 'I saw the coat in that
cupboard weeks ago. Viv told me that Gray often got shut
in the cupboard. Looking back, I suppose she said that to
make me look in there and find the coat – and be suspicious
of you. She wanted me out of the way – she probably
thought I'd run back to Australia or something if she made
me hate you.'

'You didn't run though. Not this time.'

She shook her head. 'I could never run far enough away
from you, Holt. You're here.' She clutched her clenched
hands to her chest. 'Here inside me. There's no hiding
place any more. Wherever I am, you'll be with me.'

Slowly, he walked over to the cupboard and dragged the
drab-coloured coat up from the floor. He shook out its
folds and creases then held it up in front of him. 'She used
it in her garden – when she went out to clear up the leaves
or do a bit of weeding.'

Hanging against him, it was ludicrous to believe that
Holt could ever have been the one to have worn it, Serena
saw. Her laugh was tremulous. 'You'd have had to whittle
yourself down to a size ten to get into it,' she said.
'Obviously Viv hadn't thought of that when she told
me it belonged to you.'

He sighed, shook the coat again, then delved his hand into the pockets, each in turn. There was nothing in either of them.

'How could she?' he asked, glancing up again. 'How could she tell you I was a murderer?' His face was full of disgust.

Gently she took the coat out of his hands, walked back to the cupboard and hung it on its hook again. She closed the door on it then, and went back to him.

'I need a drink,' she said huskily. 'Come on, love.' She held out a hand, knowing in that moment that his trust in his Aunt Viv had been shaken to its very foundations. Maybe one day he'd be able to forgive her though. Serena hoped so.

'How do I cope with this?' he asked as she drew him towards the big room at the end of the corridor.

His words made tears spring to her eyes, for there was no reply she could make. Viv had in effect, dug her own grave. Holt, she knew, would never feel the same about his aunt again as long as he lived.

The telephone rang as they sat in front of a fire which Holt had put a match to while Serena made some tea.

He went out into the hall. She heard him speaking to somebody. Heard the name 'Mari' mentioned.

He came back, stood uncertainly in the doorway, frowning.

'Mari!' he said.

'Yes, I heard.' He looked so worried, she rose from the sofa where she'd been cuddling Gray, and went over to him.

'She says she picked Viv up . . .' He glanced at his watch. 'Just after four this afternoon. Mari was worried because you hadn't phoned or turned up at the office. She

371

was coming here, but met Viv who told her she'd seen you walking up the lane past her house.'

Serena drew in a deep breath. 'She obviously meant to keep me in that cupboard for a lot longer then.'

He nodded, and his face took on a savage grimness. 'Anything could have happened,' he railed, 'Anything at all. She couldn't have cared less, could she? About you being in there all that time.'

She reached out a hand to him. 'Nothing did happen to me though . . .'

He dragged her into his arms and held her against his body, and she could feel him physically shaking as his arms tightened around her. 'But it could have.'

'It's over, love. I'm okay. No harm's been done.' She nuzzled her head against him, then tilted her head back so she was looking up into his face. 'Hey,' she said, 'Don't take it so badly. She won't try anything like this again . . .'

'She won't get the chance,' he said bitterly. 'She's crazy! She's not safe to be let loose on human society . . .'

'Hey! Don't . . .' She wriggled herself free a little. 'Holt,' she warned softly, 'Don't get eaten up with hatred. I know what it's like – I've been there, remember? And sometimes you don't get a second chance to make amends.'

He shook his head. 'I don't want a second chance with *her*. She sickens me. I'll never forgive her for this . . .'

She cut in, 'Maybe if we could both go and talk to her? Convince her I'm not going to push her out of your life?'

He gazed down at her. 'She's not at home,' he said in a more sober tone of voice. 'That's what Mari rang to tell me. She picked her up in the car, took her down to Caindale and left Viv at the little shop down there while she went up the hill to see if you'd gone to visit Ryan and Kirsty.'

'Viv's at Wintersgill then? With Mari?'

Again he shook his head. 'No! When Mari got back to the shop, Viv had disappeared.'

'She'll be at home, I suppose.'

He frowned. 'The place was in darkness when I came past there. And Mari can't get any answer when she phones.'

'Oh, heck!'

'It's dark,' he said. 'She could be anywhere!'

'We ought to go and look at the cottage first.' Serena was pulling away from him completely now. 'She's not well, Holt.'

Against his better judgement, it seemed, he said grudgingly, 'She can't stay out all night. Hell! What's got into her?'

Serena didn't answer. If she had done, it would have needed only one word, she knew, to explain Viv's unreasonable behaviour just lately.

And that word was 'Jealousy'!

At midnight, Holt called the police from his mobile phone as they stood, a silent little crowd, on Caindale beach.

Smothering an oath then, he rounded on Serena, Mari, and the handful of Caindale residents who had joined in the search of the surrounding hillsides, the cliff tops and the beach.

'They can't class her as a "missing person",' he stormed. 'They said she could have gone to the cinema, be visiting friends, or else have taken herself off on a holiday – a holiday! I ask you! Would Viv go off on a holiday, just like that?'

Mari said soothingly, 'The police don't know Viv as well as we do, Holt.'

'She's a damnable woman.' He thrust the phone back into his pocket and glared at them all. Then he let out a huge sigh. 'There's nothing else we can do, is there?'

George had ambled out of the 'Old Bachelor' and stood glumly by as word spread that Vivian had gone missing. He came forward now. 'Could have been swept out on the tide,' he said. 'Didn't nobody think o' that?'

Mari said, 'Viv hated water. She was terrified of the sea.'

George shrugged. 'Just a thought.'

Holt thanked the few who had helped in the search, and slowly they drifted away.

'What about t'works yard?' George said. 'There's wagons and castings all over t'place up at t'foundry. She could be 'iding. She could be in 'ospital? Have y' thought o' that?'

'We haven't searched the works,' Serena said.

Mari came forward. 'We have phoned round all the hospitals though. Look, let's leave it till morning,' she said. 'Viv could be laughing at us, you know – playing some silly game of hide and seek with us. She's most probably gone off to an hotel somewhere – or a little guest house just to give us all a fright. She'll turn up right as rain tomorrow, and have the last laugh on all of us.'

George shuffled off home. Holt, Serena, and Mari were left alone.

'Do you really believe that?' Holt asked.

Subdued, Mari shook her head. 'No. But I don't think any good can come of us trying to find her now. It's too dark, for one thing.'

'She could be lying injured somewhere . . .' Serena was feeling the strain of the last few hours. She desperately needed to know where Viv was. 'She was so upset this morning . . .' She broke off, unable to continue. 'I should never have told her we were going to get married.'

'It's not your fault.' Holt draped an arm round her shoulders. 'She had to know sometime.'

Mari cut in, 'And there's no excuse for what she did, Serena. It was childish in the extreme to shut you up in that cupboard.'

'Come back with us, Mari,' Holt said. 'Come and stay the night. It's too late for you to go back to Wintersgill.'

'I do have my car,' Mari said, with a smile. 'And I'm not scared of the dark.'

Holt's face was drawn. 'I don't like to think of Viv being just anywhere,' he said. 'She's not to be trusted after what she did to Serena today.'

Mari shivered. 'You've convinced me,' she said. 'I hope your spare room's well aired.'

At dawn they were up again, searching the cliffs, going over Viv's house – for which Holt had a key – from top to bottom. There was no sign of Viv though. The house was spick and span as it always was. They opened doors and cupboards; all Viv's clothes were in her wardrobe. Nothing had been taken away. The only things missing were her lilac-coloured coat and a grey wool suit, Mari said.

'She was dressed in those things yesterday.' Serena's voice was strained.

Mari moved away to the little cloakroom at the bottom of the stairs, and suddenly shouted, 'Come and look here.'

Scattered on the floor underneath the washbasin they found several little white pills. Mari pointed to the lavatory. They peered inside. There was a pile of white powder in the water at the bottom of the bowl.

'Her pills.'

They stared at Mari.

Serena swallowed and gripped hold of Holt's hand.

Mari pushed past them and went into the kitchen, where they followed to find her wrenching open drawers, opening cupboards, her eyes scanning each one. After what seemed like an age, she turned round to them. 'All her heart pills are missing. There are none here at all, and there were none upstairs in the drawer beside her bed.'

Holt's voice was raw. 'It looks as if she threw them away deliberately.'

'Yes!' Mari hurried across to the kitchen waste bin, flipped up its top, then turned to them, an empty pill bottle in her hand.

Serena whispered, 'Oh, no.'

'The police have got to take this seriously,' Holt fumed. Springing to life, and without another word to either of them, he strode tight-lipped over to Viv's telephone and dialled the emergency number.

CHAPTER 30

Nearly everybody in Caindale knew that Viv was missing.

The residents of the village stood around in silent little clumps, watching the police who were swarming the hillsides, some with dogs, some scrambling alone, but all with the same intent – finding a woman who, it seemed, had decided to take her own life.

'I feel so useless.' Holt thrust his hands into the pockets of his leather jacket as Serena joined him again at the sea shore.

'Ryan wanted to come and help look for her.' She grimaced slightly. 'Kirsty made him sit down and watch from the window of the caravan though. He feels helpless – just like we do,' she added.

'It's the waiting.'

He linked his arm in hers and they started to walk towards the nearest police car where they could hear a radio conversation.

'They're all in touch with one another.' She glanced round at the hillsides, then shivered as she spotted a silent white ambulance just crawling into the valley from the direction of the main road.

'It's just a precaution,' Holt said, his voice stony. 'The ambulance. It doesn't mean that they'll need it.'

'No. Of course not.'

They reached the police car. Holt bent down against the open window. 'Any news?'

The officer inside shook his head. 'They've just radioed through to say they're outside a derelict ironstone mine. It's locked though. Do you know who might have the keys?'

Serena said quickly. 'I do . . .' Then remembering, she frowned. 'No, I don't, do I?' She glanced up at Holt. 'That Sunday afternoon . . .'

She didn't have to say more. He clapped his hand to his forehead.

'God! I forgot about the keys. I had them . . .' His brow furrowed. 'What the hell did I do with them . . .?'

'I don't know . . .'

'Viv's!' he said, suddenly recalling what had happened. 'The keys – they fell out of my coat pocket. Viv picked them up – put them on one side in her kitchen – I don't remember seeing them again. I certainly didn't take them with me.' He stared at her. 'No,' he said softly. 'Oh, no. I mustn't even think that she's gone down there. If that's the case, she could have been planning something like this for ages . . .'

'Come on.' She shook his arm. 'Come on, Holt. We've got to get there . . . to the mine.'

They raced off up the road. Behind them, they heard the radio come on in the police car again.

The officer leaned out of the window and yelled, 'They've got the keys . . . found them on the ground up there . . . there's no hurry . . .'

But Serena and Holt ignored him.

Two of Rivelyn's fire crew, wearing breathing apparatus, had carried Viv out of the drift-mine and laid her on the ground by the time Holt and Serena arrived.

Holt rushed towards the lifeless figure as the firemen made way for paramedics, and pulled off their masks and shrugged out of their oxygen harnesses.

It was pitifully obvious there was nothing anyone could do to help Viv.

Serena stood beside Holt as they lifted Viv gently onto a stretcher, covered her over from head to toe, and carried her to the ambulance.

There was no rush. No hurry.

In the silent valley, it seemed as if everything had ground to a stop. The hills were quiet – the shouting over. Villagers huddled in their groups and bowed their heads. Viv had been a familiar figure to them. They'd had no quarrel with her.

Holt stood ram-rod still, stiff and unbending as he watched the ambulance drive away. His face could have been carved out of stone, Serena thought.

She slipped her hand into his.

Someone in uniform came up to them. 'I'm sorry it had to end like this.'

She saw a muscle twitch in Holt's jaw. Then he looked at the man and said, 'Thanks! Thanks for all you've done.'

'There were letters. She'd left letters. If you could come to the police station – perhaps tomorrow when the coroner's seen them. There'll have to be a post-mortem of course.'

'Letters?' Holt repeated the one word and stared at the man.

'Looks like she meant to do it. There was one addressed to you, sir. One to somebody called Mari, and another for us. They were in her hand bag.'

'I see.' Holt's voice was husky with emotion.

Serena led him away from the scene, back to the foundry yard where her car was parked. He walked round to the driver's side, but she checked him with her hand on his. 'No. I'll drive.'

'I'm okay, Serena.' He stared at her, his eyes dull.

'All the same, I'll drive. Okay?'

He hesitated for only a moment, and at last he nodded.

'Okay!' A faint smile touched his lips. 'Okay, love. Let's go home, shall we?'

'It was an accident,' Mari said. 'Max's death was an accident, even though Viv *was* up there on the headland with him when he fell.'

She placed the letter on the coffee table in front of the fire at Holt's house. 'You can read it. She explained everything in it. She was in love with Max from the first day she met him when she was sixteen. She must have grown to hate me so much though . . .' Her voice tailed away. There were no tears however.

'I've shed so many these past few months since Max died that I don't think there are any more left,' she explained, her face twisting miserably.

Holt got up and went to sit beside Mari. 'Viv had got everything out of proportion,' he said gently. 'She'd allowed herself to get terribly embittered, but it's over now. It's something we've got to try and forget.'

'Can we do that?' Serena walked across the big room towards them carrying a tray laden with tea things. She placed it on the table beside Mari's letter.

She straightened then and looked first at Holt, then at Mari. 'Can we be happy, I wonder, knowing what she went through?'

380

'Jealousy is a terrible thing.' Mari took a tissue out of her bag and blew her nose.

Serena perched opposite Mari on an easy chair and said, 'You knew, didn't you? You knew Viv had something to do with Dad's death?'

Mari's head came up slowly, her eyes meeting those of the girl. She nodded. 'I – had a suspicion.'

'More than that, Mari.' Serena was very still, very positive.

'Yes.' Mari said nothing more for a few moments, then went on, 'I knew she had that duffel coat. I knew she could have been on the cliffs that day because she was looking after Gray, and she often walked up to the headland after she'd been to Holt's house to feed the cat.'

'And Gray was always following her about,' Holt said. 'So I think we can take it as read that Viv told the truth in her letters to us – that Gray was there when Max died.'

Serena started to pour tea into the cups. 'Gray can't be blamed.'

'No.' Mari smiled as the cat got up from the hearthrug on hearing its name, stretched, then walked over to them and miaowed. Mari bent down and ran her fingers through Gray's thick fur. 'Lucky you didn't go over the edge too,' she said drily. 'It was more than lucky, however, that Viv had a soft spot for you and grabbed you before you fell.'

'At least she had some human feelings.' Holt's voice was cold to the point of iciness.

'We've all got to try and forgive her,' Mari said.

'It's going to be hard.' Holt got suddenly to his feet, walked over to the fireplace, leaned his hand on the high mantel, and stared down into the fire. Then slowly he turned back to face them. 'I don't know if I can ever forgive her,' he said then. 'You do know, don't you, Mari,

381

that Viv kept those keys to the mine with a very different purpose in mind to the one she eventually found for them.'

Mari's face registered alarm. 'What do you mean?'

Holt went over to a desk in the corner of the room, took out a letter in an identical envelope to the one Mari had, and brought it to the table. He threw it down in front of Mari. 'Read it,' he ordered. 'Viv decided to clear her conscience apparently, before killing herself.'

Mari's face paled. 'No. I don't want to touch it. You tell me what it says.'

'It's almost the same confession as she wrote for you, and for the police,' Holt said savagely. 'Except that I got a few more lines tagged on the end of my letter. Viv kept those keys intending to lure Serena to the mine and get rid of her in there.'

'Lock her in? But what would that achieve? Somebody would have found her. She could have called for help . . .' Mari's voice tailed away. 'Oh, God, she didn't have anything more devious in mind, did she?'

'Oh, nothing definite,' Holt said. 'She just had an urge to rid the world of Corders, I think. There was mention of popping some of her very potent sleeping pills into a flask of coffee – then asking Serena to take her to see inside the mine.'

'A deadly picnic!' Serena's head fell forward into her hands. She felt Holt's arms go round her, and looked up, blinking away tears.

Mari was speechless. Her mouth had just dropped open. When the truth had sunk in, she gasped, 'You mean . . .'

'She was going to drug me with the coffee once we got there; she intended letting me get inside, then she was going to pour out the coffee. While I drank mine, she was going to pour hers, but "accidentally" drop the flask so

382

she didn't have to drink any herself. Then, she was going to leave me there . . .'

She couldn't carry on. Holt finished the sentence for her. 'Hoping,' he said in a ferocious voice, 'that Serena would probably stagger further inside the mine for warmth, and succumb to the black damp inside the mine . . .'

'The gas! The gas that killed *her*. Oh, my God . . .' Mari closed her eyes momentarily.

Holt's lips twisted wryly. 'She's already won round one. Her funeral's on the day Serena and I should have been married. We've had to postpone the wedding.'

Mari nodded. 'Yes. I know. Serena told me on the phone, didn't you, love?'

Serena looked up at Holt. 'Is this nightmare ever going to end?'

His jaw was set and decisive. 'Yes,' he said. 'It will end. Believe me, it will end now Viv's gone.'

There was a noise outside the house.

'A car?' Mari's head jerked round. 'I'd better be off if you're expecting company.'

'No.' Serena twisted round too, then she got up from the chair and walked to the door. 'No – we're not expecting anybody. Just hang on a minute, Mari.'

She went out into the hall, down the long corridor to the front door and opened it. Mark grinned at her from the cab of his big black taxi, then he opened its door, got out and held the back door open.

Kirsty and the baby got out first, then from the other side of the car, Ryan appeared, carrying a huge bunch of flowers. He hurried towards her, thrust them into her arms. 'Here, take them. I feel a right pansy carrying flowers, but I wanted to cheer you up.'

'Ryan!' She laughed up into his face.

'Er . . . do we get tea offered – or shall I tell Mark to wait for us?' he wanted to know.

'Tell him to go,' she whispered. 'I'll run you back to the caravan after tea.'

The black car pulled away and Serena led the way into the house.

Mari admired the baby; Holt went and put the kettle on again, and then came back with a huge vase full of water.

'Put the flowers in this,' he said, laughing softly as she peered out at him from behind a mass of yellow laburnum blooms and white carnations from Maddie's shop in the village.

Mari took the baby from Kirsty and rocked her.

Kirsty went and stood beside Ryan in front of the fire.

Serena placed the flowers in the vase. 'Nobody ever brings flowers like this unless they've got a guilty conscience,' she teased, turning to face them.

'They're a softener,' Ryan said, his face reddening.

'A softener for what?' she asked with suspicion.

'A softener for not inviting you to the wedding this morning.'

Kirsty shot out a hand, her left hand, on which gleamed a shining gold ring, and laughed breathlessly.

There were kisses all round, and tears as well.

'We're going back to Australia,' Ryan explained. 'Next week.'

Serena felt overwhelmed by it all. 'No,' she said weakly, 'You can't do that . . .'

'Yes they can.' Holt was beside her. Holding her. Squeezing her shoulders tightly. Looking down into her upturned face and telling her with his eyes that things were changing now.

Solemnly, she nodded up at him. 'Yes,' she said. 'I see what you mean. We've all got to make a new start.'

Ryan came over and dropped a kiss on her forehead. 'I went back to the hospital at Rivelyn yesterday,' he said, looking directly at her. Then, without beating about the bush, he continued, 'There's no change in my condition, love. The bullet's still there, the damage is still the same.'

She felt her face beginning to crumple. He was so matter of fact about it now. She felt as if he'd accepted what had happened, and was accepting too what would almost certainly happen in the not too distant future.

'Don't cry!' It was an order. 'I'm happy. We'll get by – Kirsty and me,' he said gently.

Kirsty came up to them too. 'We're not just going to sit and wait for it to happen,' she said. 'We've heard of a surgeon – in America. New York. He's done marvellous things with injuries like Ryan's.'

Serena turned her head into Holt's shirt and sobbed like a baby.

'I said not to cry.' Ryan gave an exasperated sigh and grasped hold of her shoulder, pulling her round to face him again.

Holt handed her a clean hanky. 'Mop up,' he said. 'This is a wedding day, for heaven's sake.'

Kirsty pushed her hand into the pocket of her smart new cream-coloured jacket and pulled something out.

'Here!' she said, holding up a small stone that could only have been three or four inches at its widest part.

Serena stared at her.

'A luck-stone,' she said. 'It has a hole in it, see? I found it on the beach when the fishing boats were being blessed. It was the day I found Ryan again too. It brought me luck.

We don't need it now. We have each other – and baby
Reanne. I want you to have it, Sera. I want you and Holt to
be as happy as we are.'

'I – I couldn't . . .' Serena held back, knowing that
whatever happiness Ryan and Kirsty had found, they
still had a long way to go before their troubles were
over.

Kirsty grinned. 'We won't be here for your wedding.
And we're poor as church mice so we can't afford to buy
you a present.' Determined not to take no for an answer,
Kirsty grabbed her hand and placed the stone in her palm,
bending her fingers up over it,' then squeezing Serena's
hand tightly in her own. 'Take it,' she whispered. 'You've
gone through so much this past week – you must be reeling
with the shock of it all.'

And then she was gone. Gone back to sit beside Mari
and talk about babies, and Ryan was wheeling away too.
Reanne was the centre of their universe, that much was
obvious.

They stood alone on the headland, hands linked. To the
right of them, most of Caindale still slumbered on. To
their left, the grey ocean stretched out beyond eternity.

The tide was full and almost on the turn. Bright-
coloured fishing cobles were massing round the jetty,
and one by one heading out into the pearly mist-shrouded
dawn.

'Is this why you couldn't sleep? Because you wanted to
see the cobles going out to sea?' Holt asked.

Serena turned her head towards him. 'No,' she said
simply. 'I couldn't sleep because this is the day my life is
going to change, the most important day of my life, and I
don't want to miss one minute of it.'

His smile was broad. 'In exactly seven and a half hours we'll be an old married couple, huh?'

'I'll really belong then, won't I?'

'Belong?' He frowned slightly. 'Haven't you always belonged?'

'Not like this. Never like this before. Now, I know how Dad felt, I think.'

'About Caindale.'

She nodded and turned away again to watch the last of the boats leaving the shore. 'It's beautiful, isn't it?'

He laughed softly. 'You've only just started to look at it, haven't you? To me it's always been beautiful – the hills, those solid little houses, even the gaudy pigeon sheds . . . Caindale was beautiful because you were a part of it – because you'll always be a part of it, Serena.'

She twisted her head round to look at him. 'It's growing on me – with every day that passes, it's giving me an anchor, a reason for being here.'

'It's that sort of place.'

'I've never really looked at it before. Now though, I can't ever imagine leaving Caindale again. It needs me. It needs the foundry to survive, and I'm going to help it do that.' She grinned suddenly. 'And I'll move heaven and earth to manufacture those blessed doors, you see if I don't.'

'You're growing to love it already.'

She said, 'Am I? Can you feel that too?'

'You always did, you know,' he said, pulling her close to his side. 'You always did, my Serena. It just took you a bit longer than the rest of us to discover the magic, that's all.'

'And to love you? That took a bit longer – ten years *too long* in fact.'

'Ah, you loved me all along the way,' he said. 'That's why you never found a proper hiding place – not even at the other end of the earth.'

She went into his arms. 'So, love me,' she said. 'Love me, and never stop loving me.'

'I do.' He bent his head and kissed her. 'I do, and I always will.'

THE EXCITING NEW NAME IN WOMEN'S FICTION!

PLEASE HELP ME TO HELP YOU!

Dear *Scarlet* Reader,

The end of July will see our first super Prize Draw, which means that **you could win 6 months' worth of free Scarlets!** Just return your completed questionnaire to us (see addresses at end of questionnaire) before 31 July 1997 and you will automatically be entered in the draw that takes place on that day. If you are lucky enough to be one of the first two names out of the hat we will send you four new *Scarlet* romances every month for six months, and for each of twenty runners up there will be a sassy *Scarlet* T-shirt.

So don't delay – return your form straight away!*

Sally Cooper

Editor-in-Chief, *Scarlet*

---

*Prize draw offer available only in the UK, USA or Canada. Draw is not open to employees of Robinson Publishing, or of their agents, families or households. Winners will be informed by post, and details of winners can be obtained after 31 July 1997, by sending a stamped addressed envelope to address given at end of questionnaire.

Note: further offers which might be of interest may be sent to you by other, carefully selected, companies. If you do not want to receive them, please write to Robinson Publishing Ltd, 7 Kensington Church Court, London W8 4SP, UK.

QUESTIONNAIRE

Please tick the appropriate boxes to indicate your answers

1 Where did you get this Scarlet title?
Bought in supermarket ☐
Bought at my local bookstore ☐ Bought at chain bookstore ☐
Bought at book exchange or used bookstore ☐
Borrowed from a friend ☐
Other (please indicate) _____

2 Did you enjoy reading it?
A lot ☐   A little ☐   Not at all ☐

3 What did you particularly like about this book?
Believable characters ☐   Easy to read ☐
Good value for money ☐   Enjoyable locations ☐
Interesting story ☐   Modern setting ☐
Other _____

4 What did you particularly dislike about this book?
_____

5 Would you buy another Scarlet book?
Yes ☐   No ☐

6 What other kinds of book do you enjoy reading?
Horror ☐   Puzzle books ☐   Historical fiction ☐
General fiction ☐   Crime/Detective ☐   Cookery ☐
Other (please indicate) _____

7 Which magazines do you enjoy reading?
1. _____
2. _____
3. _____

And now a little about you –
8 How old are you?
Under 25 ☐   25–34 ☐   35–44 ☐
45–54 ☐   55–64 ☐   over 65 ☐

cont.

9 What is your marital status?
   Single ☐   Married/living with partner ☐
   Widowed ☐   Separated/divorced ☐

10 What is your current occupation?
   Employed full-time ☐   Employed part-time ☐
   Student ☐   Housewife full-time ☐
   Unemployed ☐   Retired ☐

11 Do you have children? If so, how many and how old are they?
   _____
   _____

12 What is your annual household income?
   under $15,000 ☐ or £10,000 ☐
   $15–25,000 ☐ or £10–20,000 ☐
   $25–35,000 ☐ or £20–30,000 ☐
   $35–50,000 ☐ or £30–40,000 ☐
   over $50,000 ☐ or £40,000 ☐

Miss/Mrs/Ms _____
Address _____
_____
_____

Thank you for completing this questionnaire. Now tear it out – put it in an envelope and send it to:

Sally Cooper, Editor-in-Chief

USA/Can. address
SCARLET c/o London Bridge
85 River Rock Drive
Suite 202
Buffalo
NY 14207
USA

UK address/No stamp required
SCARLET
FREEPOST LON 3335
LONDON W8 4BR
Please use block capitals for address

CHHEA/5/97

Scarlet titles coming next month:

REVENGE IS SWEET Jill Sheldon
Chloe Walker is a soft touch for anyone in trouble. Thomas McGuirre is a man with no heart, set on revenge, no matter who gets in his way. So something (or someone!) has to give! But will it be Chloe . . . or Thomas?

GAME, SET AND MATCH Kathryn Bellamy
Melissa Farrell's career on the professional tennis circuit is just taking off. One day, with a lot of hard work and dedication, she may achieve her dream of winning Wimbledon. But Nick Lennox isn't prepared to wait for her. Unlike the attractive bad boy of tennis, Ace Delaney . . .

MARRIED TO SINCLAIR Danielle Shaw
Jenny has been engaged to Cameron for several years, but he calls it a day when he realizes that the family firm is far more important to her than he could ever be. Then Jenny meets Paul Hadley and realizes what love is all about. But Paul is married to the glamorous Gina, who will never let him go.

DARK CANVAS Julia Wild
Abbey has a steady, if dull, boyfriend and is at the height of her career. But then someone begins to threaten her, and Jake Westaway appoints himself her protector. But then he starts to *want* her . . . even though she's his best friend's woman!